I0678223

Morland Blood

Megan Allen

This is a work of fiction. Names, characters, businesses, places, events, locales, and incidents are either the products of the author's imagination or used in a fictitious manner. Any resemblance to actual persons, living or dead, or actual events is purely coincidental.

I am a christian and while I believe that God reigns over every part of the universe, I don't think there are magic worlds out there. I also know that the Bible says that those who practice witchcraft will suffer a fiery lake but I can also pretend and imagine worlds where that wouldn't be true. I can imagine a world where God would grant power over elements to people. Didn't Moses part the red sea? Didn't Daniel and Jospeh interpret dreams? Didn't Elijah call down fire from heaven? Didn't Paul and other raise people from the dead? God is all powerful and sometimes let us mortal call upon that power. So don't try to do any witchcraft here on Earth but it's still fun to imagine a reality where our spiritual gifts were displayed externally instead of internally.

So please forgive any liberties I take as I create a christian fantasy world. I just know that if there are any other planets inhabited out there in our universe God would be with them, too.

Copyright © Megan Allen 2018

All rights reserved.

www.MeganAllen.com

ISBN-13: 978-0-578-44286-0 (Allen Books)

ISBN-10: 0-578-44286-0

Cover design by Nathalia Suellen

Big thanks to all my kindred spirits who loved

Magic Headaches so much that I just had to share what happens next.

<u>Magic Headaches</u>

Magic Headaches

The Morland Prince

Morland Blood

Chapter 1

Elinor

Elinor took several deep breaths as she watched Derek pull a knife from the first aid bag. Her arm was wrapped around her stomach and held tight by layers of bandages and blood, both old and new. Using her arm to keep the wound closed had been the only option they had had at the time and she was nervous to see the damage that lay underneath.

Derek met her eyes and then sliced the bandage off. The bandage didn't fall off like she'd thought it would. It *stuck* and he had to *peel* it off. She let out a deep breath when he lifted her arm off the wound. She was glad she was already laying down.

"It's..." Derek said looking from the wound on her stomach to her face. "I'm surprised you didn't go into shock. It's deep, like you said. And obviously there was a lot of blood. Man, this must hurt."

"It's coming to me now," Elinor said trying, and failing, not to look at the claw marks that stretched across her stomach. The creature that had done those was the stuff of nightmares. It was impossibly made of both smoke and claws and had somehow attacked her from a world away, Morland. Elinor's magic ability made her able to *see* the magic planet of Morland but this was the first time something from Morland had been able to see her.

And now they were *in* Morland. She had climbed a magic portal in a tree in Waxhaw, North Carolina and was now on another planet. But only for a short trip, an hour tops. Derek would treat her wound and then they would be safely back home via the portal in the tree. Because Morland wasn't a place to linger.

The man gently touching her shredded stomach was so different from the Derek she'd seen just moment ago. His short hair had turned long. His jeans and t-shirt were now leather armor accessorized with swords. Studying him distracted her for a moment. He was somehow more handsome than before but also so much more dangerous. Elinor made herself take a couple deep breaths and calm herself. The blood loss was making her a little lightheaded.

"Oh man. That's bad," Ryan said sitting down next to her and reaching for her hand. He was such a good brother. Elinor was infinitely relieved to have him with her. "It's really bad," he said frowning. "Can you fix this, Derek? Is there someone else we can take her to?"

"Ha," Derek said simply. "Have you listened at all? The point of this whole reconnaissance is not to *see* anyone or be *seen*. Also, there is no one I trust." He paused a moment in thought and then said, "And yes, I'll do a good enough job. I've got more experience than just our first aid class." He started to look through the bag and then he was throwing things on the ground as his search became more frantic.

"Bloody hell," he muttered after a minute, shaking his head.

"What is it?" Peter asked. "Did you forget something? Can we still do it? Do you need me to go get something?"

"Oh, I can still do it," Derek said, his voice a thick mockery. "It's just a matter if our little princess can do it."

"What?" Elinor said. "What do you mean?"

"The nice local anesthetic I packed for you is gone. In its place is this," he said holding up a red plant.

"What is that?" she asked.

"Bloodroot."

"Of course it is," Elinor said rolling her eyes. "What does it do?" The pain was making her snippy. She could take her pulse from her pounding wound now that her arm wasn't the stopper over the claw marks on her stomach.

4

"It'll make you unconscious for a couple hours. Or it would if I ground it up and brewed it into a tea."

"A couple hours!" Elinor said. The plan was to only be in Morland for a couple *minutes*. She knew enough of Derek's history with Morland that the idea of staying longer made her *very* nervous. This world seemed to have a way of taking a person and changing them into their worst possible self.

"How is this going to work? I don't know," Elinor said shaking her head. "If I was unconscious you'd have to drag me up that tree and then dump me over or worse we'd have to wait it out here. No way!"

Derek stared at her a moment.

"Yes, those are our options," he said. "Not taking it though... I don't think you could handle it."

Elinor felt torn. She *hated* being a burden. "I don't want to slow us down..."

"Why don't we just take Elinor and the bloodroot back through the portal, shoot her up with the local anesthetic, and then bring her back?" Peter said.

"It's too late to move her," Derek said looking at Peter. "The wounds are bad and we've opened them up. For her to stand up, climb the tree, jump down, and then do that again would be too much. Also we might only be injecting her Earth body. And then it would all have been for nothing."

"Okay. Then make the tea. El, I'll carry you up that stupid tree myself when we are done or we could make a pulley system to carry you up and down to the other side, okay?" Ryan said.

"Can we just try it without first?" Elinor asked.

Derek looked visibly relieved.

"Yeah. I'm glad you said that because making the tea would mean making a fire and... I'll be very gentle. Alright, here we go," Derek said. "Oh, remember to breathe."

Elinor closed her eyes and tried to think of anything else. When Derek cleaned the wound with water and clean cloths, Elinor hissed through closed teeth. *I can do this*, she told herself, *it can't be worse than a headache*. But the pain of the needle diving deep in her sensitive, angry wound made her lose herself for a moment. She arched up as a single solitary scream burst from her lips. Derek did not hesitate. In one powerful punch, he knocked her unconscious.

Ryan

"What the hell?" Ryan yelled as Derek continued to sew. Derek was a maniac and Ryan was an idiot for trusting him.

"I commend her for trying," Derek said. "But I couldn't have her yelling the whole time and now we get the effect of bloodroot without making a fire. Win-win."

And then Derek actually smiled.

Ryan extricated himself from Elinor and had to take a couple deep breaths.

"You are such an asshole. You know that?" Ryan said pacing around the clearing. He didn't want to yell at Derek since he was sewing his sister's stomach back together so he turned to Peter. It was as much his fault anyway. "I don't get it, Peter. You seem like an okay guy. How can you be around him and not want to kill him all the time? When we get out of here..."

"Hey. Just calm down a minute," Peter implored, following Ryan as he paced.

"He punched my sister in the face," Ryan said.

"She was screaming," Derek said matter-of-factly.

6

"You could have made the bloodroot tea," Ryan said

"We are not making a fire," Derek said without lifting his eyes from his work.

"She already has bad headaches every day. She didn't need a knock-out punch," Ryan said.

"Then she'll probably hardly notice any difference when she wakes up," Derek said with the hint of a chuckle. Ryan started to see red.

"Derek..." Peter groaned.

"You..." Ryan said coming towards Derek.

"Shut up," Derek said

"What!" Ryan growled.

"No, shut up," Derek said standing as he dropped everything. He stood completely still. His hands were covered in Elinor's blood and he just listened. The sight made Ryan's heart stutter and he listened too. Then he heard it: noise and the shout of men. Derek brought a finger to his lips. He knelt down to Elinor and frantically tried to finish. He motioned for Ryan to come over to start wrapping her torso with the bandages he had laid out.

"How is your Scottish accent?" Derek whispered to them

"I don't know. You tell me," Ryan said in a jilted whisper.

"You dunna have to worry about me, laddie," Peter whispered with a wink.

"Okay, neither of you say anything. We are from the South. Traveling home after some bad luck trading with the nomads. Bind her wound quick, doesn't matter how." Derek said as he stood to face three armed men walking towards them.

Derek

It took an effort for Derek not to sigh. Of course, they had been found. What had he really expected. He *knew* that Morland was the worst. He'd been trapped on this stupid, garbage, magic planet for five years. And he'd allowed a pair of doe eyes to drag him back. He deserved everything that was coming for him.

"What have we got here?" said the first man. He was all muscle and just as tall as Derek. But his uniform named him a low born, nothing to worry about. One of the other men was just a solider as well but the third one was dressed well and bore himself well. He had brown hair pulled back to his neck and he looked at Derek keenly. He was the one to worry about. Derek nicknamed them Dumb Muscles, Other, and Officer Trouble.

Derek didn't relax his right hand from the hilt of his sword. The other two men stayed back watching as the first man kicked their bags around until he came to Ryan binding Elinor's stomach.

"Is this the scream we heard earlier? You all having a little fun? Since she's asleep she wouldn't mind three more, I don't think," Dumb Muscles said laughing as he tugged at his belt.

"Don't touch my sister!" Ryan growled in a thick Scottish accent. Derek glared at him.

"Oh now," said Officer Trouble as he walked closer, his interest piqued. Derek silently cursed. *Bloody hell.* He'd made some mistake. "What do we have here, indeed?" the man said.

Derek kept his pose with difficulty. This man was a highborn officer, not some hired muscle that joined the army. Someone with family, money, clout. Someone he might have known, who might have known him, who certainly knew the Queen. If she was still around...

"Now what are boys from the South Coast doing here? Or anywhere?" the officer laughed. Ryan looked at Derek helplessly. Derek hid his confusion. He'd thought picking to be from the South would be a safe bet. It was far enough away from where they were that no one would know enough to doubt them.

And the South was a big port so even though the natives were mostly dark skinned there were so many merchants and visitors that it would be impossible to keep track of who came and went. But something must have happened...

"We are on our way home. We had bad luck trading and we are heading back south," Derek said falling effortlessly into the brogue.

"Trading with who?" the officer said with narrowed eyes.

"Bloody nomads."

The officer's face blanked and then he burst out laughing. The other two soldiers looked on unsmiling. Peter and Ryan looked about to wet themselves. Derek made himself take a deep breath.

"Now, now," the officer said still laughing softly as he shook his head. "If I don't kill you for lying to an officer of the Queen. I may recommend you as court jester," he chuckled again. "And you did it so straight-faced." He tapped his finger to his chin. "What should I do with you?"

"You could let us go?" Derek said with a wicked grin. *Hide it. Hide it,* Derek told himself as his fear, panic, and confusion rose to take control. He could find out what happened later. Something was wrong in Morland and he felt chills rising up his spine as he waited for the next blow. And the Queen was still alive. Of course she was.

"Ah no," he said without taking his eyes from Derek. "The General will want to speak with you. You'll be coming with us. And where would you go anyway? The whole South Coast is just ash after all. You could have thought of a better story... and nomads. Who can even find two nomads to rub together, let alone trade with?" He barked a laugh as Derek felt his heart drop to the floor. There it was.

Officer Trouble motioned for Dumb Muscles and Other to collect them. Derek didn't move. The two soldiers moved to fight him but Office Trouble laughed again.

"Such spirit. You might be able to take these two but," he said as he raised his hand to his ear, "there will be five dozen men passing by soon. Shall we make this fight a bit more challenging? How many more would come if she screamed again? A dozen? All of them? I am accompanied by the General and I am one of his men. You may be good with that sword but not that good. No one has ever beaten him. And none of your other companions are even armed and your girl is still unconscious. What did you do to her anyway?" he said raising his eyebrow.

"Come," he said with no humor this time. "Carry the girl," he said to Dumb Muscles. Ryan protested and received a sharp punch in the stomach as the man lifted Elinor into his arms.

Chapter 2

Derek

The soldiers led them a few miles to a main caravan. There were a lot of soldiers milling around and Derek didn't look forward to meeting with the General. The General and Derek had not been on the best of terms when Derek had left but the man had seemed ancient when Derek was just a kid. Maybe he had finally retired and the new General wouldn't know him. *There is no chance of that,* Derek thought. *Morland doesn't give lucky breaks, at least not to me.*

Derek, Ryan, and Peter were kept together as they were added to one of many rolling prisons wagons. They were made of four walls of iron bars with wooden floors and roofs. Each had four large wheels that seemed able to roll over large debris to the great discomfort of the occupants.

Derek had employed such vehicles before but he'd never been trapped in one. And never with two other men he was responsible for, and Elinor as well. They had tried to argue to keep Elinor with them but she'd been carried off to who knows where and she had still been unconscious. He hadn't meant to hit her that hard…

As soon as Derek was in their wagon he looked for something to cover himself with. His red hair was too noticeable. Their supply packs had been taken, of course, along with their weapons. He found a scrap of fabric, last remains of someone else's shirt but he tied it over his head like hood.

As the wagons started to move, he looked around and his eyes fell on the ground. Shock crashed into his like a tidal wave. They were on a road. This was definitely new. How had Elinor never seen this road? She must have never driven down to South Carolina. Waxhaw was right on the border and that's the direction the road had been in. He felt like a fool for not driving around for more reconnaissance. They had only driven looking for Morland landmarks that *one* day.

Everything coming for us is my fault.

It had been six years since Derek had left Morland but he wondered if somehow more time had passed here. The Queen still lived but she was almost eternal and the nomads were gone. How could that be?

When he was last here they had been a vibrant people. Four distinct clans: North. South. East. West. Each as different as their compass points. The Queen had not been pleased with them but there were many of them. How could they be gone? And why? Had they stood against her? Was she so strong? And what about the South Coast? *Ash.* That word. Why had they used that word? They could have said it had burned but no, they had said it was all ash. It stirred something in him. Something he had wanted to keep forgotten, his worst memory. But he forced it down. *One terrible thing at a time.*

"Eww, Derek," said Peter reaching his finger but not quite touching the fabric on Derek's head. "I wouldn't touch that." Peter's accent was horrible but at least he had remembered.

"Dunna speak," Derek said in a harsh whisper.

Ryan hadn't looked at him since they'd been captured. He sat with his knees up and his fist under his chin looking out through the bars. Derek could see his clenched jaw from across the wagon.

Derek had replayed what had happened in his mind a hundred times since they had been captured. He should have done this. He should have done that. Maybe if he'd given Elinor the bloodroot she might not have screamed and attracted the soldiers. But the bloodroot had to be brewed into a tea and seeped. The army was obviously close to be able to hear her short scream and to get there so quickly. And the fire surely would have had the same result. They would have seen the smoke.

They had been doomed from the start.

If they had only come through the portal earlier or later but they hadn't. It was no use wishing. He, of all people, should have learned that lesson. *It was what it was.* They had come through the portal when they had and been caught. And he knew Peter and Ryan blamed him for it. He tried to tell himself that Elinor was all right. But then he heard her scream.

Ryan's expression turned frantic and then dark and violent as the screaming stopped. "Whatever has been done to her," Ryan said as he grabbed a fist-full of Derek's shirt, "You will pay for this. You'll pay for it." Derek nodded his head. He had no doubt be would pay for it. Morland always took her pound of flesh. Derek strained his ears to hear more.

Elinor

Elinor screamed herself awake as a heavy weight slammed on her stomach and the pain was so sharp and intense that her vision blurred. She couldn't remember where she was. Something was tugging at her clothes and she was swaying back and forth like she was on a ship. Her vision cleared in an instant as she remembered where she was, Morland. She saw she was in the back of a wagon and the heavy weight on her stomach was a man as he pinned her down and reached for his belt.

"Get off me!" Elinor yelled frantically trying to get out from under him. Her stomach was throbbing and bleeding.

"Well good morning, my dear," he said straddling her, running a hand down her chin while bending closer to kiss her. He was too big but she didn't stop fighting. She had to get away. *Oh God! Help me,* Elinor prayed and then yelled "Ryan! Derek! Peter!"

"Shut your mouth!" The man yelled shaking her hard enough to rattle her teeth and send her head spinning again. "Or I'll give you a bruise to match the other side. Now nice and still," he said as one hand slid up her leg.

She didn't stop fighting. *Let him hit me,* she thought. *It was better than what he had in mind. I'm never going to stop fighting. Never!*

"Ryan!" she screamed and then she saw him. She was suddenly with him, inside a wagon filled with several men. Derek and Peter were there as well. Derek had a dirty cloth over his head. Elinor reached out her hand to touch them but she went right through them like she was a ghost.

"Ryan! Can you hear me? Derek! Peter! Can you see me?" she said frantically. They were right there but she couldn't touch them and they didn't look up. Then just as suddenly she was back in the wagon with the man on top of her trying to hold down her arms. *What is happening to me? God help me!* Elinor prayed again and as if in answer a man on horseback suddenly rode up.

"What is going on here?" he said pulling the man off of Elinor by his shirt back. "Were you really going to rape a wounded prisoner in a moving wagon in broad daylight?"

"Not even worth it. This one is mad," her attacker said.

"Then get off her. What were you thinking? What kind of behavior is this? Report to my tent tonight." The man on horseback was handsome. He looked to be in his late twenties with long dark hair. He had a scar running along the left side of his face. Elinor could have married him for saving her. Tears of relief trickled from her eyes as the bad man got off of her.

"Thank goodness," she said softly to herself.

"The Goodness is long gone," said her attacker as he went to sit at the front of cart. "Only the Darkness and the Queen. Save your prayers," he said spitting on her. She wiped it off with her sleeve and glared at him.

"Move her to the women's wagon," the man on horseback said to the two men walking beside him.

"Where is my brother?" she asked as she scrambled out of the wagon. Her knees suddenly buckled underneath her. Her adrenaline had left her system and her legs were wobbly and shaking.

"Carry her, Luke," the man on horseback said. "And when you are done, come find me. We have a lot to talk about."

14

"Yes, sir," Luke said lifting Elinor into his arms as if she weighed nothing. She sucked in her breath as her stomach was scrunched up. "You aren't a Southie," he said accusingly.

"A what?" she asked

"Your brother spoke like a Southie."

Elinor thought quickly. She must have missed something in the time she was unconscious.

"He's my step brother," she said slowly sliding into a soft British accent. She remembered Jol's warning from Derek's blog. Speaking with the correct accent was very important. "We have different parents." Which was the truth and hopefully also applied to whatever scheme the boys had concocted.

"Hmm," he said. He didn't look convinced. From his arms, she studied him. He wasn't a brutish looking man and the ornaments on his jacket made her think he might be something more than just a foot solider. His brown hair was tied back at his neck and he had sharp eyes that Elinor worried saw too much. He looked polished and refined, not so much like royalty but more like a sword.

Elinor's gaze was pulled from Luke when a familiar face sent a shockwave through her. "Ryan," Elinor said in relief as she passed a wagon full of forlorn men. "Are you okay?" she asked breaking free from Luke's arms.

She grabbed Ryan's hands through the bars, making sure he was real. What in the world had happened earlier? Had she finally gone round the bend? Or were her magic visions changing somehow? Because she'd seen this wagon before. When she was being attacked she saw this wagon as clear as day, like a vision or something. And it had felt like she'd really been there for a moment.

"Oh Elinor!" Ryan said squeezing her hands tight. "Are you okay? Did they hurt you?" His voice was rough and his eyes were brimming.

"I'm fine," she said looking to make sure Derek and Peter were there. Ryan tilted her head to see the bruise that must be growing on her face. She sure felt it. "Just this. Not sure when it happened." Ryan shot a venomous look at Derek but Elinor continued, "I think it was the bad guard who was holding me. Wait," she said as she was being pulled back by Luke. "Put me in there!" she pleaded.

"No, it's full. Anyway, we don't mix. I'll put you in the women's wagon."

"No, that's my brother. I'll be fine," she said as he pried her fingers from the bar.

"We'll find you when we stop," Ryan said.

"Please go back," she cried to Luke but he just held her elbow and led her away. Tears fell as she looked back to see all three of them with their faces pressed against the bars. The pitiful sight made her smile a moment. *They look like puppies in a pet store window,* she thought.

She passed five more wagons before she got to the one full of only women. Luke said nothing as he unlocked it and closed her in. She didn't know what she expected to see in a rolling prison wagon full of women but she was *by far* the most bedraggled of the bunch. With her bleeding bandaged stomach, her bruising jaw, and her blood stained clothes, she wasn't surprised when no one greeted her.

There were eight women sitting on the dirty floor. They seemed youngish but the grime and grimaces covering all of them made it hard to pin down an age.

In the awkward silence, Elinor took stock of her wound. She peeled back the bandage and sighed in relief. Derek had sewn her up. It wasn't textbook but it would keep her insides inside. But it hurt like the devil. She wished there was room to lie down. The sitting position was making her wounds scrunch up. 'Scrunch' was not a word one liked to apply to newly stitched up wounds. Elinor tried to control the rising nausea.

What am I supposed to do now? Elinor thought trying to distract herself. *How am I going to get home?* She was locked up in this rolling prison and the boys were five wagons ahead of her. Not close enough to see each other, let alone speak to make a plan. What was she supposed to do? Had they discussed things while she'd been unconscious? She looked around and studied the other women locked up with her. Who were these women that they were here with her? Did the soldiers just imprison everyone walking around? Seemed silly because now what were they going to do with them? They couldn't imprison everyone on the planet, could they?

After a couple minutes, the brunette sitting across from her said, "Have a rough tumble with one of the soldiers?" Her face was a cold sneer and she twirled the bottom of her skirt suggestively while she talked.

"No," Elinor said in disgust. Then she realized that these people were her only source of friendship and information for possibly a long while yet. "He did try," she said wryly. "But I got the better of him and made him think twice about it." Elinor took a long look around, considering before she went on. She really did need information. "My brother, some friends, and I got captured earlier this morning. Do any of you know where we are headed?"

"The prison," said the woman.

"Are we to see the Queen then?" Elinor asked fearful, worried for Derek.

"No, you idiot. What would the Queen want with you? We'll be made to be slaves in the mines or worse," she said eyeing Elinor's bedraggled self.

"Have any of you seen the Queen?" Elinor asked. Her curiosity to be speaking to people who really lived in Morland was too much. She understood a little of Peter's excitement.

"So many questions! Ask that nomad over there."

Everyone turned their gaze to the corner of the wagon where a hooded young women sat ignoring everyone like it was an active violent thing inside of a passive dismissal.

"Well," said the brunette, "have you seen the Queen?" When the nomad didn't reply she was given a hard elbow to the side from the woman next to her and the nomad's hood slid down revealing beautiful soft pink hair. There was a collective sigh from the group. *A real live nomad with pink hair.* Elinor was enchanted.

"You are very beautiful. Do you all have pink hair?" Elinor said unable to stop herself.

The nomad glared around the wagon at everyone in turn and then locked her eyes on Elinor. She seemed surprised at what she saw. *I must look worse than I imagine I do.*

Elinor cringed wishing with all her might for a shower and a fresh clean bandage for her stomach. But the nomad wasn't repulsed. She just nodded to herself as if in dismissal but her wide eyes betrayed her interest.

The nomad's soft Irish accent made everyone somehow quieter. Her words were like a spell. "The women did. Have pink hair, I mean. We dyed our hair with special seeds. My mother did it and my sisters and when I had daughters they would have... so one day those born would have pink hair and all those after. It would be something we would be known for," she said her voice growing dark. "But now it only means death. And I am the last one.

"But... you asked who has met the Queen. I have but only from afar. Not close enough to do anything. This hair I prized," she said running her fingers though it to undo the braid and then quickly re-braiding it again, "which you find beautiful made it impossible to run. But is it not shameful to run when everyone else is dead? I too should face my fate. You all should prepare yourselves as well. There is no happy ending where we are going. There are no happy endings as long as that witch rules Morland." But despite her cryptic words her eyes were alight and they didn't leave Elinor's face even when Elinor broke contact and turned away.

So, Elinor thought reviewing the facts, *we are going to the prison, not to the castle. That had to be good. Right? That means 'She' must not know Derek is in Morland. There is still a chance we can get out of this.* She pushed the nomad girl's warning down. Elinor didn't give up on happy endings so easily.

18

She had been gazing through the bars watching the scenery when she saw Derek go by. It took her a moment to say his name because her mind knew him to be five wagons ahead of her with a dirty blanket wrapped over his head. And here he was walking without a care in the world sans blanket. He might as well have been whistling he walked so carefree.

"Derek?" she said as he passed. He looked genuinely surprised and scanned the wagon as Elinor said, "Over here!" By then everyone in the wagon was staring at her and looking around but she didn't care. How had he gotten out? Was he here to get her out as well?

But all he said was, "Shhh" putting a finger to his lips. He came over very close and whispered in her ear, "Turn your back to them and lean into the side of the wagon like you are going try to get some sleep." She looked at him strangely but did as he said.

To Elinor's amazement, Derek came so close that he was half in and half out of the bars, walking in step with the wagon.

He said, "If you whisper very quietly they won't hear you, but I'll hear you fine."

She barely held in her gasp. It wasn't Derek after all, well not her Derek. She mentally shook herself. No Derek was *her Derek*. She didn't have a Derek but it wasn't Earth Derek. It was Derek's soul. He looked just like Derek, same long red hair but rougher and older and... kinder. He didn't have the same aura of rage about him.

"Now how is it a beautiful girl such as yourself can see and hear me?" he asked with a charming grin spreading across his face. Elinor didn't know him at all. It was Derek's face but it wasn't. She didn't know it could do that.

This was Derek's soul. She was meeting Derek's soul. She had been seeing him in visions for over a year since the day her brain broke and she had started to see Morland whenever she blinked. And now she was seeing him in person. She suddenly felt a little shy.

"You don't know me?" she asked softly a little surprised and hurt. There were times she'd sworn they had been looking right at each other. She had thought he could see through to Earth or at least see her Morland projection.

"Should I?" he asked tilting his head like an inquisitive dog. "I'm sure I'd remember you. I don't talk to many people. I don't talk to anyone anymore. But more curiously, how do you know me? How do you know my name, little woman?" he said leaning closer.

"I know the other Derek. From Earth," she said. His eyes grew wide and his mouth actually dropped open. He reached out his hand to touch her but it passed right through. He closed his eyes then and brought his hand back to his side. And suddenly she was looking at her Derek. His face became a mask.

"Forgive me. I sometimes... forget. Tell me where are you from? And how are you here?" he continued.

"We are in quite the predicament. I'm from Earth, as well. I live down the street from him in Waxhaw. We are all here because..." But he interrupted her.

"Wait. Who is *all*? Who is all here with you?" he asked urgently.

"Derek, my brother, and a friend of ours," Elinor said struggling to keep her voice a whisper.

"Where is he? Is he well? Does she have him? Why would you bring him here?" He was yelling. Elinor turned around but no one in the wagon could hear or see him.

She turned back to him.

"Derek is here. He was safe when I saw him less than an hour ago. He's several wagons ahead with a dirty blanket over his head trying to stay hidden. I'm sorry I brought him here. We didn't have a choice. I'm so sorry."

But he was already gone.

Chapter 3

Derek

He was there as silently as ever. Derek knew better than to call to him in a mixed group like this and there was no need for him to do their secret whistle. Not when his soul was grinning like a Cheshire cat and walking straight towards him. Derek couldn't stop himself from smiling back and shaking his head a little. This wasn't the worst mess he'd been in but it was close. And it gave his soul no little joy in seeing Derek caught with his hand in the cookie jar.

"Stealing apples again, littlest prince?" his soul asked once he was close enough Derek could respond back without being overheard. Derek turned to have his back to everyone else.

"You know me, Soul. I've always been a fox in the hen house. Can't help myself," he said quietly, allowing himself a sly grin. It felt stiff but he still found his way back into their old familiar banter.

"I know," his soul said turning serious. "But I wish you could have tried just this one time. Why did you come back? What are you doing here? Not for me, right?"

"No, not for you," Derek said looking down for a moment. The guilt and the 'feelings' were already coming back and he'd only been with his soul for two minutes. *It was good to be back? Maybe. Probably not.*

"For her?" his soul asked.

"What?" Derek said too loudly then caught himself. "How do you know about her?" he whispered, frustrated that he had to whisper and angry at himself for slipping up. He knew better. He didn't look around but he was sure everyone in the wagon was still watching him.

"She saw me and told me where you were. Why would you come back for some girl? Bringing her home to meet mom?" his soul said raising an eyebrow. "And how can she see me?"

"That's a lot of questions. First, I'd never planned on coming back and I had assumed you'd be with me when I left. I thought we'd go home… together. It was the cost of the flower. To be separated from you. I knew it the second I ate it. I felt this voice, almost. This certainty telling me the cost. Did you know it too?"

His soul nodded.

When Derek had first arrived on Morland eleven years ago, his soul had been ripped from his body. He'd been only visible to Derek and had been Derek's constant friend and confidant. Derek never would have left him behind on Morland on purpose.

But when the Mage gave Derek a way to go home to Earth, a strange red flower, Derek had taken the gamble. The Mage had said that there would be a cost but Derek hadn't given it a single thought. He'd known that anything was better than staying on Morland where the Queen was going to destroy his soul and fill him with Darkness.

Derek had eaten the flower and had returned to Earth but the cost… His soul had had to stay behind on Morland. On Morland where he could touch nothing, feel nothing, and eat nothing. Where no one could see him or talk to him and where he could see everything but talk to no one. A ghost.

Derek hesitated a moment before he asked his next question, "Have you been alone all this time?"

His soul stared back.

"Yes. But it was a fair price for your freedom. Knowing you were home, beyond her reach." He smiled a moment and then it faded. "But you came back on purpose. Was it on purpose?"

Derek nodded.

"She still hunts you," his soul said.

"I know," Derek said.

"No, you don't know. You don't know anything. Though I have been alone, I have not wasted my years. There is so much I have to tell you, but you first. Why have you wasted our sacrifice?"

Derek told him quickly and concisely what had happened to Elinor and the why and how of their return trip. His soul walked silently in sync as the wagon rolled. When Derek was done his soul took a deep breath and said "It was very *good* of you to come back to save this girl. More good than I've seen in you since... our sister. But you still shouldn't have come."

"We were only supposed to be here an hour tops. Everything has just gone the worst it could have possibly gone."

His soul smiled a broad smile but it wasn't in his eyes. "This place is your Kryptonite. This place is your Achilles heel. This place is Murphy's Law incarnate for you. How could you ever forget it?" he asked shaking his head.

"I didn't," Derek hissed through his teeth. "I took a gamble on an hour. I thought it owed me an hour."

"Morland owes you nothing!" he spat. "She will not stop until your blood is drained from your veins and your bones are bleached on the shore and I am the Darkness and the Darkness is me. I'm surprised there wasn't a noose waiting for you as you dropped from the portal."

"I couldn't let... I couldn't watch her die," Derek said simply. And even with the restraint of having to whisper, he hadn't wanted to yell back.

"I know," his soul said finally softening. "I know. I don't know why. But I know. I'm not mad anymore. We'll figure something out. We always do, you dumb idiot." But then his tone turned frantic. "Do you know the way back? Did you mark the tree?"

"Yes," Derek said. "I know where the portal is and it works both ways. If I'm not murdered and turned into a mindless minion of Darkness, I'll be able to find the way back. For both of us."

His soul nodded but was quiet.

"Okay your turn, Soul. Tell me the news," Derek said.

"The Midsummer banquet was really something last year. They served roasted duck."

"Ha ha you're as funny as ever," Derek said as his eyes narrowed.

"She never stopped waiting for you. She doesn't wonder where you are or how you left which worries me. You know how she talks most things out loud when she's frustrated? Well she never mentions it. Why isn't she cursing the evening star that you are still missing? I don't like it. It's like she knows something. I don't like it at all."

"Maybe Jol... He wouldn't, would he?" Derek mused. The old mage had been Derek's guardian and almost friend. He'd found Derek that first dark day when Derek had fallen into Morland. Jol was the only one who had known Derek's secret, that he was from another world.

"No, I don't think it was him. I've watched him from time to time. It's easier now that he's in the prison."

"He's in the prison? Why?"

"She didn't like that you had been to see Jol when she ordered you back to the castle. This is going to take a long time. There is so much you missed..."

"Did she ever adopt more children?" Derek asked. He needed to know and yet dreaded knowing. It had haunted him that he might not have done any good in his whole time here, that he just broke things. That maybe he shouldn't have been born for all the wrong he would do and that his sacrifices hadn't even slowed her down.

When Derek had been in Morland last time he had been a solider. It seemed to him that maybe he never stopped being one. After years of killing, he'd accidentally won a competition that drew the Queen's eye and impossibly named him 'Prince'. Through some spell he'd become not just a prince of Morland but her adoptive child. He felt a pull towards her. He felt an invisible binding that he didn't know how to break free from. Even Earth wasn't far enough away to sever it.

The Queen had made a total of seven children. All of them were forgettable except one, his dear sister, Brigitte. But Derek had killed her and then killed all five of the others. He hadn't wanted to but his mother had turned them into empty vessels of the Darkness and Brigitte had begged him to release her. And he'd done it. And even now, years later, it still made his stomach turn to remember. He'd done it all to stop *her,* the monster of a queen mother of theirs.

"No," his soul said and waited a breath before speaking more. "Not exactly. She's tried. She tried a lot at first. It was pretty horrible to watch. I had to stop after a while. It was too much for me," his soul said looking down. "But it never stuck. After a while she gave it up. No tournament, no scouring the countryside. It's like she used up all that type of power she had on you seven. That's why I think she's searched for you for so long. You are her last hope. That's why coming back here was the worst thing you've ever done. I'm amazed you weren't recognized yet."

"Is there someone here I knew?" Derek said stopping himself from turning to scan the area.

His soul looked around for him. "Probably. Statistically. But I meant that your face is everywhere. Paintings. Posters. There is even a ..." He chuckled. And Derek smiled at him. It felt good. "There is even this statue of you. It's rich. You'll love it. I love it. It's like you never left," he laughed softly again. "But really it's just a matter of time until they figure it out. You are almost the first face every newborn sees. That disgusting rag won't hide you forever. Nor will being a Southie."

Derek smiled slowly, "You heard all that?"

"Oh, I hear things. I didn't imagine for an instant that it was you who was being so stupid but really that's on me for not guessing," his soul said shrugging with a big grin.

"The military looks as strong as ever," Derek commented to change the subject. Being a solider was *the* occupation for the young generation. They bared little malice for a queen that had always been there and it paid well. It was inevitable. They were the generation that truly accepted the Queen and that this crap was just how life was. Their parents had been fed the injustice from their parents and they became bitter. But that trickled down into a dull resignation. It was what it was. So why not make the most of it? Join the military. That way *they* got to be the ones with the weapons. He'd done it himself, not that there had been a single other option to choose.

"Yeah, recruitments are way up. She's planning *something*. She doesn't talk about it. Why doesn't she talk about it?" His soul said agitated and then sighed. "Well our two half heads will think of something." They were both silent for a moment thinking when his soul spoke again.

"How can she see Morland and me?" his soul asked.

"I don't know. Like I said, she started getting bad headaches a year ago and she also started seeing Morland the same day. It scared the crap out of me when she told me. There is something there. Something to her. Something we don't know. That she doesn't know. We think she has been projecting her spirit into Morland and then pulling it back to Earth every time she blinks."

"Projecting her spirit into Morland?" his soul asked.

"Yeah that's how she got attacked by the creature of Darkness," Derek said. "She's been sending a part of herself here. Well maybe. We know nothing about it."

"Could it be her?" his soul said softly to himself but at Derek's raised eyebrows he just shook his head. "And who are those twin idiots you brought?"

"The blond scraggly looking one is Peter. It's amazing to me that you don't know him. I guess I met him later. I had a... hard adjustment home. We can talk about that later. Anyway Peter is a good friend. Even if he is a fool for coming when he knew full well what it was like. And the other one is her brother, Ryan. He wouldn't leave her. He's a good brother."

"So they are both liabilities. Great. Any combat experience?"

"No. Peter was a Boy Scout with me so he..."

His soul laughed so loud Derek jumped drawing the attention of the other prisoners.

"A Boy Scout!" his soul said slapping his thigh. "Oh I never thought you'd have so many things to tell me." He smiled all the way to his eyes and didn't stop laughing for a few minutes.

Derek flushed. "I told you I had a difficult adjustment. They thought I was crazy, Mom and Dad. They didn't believe me. I haven't mentioned yet... but no time had passed. Not a second not a year. I came back the moment we left. It was like how we always said they probably wouldn't even know we were gone." Derek barked a cruel laugh, becoming himself again.

He had slipped into his old clothes but they didn't fit right anymore. He wasn't the kid he was before but he wasn't his Morland self either. "And they locked me up. Sent me to a psychiatrist and a nice stay at the pediatric mental ward. I couldn't leave until I'd renounced it all. I was just a dumb thirteen-year old kid to them. So I said I made it up."

"It hasn't been a picnic on this side either," his soul said but then he waved his hand in the air as if to erase what he'd shared.

"Do you know where we are going?" Derek asked.

"We are going due north," he said. "So where did you think we are going? We are off to the prison and then we'll be sorted. Most for labor at the mines and some will be killed, you know, for fun.

"Mines?" Derek said. "Where?"

"East of the prison. Those little red foothills of the North mountains where the soil gets crappy. She's demolishing those foothills with mining. I don't know how they don't tunnel right through and fall into the ocean. You know that on the other side of the mountains is sheer cliffs and then the water. But she is single-mindedly looking for something there.

"I haven't been over there very much since it's swarming with those creatures of Darkness. Maybe if you get sent there you can figure the mystery out. I mean what's she doing in those mines? For the past couple years, she's been getting every free, or not so free, man she can find to work until they die in those stupid mines under the mountains. But honestly, if we are lucky, your best case scenario could be that you'll live out the rest of your days in a dark mine and the Queen will be none the wiser." His wry grin told Derek that his soul had a couple plans already brewing in his brain.

"How much time has passed here? It's been six years in Waxhaw." Derek said, putting the pieces together of how much the world had changed. "Is she older?"

"Same here. Six years. And you already know the answer to that. Not a day," his soul said with hard eyes that were like looking in the mirror. His soul just stared at him. "I wondered if I'd disappear when you died. I imagined you were married with a couple kids. Happy. Successful. Normal. Seeing you this age again... is surprising."

"You've aged. How can that be?" Derek said looking at his soul. He did look older than Derek's current nineteen. He looked... "You look like my real age. Twenty-five looks good on us. But it's so strange."

"Yeah, strange," he echoed.

Derek and his soul talked late into the night while the guards and prisoners slept. Peter had fallen asleep easily while Ryan stared between the bars with glazed eyes for a long time before finally giving in to sleep.

"What has happened to the world?" Derek asked. "It seems impossible but I think it got worse since I left."

28

"Yeah who would have thought? I'd assumed you were what was really wrong with Morland," his soul chuckled but then continued. "A lot of things. The biggest two you landed into head-first like you always do. The nomads stopped liking it when the Queen stole their children. They only managed the first baby steps of a rebellion before she shut them down. There are some still scattered around, hiding but she'll find them. She wants to destroy the whole people. It was hard to watch," he said looking up at the night sky.

"And... the South Coast?" Derek asked. "They said it was 'ash'."

"It wasn't Brigitte. You know that," his soul said answering the unsaid plea in his words. "The people of the South Coast were aiding the Southies. You know their biggest port is in Southtown. The non-nomad locals tried to evacuate them all before she could come but she is the quickest," he said crinkling his eyes. "The fire flew from her hands like I've never seen. It killed everyone. It scorched the very ground."

"I wonder if she would have been happy seeing it?" Derek asked, not meaning the Queen.

"She wouldn't have, Derek. The true Brigitte would not have wanted all those innocent people killed. The Darkness wanted it. The Darkness fed the desires through her. She would have wept to see the ash..."

"Speaking of the Darkness, is it just me or does it feel... less?" Derek said.

"I can't tell. Maybe you had just remembered it worse or maybe it is. Maybe what you did made a difference but maybe not. I don't notice a difference."

"Just as well," Derek said unable to look at his soul, turning to settle in for sleep.

"See you in the morning," his soul said before slipping off into the night.

Chapter 4

Derek

Derek stirred as the early sunlight shone off the bars of the wagon cell and directly into his eyes giving him an instant headache. *Is this how Elinor feels all the time?* He caught himself thinking. He knew without looking that he was the first one awake. There wasn't much sound in the world. There were probably a couple guards close by but they were moving slowly in the new day.

He took a deep breath and stretched his arms up grazing the roof with his fingertips from his seated pose. Not being able to stand made him stir crazy. He knew they did it on purpose. He had. No one wanted agile, rested prisoners that might escape. They needed to feel constantly sore and tight. It would take precious minutes for them to accustom themselves to running and that would be enough time to catch them.

He scanned quickly for his soul. Derek wanted to know what he had discovered over the night. His soul didn't need sleep, water, or food. Derek yawned long and forceful. He had slept so poorly, feeling haunted all night, like being in a real life nightmare, which, of course, he was. But his sleep wasn't the dreamless sleep of the damned. No, he'd dreamed vividly and it still clung to him. He couldn't quite shake it off.

It had been a strange dream, to say the least. It wasn't the normal kind of strange dream where he was in a Taco Bell but it was also his house and his feet were glued to the floor so he'd be late for school. The strangest part of last night's dream was that he hadn't been himself. It had been like watching a documentary from someone else's eyes. A woman's eyes. A woman he didn't know.

She left behind no clues as to her identity except her signature of hate as an introduction. He could still taste the metallic tang of her hate in his mouth. It had been a dream of deep, confused, angry emotions. But hate and fear were the two most nameable. But a dream was a dream and he had enough real life hate and fear that he didn't need to take on imaginary versions as well. With another yawn, he leaned his head against the bar to rest for just another moment tucking the filthy fabric around him like a pillow hat.

Eventually he heard the stirrings of life. He creaked his neck from side to side. He reflexively ran his fingers through his long hair. It still felt strange to be this version of himself again. Long hair. The blanket must have fallen while he'd dozed for a minute. Before he could reach down to reattach the cloth he had locked eyes with a guard doing his morning chores. Derek ducked his head slowly, stretching nonchalantly. But it was too late. The guard raised a shout and more came over.

"Hello, Princeling. You are looking well," a guard said inches from the bar. Derek tried to keep his face neutral. There might still be a way he could get out of this.

"I told you it was him," another guard said coming over holding a poster in his hand. Derek grimaced. It was his face with another six years added, his soul's face. He'd never stood a bloody chance. He heard the others in the wagon starting to wake up and his eyes glanced over at Peter and Ryan. Peter met his eyes and started to say something. Derek had to make sure they stayed out of it. Someone should get to go home. Someone needed to rescue Elinor. So before the two of them could ruin it, he spoke.

"That's Your Royal Highness to you. Open the door. I need to stretch my legs." The guards looked around at each other, unsure if they should obey the prince, when a deep voice spoke.

"Open the door. Get him away from the other prisoners before he corrupts them. I'd hate to have to kill the whole load. And get him on a horse. We ride for the castle at once," said the most familiar voice. Derek struggled to keep his mouth closed. It may have been six years but he'd know Garrison anywhere.

His long dark hair was at his chin not hiding his scar but somehow accentuating it. Derek had been there when that scar had been born and for much more. Garrison had been his best friend and partner in crime until he'd been made prince. He had never thought he'd ever see him again. Derek shuffled around as if looking for something. He then grabbed Peter's neck and whispered. "Get her out of here. You all need to leave."

"Leave you?" Peter whispered angrily. "No way."

"Do as I say," Derek roared and Peter finally saw the prince in him. Derek kicked at the ground right next to Peter and raised his eyes. Peter obediently clutched his stomach moaning.

"Took you long enough to get me out of there," Derek said looking the guards up and down as he showed his disapproval. He couldn't stop himself for scanning for his soul. *Where is he? Where is he?* He was never there when Derek needed him. Derek made himself calm his nerves. They would find each other eventually. It probably wouldn't be too late.

Derek's hands were tied to the pommel of his horse's saddle and another rope tied around his neck was held by a solider a foot away. Derek saw his soul right before he rode off and whispered "Tell Elinor. Tell the guys. They need to escape. You need to get them home." His soul looked back watching as he rode away. Derek was riding to the castle. He took what would probably be his last free, deep breath. He was going to see *her* again.

Elinor

"Elinor! Elinor! Elinor!"

She woke up to someone yelling her name. She sat up suddenly, startling a couple of women in the wagon. Derek was yelling at her from outside the wagon.

"Derek, what is it?" Elinor said.

"Shh. It's not him. It's me."

"What's happened?" Elinor whispered to Derek's soul.

"Derek was recognized. You need to escape. He asked me to get you out of here."

"How?" Elinor said in despair looking at her cell and the guards pacing around. "Will Derek be okay?"

"No. That's why we have to get you out. You are all I've got to help Derek."

"But how do I escape?"

"I... I don't know yet. Our best chance will be tonight. That gives us both a couple hours to think of something."

"We aren't leaving without my brother and Peter."

Derek's soul looked at her thinking. "Yes, of course. We couldn't leave without them. Now use your brain, pretty girl. Show me that you were worth saving." He leaned through the bars and kissed the top of her head. She couldn't feel it, of course, but it gave her courage. She could do this. She'd seen movies and read books about this exact situation. It was very doable. She just needed to think.

When they were allowed to leave the wagon one at a time for a bathroom break, the nomad girl changed her spot and was sitting next to Elinor. It naturally upset everyone. People liked their spots. But the nomad just eyed them down and the group adjusted to the change.

Elinor didn't know if she was supposed to speak. She'd been berating herself for coming on so strong to everyone earlier. She was running out of time, the sun would set before she was ready and they all thought she was putting her nose where it didn't belong. But then the nomad spoke.

"My name is Winter," she whispered and her Irish accent was almost as mesmerizing as her pink hair.

Winter had turned her back to the others and was speaking very close to Elinor's face.

"Hello. My name is Elinor," Elinor whispered back.

"I sense something. What is your gift? Can you speak to the dead?"

Elinor stiffened. So her chats with Derek's soul hadn't gone unnoticed. What was she supposed to say? She didn't want to do the wrong thing and make this all worse somehow. Winter saw her struggle and guessed the answer.

"Can you speak to my loved ones?" she asked.

"No," Elinor said shaking her head, "I can only speak to one spirit."

"That is a shame," Winter said looking past Elinor through the bars. "When are you planning on leaving?" she said.

Always an open book. Sigh Elinor tried to keep calm. She didn't know this lady. Winter could be a secret spy. She could turn her into the guards. But Elinor decided that a fellow prisoner wasn't likely to rat her out. And she remembered what Winter had said earlier. She wasn't a fan of the Queen. She was probably as safe an ally as could be found on short notice. Elinor took the risk.

"Tonight."

"Why did you ask about the Queen? No one ever asks about her," Winter said. Elinor guessed that made sense. The other women in the wagon had nearly fallen over each other to hear what Winter had to say about her.

"She wants to hurt my friend. I'm not going to let that happen."

"And how do you propose to deny the Queen anything?"

"I'm not entirely sure. First step is escaping tonight. The spirit I speak to is preparing a plan but I need to come up with my own in case he doesn't show up. Then I need to free my brother and friend who are five wagons up. Then we head to the castle and rescue Derek. I'll wrest him from the Queen with my bare hands if I have to."

"I will help you," Winter said.

"What? Really?" Elinor was floored.

"Yes."

"Why?"

"Because you have a fire within you and I want to set it loose in the dry brush. I had given up. I was prepared to face the noose and accept the curse of my people but… I can sense your magic. I don't know what it is but I am breathing it in like I've been suffocating. You have no fear and all I want is to aid you."

Elinor leaned back but there was nowhere to go. That was maybe the nicest, most intense thing anyone had ever said to her.

"You will help me avenge my people. Your power is great. It tastes like vengeance," Winter said.

Elinor didn't know what to say to *that* so she nodded and then stared out into the trees as she waited for night. It came fast and she was nervous that she still didn't know the plan. Whenever she had started to bring it up, Winter would stare her down. Elinor stopped asking. She wished Derek's soul would at least stop by but he didn't. The wagon train stopped when dusk began to settle and before Elinor could try to ask Winter again, the ground exploded in an earthquake.

Elinor grabbed the sides of the wagon as the ground shook. But Winter wrenched her hands free and pulled her outside through the somehow open door. Winter walked as if the ground wasn't bursting to life beneath them.

Winter held Elinor's hand and the two of them walked easily as the ground came to life around them. Winter grabbed something from a cart and walked quickly to Peter and Ryan's wagon. The door was open before Elinor even knew what was happening. And they were all running just as the ground stilled.

Derek

Derek tried not to look at him. They had been riding all day. Night was falling fast and Garrison still hadn't said a word. Each step closer to the Queen and farther from his friends was killing him. Derek hoped that Garrison might still have some kind feelings toward him. Maybe he had enough to help Derek escape, so Derek played nice and let the guards think he wouldn't run. He was not pleased to see that Garrison's number two was the officer who had captured him and then had carried Elinor off to the women's wagon.

Derek shouldn't have been surprised at Garrison's apathy. What had he expected? He'd abandoned Garrison just like he'd abandoned his soul. He'd left them to deal with Morland's decline alone. He hadn't even told Garrison he was leaving. Derek lay looking at the stars wondering if he'd have any friends by the time this was over, when he felt a strong pair of arms pull him back into the woods.

"So you're back," Garrison said once they were out of earshot of the other men.

"Yes. And you are the General now?" Derek said.

"Long story but time continues on for some of us," he said with raised eyebrows. "I was surprised it took a whole day for someone to recognize you. I'd know your stupid face anywhere," he said grinning as he extended his hand.

"It's good to see you too," Derek said taking his hand.

"It's been pretty dull without you but I have a horrible feeling that is all about to change."

"Can you let me go?" Derek asked.

"No. My men are good. They'd find you in a couple hours and then we'd both be in trouble. But I've got a couple ideas. Play nice. If my men hate you, it'll make what I'm planning difficult."

"I can be nice," Derek said.

"Uh huh. Just be that charming prince I heard about. I'm sure he's in there somewhere. Under that baby face of yours," Garrison said slapping his face sharply but playfully as he lead them back towards the sleeping group.

Derek tried to get comfortable on the cold hard ground with only a thin woven blanket to provide comfort against the giant Morland sky. Another night in Morland. *I'm never going home. It starts with one night and then two and then five years.*

And then impossibly he started to get tired and he knew he'd be asleep in a moment. It should have shocked him awake how easily his body felt at ease. Yeah, he was never going home.

Chapter 5

Elinor

Her stomach pulsed. Elinor could feel the warm blood leaking through the bandage as she ran in the dark woods. She locked her teeth as she wrapped an arm tighter around her middle. She wouldn't yell out this time. She wouldn't make a noise. They had to get away. It wouldn't be her fault they got caught this time.

The forest was so dark and everyone but Winter was stumbling. Time must have been passing but it felt endless. Elinor hardly noticed as the sky began to lighten and her visibility increased imperceptibly. Ryan was next to her holding her hand tightly as he used it as leverage to navigate her. She wondered how long he'd been doing that. Maybe she'd been falling behind.

It had been too easy.

Winter had started an earthquake.

Winter had somehow started an earthquake. Winter had walked with such purpose during the quake, guiding Elinor effortlessly. Winter had then grabbed her satchel from a cart. She must have kept an eye on her bag from the moment it was taken. Elinor wished she'd known where their things were but there hadn't been time to look.

Thankfully Ryan and Peter had been next to each other in their wagon and they looked ready to bolt. And then they were all running into the trees. *Easy as pie,* Elinor thought. It worried her. It broke Elinor's mind trying to think about it. So she didn't. She just tried to keep moving.

The budding light brought more pressing concerns. Elinor was able to see how slow she was really going. Ryan must have grabbed her hand to force her to keep up. Winter and Peter were so far ahead that she could hardly see them. She took a deep breath. The arm she had wrapped around her middle was sticky and covered in more blood than she could have imagined in the dark but she made herself push on.

I can do this, she told herself. *We will probably have to stop soon. We will have to stop soon. I can do this,* she repeated. She must have spoken out loud on accident because Ryan yelled out to Winter and Peter.

"Hey! We gotta stop. She can't take anymore. Please," he said looking at Winter. She turned around and took a look up and down Elinor and nodded. Peter went instantly pale and was at her side holding her up. It was so much easier with him holding her also. *Why hadn't they been doing that the whole time?* She wondered. Winter led the group, making a sharp left to a cluster of large rocks and a small stream. It was the perfect place. If Ryan hadn't have spoken up would they have passed by this oasis? Elinor collapsed within a foot of the stream.

"Almost," Winter said. "Move her over a bit. We need to be hidden behind the rocks." The guys pulled Elinor over and before her weight settled fully on the ground, Winter was undressing her.

"Whoa!" said Peter turning red and looking away quickly.

"I know this isn't anything either of you particularly want to see but one of you is going to have to help me. There, I've covered her up a bit. Open my bag, my hands are all bloody," she directed to the boys in general.

Ryan and Peter exchanged glances.

"I could..." said Peter.

"Uh. I'm her brother. Family should probably do it. Oh man," said Ryan.

Ryan

Elinor's chest was covered with the bloody bandage remnants and her breeches were shimmied down an uncomfortable amount but Ryan steeled himself. She needed him. He was her brother and she needed him.

"You, the brother one, hand me my sewing kit and start shredding that white shirt into strips." The Irish girl with pink hair gave orders without looking, soothing Elinor's brow with fingers covered in her blood. Ryan rummaged through her bag.

He wished they'd been able to grab their gear but this lady was seriously stocked. He'd noticed the long staff that had been tied to the side of her pack and now that he was rummaging through he saw that she had at least four knives. Yeah, her pack was probably much more useful than his bag full of clothes and toiletries. But a change of clothes and a quick teeth brushing would have been heavenly.

"You, other boy..." she said motioning at Peter.

"It's Peter," he said.

"Sure. Peter," she said rolling her eyes like it was nonsense to exchange names. "I'm going to need a bunch of water. I have a cup in my bag, brother?" she said. Ryan found the cup and tossed it to Peter.

"Thanks and all but who are you?" Ryan asked.

Elinor had said something while they were running but it hadn't made any sense.

"I'm Winter," she said as she dipped a strip of cloth into the water and cleaned the wound. "I'm helping Elinor because she is going to help me avenge my family." Ryan tried to stifle his groan. He didn't care what the crazy lady wanted as long as she helped Elinor.

The wounds were cleared of dried blood and everyone sucked in their breath. Ryan had seen the wounds before but the transformation was horrible. Besides the deep red blood leaking from her, the wounds were angry, very angry, especially the biggest one. It had ripped through three quarters of the stitches and looked like it had grown an inch on each end. Ryan noticed Elinor set her jaw. The muscles flexed and locked under the skin. She was going to try and do it awake again.

"Winter," Ryan said. He didn't need to know anything about her except that she wanted to help Elinor but he wasn't going to relinquish all control again. "She's not doing it without bloodroot this time. I'm sorry we'll have to start a fire and she'll be unconscious for a bit but that's just the way it is. I'll carry her myself when we are done if that's the only option."

Winter cocked her head up at Ryan, thinking.

"Ryan," Elinor said, "I'll be fine this time. I'm prepared. I know how bad it's going to be."

"No, you don't," Peter said joining Ryan next to her. "It looks much worse," he said stroking her matted hair.

"Winter?" Ryan asked.

She grabbed the cup from Peter and splashed her hands clean and then wiped them on her pants. "Give me that red pouch," she said to Ryan. "It's probably for the best anyway," she said as she rummaged through her things. "We are going to have cauterize it this time. Only the deepest one. Well we might as well do all three." Everyone stiffened. Elinor moaned a little bit.

"It's the only way," Winter said ignoring everyone. "We have to be able to move in a couple hours and the stitches will just keep ripping. Ah." She said pulling out a small green vine from the pouch. "I thought I might have some of this left."

"That is not bloodroot," Ryan said.

"No, it's not. Only the wealthy can afford that stuff. This will work fine. As long as she stays calm, that is."

"What is it?" said Ryan unconvinced. He was feeling less trusting this go-around.

"Spula vine. It's not a pain-killer. It's a light hallucinogenic. Calm down," she said raising her hands at Ryan's instant uproar. "She'll be fine. And where is my fire? You can build one right, Peter? The vine will only last an hour. It'll be close but I'll be quick. The spula vine will just take her mind somewhere else. She'll be floating in the clouds, disoriented from her body. She'll be fine," she said. "It's very common for... recreational uses. You may have to talk to her to keep her calm and distracted."

Winter began grounding the vine in between two stones, being careful not to touch it. It turned into a bright green gel.

"Not a peep," Winter said to Elinor who nodded. Winter unsheathed her knife and sliced a gash in Elinor's forearm. She kept quiet but Ryan and Peter exploded.

"Shh! You are making me mad," Winter hissed. "If I wanted to kill her I would have just let her bleed out and fester. It needs to go in her veins. If I had her inhale it, we'd all be in the clouds. And it lasts a little longer this way." She scooped up the green gel with her knife and pressed it into the wound. Elinor hissed but didn't cry out. "Good job," Winter said patting Elinor's shoulder. After two shuddering breaths, Elinor sighed and closed her eyes as her whole body visibly relaxed.

Elinor

It was just as Winter described it. It was like being in the clouds. It was like Elinor's consciousness was just off to the side, unfettered, unconnected, and unconcerned. *I could stay here forever.*

Elinor felt an overall certainty that everything was going to be okay. She felt a presence of... lightness, of light. She could have stayed in this place forever. The Darkness felt far, far away. The relief from its oppression was very noticeable. She didn't want to ever leave. The awareness of pain was like waves lapping on a distant shore. A presence seems to hover close by. But she wasn't afraid. It was a good feeling.

Then she smelled something wrong and suddenly the waves became more persistent and closer. She tried to get out of the way so they couldn't reach her but she felt sluggish like someone else was responsible for moving her arms but she couldn't remember who. The weights of pain and wrongness were choking her and she couldn't pull herself up out of it. The clouds were dark and she couldn't find the way. She wanted to scream but couldn't remember how.

Peter

"You need to hold her still, Brother," Winter said through gritted teeth laying the knife back in the coals. "I'm not half done yet." Ryan obediently held Elinor down, gripping her wrist together above her head while he tried to hold her legs still with the rest of him. But Elinor thrashed wildly and broke from his grips. Her eyes suddenly shot open, unseeing and frantic.

"Oh no," Winter said staring down at Elinor. "She's panicking. If we don't calm her down, it'll wear off and we'll have to do it with her fully awake. Peter, you need to calm her down. Take this," she said tossing him the rock covered in the vine goo. "She can't hear us from out here." She handed him a dagger from her boot. "You need to be a calming agent in there. Do you hear me? Keep her from losing herself."

Peter didn't hesitate. He was actually able to help her. The relief was intoxicating. He cut his arm and smeared in the gel, and unfortunately lots of dirt, into his open bleeding wound. It stung alcohol.

He took two deep breaths as he lay down and then he was gone. *The clouds' had been a really a great description,* Peter thought. He looked around at the soothing whiteness. He couldn't see Elinor but he called for her not letting himself get distracted by how bizarre he felt floating in the emptiness. She came to him out of the light. And he could *feel* her screaming.

"Elinor! Elinor," he called to her. She looked around wildly. He didn't know if he moved or if she did or if it was even physically possible to move but suddenly she was in his arms. Tears streamed from her eyes floating around them like suspended rain.

"Shh. Shh," he said. "I'm here. Calm down." She was clinging to him, her body shaking. "Hey El. It's me, Peter. It's okay. Shh. It's all going to be okay. You need to calm down." Her breathing finally slowed into shuttering gasps.

"Peter," she said looking up at him. Her face was so open and trusting. They stayed there a minute just holding each other when suddenly she seemed to dissolve around him, her mouth gasping for air as if she was drowning.

"El, El! Come back to me. Hey! Stay with me." She faded and then brightened and then faded again. "Hey girl, stay with me," Peter pleaded. He tried to hold her tighter but she felt insubstantial, like the white clouds around them.

Winter must be doing more cauterizing. He could almost hear her Irish hissing at him to calm Elinor down. Elinor was looking at him, her eyes begging him to do something and he did the only thing he could think to do. He pulled his hands from her waist and held her face. Before he could think himself out of it, he was kissing her. He felt her fade for a moment and he worried he'd made a terrible mistake but then her hands were wrapped around his neck and she felt solid in his arms. She was kissing him back, meeting his desperation with her need.

He was the first to pull apart. He smiled, tracing his thumb across her jaw. "I was supposed to be keeping you calm," he murmured. "I'm not sure that qualified." She stared up at him smiling and then faded completely out. It must have hit an hour. He wondered how long they had been kissing and how much longer he'd be in this void waiting to see her again.

Elinor

She faded back into her body in bits at a time. First was the pain: Her sore feet, her jaw, and then her stomach. Then she felt cold. There was a beautiful cold cloth on her face. She breathed it in. She felt the dirt under her nails. She felt the breeze trying to soothe her burned abdomen. She heard voices.

"Finally. She's coming around. I don't know what he did to calm her but it worked."

She opened her eyes and could see Ryan and Winter standing above her watching.

"Hey sis," Ryan said softly crouching down next to her. "How do you feel?"

"Not amazing but not so bad," she said trying to sit up.

"Hey, let's give it a minute." Ryan said laying a hand on her shoulder to push her back down.

"Actually," said Winter, "she should sit up. We'll need to leave soon. As soon as he is back." She pointed to Peter snoring softly. Elinor flushed crimson, remembering.

"Ah, that explains it," Winter said with a raised eyebrow, helping Elinor sit up. She sucked in a breath as she rose.

"I can really walk without busting this open?"

"I hope so. You'll just have to be careful."

When Elinor sat up fully, her makeshift covering slipped. Ryan turned away quickly when the bloody bandage fell to the ground. Winter began binding her middle and Elinor couldn't be bothered to be modest in front of this near stranger. She was so tired, bone tired.

The wound was not pretty, to say the least. She couldn't bear to look at it for more than a moment. If it hadn't been on her body, she could have looked at it all day. But it was *her* burned stomach and it made her want to vomit, which would have made them have to start this whole nightmare over. So she stared off into the trees.

46

After Winter was done, she gave Elinor a wet cloth to wipe off the remaining dried blood from her chest. She put on her old shirt and undershirt, which they had washed as she slept. They were still slightly pink and damp but they were soft and clean. Being free of dried blood and wearing a clean shirt made her feel like a new woman. She heard Peter stir as Winter encouraged everyone to drink plenty of water before they started back up.

Elinor kneeled over Peter wondering how aware he was. She remembered her slow return to consciousness. "Good morning, sleepyhead," she said. Then he smiled. His smile. It hit Elinor suddenly what it all meant and she stood up too fast getting lightheaded. Ryan grabbed her elbow.

"Whoa there. You okay?" Ryan asked.

"Yeah. I just got up too fast," Elinor said standing on her own. It had nothing to do with the look in Peter's eyes or the fact that she had had her first real kiss in a drug-induced cloud land. Yeah, she'd just stood up too fast.

"So how was your first experience with recreational drugs? It was your first time right?" Ryan said not smiling.

"Yes, big brother," she said. "I don't think I ever want to do that again."

"I disagree," Peter said chuckling as he stood up.

"Well you weren't getting hot steel melted onto your abdomen. I felt like I was drowning. Like I couldn't move to get air. It was terrifying," she said.

"That's why we sent Peter in," Ryan said. "You were thrashing around like crazy."

"It *was* better when you came," Elinor said to Peter not able to make her eyes reach his.

"Yeah, I'd hope so," Peter said grinning.

"Come on. We've been here too long already. I want to get going," Winter said. "Brother, hold her elbow. She'll need to be supported for a while. We have a long day ahead of us."

"Where are we going?" Elinor asked.

"To get help, I hope," Winter said.

Chapter 6

Derek

Derek woke up with a start as the bright sun suddenly found a path through the dense trees directly into his face. He was already drenched in sweat and he could almost smell soot in the air. The dream had felt too real. Derek was startled when Garrison appeared at his side scanning the woods. "What is it?" he asked

"Nothing. A dream," Derek said shaking his head.

Garrison did not look convinced. "I've seen you have nightmares before and this was different." He waited for Derek to speak. Garrison knew him so well. He knew that Derek liked to process things and that he would just as soon do it internally if someone else spoke too soon. After a couple minutes, Derek spoke.

"I've been having these dreams since I've been back, visions more like. At first I thought they were unrelated. I thought they were just strange dreams, the product of being back here and feeling so small again." Derek knew how strange that sounded. Garrison stood just an inch shorter than him at six foot one. But being back in Morland made him feel out of control and that scared him.

"So in the dreams, I'm not myself. I'm a woman," Derek said and at Garrison's leering look he rolled his eyes. "Not like that, unfortunately. At first it was just her in a room, everything was on fire. But not just any fire. It seemed like it meant something," Derek looked to Garrison to play interpreter and soothsayer.

"This whole land has been ravaged by fires one way or another," Garrison said. "And if it was an enchanted fire that does little to narrow it down. Maybe the dream was just a reaction to hearing about... you know, the coast. I know that's where your sister was from."

"Maybe at first that could have explained it. The dream from before was only images, feelings, and fire. But last night it changed. I think it's a story. The images are connecting. Last night I saw something and I think it's important. Ah!" Derek said massaging his forehead. "I'm already forgetting some of it. I wish I could write it down."

"Your wish is my command, my prince." Garrison said with a mock-bow leaving and then returning moments later with ink and paper from his sack. He tried to write exactly what it felt like. What he heard and felt and saw. He didn't know what it meant but he thought they were supernatural dreams and that was all the more reason to write down every single word.

"The woman in my dreams <u>hates</u>. She hates something. The hate is so strong. This time I think I saw someone else in the fire. A man? I couldn't tell. Maybe if I keep writing I'll find some meaning to these nightmares. Or maybe there is nothing to them. Maybe Morland has a new game to play…"

After they had been riding for an hour and the sun was clearly visible, Garrison spoke without preamble. "So before this little prince was a prince he was arrested in the North Woods. Apparently he bore a passing resemblance to the best looking young thief of the time," he said winking.

Derek was surprised Garrison was telling his men of his criminal background but they were all grinning and must have known something of his past.

"He, somehow," Garrison continued shaking head, "convinced the Mage that he wasn't me. How he charmed that old rock I'll never know. But that put the heat back on me. I was passing closer to town than I usually did but it was winter and I was starving. There were only a few guards but they started to follow me. Then I ran face first into this kid and we both crash to the floor. The guards were closing in, pulling out their manacles when Derek clasps me over the shoulder and says 'It's about time. Jol has been waiting a week for you to arrive. It's not good to keep your uncle waiting. Come on.'

"And he leads me away without looking back. I was free and clear. Rumor spread that I was the Mage's nephew and I became untouchable. I've never met someone so quick thinking. You saved my life," Garrison said and Derek was surprised. Garrison owed him nothing after all they'd been through. Their tally for saving each other's butts was long. And all the times Derek had done Garrison wrong had cancelled whatever good he'd done, surely.

"Yeah and what good did it ever do me?" Derek said with a hint of a grin. "You got me in more trouble than I could have done on my own in lifetimes. Do you guys see this?" Derek said pulling down his collar to reveal a thick scar that circled down his back. "This genius thought that if we broke into a pretty girl's house in the middle of the night with a bouquet of stolen flowers that she'd give us a kiss for our efforts and not scream bloody murder. Well she did one better and sent her four hounds after us. Garrison threw me behind him and high tailed it out of there. I had had a couple drinks and wasn't as quick. I stumbled and the dogs were on me going right for my neck."

"I came back for you," Garrison said wryly.

"Yeah. That's only because I still owed you money for the drinks. I hope you all know what you are getting into with this one," Derek said and watched as each one of them uncovered scars on different places and everyone was laughing.

"Ha. Ha," said Garrison not laughing but smiling. "I won't be ganged up on." He then smiled and pulled out a heavy emerald necklace. "I'm in charge as long as I have this. He with the biggest prize gets to lead. This is what started this whole thing in the first place."

"Is that it? Is that what got me arrested?" Derek said incredulously. "It's hideous."

"The woman wearing it wasn't," he said with a grin.

"Why do you still have it after all this time? I know you could have used the money. Why not sell it? You were starving when I met you," Derek said.

"It has sentimental value. At first it was too hot to sell and then… Then I was at the citadel and had a proper income and didn't need to sell it but… I kept it as a life line. Just in case things got too bad or I got kicked out for getting into trouble with you. But then you were gone and things were really bad but I kept it cause it felt like a win. Like I'd showed the world that I'd won at least one fight. As long as I had this they hadn't taken everything from me. I guess it's my lucky charm."

Derek's soul caught up to them as they stopped to make camp. He waited until everyone was busy with meals and tending to the horses until he started talking.

"How's it looking with Garrison?" his soul asked.

"Good, I think. He's got something cooking. I think we are going to try to turn his men. Men trained by Garrison would be an invaluable asset. How's Elinor and Peter? How are they doing? Did they escape?"

"Yeah. A nomad is helping them? I don't know how that happened," he said answering Derek's doubtful look. "Last I saw them, Elinor was bleeding up a storm and they were heading north. It looked like they were making a straight shot for the prison. I don't know. I'll try to find her somehow, maybe later tonight," his soul said looking behind Derek into the dark. "Are you okay? How are you holding up?"

"Okay, all things considered. I'm still free, well free-ish. I've been having bad dreams, nightmares."

His soul furrowed his brows. "Why are you telling me this? What is wrong with these nightmares?"

"I don't know. Maybe it's nothing. I just wanted you to know. I want you to have all the puzzle piece. You are the cleverer of the two of us. Maybe you'll make sense of it all."

"Okay. Okay. Keep me posted. I'll try to be back by the morning. I hope I can find her. Is there anything you want me to tell her?"

Derek was silent for a moment. The words he wanted, no needed to say were so far away. It would take him days to sort it out.

"I guess," he finally said "Tell her I'm sorry."

"Will do, boss," his soul said biting his cheek. "Don't get killed till I get back."

"I'll do my best. Will you wait to go?"

"Yeah. I'll stay until you are asleep. Just like old times."

"Yeah, nothing at all has changed."

Elinor

They finally stopped for the night an hour past true dark. Elinor didn't realize at first that her feet had stopped moving. She'd been unaware of anything for a while. The pain of her stomach had filled her whole being. Each breath had been its own little nightmare to survive. The movement of her stomach with each inhale and exhale had taken all her headache meditation training to endure.

"Ryan," she said pulling her brother down. She was surprised to find she was sitting. She forgot what she was going to say when she felt something... Something wrong or missing. And then she found the name of it. Her head didn't hurt.

"My head doesn't hurt," Elinor said saying the words out loud in strange wonder.

"Okay?" Ryan said placing a hand on her forehead anyway.

"No. My headache is gone," she said. She closed her eyes for a moment so she could really check, take invisible stock. And when she opened her eyes she felt a smile bloom from her soul to her face. There was no headache in there. There was no headache at all. It was blissfully quiet for the first time in over a year.

"Your head doesn't hurt? At all?" Peter asked coming over.

"Not at all," she said. "I can't believe it. I never thought..."

"How is your stomach?" Winter asked as she started pulling food for dinner from her bag.

"It hurts very very much," Elinor said still smiling. Winter also reached over to touch her forehead.

"She is a little warm," Winter said to Ryan. Elinor reached up and grabbed her hand between both of hers.

"Winter, did you heal me?"

"What? I only cauterized your stomach," Winter said trying to extricate her hand from Elinor's.

"You have no idea what you've done for me," Elinor said, tears brimming in her eyes.

"Elinor," Peter said, "not that Winter doesn't deserve your thanks but I don't think she healed you."

Elinor turned to Peter and she felt herself flush crimson "Peter. Did you... When we?" She couldn't find the words to ask him.

"Oh El!" he said laughing. "I so wish my kisses had the power to heal you. But unfortunately I think your headaches are gone because we are in Morland."

When no one spoke Peter continued, "I've always thought that your headaches were linked to your sight, that your spirit has been shuttling itself between Morland and Earth. Now that we are here your spirit isn't doing that anymore. You wouldn't have noticed your lack of headache when we first got here because the pain of your stomach and the presence of the Darkness were such new intense sensations for you. And since then you've been terrified, in pain, or in danger. Now that your wound is treated and you are the safest you've been in a while, your body is taking stock and noticing what's missing."

Elinor blinked her eyes a couple times. Her headache didn't appear and her vision didn't switch. She only saw Morland and her head didn't hurt. Peter was studying her closely and he leaned in to look at her eyes.

"I don't know what this means but your eyes aren't switching anymore. They are both stuck with the yellow ring," Ryan said leaning to look also.

"Hmm," Elinor said softly. "I don't know that that's a good thing."

"I think that's because you aren't capable of seeing Earth like you've been seeing Morland. I mean otherwise you'd still have headaches and your vision would switch over at every blink. But that's not what is happening," Peter said grinning. "Have you noticed any other changes since we've been here? Not that you've been conscious for too much of it."

"I don't think anything has been different except, well… I'm sure you guys heard me yelling when we were captured." Peter and Ryan both paled and nodded.

"I meant to ask about that but you know the running and the bleeding. Did someone hurt you?" Ryan asked. His face was set and his anger was a palpable force.

"Kind of. Okay let me start from the beginning," she said seeing their faces were already in agony. She needed to tell it quickly and concisely. "So I woke up on a cart with a man on top of me. He tried to… but he didn't. A man rode up and had me moved to the women's wagon. But when the first man was trying to, you know… I was calling for you and suddenly I was in the wagon with you. But I'd never seen the wagon. I could see you all but I couldn't touch you. Like you were all ghosts. It only lasted a moment and then I was back in the cart. I don't know what that was. Maybe in my desperation I saw what I wanted to see. But I saw Derek with a blanket over his head and I couldn't have known that."

Peter's face kept getting brighter and brighter as she reached the end of her story. He was practically bouncing waiting for her to finish talking.

"Elinor," he said, "I think we've had your gift all wrong."

"What?" she said.

"I just assumed that your ability was to see Morland from Earth. That somehow you'd found some link between Earth and Morland and were able to jump your spirit between the two. Like you found a secret road that could take you back and forth. But your sight has nothing to do with Earth. It's just a very weird coincidence you were born there. Your ability is to scry Morland."

"Scry? What's that? And how is that different from *seeing?*" Ryan asked, his grimace the complete opposite from Peter's beaming grin.

"Seeing is seeing what is around you, right? What your two eyes can show you. Scrying is seeing things that aren't normally seen. Being able to look anywhere and see anything."

"Like a scrying bowl?" Winter asked with wide eyes.

"Yes. Except Elinor doesn't need one. She is one."

"What is a scrying bowl?" Elinor asked.

"You've probably seen them in a movie or read about one in a fantasy book. Oh, okay it's kind of like a pensieve from Harry Potter except the magician using it can see anything they focus on, not just memories they've saved. I can tell you don't believe me. So let's test it. Think about Derek. Focus on him. Say his name out loud if that helps and let's just see what happens." Peter was nearly hopping with excitement.

She closed her eyes and thought about Derek. Where was he? Was he hurt? Had he seen the Queen yet?

"Derek," she whispered closing her eyes. "Derek. Derek." And suddenly she wasn't in the same woods anymore. There was a large bonfire surrounded by over a dozen men and Derek was sitting alone off to the side.

She heard someone say "Wait, what is that?" and she turned to look at double Dereks.

"Derek," Elinor said looking between the two men, one of them must be the soul but she couldn't tell the difference in the dim light. "Derek, can you see me?" she said taking a step forward. Only one of them moved toward her, it was like she had broken his trance by taking the first step.

"Hello," Derek's soul said as he walked toward Elinor.

"What is it?" Derek asked his soul.

"It's Elinor," his soul said reaching for her as if he could touch her. But when his hands touched her shoulders, she felt him. The shock on his face made Derek stand up.

"What is it?" Derek asked. "Is she okay?" He was scanning the trees as if he could will himself to see her.

"I'm… I'm touching her," his soul told Derek and then turning to Elinor he said, "Can you feel this?" He tightened his hold on her shoulders.

"Yes," she said looking at him and looking at herself. She wasn't misty or see-through. She looked solid. It didn't make sense but she didn't really care. "Can you feel this?" she said resting her hand on his cheek. His exhale was the most intimate sound she'd ever heard. She moved to pull her hand away when Derek's soul pulled her into a hug.

"Oh Elinor," he said. "It has been so long since I've been able to touch anyone." He rested a hand on the base of her neck and set his chin on the top of her head holding her tight. "You can't know how amazing this is,." When he finally releasing her, his face was transformed and she couldn't take her eyes off him.

"You don't look so good," he said and she noticed she was swaying on her feet. "You need to go. I'll come find you. Where are you?"

"I don't know. On the road somewh…"

But Elinor was thrust back into her body, exhausted.

"Did you see him?" Peter asked.

"Did you see her eyes?" Ryan asked.

"What about my eyes? I thought they were closed," Elinor said. Everyone just stared at her and she paled.

"What is it? What fresh hell?" she said sighing.

"Your eyes were pulsing. Like gold rings pulsing from the center and the rest of your iris changed shades of green like a kaleidoscope," Peter said.

"Oh good. I was worried it was something weird," she said sarcastically. "Well what's one more thing, right?"

"So did you see him?" Peter asked.

"Yes. He's with a bunch of men. And his soul is with him. I think he's okay. But I'm so tired. I don't think I can do it again," Elinor said. "I just need to go to sleep."

"Nope. You need to eat first," Winter said giving her some bread and hard cheese. "Let's not do that again until you are healed up a bit. And don't fall asleep until I rebind your wound. I'm going to go look for some herbs that might help," she said tossing the boys their dinners.

Elinor dutifully stayed awake until Winter wrapped her stomach with a poultice. She then drank the vile herbs Winter mixed in a cup of water and she felt its effect very fast.

"I hope I get to see Derek's soul again," Elinor said as she lay down to sleep. Whatever the herbs were, they were knocking her out. She felt loose like liquid. And gravity felt like it had increased its pull ten times.

"Don't go looking for him," Ryan said.

"I won't. But we should give him a name," she said succumbing to the weight of her heavy eyelids.

"Sure," Peter said and she could hear the smile.

"James," she said.

"Why not?"

And she was asleep.

Ryan

"What does this all mean?" Ryan asked Peter as they sat in the dark. Elinor had fallen asleep quickly but Ryan was restless. Winter wouldn't let them have a fire so they stared into the dark night.

"I don't know. I'm just making a bunch of educated guesses here. I could be wrong about all this."

"Will her headaches come back when we go home?"

Peter didn't answer at first. He cleaned his glasses with the edge of his shirt. His glasses had changed just like everything else. They looked like antiques or early glasses prototypes. Peter probably loved them. After a minute he said, "I don't know. This is all new to me. I'm not an expert or anything."

Ryan waited.

"Um okay. If I had to guess, then yes, I think her body will always want to see Morland. I think as soon as she goes back it will all start again. No treatment will be able to fix what is going on inside her. But maybe I'll be wrong. I'd love to be wrong. Maybe she'll get it all out of her system. Maybe something *here* can fix her. Maybe we'll figure something out. Because..."

Ryan finished it for him. "Because she'll either live the rest of her life in constant pain or have to stay here forever. How could this have happened to her? Why can she see Morland? It's the weirdest, most horrible coincidence ever. Could Derek have done this to her somehow?"

"No. He would never do this to someone on purpose and I don't think he could have done it on accident. He hadn't even met her yet."

"It's all just... I can't believe this is all real. I'm here. I'm living this hell but I still can't believe this is all happening. It's strange. This, this is the strangest thing that has ever happened to me. The moment I crossed through the portal all I noticed was how amazing I felt. I'd been feeling so tired lately and crossing over the portal was like getting a shot of adrenaline. Part of it was that I wasn't convinced Morland was real at all. I almost expected us to climb that tree and for nothing to happen. But I knew right away that something had happened. I felt awake and strong. I felt like everything that was broken inside me got suddenly fixed. I felt the Darkness a little but nothing like how Elinor did. What did you feel?"

"I felt exhilarated. I thought I was going on an adventure. Even after all Derek's warnings, I was so pumped. But nothing supernatural about it. I felt the Darkness too but it felt like a smog or something. Not like Elinor, either."

"There has to be another option. There has to be a way to get rid of it. All of it. Her headaches and her ability," Ryan said. There had to be a way.

Elinor

"Hey, my little mist girl," Derek said leaning above Elinor.

"Derek?" Elinor mumbled, slowly waking up.

"Almost," he chuckled.

"Oh, James," she said yawning.

"What's that now?"

"I've been trying to figure out what to call you. Derek's soul or Derek's shadow is a bit of a mouthful. Then I remembered that Derek's middle name is James and it felt so right. You are Derek's missing middle after all. The soft caramel center," she said yawning.

"Hmm. I like that," he said smiling. "I'm so sorry for my rudeness earlier in the wagon. I didn't have time to tell you that you are the loveliest person I've ever talked to."

"That's not saying much," Elinor said smiling back.

"Maybe not. But it's an honest compliment. Especially since you've been haunting me."

"What?" Elinor said trying to sit up but falling back as she sucked in her breath.

James was at her side in a moment as he tried to support her. His face fell when he passed right through her. "You aren't looking so hot. I mean you are, of course, as attractive as ever. Is that your wound? The one that brought you here," he said motioning to her stomach as he leaned forward as if to see through the bandages.

"Yeah. Cauterizing isn't as fun as the movies make it," she said turning on her side to rise a little slower.

"Will you be okay?" he asked sitting knee to knee with her.

"She tells me I will. Winter, she's the one who patched me up," Elinor said pointing off to where the pink-haired lady slept. "Oh," she said suddenly turning back to him. "What are we going to do about Derek?"

James leaned back a little as he rolled his eyes and smiled. "That dummy? He'll be fine. We still have more than two weeks until the full moon, plenty of time to figure something out. But I'm more interested in your plans, my little ghost."

"Ghost?"

"Yes. As your stomach attests, you've been sending a piece of yourself here into Morland. I've been seeing you for quite some time. You looked like a woman made out of mist and shadow. Your hair blew from some wind I could never find. Moonlight for hair."

"Why am I not misty anymore," Elinor asked. When she'd scried to Derek earlier she'd looked normal. Solid. Real.

"Well I was wondering about that too," he said. "I've talked to Derek about you and he said that he thinks you've been sending a bit of your soul here from Earth. But just a bit of it, like a broken fragment. I wonder if your headaches were a sign that you were being shattered. I wonder if after enough time your spirit would have broken off bit by bit. But you are here. We'll get you all sorted out. Just add it to our to-do list. By the way how did you find me? In all of Morland how did you find *me*?"

"I don't know. I wasn't looking for you. It must have been chance. The first time I saw you I hadn't even met Derek yet," Elinor said.

James raised his eyebrows. "Huh. Morland is a big place and maybe it was chance. The first time I saw you I was in the woods not far from where we think the portal is. I remember it so clearly. It was just a moment. You looked towards me and then disappeared into mist. I'd thought you were a reaper come to take me to the underworld but then right as you faded you turned back for a moment and I'd have sworn you smiled. I worried I was crazy for a while. It would have been one too many bad things. But then I saw you the second time and I knew that whatever you were, you were here for me. Seems dumb now, I know."

Elinor felt a pang of kinship. She remembered her sudden fear that she might be crazy when her visions first started and she started seeing a strange sword-wielding man in an imaginary wood. But then later that man had been a solace, a comfort. She had known somehow that he was real and that she wasn't crazy.

Then after she had found out who he was she had felt even more drawn to him. He had been one of the only people who had been there for her. She remembered one of his silent vigils when she'd had an extra bad headache. It had been so nice to not be truly alone.

"Where you always in the woods when you saw me?" she asked.

"No. At first I was all over."

"So I was seeing you when you weren't close by?"

"Oh yeah. The second and third time I was north, close to the mountains. But soon after that I tried to I stay near the woods."

"Why?" Elinor asked.

He took a moment to respond. "Is it foolish to say I was looking for you? Waiting for you? And I did see you more after I stayed close."

"It's not foolish. I think I was looking for you, too. I must have been scrying without knowing it. I remember a couple times I'd think about you and wonder where you were and then I'd suddenly see you."

"See you are a ghost. You were haunting me," James said grinning wide. "Most times I'd just get a glimpse of you. Then one night you were there for hours. I tried once to touch your cheek... I'm sorry I didn't recognize you when we first met. Now, when I squint," he said looking at her closely, leaning across the empty space between them. "I can almost see her in you, the traces of a wild thing made of smoke and magic."

Elinor didn't know what to say to any of that. Speaking to James like this, while he wore Derek's face was so very strange.

"I think you did touch me that night," Elinor said flushing. "But why can't we touch now?" she said passing a hand through his.

"I've been thinking about that a lot over the past hours. Your ability must have passive and active traits. When you actively use your gift, you are coming into the spirit world. And that's where I am," he said smiling. "But right now since you aren't using your gift, you are on the other side of the veil like everyone else. But you can still see me due to some passive trait. Are you strong enough to test my theory?" he asked with a crooked grin.

"Yes. Just for a moment," she said. Elinor focused on trying to be outside her body. She looked around wondering if it worked when she saw herself sitting on the ground staring into the woods with pulsing eyes.

"This is very strange," she said pacing around herself. But James stopped her with a hand at her wrist.

"Not as strange as this," he said kissing the back of her hand. "Hello," he said introducing himself. "I'm called James. It's a pleasure to meet you," he said bowing without letting go of her hand.

"Hello, James. What a lovely name. Whoever named you must have been amazing and clever," she said smiling. "I'm Elinor and…" She stopped talking as she felt the tug to return to her body. "I think my time limit is striking midnight, better leave before I turn back into a pumpkin. Goodbye," she said kissing his knuckles before fading back into herself.

She was laying on the ground and they were a world away from each other again.

"It was weird seeing myself from the outside," she said smiling, not trying to sit up, just gazing at the stars and him.

"Yes, I can agree with that."

"Yeah. I guess you'd know. But James… Is my soul leaving my body?"

"No. Maybe. You are still whole though. Maybe you are only projecting into the spirit world. You are really only here. But you are also in both places. I don't know."

"I don't know either," she said chuckling as her eyelids became heavy.

"I'd better go," he said hovering over her. "Goodnight. I'll see you soon."

Chapter 7

Elinor

"What's our plan?" Peter asked after they had been walking for a couple hours the next morning. "How will we save Derek? How much longer till we make it to the castle?"

Elinor shook her head, smiling. Peter was a lover of plans. And even though not even one percent of their previous plans had worked out, he was undeterred.

"We aren't going to the castle," Winter said without turning around.

"But that's where Derek is going. Right, Elinor?" Peter said.

"Yes, that's where the prince is going but we are going to the prison," Winter said still leading the way with her pink hair braided tight and hanging down her back.

"Isn't that where we were already heading before we escaped?" Ryan asked.

"Yes," Winter said

"Isn't that where all the soldiers are headed? Why would we want to go there?" Ryan asked grabbing her arm to make her face him.

"Yes. But that's where the Mage is," she said. Then upon seeing their blank expressions she continued "Jol, the Mage. Have you really never heard of him? How is that even possible? His arrest was the greatest scandal since the rebel prince. Where are you from exactly?"

"Oh Jol. Yeah we've heard of him. But how is he locked in prison. I thought he was the Queen's man and he has magic," Peter said.

"The Queen and he had a bit of a falling out, I guess, and he can't use his magic right now. But once he's free..." A smile spread wide across her face. "He'll burn them all." Elinor felt a chill pass over her.

"What is his magic? Fire?" asked Ryan.

"Yup. Just like the Queen," said Winter.

"Well why hasn't he just burned the prison down and escaped?" Ryan asked.

"Because his magic only comes out of his dominant hand and rumor is she keeps that locked up. So no magic."

"Sure. But why aren't we going to the castle?" Peter asked. "I get that the Mage is locked away but it's more important to free Derek."

"How do you propose we do that? Do you have magic? Do you have any combat skills? How will you take down an army or even a small band of men? How will you repel her fire magic before it burns you to ash or the Darkness before it destroys your soul? Exactly," Winter said at their silence. "The prince is beyond our reach. So we are going to get the only person who might be able to reach that far."

"Okay, so we find the Mage and then what?" Peter asked.

"Then we find a way to kill the Queen," she said smiling widely.

"Or," Ryan said, "we go home. Derek has been here before. He's escaped here before. Elinor, let's go home. Peter, you can stay if you want but we are gonna go. We can figure your headaches out later, Elinor."

Peter jerked back and was about to say something when Elinor spoke.

"No, Ryan. We can't leave him here. We have to try to save him. He wouldn't leave us."

Ryan snorted and rolled his eyes.

"He wouldn't," Elinor said. "He came here for me. I can't leave him."

Ryan

As the sun set, they ate Winter's bread, dried meat, and cheese. Elinor could hardly keep her eyes open. At least she would sleep well. Ryan didn't like her being so tired while her stomach was still healing. She had been moving much better since she'd been cauterized but she wasn't out of danger completely.

Peter fell asleep shortly after Elinor but Ryan was restless. Always restless now. He was itching to be gone and contemplated kidnapping Elinor and dragging her home. But he wasn't sure he could find the tree without her cooperation.

"You can go to sleep," Winter told Ryan. "I'm going to stay up tonight since we are so close to the prison." As if to illustrate her point, she pulled several knives from her bag and attached them to hidden sheathes sewn into her belt and boots.

"I can't sleep," Ryan said watching the knives disappear.

"Alright."

"Why are you helping us?" Ryan asked her plainly.

"Your sister is something special. I think she can do what she plans to do."

"And what is that?"

"She wants to save the prince but I think she might be able to save the world."

"Why?" Ryan asked. He didn't ask how because he didn't care how. He didn't want Elinor to be special. He didn't like that she was able to see things. He didn't want her to be able to help anyone. He just wanted her to go home.

Maybe everyone could tell that there was something special about Elinor. He had thought of it as her 'muchness', like from *Alice in Wonderland*. It just felt like there was more to her than most people. He had always thought she had *more* than him, more of the indefinable quality that made people take a second look. Maybe she was always meant for this. He did not like that thought.

"It's hard to describe," Winter said thoughtfully. "I felt it immediately. The moment she entered the wagon. She is a beacon of light. No, that's not quite it. Having learned a little more about her gift, I think she is a bridge to the light. I think she pulls over bits of the Goodness with her wherever she goes. I can't believe everyone doesn't feel it. Maybe it's because I have magic."

Ryan groaned. Of course she had magic. They had never discussed the earthquake. "What is it?" he asked cringing in advance.

"It's an affinity to the ground. I can sense the rocks in the soil. I can feel that the ground will rise before I can see a hill. When I'm not with your sister, it feels like the Darkness is smothering my ability, like I'm underwater. But when I saw her, it was like the water fell away and I could feel every inch of the ground for miles. I grabbed a rock when we had our break and I knew I could manipulate it. I'd done it years ago when we had found a safe haven and we could feel the source, the Goodness. I turned the rock into a key. I knew it would fit the lock. I decided to free her before we'd even spoken. She was speaking softly to herself and I knew she was something... more."

Ryan sighed. It was inevitable, their being on this journey. He faced it with a resigned determination. He just needed to bring her home alive.

"My only goal is to protect her. I don't want her involved in any of this. I just want to take her home. Take her away from all this," he said motioning to the whole damn world.

"Where is your home that it's far enough to escape this?"

Ryan kept his lips closed. She already knew enough. They had stopped their weak show of having accents as soon as they escaped and she hadn't questioned them about it.

"How did you end up captured if you have magic?" Ryan asked.

"Like I said, my magic was dampened. And I was so tired of running. It's not easy to hide with this hair," she said tugging on her pink braid.

"Why didn't you stop coloring it? You color it right?"

She stared at him like he'd asked the most important question. She sighed before she answered.

"I haven't colored it since my family was killed."

Her face hardened into a sneer as she continued. "We'd been waiting for the color to take, for it to become natural and it was an excited honor awaiting a lucky woman. But for it to be me... the last survivor, the coward... It's almost too much to bear. If you are staying up, then I am going to get some rest," she said brushing his arm as she stood. "If you get tired wake me up. And Ryan, I mean your sister no harm. I just can't help but hope."

Ryan watched Winter sleep unable to slow his mind. He was warring within himself. He should just grab Elinor and go straight back to the portal, if he could even find it. Derek made it home once, he'd probably be fine this time.

Ryan didn't want to trust Winter. He didn't want to hear the truth she spoke. He didn't want to watch the blanket fall and rise as she slept. He didn't want to think that she was a different kind of woman than the ones he'd met at college and that her beauty, unspoiled by her hardship, was exactly his favorite kind. He instead stared into the woods and recited every song lyric he could think of and waited for the sun to rise.

Peter woke up a couple hours before the sun and switched duty with Ryan. Ryan was glad to give Winter a solid night's sleep. He woke up again with the sound of talking.

"It's time to go," Winter said laying a hand on his chest. "We are too close to tarry. We'll be there by early afternoon."

Elinor

Elinor didn't think that she'd walk recreationally *ever* again. She'd never been more tired in her life. Her stomach wasn't oozing but it still hurt like a beast. She was able to keep her complaining internal until an arrow pierced her through the leg.

"Bloody hell!" Elinor yelled staggering back. Winter shoved her to the right and Ryan and Peter followed.

"Elinor, I know it hurts but I need you to tell me where they are," Winter said grabbing rocks from around her. The edges of the rocks seemed to disintegrate in her hand leaving behind deadly-looking stone arrows in an instant. Elinor would have cared if not for *the arrow in her leg*. She was unimpressible at the moment.

"I don't know where they are," Elinor hissed through her teeth, trying to keep the pain in. How was she supposed to know who shot her? If she knew where they were she would have moved out of the way.

"You can scry. You can find them. Close your eyes and tell me where they are."

Elinor did as Winter demanded. She closed her eyes and felt her awareness rise above her body. She walked around and saw them. Elinor tried to memorize their positions as she returned to her body to tell Winter.

"There is one in the trees. He's that way," Elinor said pointing behind her in the direction of a grove of trees. "You'll be able to see him by the patch of moss. It's just above his ear on the tree." Elinor heard the whistle of flying stone and then a thump as the man fell to the ground.

"Then there are four more," Elinor said. "They are all on the ground and armed with swords. That way," Elinor pointed in front of them. The first two fell easily but the second two started running towards them. Winter commanded Ryan and Peter to stay back as she ran forward to meet them.

Her thick staff met the swords without breaking and she had one of them on his back in an instant. She ducked the other man's sword by a half inch and on her way back up she stabbed him in the gut with a blade from her boot.

He was on the ground as the second one got up and started to run. She extended her hand and stone spikes shot up out the ground and impaled him. Elinor felt double sick to her stomach. Once from the pain of the old wound and new wound and once because she was now an accessory to murder. She'd helped Winter kill those men. She moaned a little. *One thing at a time, Elinor,* she told herself. *Existential crisis comes after leg wound.*

"My God," Ryan exhaled looking between Winter and Elinor's leg. He seemed to be having trouble on where his focus should be. But Elinor's tears and the arrow that was still sticking through her leg won and he rushed over.

"Hey 'Ninja Warrior," Peter said to Winter. "Get over her and help Elinor."

"I'm sorry that I didn't save our lives fast enough," Winter said wiping the blood from her hands.

"Why didn't you know they were coming?" Ryan asked Winter sharply.

"I did feel something but I thought it was wildlife. They moved so well in the forest."

Ryan rolled his eyes and said, "Let's get her patched up. Do we need to cauterize it?"

"No," Winter said snapping the arrow in two above the wound and sliding it deftly out. Elinor growled. "One of you go look over there," she said pointing to her right, "by those dark boulders, there might be some kingsmar. It's a green weed that is shaped like a cross and it sometimes grows on those type of dark stones."

"Well done," Winter said to Elinor as she splashed water over the wound. "You saved us. I know you'll be tired once this is bound but you'll need to scan ahead until we get there. Those men were looking for something. I sure hope it wasn't us." Winter made a poultice from the kingsmar and packed it deep into the wound. Elinor started a low constant moan.

"We probably should cauterize this," Winter said to herself. "But there just isn't time. Oh well."

"Have I mentioned how much I hate Morland?" Elinor said when they were finally done. She was supported by Ryan and Peter doing more bloody walking. "I mean like really, truly hate it. Like so much."

Chapter 8

Jol

He knew how many bricks where in his cell. He knew when the meals would come. He knew what time the sun would be setting without a window to tell the time. He knew when the young woman next door would start crying in her sleep. He knew that no matter how he raged he could not melt the metal that held his magic prisoner.

His fire came from his dominant hand and the metal sleeve that covered from fingertips to forearm was special. The metal made of a dark ore could only be melted once. The blacksmith working with it had to be quick because once the metal cooled it could never be melted again. If it were tossed into a volcano it would never melt. So it was the perfect way to imprison a fire mage and the Queen had had it commissioned just for him.

Jol was brought sharply from his thoughts when the door at the end of the hallway creaked open. He stood suddenly ready for anything. No one ever came to his cell at this time of day. His cell was situated in the dankest, most forgotten part of the prison. Of the six cells, only his and hers were filled. So when he heard noise, he grabbed his small stool, the only furniture afforded an old man, and prepared to attack. This couldn't be good. Maybe she'd finally decided he was better off dead.

"It's so dark in here," came a young man's voice.

"Shh," hissed a woman. Then he heard it. The word he thought never to hear again. His name.

"Jol," the woman whispered, "are you in here, Mage?"

He heard a clattering sound at the cell next door and he found his voice.

"Leave her alone. I'm in here," he said kicking the door with his foot. *So they weren't guards,* Jol thought because they certainly knew which cell was his. The noise moved to his door and after a moment the lock clicked open.

"Who are you?" Jol growled. His long life had taught him not to jump from the frying pan into the oven.

"Jol, we are here to get you out. We need your help," the woman said, she sounded like an Eastie? He couldn't make out how many people were in his cell but it was more than just the two voices he'd heard so far.

"You need my help?" Jol asked. "I have nothing to offer you or anyone."

"What about Derek?" came another female voice and her accent was different. Maybe all of their accents were different. But he didn't care.

They'd just said Derek's name.

"What?" Jol said striding to the group in one large step. "He's here? The boy?" Jol had overheard Emmaline talking in her sleep last night and he'd hoped it was just a dream. But her dreams usually tended towards the truth. When the voices answered in the affirmative he said, "And you are his friends?" It was a fair question. Derek had only ever had two friends and these were not them.

"Yes," said a young man's voice. "We would do anything to save him."

"Everyone always says that," Jol said tired. Youths were exhausting. Always high stakes, always ready to sacrifice everything. "Fine. Tell me more later. We need to get out of here. I hope you all have a plan and we don't get covered in arrows the second we step through that door. Can you release me from this torture device?" he said rattling the metal box that kept his hand imprisoned. "It's the shortest key," he said waiting to hear the jangle of keys but he didn't. And somehow he was freed anyway.

74

"Oh," he said, "that feels good." He lit a small fire in his palm and the fire was so beautiful, like always. He lifted the flame out to see his rescuers better. "But you are all children," he said. Jol examined his rescue party with bemusement. The two men were nearly boys. The nomad might be an asset but the other girl had an unstable gait and a bandaged stomach and leg. It was the most pathetic group of adventurers he had ever seen.

"Hardly," the nomad girl said, her pink hair glowing in the light. "Are you coming?"

"Of course I am. Oh and free the young woman in the cell next door. She deserves to die in the sun."

Peter

They'd broken into the prison with surprising ease. It was lucky for them that Jol was in the old part of the prison, the part of the prison that was for forgotten things, it was old and empty. Maybe it was for the people that the Queen didn't want to remember or maybe people that were too dangerous to socialize with the other prisoners.

The main entrance to the prison proper had looked ancient to Peter until they'd skirted around the side and seen what a true old building looked like. It was a small building that must have been the original prison when Morland was first founded. It looked a million years old.

It was attached to the main building by a mismatched hallway. The main prison was a dozen times bigger than the small one they were going to, which was so lucky for them. Elinor guided them in, giving them instructions on which way to go to avoid the guards. They rescued Jol but he insisted they bring the prisoner from the cell next door as well. She'd been sleeping and Peter picked her up and carried her out.

Peter held the slender woman in his arms. She didn't stir. Her black hair fell across him like an inky breeze as he walked. She looked about his age but was so thin and wretched looking. He could have carried her all day she weighed so little. Her breathing was steady and her eyes darted under her closed lids. Her skin almost shimmered and he realized it was because her arms and legs were covered in a crisscross of faint white lines. And they weren't just on her arms and legs they were on her neck and... he was pretty sure they were everywhere. And he didn't think they were just lines, they looked like scars. What had happened to her and how long it had been since she'd been out of that cell?

With Elinor's scrying directions, Winter led them as easily out of the prison as they had made it inside, avoiding the few guards with ease, almost like a video game maze puzzle. She seemed to be walking with a purpose and Peter followed along silently, watching the sleeping woman in his arms.

"There is a cave up here," Winter said. "Is it empty?" Elinor stopped walking, sat down, and then nodded as she walked on with Ryan supporting her. Once they were inside the cave, Winter raised her hands and rocks covered three-quarters of the opening, hiding them. It made Peter feel claustrophobic.

Jol

Jol raised his eyebrows. A nomad and a mage. He was very impressed that she had avoided notice. "Tell me how Derek got captured," Jol said sitting down on the ground. "He's been captured, correct? I assume that's why you were sent to get me."

"Yes, he has been captured," said the wounded girl exhaling as she sat down and leaned against the wall. "We weren't *sent* to get you exactly. You are kind of our last ditch effort. Winter," she said motioning to the nomad girl "thought you might be able to help. I know you were close with Derek."

"Pah!" he said. "What you all seem to know wouldn't fill a thimble. Let's start at the beginning. Who are you?"

One of young men spoke up, the one that had been helping the wounded one. But Jol watched the other man as he set Emmaline down gently on the stone floor.

"I'm Ryan and this is my sister, Elinor," he said motioning to the injured one. "That is Peter, Derek's friend. And we only met Winter a couple days ago. We arrived here from Earth five days ago. God, it's almost been a week," he said.

If Jol had thought he'd never hear someone say his name again... hearing someone say 'Earth' was like a loving embrace followed by a punch in the gut. These children were from Earth. They must have found a portal.

"What did you just say?" he said looking Ryan in the eyes.

"We met Derek in Waxhaw, North Carolina on the planet Earth. We know all about his history with Morland," Ryan said.

The other young man, Peter added, "Minutes after arriving in Morland, Derek was captured and later recognized. He's on his way to the castle and we need to save him before the full moon. Can you help us?"

Jol's eyes narrowed. "If you know Derek's history than why would you ever make him come back here? You are no friends of his," he spat.

"James said the same thing," Elinor murmured.

"Who is James?"

"Oh that's what I call Derek's soul. It's just easier and he doesn't mind. He was really mad at first when he learned Derek was here."

"His what?"

"Oh I guess he never told you. Derek's soul is separated from his body. His soul has been here on Morland while Derek has been on Earth.

77

"You can see his spirit? You can talk to him?" Jol asked. He didn't doubt her. What cause would she have to lie to him but it was strange. And also made a bit of sense. It filled in some inconsistencies and oddities he'd noticed in Derek over the years.

"Yes, I can talk to him."

"Can you see him right now?"

"No. He checked in with me yesterday. Hopefully we'll see him soon. But I could try to find him if we need him."

"Okay so what's your plan, old man?" Ryan asked.

"Well first we'll need to..." He stopped talking a second before Emmaline starting crying. Everyone turned as if the sound was a string that pulled their attention.

Jol had never actually seen it. He'd only suffered alongside her, a stone wall away. Every day like clockwork, after she'd been asleep about two hours, she'd start crying. She slept in the afternoon for a couple hours and then at night.

"It's best not to wake her," Jol said softly as he pulled his eyes away. He wondered if now that she was free she'd tell him. He knew nothing but her name. He had his suspicions but they couldn't be right.

"Who is she?" Peter asked still watching the small woman sleep sob.

"None of your business," Jol barked. "She has nothing to do with any of this. She just needs to be free. What do you want from me?"

"We want you to help Derek," Elinor said.

"We want you to help us kill the Queen," Winter said after her.

"Hmm. Well first things first, I've got to remove this bloody beard," he said setting his face on fire. He enjoyed that parlor trick around people who hadn't seen it. He wasn't able to burn himself or another fire mage with his magic. It was nice for shaving but it meant he couldn't use his magic to harm the Queen.

Elinor

Elinor had been as surprised as everyone else when the Mage's fire didn't burn his face off. It just proved to her that she knew nothing of magic, hers or anyone else's. Her ignorance terrified her. But who could help her?

The Mage didn't look any friendlier without his beard. His blue eyes were steel and his forehead seemed to be in a constant state of disapproval. And the eyebrows! Derek had not been wrong. They seemed to be creatures of their own. Always furrowed. She couldn't pull her eyes away. But there was something else about him.

A memory of a dream.

A memory of a single photograph on her grandmother's nightstand. Her legs buckled under her as she tried to jump to her feet. Ryan came over to lift her up but she brushed past him and stood behind Jol.

"What is your last name?" she asked him with tears already brimming in her eyes.

"I don't have a last name. I am Jol, the Mage."

"If you had to pick a last name, what would you pick?"

He turned around then and was surprised to find tears spilling down Elinor's eyes. She reached for his hands and said, "Is this where you have been all this time, Grandpa Lirdin?"

Elinor watched his face cloud over in confusion and then she saw it. A flicker passed through his eyes.

"Who is your father?" he whispered.

"George Joseph Lirdin. And I am Elinor Marie Lirdin."

He closed his eyes still holding her hands tightly in his.

"It can't be," he said. "You are a dream. But..." he said tucking her hair behind her ears. She knew exactly what he was looking for. Her father had a small crimp on the top of his right ear while the other ear was a normal little round ear. Elinor had inherited the crimp as had Katie. She pulled back his hair and found where it had come from. He looked at her and then turned to Ryan.

"Him too?" Jol asked.

"No. He's my stepbrother. You've only got me. Well, no, you've two more besides me. Colton is ten and Katie is eight. Oh grandpa," she said closing the hesitation between them and embracing him. He kissed the top of her head and let out a deep breath. After a moment they each pulled back and stared at each other.

"Have you been here all this time?" Elinor asked again.

Jol

Jol had to look down to be sure the floor was still firmly underneath him. He felt dizzy. A granddaughter. He had a granddaughter and she had found him. His heart had been shriveled to the size of a raisin and this new feeling made him feel that it might burst from his chest.

"Yes, little one. I've been here since I left. Morland always takes back her own."

He watched as Elinor looked at him closely. "Why didn't you come back?" she said.

"It's not so easy. If it were, Derek wouldn't have been trapped here for five years."

"But he came back," she said not yielding an inch.

"Yes, because that's where he was born," he said. When she just looked at him he explained. "The way he left only worked because it sent him back to his birthplace. When I tried it, I was sent instead to Alentar, my birthplace, which is of course on Morland. Like Derek, I could not recreate the way I had come. I don't think the portals work both ways."

Elinor's eyes flashed at that but she didn't elaborate.

"But you wanted to come back, right? You tried really hard?" she said as tears threatened to spill again. Jol's heart started to crack. He had tried not to imagine the mess he had left behind when Morland had sucked him back across time and space. He liked to think they hadn't noticed or that they were happier without him. But the girl's face realized his worst fear, that his disappearance had destroyed them.

He had relived that day in his mind, the day he left, so many times that when he closed his eyes it replayed like a movie on repeat. He had been fading. It was the only way he could describe the feeling. It was a sense of being tugged out of the fabric of Earth. There were days he had felt so frail that he thought he might blow away.

It was a Tuesday and he'd taken a nap on the recliner. He'd just turned fifty-seven the previous week but felt much older, like time was costing him double what it cost others. He'd woken up from his nap with a jolt and was falling but not on the floor.

In an instant, he was gone and then he was in Morland in the same meadow he had left seventeen years earlier. He didn't know right away that no time had passed, that he hadn't even lost a day in Morland. His home world didn't want to lose any time with him. He was younger again. He felt strong and he could feel the years were gone without having to look in a mirror.

Morland had taken every trace of his dalliance, every wrinkle, every gray hair, even the scar on his thumb he'd gotten building his son a bike. They were erased as if the last seventeen years had never happened, like it had all just been a dream. The despair he felt could never be described or understood. It was all consuming and crippling. He'd walked in and out of the sunlight a thousand times. He ran through the meadow for days. He slept there for weeks. But whatever magic had transported him there had dissipated. He was trapped and his family was alone.

He had traveled the length and breadth of the land but no one had ever heard of another world and he found no trace of Earth. He heard a folktale about a deserted widow in a foreign land who had eaten a flower and was transported back to the land of her family and her birth. He'd found the flower and eaten it. But the legend didn't say there was a cost.

He'd eaten the flower and had wished to see his family again. And he had. He had told himself over and over that it had been a trick. That it had been a nightmare. But for the first time he believed it might be true. He'd seen a vision of his wife with vacant eyes and his son sobbing at her feet holding his wallet and shoes.

What had they thought when he'd left without a dollar and not even a pair of shoes missing? When the vision ended he was in the town of his birth and he'd wept.

"I looked harder than any man has ever looked for anything," Jol said cupping her face. "I loved your father and my wife as truly and deeply as any man can love." She looked pitifully into his eyes and he hoped she believed him.

"Is that why I have magic? Because I'm your granddaughter?" Elinor asked.

She has magic? Jol thought. He hadn't understood why she say down so often but he should have put it together. This was unexpected. She could only be a quarter Morlander and yet she had magic. And Earth hated magic. He'd have to learn more about her.

"Is it fire?" he asked.

"No. We aren't sure exactly what to call it but I can *see* Morland. Anywhere. I could see Morland from Earth. Peter thinks it might be scrying. I can look for Derek and see him wherever he is."

Jol had never heard of someone with such a gift and he had a feeling she could do more than just see it. But he didn't say so. He needed more information. She was a very interesting new puzzle piece. Maybe…

"Sorry to break up the reunion but the hour is getting late. We don't have much time until sundown. We need to put some distance between us and the prison," Winter said standing.

"Where do you propose we go?" Jol asked.

"To see Sister," Emmaline said startling them all as she suddenly joined the group. He hadn't even noticed she was awake. She smiled as she stretched. "I've always wanted to meet her. I bet she'll give us some warriors."

Chapter 9

Derek

Garrison was a sly, clever devil, Derek had to admit. If Garrison had just told his men outright that he wanted them to rebel against their Queen by backing the 'Rebel Prince', as Derek had been termed after he'd left, they would have laughed in his face. But Garrison had started slow, like a river wearing down a stone.

He told them the stories of their adventures in more personal details than Derek was comfortable with and every night Garrison dueled with him. At first Derek had been so out of shape that it had been a pity fight but once his muscles remembered and his brain turned off, he was close to as good as he'd been before he left. He had Garrison panting and their matches became fifty-fifty again.

Eventually several of the bolder men would challenge Derek afterwards. Derek did not go easy on them. He knew this game. He had been in the Queen's forces long enough to know that the quickest way to earn a man's respect was to *show* him why you deserved to be respected. Derek was by no means the best swordsman in Morland. He probably wasn't even truly better than Garrison. But he unnerved people and they made mistakes.

First, it was strange to fight a prince. Derek had lived in the castle and called the Queen 'Mother', even if it had been six years ago.

And that led to the second thing, where had he been for six years that he hadn't aged a day? He heard them talking about it when they thought he was asleep.

The third reason he beat them was because he cheated, all the time. He had never just fought with his sword. He considered his whole body as a weapon in the fight. He'd punch them in the face or trip them or kick dirt in their face. Garrison must have taught them a couple of the tricks but even he didn't know all of Derek's moves.

When they were days from the castle, Derek was somehow possibly winning them over. The stories being told stopped starring Garrison and were mostly answers to questions from the men. He tried to keep his stories light and funny, like the ones Garrison told. But Derek didn't have many stories that could be turned funny with a clever retelling. Most of his tales were dark and cruel and his attempt at humor turned them sarcastic and bitter.

But the men listened in rapture. He didn't tell them everything but he did paint the Queen with true strokes. He knew that the only way they would side with him when the fighting came was if they knew who their monarch really was.

He told them about how everyone with magic was murdered. He told them about the rituals that stole his siblings' souls and filled them with the forces of Darkness turning them into evil husks of themselves. He couldn't tell them about Brigitte or his actions after her death but there was already enough speculation that his silence spoke louder and they filled in the blanks with their own horrible details that could not have been worse than the truth.

Even though he'd ridden for longer and harder when he was last in Morland, he was exhausted. It was hard to be charming and nice all the time when he was not really either. All day he entertained them with stories and in the evenings they sparred. Then at night he'd talk to James for a little bit and then he'd dream about fire and hate.

In the mornings he'd wake with a start and write down the latest dream. They were getting more clear. The images and feelings were definitely telling a narrative and he didn't like where it was going. But he didn't let himself think about it. It would have been too much. His plate was too full and dissecting his horrible hate dreams was too Freudian even for him.

So he wrote them down and then made himself forget them. The dreams were not for the daytime. He had too much to do to try to interpret them. He had to win over the men and stop their journey to the castle. They were getting closer and closer and he found it harder to be charming and nice. He couldn't keep it up indefinitely but he had to win this challenge. Garrison and his men were his last chance of escape.

"Where did you go?" Garrison finally asked him.

Derek had felt the question hanging in the air for days. Everyone stilled for a moment, not hiding that they had been eavesdropping. Derek guessed it was time for the gamble. Time to find out if Garrison's men could be trusted.

"Home," Derek said simply and then after a deep breath he dove in. He told them about Earth and how he'd come here on accident. He told them about meeting Jol and finding Garrison. He told them about becoming a prince and Brigitte. He told them how he'd killed his siblings, each and every one of them in an effort to save them from the Darkness and hinder the Queen. Then he told them how he'd fled home and had never ever planned on coming back.

Their silence made the air feel thick and slow, like time had stopped moving for the moment.

"What do you know about the mines?" Garrison asked. His men somehow increased their intensity as they looked to Derek. He could feel it in the air.

Derek was surprised. That was not the question he had been expecting.

"Little to nothing. She started them after I left. Why?"

"It is her sole focus right now," Garrison said. "Every free man she can brand a criminal is sent there."

Derek raised his shoulders asking, *So?*

"I don't think the Queen has told many people but she says she is looking for a door," Garrison said. Derek blanched. He did not like the sound of that.

"Is that how you travel to your world?" Luke, Garrison's number two asked.

"No. The way to my world is in the woods. I've never heard of a door. Let alone in a mountain. In a mine. Tell me everything."

"Even as her General I know little more than that. She started the project a year or so after you left. All she told me was that there was a door at the heart of those red hills and that it would lead to somewhere *else*."

Derek felt chills rise on his body.

What if there were two portals to Earth? The thought of the Queen and the Darkness being unleashed on Earth made him want to vomit. It was not a thought he could entertain for long. She could not be allowed to spread her reign of terror to another world. It had to end here.

"Can you stop her?" Luke asked.

"I don't know. But I won't leave without trying," Derek said and found that he meant it. The man nodded once and slowly one by one everyone else did, except Garrison.

"I thought you were dead," Garrison said and Derek didn't know how to respond.

"I feel like I'm a little dead," Derek said.

Garrison nodded then and that was that. He was somehow forgiven, forgiven without a word or an argument. It was gone. The past no longer hung between them like a wall. Derek couldn't fathom it.

If only the castle wasn't a day away. But that would have to be enough time. And then he'd have to figure out what to do about the damn door that lead 'somewhere else'. He thought he knew all of Morland's secrets but maybe there were more.

Jol

"Emmaline," Jol asked, "where are we going? There is nothing but woods here. I am sure of that."

88

"You would never have found them. They are hidden by magic," Emmaline said.

"They? How many?" he asked.

"Not all," she said sadly. "But some."

"When will we be there?" Jol asked trying to pry some details out of her. He didn't like not knowing the plan. They were making camp after another day of walking northward in uncharted woods to some refuge Emmaline was somehow aware of even though she had been trapped in the prison with him for years.

Emmaline looked up at the morning sun and said "We'll be there when there is not a bit of moon."

"So tomorrow or the next day?" Jol asked.

"I don't know. I don't control the moon," Emmaline said. Jol exhaled and couldn't hide his eye roll.

"I think we should head to the castle," Peter said shaking his head and ignoring Emmaline. "I don't know where she is leading us but Derek needs us. We've been wandering for days and Emmaline won't even tell us where we are going."

"How do you propose to save Derek?" Jol asked. "Do you have magic that will work against the Queen? Do you have an army? Do you have a magic lantern that will clear the world of Darkness? Because I don't have any of those things. Emmaline is strange but I'm inclined to trust her. I have a strong feeling that what she says comes true. If there is an army hiding in these woods, then I want to meet them and I want them on our side. We've still got time. We still have fifteen days until the full moon. That will be enough time.

Peter

Peter was glad that Elinor had found her deadbeat grandfather but he didn't trust Jol an inch. Derek had always been distrustful of Jol. He'd always felt like he'd been hiding something and here it was! Jol had been to Earth! He'd had a family there.

Would that not have been good for Derek to know? Would that not have helped him hold on to his humanity? Derek had been in hell the five years he'd lived in Morland. And here was a man who understood completely and he'd left Derek to figure it all out on his own.

Peter could see that Elinor didn't exactly know what to make of her grandfather. She had been so excited at first that she had forgotten who he was and what she already knew of him. She had just been so glad that he hadn't wanted to leave her father and that he had loved him that it took her a while to remember what he had done to Derek and to doubt him.

"Grandpa?" Elinor asked. "Can we trust you? Will you really do right by Derek this time?"

"Did Derek talk about me that much?" Jol asked pitifully.

"A little bit," Elinor said and Peter was listening, waiting. He had wanted to plague Jol with questions the moment they'd found him but Peter had held back. He'd let Elinor have time with grandfather but now that Elinor was voicing her doubts he felt entitled to add his own.

"We know what you did for the Queen," Peter said.

"I won't lie and tell you that I hoped you'd never know any of that, Elinor. I hoped we could have a fresh start but fate is not so kind. Yes, I did many things for the Queen. I was her assassin and her spy. I was a coward who didn't want to die. Killing mages for her meant I got to live. But you have to understand. I had lost everything, everyone. Your father and grandmother were lost to me forever. I was a man without hope but even then I couldn't die with dignity. Do I regret what I have done? Every day. Every bloody day. When I met Derek, I changed. I protected him."

Peter rolled his eyes and a growl escaped. He couldn't keep quiet. "You are a manipulator. You used Derek as your sword to kill his siblings and weaken the Queen. You *never* protected Derek. You only ever protected yourself. If Derek exposed Earth that might have hurt you in some way. You needed him quiet but alive, in case he found the way back. I don't know why we are letting you come with us. If there are people resisting the Queen, then you are the last person I want meeting them."

Elinor was quiet while Peter had talked but her eyes were pleading her grandfather to defend himself, to provide evidence that would clear him. But Peter knew there couldn't be any. Jol moved from his seat and kneeled before Elinor.

"I cannot change what I've done. But I swear that you can trust me. You are my flesh and blood and I won't fail Derek again. What can I swear on that you will believe me?" Jol said.

"I… I don't know," Elinor said. "Time. Time will prove you. Show me who you really are. Let me see my father in you."

Jol bowed his head. Peter sighed and walked a couple steps into the woods. Elinor was just so nice. Too nice. Of course she'd give Jol a chance. Peter jumped about a foot off the ground when he felt a hand slide into his.

"Don't worry about the Mage," Emmaline said gripping his hand. "He loves Elinor. And he mostly wants to do the right thing."

"Mostly?" Peter said trying to pull his hand free.

"Mostly is more than most people." Emmaline said looking into the trees without releasing his hand.

Peter down looked at her and saw that she was much improved. A bath in a stream and Winter's spare clothes had restored her so she didn't look so much like a wild cave fairy anymore. Her head was just taller than his shoulder but she looked grown up. She wasn't a child but a young woman probably close to his age. Maybe it was her hand in his or maybe it was the moonlight in the trees but she was beautiful.

"Who will you kill?" she asked him quietly. He jerked his hand away and was restored to his sense.

"What are you talking about? No one. I'm not killing any one," Peter said backing away.

"It's hard to tell. The blood on your hands is red and black and white. What does that mean?" she said walking into the woods muttering a soft song to herself that Peter couldn't quite hear. He couldn't wait until they reached where they were going and Emmaline and he could go their separate ways.

Elinor

Elinor was so tired and everything but her head hurt which a month ago she'd have thought would have been a fair trade but she'd rather nothing hurt if she got to choose. But she didn't get to choose.

"Hey, how are you doing?" James asked startling her as he came out of the dark trees and sat down across from her. It was so good to see him. She hadn't seen him in a couple days.

"Not so good. I hope were are almost wherever we are going. I don't think I can keep this up much longer and I think Peter and Ryan are getting tired of supporting me all day. I know they are tired too."

"I can't stay long. Derek is too close to the castle but," James said with raised eyebrows, "where did you find the Mage and the strange little woman and where are you going?"

Elinor couldn't help but chuckle a little. "We freed him from a prison. I know nothing of Emmaline except that she is exactly a 'strange little woman' and she is leading us somewhere northish. That is all we know. Oh. I don't feel good," Elinor said swaying. "I'm sorry, James. Winter gives me a sleep draft every night to help my pain and sometimes it hits me fast. Will I see you tomorrow?"

"No. I won't leave Derek while he's at the castle. Make a plan with the Mage and I'll see you in a couple days if not sooner. If I need you, I'll find you and I know you can find me," he said with a wink as Elinor crashed to her mat.

"Goodnight," Elinor whispered

"Goodnight, my little mist girl," he said kissing her forehead even though neither of them could feel it.

Derek's papers: Full moon in 14 days

The dreams are strange because they don't feel like mine. They feel like I'm eavesdropping on someone else's nightmare. A woman's nightmare. I don't know her but I am aware that it's her eyes I'm seeing from, her memories. And her fear and hate of the fire.

The first thing I always remember when I wake up is the fire. The fire and then the hate. The hate comes quickly on the fire's heels. There is so much of each, feeding off of each other, that I can't tell where one starts or ends. The fire is everywhere. All around me. I can feel it. I can sense it. The smoke blocks out everything else. I feel the ground below me and it seems like I'm in a dark box until suddenly the flames reach high enough and the roof caves in.

Beams fall around me and the fire only grows and grows with the fresh air. My feet don't move. There is too much fire and it's too close and too hot. I can feel myself sweating even though I dream.

It is just a dream but I don't know it yet. All I know is that I'm going to die in the fire and I don't move one inch to get away. I don't know I'm dreaming until I wake up. But it's not just a dream. What in Morland has ever been what it seemed? I am the stupid bloody Morland Prince after all. And these dreams are not good and I wish I didn't feel so strongly compelled to write them down. I wish I could forget them. I wish I could forget that I even existed. I wish I didn't smell like smoke every morning.

Chapter 10

Derek

After Derek finished writing his dream, he gathered his gear and went looking for Garrison. And Garrison's silence told Derek everything he needed to know.

Derek felt like such a fool and his anger burst forth, finally free from the tightly locked cage of civility he'd been pretending was his true self. He had nothing to lose now.

"No," Derek said loud and clear. The men stopped breaking down camp and turned to look. Derek had never stood a chance. He couldn't even get this small troop of men to believe in him. "No," Derek repeated. "Garrison, you can't take me to her! I won't go." Derek pulled a sword free from one of the men's scabbards so fast that the man didn't even have time to move. And Derek pointed it at his once friend. Derek's soul stood silent, unmoving, and heartbroken.

"Don't fight me on this. It is what it is," Garrison said.

"No! You don't get to say that me. She is going to take my soul. You are the only chance I have!"

"I'm sorry, my friend but you ask too much. If you were a simple farmer, I could hide you somewhere and no one would care to even look for you. But you are the bloody prince and you already know that she knows you are here. And even if I were to betray my Queen, where could I take you? Where could I hide you that she wouldn't find you? No, Derek. I cannot. Even for you."

Derek stared at Garrison's face and saw a resigned determination that simultaneously knocked the breath out of him and stirred a rage in his soulless frame. Garrison's men had seen the look as well and they were getting ready. Derek could have taken a couple of them but not all and not at once. He threw the sword down and allowed his hands to be bound.

Despite everything he still didn't want to die and he didn't want to kill.

They'd be at the castle soon. If he wasn't such a coward he'd let Garrison kill him now but… He couldn't give up a sliver of hope that somehow it might be alright and *that* hope was scarier to him than anything else that lay ahead.

Derek had trouble keeping the dreams out of his mind after his argument with Garrison. They kept flashing to his consciousness as they rode closer and closer. He wouldn't think about the dreams. He made himself think of something else every time they touched the edges of his consciousness.

The dreams had not gotten much clearer. Always the woman and the fire and the hate. Now there was someone else in the fire and he'd wake up sweating with feelings of fear and horror that had not originated from him. Apparently he was not allowed one moment of reprieve, even his sleep was a battlefront. He sighed and looked back up at the castle as it rose on the horizon, the real nightmare lay ahead in solid stone. He had to go in, didn't he?

The morning sun was shining down on the castle and it looked as enchanted and haunted as ever. He remembered what he'd thought the first time he'd seen it. It had looked every bit the fantasy he'd expected from a magic world. It looked like a stone city with shining armor on. He'd been such an idiot then, yet to learn that Morland wanted his blood, every bleeding drop of it and that all the magic it possessed was dark and spoiled.

The castle was a stone monstrosity much older than the Queen's time but she'd added her touch to it. Somehow she'd melted sand or stone on the walls to make black glittering glass. It looked like the walls were the teeth of a subterranean monster that was just waiting for enough people to enter before it snapped closed.

It had three main levels that slowly rose up the hill. The thickest outermost wall held the city village. It was full of shops and houses and so many people. On a quiet day it took thirty minutes to walk through to the next level.

Above the city village was another wall three stories above the shops below. That was where the Citadel and the barracks were, the living quarters for soldiers when they weren't out fighting the Queen's own subjects. It had been his home for a long time.

Then above that was the actual castle. He knew every step of its five towers and many rooms and he had hoped to never see a single one of those stones again. But life seemed to laugh at him and fate spat in his face.

"Anything to say to me?" Derek asked his soul but it was Garrison who answered.

"Give me a little time," Garrison whispered walking beside him. "I've got some plans I'm working on. I'm not giving up on you."

"You have until the full moon. Please, Garrison. Two weeks," Derek said with a last look as he walked past him and he went inside the castle doors. Garrison followed close behind, transforming into the General in an instant with his straight shoulders and blank face. His friend was gone.

Derek had trouble making his feet keep walking and he had to suppress the overwhelming need to run the opposite direction as fast as he could. And when the large iron gate slammed shut behind him and only the castle lay before him, the small hope that had been building was quickly snuffed.

The nostalgia of entering the great hall was a sickening deja vu. He hated the mirror lined walls when it was empty almost as much as he hated it when it was full of people. Two lone thrones stood up on the dais where there had once been eight. *Why are there still two?* That thought was still unpleasant to digest. Had she really waited so long for him? But the great hall was not to be his final destination. He wished it had been. He would rather have faced her as a Queen with her crown and her guards and ten feet between them. But he was being taken to her bedroom and he would have to face her as Mother.

He only knew where her room was because his soul had watched her many nights as she paced and talked to herself. Derek had never been there in the flesh. The doors to her bedroom were heavy and wooden with flames and flowers carved into them. It was hard to tell if the flames were devouring the flowers or the other way around but he didn't have to guess. She was a fire mage, after all.

It was all happening too quickly. Derek planted his feet at the doors. But a sharp shove to the back made him stumble into the room.

When his eyes found a shape in the dim bedroom, he took an involuntary step back but was stopped by the small band of castle guards that had followed him into the room. Derek had fed the small delusion that his mother couldn't really be real. Or in the least she couldn't still be alive. Derek's soul was able to take the steps back and Derek didn't blame him when he went back down the hallway.

He'd wanted to believe the lie he'd repeated over and over to doctors and his parents that there was no Morland and there was no Queen. People like her could not be real. Morland couldn't be real. But when his fictional Queen turned her head to look at him and spoke, his heart stopped. "Welcome home, my son."

Derek stood fixed as her eyes roamed over him. She was the same. Beautiful. Deadly. Black hair. Black eyes. Pale skin. Luxurious surroundings. She fingered a large necklace that hung at her throat, the green stone found light in the dimness and shimmered. "And well done, General." Her eyes flickered only a moment to Garrison and then he was completely ignored as she focused fully on Derek.

"You know what they started calling you?" his adoptive mother, the Queen asked without preamble. She was sitting at her mirror getting ready for the day and spoke with her back to him.

"They call you the 'Rebel Prince'. You can guess how much I disliked it. But the surest way to keep a thing alive is to try and kill it," she said flashing to look at him through the mirror. "I'm sure you wanted it to be that way, leaving so theatrically. And that was your downfall. But more on that later." She didn't offer him a seat. She just let him linger with the presence of guards blocking the door and only her back to focus on.

100

"You have perfect timing, as usual, my son. How could you know that just yesterday I completed work on the conservatory roof?" She smiled at her reflection. "You always did have a flair for the dramatic. Such a son of mine," she said shaking her head ruefully.

"I'm not your son," Derek said catching her eyes in the mirror.

"Oh dear heart!" she said turning to look at him levelly with raised eyebrows. "How could you ever doubt that it is my blood running through your veins? I know what you did to your siblings. And how you chose Brigitte to be first..." She tapped her fingers together thoughtfully.

"One might of thought you'd have had to build up to that one. But maybe it was gracious for her to go first. Did you kill her with your bare hands?" she asked inquisitively and he kept himself from flinching but he knew the blood had drained from his face. "It was probably sweetest that she went first. That she didn't have to fear for when someone would come for her. Not like poor Gabriel. He was so confused and hurt... and afraid," she smiled widely as she powdered her nose and turned from side to side to view her handiwork.

She looked lovingly annoyed when she spoke next. "I was sure he'd be safe in the palace. But you are just a little sneak, aren't you? Of course I didn't know it was you who killed all of your siblings until later. Jol offered that information to save his own skin. Jol is reliable like that."

She started to braid her hair, fastening bits of it slowly until it all built on top. "It has not been a picnic since you left, my son. But all will be made right. Their power is not lost only waiting and it will be returned a hundredfold after your ritual. Then you and I will be unstoppable. I'm so talkative today. But it has been so long since I last beheld you.

"If you've seen the posters, I'm sure you have, you'll notice the picture was based on what you would look like after six years. I mused to myself how strange it would be when you came back looking old enough to be my lover. Imagine my surprise to see you haven't aged a day. We'll have to trade secrets," she said conspiratorially as she raised her hand sharply and Derek was removed from her room, but not before he saw the deep grin spread across her face. He felt his chills rising up from his toes.

Derek felt like a bloody fool. How could he have ever doubted that he wouldn't end up exactly where he was now? How could there be any other path for him than kneeling in this castle awaiting death and Darkness? He had no hope and no chance. His fate was fixed and inevitable. He'd run across the universe and six years away and ended up exactly where he'd left. Nothing could save him this time.

Elinor

"We'll be there soon," Emmaline whispered into Elinor's ear. Elinor was learning not to jump. Emmaline had no concept of personal space but Elinor liked her. She was a unique young woman and she fascinated Elinor a little bit. Elinor liked that no one else had any idea what to do with Emmaline.

"I don't see anything," Winter said and Elinor knew she didn't mean with her normal sight. She was *feeling* the way ahead of them with her connection to the ground.

"Your magic won't work. You'll see it... Now!" Emmaline said as they crossed over a small stream that flowed from somewhere high up the mountains.

Elinor had seem some magic since coming to Morland. She'd seen an earthquake, rock arrows, and fire but when she stepped over the water a vibrant colorful town appeared out of nowhere.

Town wasn't the right word nor was colorful. It was a sea of wagons with hundreds of people bustling about. And it wasn't just people suddenly appearing that shook her, there was something in the air, something good and the colors were back. It was no longer a dreary sepia landscape but beautiful, normal full colors. Elinor felt like she was finally breathing after being underwater. She almost didn't notice when Winter staggered to a stop next to her and was slowly turning her head from side to side as her eyes grew wide.

"What is this place?" Winter asked Emmaline as a woman with pink hair broke from the crowd and walked toward Winter. "I thought…" Winter said to the woman as tears filled her eyes, "I thought I was the last one."

"No," the woman said, "you are just the last to come home. My name is River and it fills my heart to meet you." Winter collapsed into her arms and Elinor finally saw the girl under the warrior.

"What is this place, Emmaline?" Elinor asked repeating Winter's question.

"It's all the nomads. She's been squirreling them away. Protecting them from the Queen," Emmaline said.

"Who has?" Jol asked.

"My sister," Emmaline said before running into the arms of a beautiful young woman whose dark skin contrasted shockingly with Emmaline's pale dungeon hue.

"Welcome, little sister," said the woman in a soft Scottish accent as she watched the rest of them with her chin resting on Emmaline head. "You've brought some friends," she said leaning back to take a look at Emmaline, who pulled her down to whisper in her ear. The woman's eyes opened wide and she smiled.

Elinor wondered who this woman was and where they were. She should have picked up part of the puzzle when comprehension struck Jol like a lightning bolt and his usually guarded face was openly shocked.

"Who are you?" Elinor asked.

"I thought you knew," she said still holding Emmaline. "I'm Brigitte, Derek's, and Emmaline's, big sister."

Chapter 11

Derek

It was probably late afternoon, not that Derek could tell because there were no windows in his room. But he could feel it. He'd been back in his room for a couple hours and could feel every moment that slipped past as he stayed trapped in the castle. *Trapped in the castle.* Those words were the stuff of his nightmares and he'd been having his fair share of nightmares. The record of last night's dream was at the top of an upsettingly growing list. It had almost been a relief to wake up and realize he was in Morland. Almost.

Derek had hoped to never set a bloody foot back in Morland and here he was trapped in the stupid bloody castle again. Derek paced his bedroom. His soul followed behind him.

Derek had never liked his room in the castle. It didn't help that the door was now locked. His bedroom door had never been locked before and Derek had taken a break from trying to pick it to pace the room.

The room had always felt like a prison, even when the door opened. It was lined with plain tapestries that were supposed to keep the chill out but he always felt cold unless the fire in the fireplace was at a dangerous height. The large bed always felt too big and empty after the cramped quarters he had gotten used to at the Citadel. He paced past the bed to the desk which now held his notes from the road, notes of things he didn't really ever want to reread, notes that almost smelled of smoke.

His room really felt like a combination of everything he didn't want to think about. It held his old clothes, untouched, that still smelled like the adventures he'd had with Brigitte. It had the small couch that she'd sat on while he'd gotten ready for official dinners and events. It had the dart board that still had two daggers planted firmly in the center from her clever throws.

The whole room felt like a monument to how horrible his life had turned out and a mausoleum to his sister. Her life and death felt more real and more unbearable somehow now. He wished so desperately that she was there.

The only part of the room he didn't hate was the bookshelf. He'd spent a lot of time and money looking for any trace of Earth on Morland, like he'd later done looking for signs of Morland on Earth.

Books were not easy or cheap to acquire but once he was prince, his purse was bottomless. But none of them mentioned any other worlds or adventures outside of Morland. Maybe Morlanders just weren't terribly creative people. On Earth, people had been writing about visiting other places since the beginning of literature but maybe Morland hadn't always been a place people wanted to escape. Maybe past Morlanders were just content with their lot. He knew that wasn't the case now but it was hard to write novels during the reign of an evil Queen. Those would come from the next generation, the freed generation. *If there ever is one,* he thought.

"Enough," Derek said holding out a hand to his soul to stop his pacing even if he couldn't actually touch the spirit.

Seeing his soul in front of him again made him feel young and so very old. His soul had aged as Derek was supposed to. It was bizarre and it unnerved Derek how little he knew of the portal magic that had brought him to Morland in the first place. There were rules of the world he still didn't understand.

Derek still couldn't quite believe that he was back in Morland. He'd been safe on Earth for six years until he'd met a stupid girl and he'd somehow willingly come back to his personal hell to save her stupid life and he didn't even know if she was alive. Last he'd heard she'd recently had her stomach cauterized and was running for her life with Jol of all people. Morland did not disappoint.

"I know, Derek. I know," his soul said. "But this isn't the end. We still have until the full moon. The Queen can do nothing to us until then. We have fourteen days. Two weeks. That is enough. It will be enough. I'm not worried and I'm not going anywhere until we figure something out. Let's talk it though, like the old days."

"Okay," Derek said sitting cross-legged on the floor as his soul came to sit across from him. "The facts," he said. They always started with what they knew and with what was in front of them.

"We are in the castle," his soul said.

"Yes. *Locked* in the castle. And the Queen is alive and well." She was waiting until the full moon to destroy his soul and fill him with Darkness or maybe the other way around.

He couldn't help but replay their meeting over and over. Her words were stuck on some horrible repeat. "Welcome home, my son." He'd hoped to never ever hear those four words together again. Their interview had been so short that it had left his head spinning. He'd been dismissed and brought to his rooms to wait, for what he wasn't sure. But he knew she wasn't done. This was only the pregame show and judging by the second throne in the great hall, she'd been preparing for this game since the day he'd left.

"Yes, she's alive," his soul said. "But I think she is weaker. I've seen her use almost no magic. That's strange. And the Darkness... Maybe it's less, like you said. I think it's waiting. Like it's sleeping. But I don't know. Things are different this time around. I mean what about those dreams?" his soul said.

"Yes. Whatever they are and whatever they mean…" Derek said shrugging. "And we have a random door that may or may not exist that leads to 'somewhere else'."

"Yes but you know what?" his soul said winking. "That feels like a *future* problem. Whether there is or isn't a door doesn't really affect us now does it? That's for future us to worry about, those chumps. It can't speed up or slow down the coming of the full moon. I'd really try to put it out of your mind. Okay, now the good things. Garrison is still free and may be able to help us."

"Yeah, maybe," Derek said but he still worried that too much time had passed. Garrison was 'the General' now. That meant something. There was probably no man in Morland the Queen trusted more. But that put Garrison in the perfect position because she would never see it coming.

"Peter is still free. Along with Elinor and Ryan," Derek said. "You being able to talk with Elinor will be very helpful to us. We'll be able to relay messages right under the Queen's nose. We also have Jol, whatever that means," Derek said. He had no idea where the Mage stood. He was helping Elinor and they'd somehow freed him from the prison but that didn't mean he'd help Derek. He had told the Queen that Derek had been the one who killed his siblings.

"I think we can count on him. He never told her about you being from Earth. We can count him as an ally. We have allies this time," his soul said grinning. "That is huge. We didn't have that last time. We have allies," he said smiling and winking. "Pretty allies."

"Sure," Derek said ignoring the last comment. "What else do we know?"

"We do *not* know her plan. She's still being quiet but I'll start patrolling the castle," his soul said. The Queen used to always talk to herself, late at night when she was alone. It had been one of their greatest tools the last time around and it worried both of them that she'd suddenly stopped. Why didn't she talk to herself anymore? What had changed since last time?

"Good plan. Come back tonight and fill me in. Maybe there is some weakness we can exploit. It's been six years. Something has to be different in his bloody castle. Find it, soul," Derek said.

"And you try to find a way out. Show that lock who's the boss," he said grinning as Derek rolled his eyes.

Elinor

Elinor stood in a nomad camp that hadn't been there a moment ago. She'd crossed over a small stream and suddenly there was a huge camp with hundreds of people and bright tents and noise and the smell of good food but none of that held a candle to how amazing it all *felt*.

It was the Goodness. It was everywhere.

All of Morland was under a sepia-colored shade of Darkness but not this place. The colors were bright and Elinor found herself taking deep greedy gulps. She'd almost forgotten what it felt like to be free of the Darkness.

Elinor *was* super amazed that a whole nomad camp had appeared out of nowhere only moments ago but she didn't study the bright colors or the bustling people. Elinor's eyes stayed locked on one woman. The woman stared back at Elinor and smiled as she held Emmaline tight. Elinor's mind was running too slow, probably from blood loss and her many wounds. Because for a moment she'd thought that the woman had said her name was Brigitte and that was impossible.

"What's your name?" Elinor asked again.

"Brigitte," she repeated in her soft brogue. But even hearing it again, it didn't make sense. Brigitte was dead. Derek had killed her.

"You are Brigitte? Derek's sister?" Elinor asked. This was probably a different Brigitte. There couldn't be only *one* in all of Morland. The mass of people was sweeping Elinor along towards a central bonfire but Elinor didn't lose sight of the woman. There were so many wagons and so many people and it was loud and people were pushing her. All the sudden, exhaustion and claustrophobia gripped her tight. And nothing made sense.

Derek had had six siblings when he'd been prince of Morland. He'd killed them all. He'd killed Brigitte first but Elinor was impossibly staring her in the face.

"Yes. He's my brother," Brigitte said looking up at Elinor as she sat down in a cross-legged position around the large fire. Everyone was mimicking her as they sat and listened.

"And Emmaline is your sister?" Elinor asked looking between the two creatures who could not have been more different. Emmaline was pale, malnourished, and wraith-like with her long dark hair flowing unbound behind her. She had looked very much at home in the dark, pitiful prison Elinor had found her in. Whereas Brigitte was… so full of life. Her smile was easy and broad. She was beautiful. Maybe the most beautiful woman Elinor had ever seen in real life. She was entrancing. Her black hair was braided and wrapped around her head like a crown.

Elinor leaned closer to see what color Brigitte's eyes were. They were a golden hue that was a beautiful contrast to her dark skin. Her eyes had been a soulless black when Derek had choked the life out of her.

"Please sit down," she said patting the ground next to her. "I'll tell you everything you want to know. But first where is Derek? Is he at the castle?"

Elinor tried to sit down. But the campfire was sliding to the right and she was falling with it. She blinked and had trouble seeing for a moment as the world spun and then suddenly went still as she felt Peter's arm supporting her.

"Hey, easy there, El. Are you feeling okay?" Peter asked.

"She needs medical attention," Winter said as she moved to Elinor's other side and motioned several people to come over. Winter was explaining what had happened and what she had done to treat her while Elinor was lifted into Peter's arms.

"No, wait! Brigitte," Elinor said trying to find her as strangers swarmed her vision. She couldn't find her. *I've only had her for a minute and I've lost her. What will I tell Derek?* Maybe she'd only imaged Brigitte. But Elinor felt a warm hand on her shoulder and Brigitte said "I won't leave you. Let them treat your wounds. We'll talk when they are done."

The days of travel with a wounded body caught up with Elinor suddenly and sharply. She let herself rest on Peter's chest and be carried anywhere he wanted to take her. She was laid down on a mat and there was a flurry of activity as several people treated her wounds.

She sighed when a cream was applied to her stomach and her angry wound grew cool and tingly. Then her leg was cleaned and a new poultice was applied. Elinor couldn't remember if she'd thanked Peter for carrying her but he had drifted out of the room. She fell asleep to the sound of Emmaline's soft humming and Brigitte's assurance that she'd still be there when she woke up.

Peter

Peter told himself that Elinor was fine and he didn't need to guard her sleeping body. Ryan had left to take a walk with Winter anyway. And Brigitte and Emmaline were staying with Elinor. So Peter was probably allowed to explore and that was good because he felt like a kid in a Freaking. Candy. Store.

Before now Morland had been a huge disappointment. He'd thought he'd believed Derek when he'd said that Morland was the worst but when the tides kept rising against them over and over, Peter had felt let down. He'd really hoped that Morland would be just a *little* amazing. He'd hoped that her cities and mountains would feel otherworldly and enchanting. But all Peter had seen were trees and a prison, neither of which had been anything special. But the nomad camp... It was something else.

He walked the makeshift streets with an unstoppable smile. He was finally somewhere magical, somewhere that felt nothing like Earth. There were a couple hundred people living in the dozen or so acres clearing that was surrounded on all sides by trees. In the clearing were aisles upon aisles of wagons. They were all different colors and sizes and Peter found himself getting lost in them before he understood the layout.

The four nomad sects, North, South, East, and West, were divided and secluded from each other as much as they could be with the large bonfire in the center connecting them. At first glance he had thought that there were only wagons, spanning endlessly in all directions but when he really looked he saw that they weren't really wagons and there were several types of structures.

They weren't wagons because almost none of them actually had wheels. Some of them looked like they'd had wheels at one point and others were wagon shaped houses, with rounded tops and small windows and doors. There were also many permanent looking tents made of a thick canvas that would probably do well in all climates. There was a stable and several stone buildings. Peter could hardly keep from running.

Once he'd figured out the differences of each clan it was easy to see the dividing lines between the four nomad sects. Elinor was resting in the East nomad side. It was the easiest to find because all the women had pink hair. The men had white-blond hair and he'd guess that that's what color the women's hair would be if they didn't dye it pink. On the far perimeter of their wagons was a large herb garden. It smelled exotic and familiar at the same time. There was also a large vegetable garden and a compost heap. Fields ran along the whole eastern side of the clearing.

The East nomads spoke with soft Irish/East accents like Winter did. Their wagons were the brightest. They were painted in stripes and polka dots, bright colors and murals. They were quintessential nomad wagons: bold and made to draw attention.

They wore flowy, colorful clothing with a lots of embroidery on everything. It looked very hippie or new age-y. Loose tops and flowing skirts and dresses. Not exactly his style but he appreciated the sheer 'otherness' of it. Peter crossed paths with Winter and Ryan once or twice but they were all content to do their own thing.

Peter was glad that he was exploring on his own. He preferred it that way. But he wouldn't have minded if Derek was the one showing him Morland. He pushed his worry down as it kept threatening to overpower him. Derek wasn't a child and they would find a way to rescue him. There was nothing he could do right now anyway. He'd only just arrived at the Glen, as he'd overhead them calling the magically hidden nomad camp.

Peter figured he was doing research. Understanding more about Morland and her people could only help them. He knew more about Morland than any Earthling beside Derek and he was finding it easy to quickly fit together the puzzle pieces that were missing and match them with everything Derek had told him.

The South nomads were the fewest and he passed by their few wagons a couple times before he realized that there was only a dozen or so of them. He was terribly reminded that the whole South Coast was ash. How lost they must feel so far from the ocean, trapped in a sea of trees? Their wagons were the closest to the river that ran down from the mountains but he was sure that was the same.

Their skin was dark and their accents were strong Scottish brogues but he remembered from Derek that it was called a South accent. Their wagons were all blue, every one of them. Different shades and patterns but only blue.

Their culture and style was distinct. The women wore pants and blouses with vests or jackets that had strands of beads and woven ropes looped across. They wore beads or jewels in their hair and around their necks. The men wore dark pants and blue tops. Most of them had pierced ears with some sort of blue stone. It didn't take a genius to see their love of the sea. Their desire and yearning was painted in bright blue strokes over every aspect of their lives. He wondered if everyone could see exactly what he loved and longed for just by looking at him. He sure hoped not.

The West nomads' area was easy to spot because there were only tents, tan, brown, and white tents. No wagons in the lot of them and they were all positioned surrounding the stables. It was the epicenter of their tent village. There were not many horses but there wasn't anywhere for a horseback rider to go. Everyone one of these nomads was here because they had nowhere else to go. They were refugees of the Queen and the Darkness. Brigitte had somehow found and saved each one of them. It was a testament to her success that Jol had been as shocked as he was. Peter felt a sudden fierce protectiveness to guard these people from Jol. He still didn't know if he could believe a word Jol said.

The West nomads looked the most like Earthlings. They were tan with dark or fair hair and looked like people who spent a lot of time in the sun. They wore neutral clothes made of leather and linen. Some of them had tattoos of intricate lines on their biceps or ankles. They would not have looked out of place on the great plains of America when the country was just getting settled.

He wondered not for the first time how all these people had ended up on Morland to begin with. He imaged giant portals opening up and sucking whole cities across space to a strange land. Or there was always the remote possibility that Morland life had started just like life on Earth and they'd somehow developed the English language along with several accents. He didn't really believe it but the alternative felt just as strange.

The North nomads had the largest quarter of land. But there were the most of them, numbering just slightly over half, he'd guess. They were very distinctive looking as well. They were pale-skinned and had dark long hair either black or a deep auburn, even many of the men had long hair. Their clothes were bold and bright. Lots of blacks and reds and greens. The clothes weren't loose and flowing like the other clans. Theirs were tight, warm, and serviceable. Not a lot of frill or excess just expertly worked pieces of clothing that did their job.

There seemed to be more artists and performers among the North. He saw several people playing instruments or singing while they did their chores. Others were writing or painting. But they were not so big on smiling. They didn't want to chat with Peter so he moved along.

The Glen was large and used to the utmost efficiency. It included a track of river that was about thirty feet wide and in-between it and the camp were the fields. Peter had wondered how this many people could be secretly sustained. It looked like they were growing wheat and a corn-like plant. There was a moderate sized vegetable garden with a compost heap that accumulated their garbage. There were also small herds of sheep, pigs, goats, and chickens. No cows or large livestock because there just wasn't the room.

The Glen was a spacious, beautiful prison but there was no forgetting that that was what it was. All the way around the Glen in a circle was a ring of small stones. It demarcated how wide the circle of Goodness spanned. He'd been given only one warning before he was allowed to wander. They told him to stay inside the ring of stones because the Darkness waited outside.

He walked the whole perimeter in an hour. No one went beyond the barrier and he didn't blame them. He'd spent a week on that side and he was very glad to be on *this* side. He hadn't noticed the Darkness so much when he'd first crossed over into Morland but it had started to get to him.

Being in the smog of the Darkness was like carrying a backpack that slowly had rocks added to it day by day. Small rocks so that it wasn't terribly noticeable from one day to the next but it wore on a person, physically and mentally. Walking across the magic barrier into the Glen was like cutting the straps free and he'd almost staggered from the release. Peter finally felt like he was in Morland, the Morland he'd dreamed about.

Derek had told Peter that there wasn't much magic left in Morland. Since the Queen had come to power seventy plus years ago she'd been systematically killing everyone else who possessed magic. By the time Derek arrived on the scene the only mages left were the Queen and Jol.

It hadn't just been that the mages had been killed but something about the Darkness taking over seemed to weaken the magic that had already existed before, magic fueled by the Goodness. Peter wished he knew more. He wanted Morland to be more magical and he wished he knew how to undo what the Queen had done.

But since meeting Winter and finding the Glen, Peter felt his hope flair. *Morland is not the worst. Morland is not a lost cause.* There was hope for her and her people. Peter was just so overwhelmingly glad that he was there. Everything finally felt like it was falling into place. They'd save Derek *and* Morland. He didn't doubt it one bit.

Peter had been equally impressed with everything he saw but he stopped in his tracks when he saw the blacksmith shop. It was directly out of the pages of a novel. There were two young men working inside who looked identical if not for the five years or so age discrepancy. Peter lost his usual shyness and walked up saying "Need another set of hands?"

"And what are you supposed to be?" the older one snapped, his fair skin and dark hair named him a North nomad.

"My name is Peter. I just got here this morning."

"What direction?" he asked eyeing Peter up and down and when Peter just looked at him he said "So are you a Westie?"

"Oh no. I'm not a nomad. I came here with my friends."

"The girl?" the man said standing to face Peter. "You came with the girl and the Mage?"

"Elinor? Yes, she's resting," Peter said.

"Well then, of course I need help around here. Brigitte is always asking for more and more weapons. I was just going to ask her to send someone. My name is Ian and this is my brother, Bo. Pull up a seat," Ian said.

Winter

Winter ran. The world passed by and all there was was Ryan's hand and the enormous rush of being home. *Home.* It was headier than spula vine and more invigorating than the strongest morning coffee. The Goodness surely wove a glorious tapestry. Never in a thousand years would Winter have guessed that saving a young woman from a wagon would lead her on a journey that would bring her home. Home. Home. Home. Winter did not tire of the word. She'd always been a creature of extremes, the highest loveliest of highs and the bitterest darkest of lows. Just now she could almost feel invisible wings at her back that could allow her to soar over the whole world.

"These are the Westies," Winter said leading Ryan through a network of tents and into a small six-horse stable. "You can usually tell them from a Northies by their tan skin but not always. They live in an elaborate system of caves but..." she said locking her lips with an invisible key. "But that's a secret now."

Winter rested her forehead on the forehead of a black mare who had lowered her head for just such a purpose. Her name was carved into the wooden beam above. "Hello, Buckwheat," Winter said bowing her head slightly. "Their horses are a bit magic, I think. I spent some time in the West."

Ryan's raised eyebrows asked a question but she just smiled a wicked grin and led him away. She shouldn't have mentioned going to the West. That was... a dark time. Her darkest. She didn't want to think about that today. She led him through a meandering path and she almost started to backtrack when she stumbled into the East nomad quarter.

"Welcome again," River said hugging Winter and Winter tried not to stiffen. River had been the first East nomad Winter had seen in a long time. It was so strange to see these people that looked like her but weren't her own family. "We hear you are a mage. It is a great honor to be blessed by the Goodness in such a way. Where does your talent lie?" River asked.

"I have an affinity to the ground. To stone and rock," Winter said stopping her fingers from pulling a rock into her hand. She didn't want to show off and the magic resisted her a little which was strange.

"We have some spare room in my wagon," River said, "and I'd love for you to stay with me while you get settled."

"Thank you," Winter said. She made herself smile. This was a good thing but it still just felt like a dream. River showed them around their wagons and gardens and Winter dragged Ryan with her. When they reached the herb garden Winter looked on with real interest. There were so many different herbs and flowers. It would be nice to replenish her pack. River bent down and grabbed a handful of something and Winter stiffened when she saw them, aris berries.

"You'll be needing some of these," River said handing them over. Winter felt her face flush as she stared down at the pink berries. Aris berries were the East nomad secret for pink hair. They were ground into a dust and then mixed with water. A newborn daughter got her first application when she was just twelve hours old. Then once she was grown it became her responsibility to keep her hair pink by applying the aris berry solution to her roots as her hair grew in blonde. It was mostly a big pain to keep up with it but young girls were told that one day a daughter of the East would find favor with the Goodness and she wouldn't need the berries.

Winter knew she could not have found favor with the Goodness but… she couldn't remember the last time she'd used the berries. Her hair roots didn't grow in the white blonde they always had. They now grew in pink. Her hair stayed pink all on its own.

"I… I haven't needed them for a while now," Winter said looking down but she was forced to look up when River was silent. Winter saw silent tears falling down the woman's face.

"Oh please stop," Winter said. "It's not a big deal." *I should have taken the stupid berries and just said 'thank you'. Why didn't I lie?*

"Yes, it is," River said with shining eyes. "You know what this means. You are blessed among the East. The Goodness must have great plans for you. Welcome home, little sister. This is a new era." Several people asked if Ryan was her ayai and she had to bite back a sharp response.

Nomads didn't get married; they *found* their lochien. It was the person who was their perfect match, their other half. They searched ayai after ayai to find their lochien. Sometimes it took years, sometimes their first ayai became their lochien. She wondered if the two of them looked like they were in love or if the others were trying to decide if she was available. She hoped she made it clear that neither one of those was an option. But all the same she didn't let go of his hand.

Winter managed to slip away as a crowd grew to stare at her pink roots. Ryan's overwhelmed expression made her chuckle.

"What was all that about?" he asked.

"Family is… interesting, isn't it?"

"Did you really not know this place was here?" Ryan asked, finally having given up trying to free his hand and was letting Winter lead him windingly through the wagons.

"Obviously not. You know that. This place… this is a secret place," Winter whispered. "If Emmaline had not led the way I would never have found it. I'd like very much to know how she knew where this was."

Ryan chuckled. "I know nothing of Emmaline but that she is incapable of answering a direct question and that she knows things we cannot fathom."

Ryan was right, of course. Emmaline *knew* things. She'd made comments to Winter and the others on their journey that had everyone squirming. She foretold death and struggles. She saw the truth of things.

The first night they were on the road Emmaline had come to Winter when everyone else was asleep and had said, "Your body is painted in invisible blood. You have to wash it off or the stones will stop listening."

It still gave her chills to recall it. That prison girl had looked into her eyes and seen her soul. Never had a statement cut so close to her secret heart. Because Winter did feel it, their blood. It coated her. But she *couldn't* wash it off. It had sunken down to her bones and become invisible. She felt it when she woke in the morning and when she braided her pink hair. It was her second skin, marking her as an East nomad more blatantly than her colored hair.

The day of the blood, she'd come home from a day's journey where she'd delivered her mother's tincture to a sick child. Winter had told her mother to leave them be. Those same people would report them to the Queen's men as soon so they delivered the medicine they begged for. No one but nomads could be trusted now.

At just thirteen, Winter had already been filled with apathy for outsiders and fierce kin protectiveness. Healing smelled too strongly of magic and magic was a death sentence for all nearby just like the blue cough that moved from mother to child to neighbor and struck the patient blue in the chest until they died of suffocation. Winter knew almost every malady and how to treat it. Not all East nomads were healers but most were. It was one of the reasons why they were so easy to catch. Their caring nature was a liability.

When times were good, their payments for medicine provided amply for their wandering lifestyle. They lived nowhere for more than a month or so. In some ways it was a cheaper, simpler life. They owned their wagons and everything they could fit inside and they owed no city taxes or dues. Yet they could grow little food from their wagons or gather from scavenging and had much need of goods that could only be purchased. But there were sick people in every village and town and they paid for the nomad expertise.

But times were not good anymore and if Winter had been in charge, they'd have found somewhere to hide or somewhere they could defend themselves from ungrateful townsfolk who might as well spit in their faces as they healed their children. But she had not been in charge. She'd been a girl and only thirteen. They were not Southies who elected women as caretakers of the clan. So Winter had tried to listen and obey their clan leader, a man named Forest.

When her mother had told her the tincture was finished and needed to be delivered, Winter had grabbed her pack and headed to the town as ordered. She was the youngest of her sisters, they each had been married summers ago leaving Winter as the errand runner. She had grumbled as she walked to town and delivered the medicine. She had grumbled on her way back stopping at a blueberry bush for a snack. And she had screamed when she had arrived back at camp.

The blood had not been invisible then.

It had been every shade of red ever painted: bright red of a sunrise, rusty red of an old shovel, pink red of a crushed rose petal, blood red. She'd gone from family member to family member, checking them all. Her training somehow coming through despite her despair and screaming. She had checked her mother. She'd been warm despite the blood that had dried and cooled on her skin. Her father, her grandfather, her grandmothers, her sisters, their husbands and children, her aunts and uncles. Everyone. She had checked each one. Her cousin, Oak, had been the only one with enough life to speak.

"Cousin, what has happened here?" Winter had asked him as she had ripped her jacket to bind his wound as she had tried to slow his leaking life blood. "Who has done this?"

"Soldiers. So many. So. Fast. I'm glad you weren't here. Remember us." And then he was gone.

Winter had howled.

She had buried every one of them and laid them beneath a large pine tree. She had willed the soldiers to return to check for survivors. She would have clawed out their eyes with her own hands if she could have.

By the end, she had been covered in the blood of every kinsman she had. When she was done, she had no blessing to give and could find no words but the vow that she would indeed remember them. She would never forget. And she would be sure the Queen remembered, too.

"What is it?" Ryan asked pulling her from Emmaline's words of truth. Looking into his eyes she felt an instant peace she hadn't felt in a long time. He would be trouble. Eyes like peace were the last thing she wanted with her heart full of vengeance.

"Nothing. A shadow. Let me show you the rest. By the end you'll be begging to be a nomad. There is no greater life. Come," she said pulling him towards the sound of music. The North nomads would help chase her dark mood away. Dancing always helped.

Chapter 12

Elinor

Elinor didn't know where she was when she woke up. There was an orange light filtering through a gap in curtains and her first instinct was to shy away from it. She was supposed to hate sunlight, especially the kind that ignored curtains. But Elinor didn't hate it. It was beautiful and her head didn't hurt.

She studied the light like she'd never seen it before. Her head didn't hurt but the rest of her was in the precarious stage of numbness that would surely fade back into pain. By the color of the sunlight, she'd lost most of the day. *Nothing new there.* She couldn't count the times her headaches had cost her *all* daylight hours but Elinor didn't have headaches in Morland. *Oh yeah. I'm in Morland.*

"Feeling better?" Brigitte asked leaning over her. Brigitte was here and alive. It hadn't been a dream.

"Yes, I think," Elinor said taking stock of her wounds. Her stomach was bandaged and felt cool like a winter breeze was blowing on it. Her leg was bound as well and she couldn't name all the herbs and spices she smelled. Everything felt blissfully numb but she knew from experience that that was not going to last forever.

"Good. You'll feel even better with a full stomach. Let's get you dressed and we'll walk to the fire," Brigitte said bringing over a stacked pile of clothes. Elinor was chagrined to find she was wearing nothing under the blanket but her bandages. But it was for the best. All her clothes had been blood-caked and dirty. New clothes sounded heavenly. She accepted Brigitte's efficient assistance and tried not to blush. She'd had a lot of people working on her wounds a couple hours ago and she hadn't cared who'd seen her then as long as they'd made her feel better.

Elinor was dressed in a structured linen tank top and small shorts for her underclothes and a loose white blouse and a beautiful lilac flowing skirt with a corseted belt overtop. There were two pockets on the front of the skirt that were embroidered with a border of small green leaves.

Brigitte was alive. Elinor was in a magical nomad glen. She was wearing beautiful clothes. All was well.

The wagon she was in was large enough that she could stick her arms straight out and still have a couple feet before she touched the walls and she could stand up straight but a tall man would have had to hunch over. Brigitte led her down the three short steps of the wagon and through a maze of wagons and tents that broke into a small courtyard with a giant bonfire at its center.

Elinor sat down abruptly feeling a little light-headed. But even so she felt better than she had in weeks. Because she was with the Goodness. She felt it in the air and the ground. It was like everything around her was charged with a faint electric current. The Darkness had been weighing her down, suffocating her, poisoning her. *But this place. This place is amazing. I don't ever want to leave here,* Elinor thought.

Elinor couldn't stop studying Brigitte. It was like meeting a unicorn. Brigitte shouldn't be real but she was. Elinor had so many questions for her but mostly she couldn't wait for James to come. Derek was going to be so happy when he heard.

Brigitte smiled at her as they watched the bonfire roar in front of them. "You look like you have some questions," she said lifting her hand in a motion that quickly brought two bowls of soup over. *That is true power and authority,* Elinor thought smiling in awe. *The ability to summon soup with a hand motion.* Elinor had a new life goal.

"Yes, I have questions. But I have no right to ask any of them," Elinor said cupping the warm bowl in her hands. "You don't know me and I know so much about you."

"Then tell me about yourself and we'll be even. How do you know my brother?"

It was the simplest most expected question that Brigitte could have asked but it would reveal the one thing Derek had always kept from her. The fact that he was from another world and he had never told her. But Elinor sure wasn't going to lie to this wonderful woman and if Derek didn't want people telling his secrets than he shouldn't have gotten captured. She felt a quick burst of shame at that. Derek had done all of this for her. And she felt sure that Derek would have known that the time for secrets and lies was past. Elinor looked around at all the people sitting by the great fire and she told the truth.

"I met Derek on our home planet, Earth."

Elinor told her about how she'd first seen Derek's soul from her visions that let her see Morland from across space from Waxhaw, North Carolina. She then told her about how she'd met the real Derek at her college and wasn't not impressed with this rude, violent nature. But how after they'd learned each other's truths they'd finally... barely tolerated each other. She did not tell his sister about the kiss in the dark Boone night or the attraction they both fought tooth and nail to ignore.

Brigitte looked surprised, of course, but not mad. It looked more like the pieces were finally starting to make sense. Elinor told her about her headaches and her sight and what had happened since coming to Morland. When she mentioned James, the name she'd given Derek's soul, Brigitte stiffened and looked around.

"Is he here now?" she asked.

"No. But he will be very happy when he sees you," Elinor said smiling.

"Hearing all this," Brigitte said staring into the fire, "is like finally understanding all my brother's struggles. He kept so much from me. He wanted to protect me, I know. But it is so good to know the whole truth. Thank you, Elinor. Now I suppose it's my turn."

"Yeah, I want to hear this too," Peter said sitting down next to her. "How are you alive?" Elinor blushed at his abruptness. It was probably rude to ask a near stranger why they weren't dead by your best friend's hand.

Brigitte grew pensive and turned to face Jol. "I think this story starts with you, Mage. Tonight will be a night of coming clean." Jol stiffened a millimeter and Peter pounced.

"You knew?" Peter said understanding immediately what Elinor didn't. "How long have you known that Brigitte was alive? The whole time, right? Even when Derek was still here?" Peter said shaking his head incredulously. "I cannot freakin believe this. You've always known that Brigitte wasn't dead. And you kept it from him. I can't wait to hear you try to get out of this one."

Jol

Jol still could not believe he was where he was, seeing what he was seeing. Brigitte and her secret nomad camp. He would have preferred to stay out of it. She had ignored his instructions and... She had saved so many.

Jol was called for his account before he was ready and he wished he could tell his story without Elinor there. Then he could lie to his heart's content and not feel guilty. Guilt. It had been a long time since that feeling had broken free from the restraints in his mind. He didn't dwell on the past. He didn't dwell on his sins. But his granddaughter, Elinor, had asked him if she could trust him and he couldn't fail her at the first test.

Jol scanned the bonfire before he spoke. He took a moment and hoped that Brigitte would explain but she didn't. Elinor's eyes were pleading. He knew what she wanted to hear. She wanted to hear that the decision to keep it from Derek had been made with Derek's best interest at heart or that maybe he hadn't understood what the lie would mean. But neither of those were the truth.

Jol felt Peter's distrust radiating off him like a furnace. It made Jol smile that Derek had found such loyal friends. Jol told himself that Derek would understand why he'd done it. He'd often wished he had told Derek everything and now it looked like he'd get a second chance. Jol turned his eyes to Elinor and told her the truth about that night.

The night Derek had killed Brigitte, he'd showed up at Jol's door covered in the dirt of her grave. They'd then had more to drink than either of them had ever had in their lives. Later that night, Jol had been curious to see the body. He guessed that he'd needed to see proof that Derek had really done it. When he'd gone to the spot where Derek had dug the grave, he found it empty. His first thought had been that the Queen had found the body and could still use it but then an acorn had dropped on his head.

Brigitte had been sitting high up in a tree like nothing had happened, but something had. He had *felt* it. Jol had known without a shadow of a doubt that the Darkness was not in her. The air around her had been clean. It had flowed down like fresh air from a cloud. The air had been purified of the Darkness. It had been intoxicating after having breathed the poisoned air for so long. No one could have missed the difference.

The Darkness covered the whole planet in an oppressive cloud and yet somehow around Brigitte the Darkness receded. Somehow Brigitte had magic now. She had purified the air around her. She had cleaned it of the Darkness. And that had made his decision. Brigitte was too valuable to the Queen and too noticeable with her magic to return to any normal life. The Queen would probably do the ritual again and this time whatever had spared her life might not be able to do it again.

Brigitte had to be hidden. Somewhere where her radius of Goodness wouldn't be noticed or reported. Hidden even from Derek. Derek could never know. She would weaken his resolve and erase his need to cleanse the world of the Queen's dark taint. Derek had to finish his mission and his sister was his only weakness.

Jol had told Brigitte that Derek was away. He had explained how dangerous her gift was and that she must remain hidden away from people, always. Brigitte had appeared to agree with him. Her resurrection had removed all ties of loyalty she felt for the Queen. Brigitte had been glad to hide and she swallowed Jol's lie that it was for the 'greater good'.

Jol gave her the money he had on him and he never saw her again. Brigitte was too dangerous to ever be found and he would not lead anyone to her. He'd reasoned she was a smart girl and would find some way to take care of herself without too much notice. He'd been relieved he'd never heard her name over the six years since he'd left her.

The Queen's children of Darkness needed to be killed and Derek needed to be the one to do it. Jol had planned on telling Derek after he killed them all but the month had passed too quickly and Derek's full moon was coming for him fast. Jol had then given Derek the flower and had still not told him. Then Derek was gone.

Jol had been so weak to make the boy do it himself but... Jol had always been a coward. Maybe he could never stop being the Queen's man. He could tell that Elinor didn't like the story he told but it was the truth. He tried to soften it down, to smooth the edges but the fact was he'd known Brigitte was alive and he hadn't told Derek. It felt inexcusable when he had to say it out loud but if he'd told Derek then Derek would probably be dead. Jol's lie had allowed Derek to return to his normal life, at least for a little while. He'd bought Derek six years. Did that count for nothing?

Elinor

Jol looked at Elinor like he was waiting for something. But there was nothing for her to say. She'd known that Jol was not a *good* man. She'd read Derek's story and knew enough of Jol's past with the Queen but he was also her grandfather. And when Elinor looked at him she couldn't reconcile the two men. He couldn't be both of them. He couldn't be a heartless solider who did the Queen's bidding just to save his own neck and the man who had taught her father how to throw a baseball and tie his shoes.

She wanted him to just be her grandfather. She wanted to bring him home with her to Earth and to show her father that Jol hadn't wanted to leave. Because when Jol had gotten sucked back to Morland, he'd left her father and grandmother alone and confused.

But he wasn't just her grandfather. He was a real life, three dimensional person with a past before he came to Earth and a past since he'd been back in Morland.

But he'd told the truth. She could see what it had cost him. His eyes had kept darting to her face during the story and she knew her face had said everything. Jol had known that Brigitte was alive! It was mind-blowing. Derek loved his sister more than anything. Her death defined his life. He had killed her with his own two hands to free her from the Darkness that had consumed her and it had nearly destroyed him. It had led him down a path of blood that ended with the killing of all five of his other siblings. He'd narrowly avoided sharing their fate when Jol had given him a way back home to Earth, a way that had cost him his soul.

Elinor couldn't stop thinking about what might have happened if Derek had known Brigitte was alive. Everything would have been different. She didn't know how but seeing this nomad camp and Brigitte's powers... They might have been able to help Morland. Maybe they could have saved it six years ago. How many lives might have been spared if they'd tried? If they'd tried before she'd murdered all the South nomads and everyone else who lived on the South Coast.

But maybe it wouldn't have changed anything.

No one knew how to kill the Queen and many had tried over the years. And if Derek had known Brigitte was alive he never would have returned to Earth. He wouldn't have been in Waxhaw when Elinor's headaches started and she'd started to see Morland. She would have had no idea what was happening to herself and she probably would have thought she was insane. Things happened the way they happened and Elinor couldn't change anything from the past. It was what it was. Only the future lay unwritten before her and it was terrifying and thrilling.

"I think you meant to do the right thing," Brigitte said. "If the Queen had found me then, I would have been lost forever. It was for the best that I stayed hidden. It was not for the best that you keep Derek from me. I am not angry with you, Jol. I let that go long ago.

But I did decide that my gift should not be hidden away from everyone. It is alright that you are here now but I must give you a warning, Mage. If you betray these nomads, you will not live one breath longer. It would be the last thing you ever did."

Jol bowed his head low. "I mean you all no harm and my aim now is to destroy the Queen and protect my family," he said scanning his eyes over to Elinor.

Brigitte nodded and seemed content enough for the time being. Many of the other nomads did not look so convinced but Brigitte looked to be in charge and no wonder because she was literally buzzing with power. Elinor could feel it from across the fire.

"Okay. There is one thing I don't understand," Peter said studying Brigitte. "Derek killed you. But Jol finds you alive only a couple hours later. How?"

"My brother did kill me," Brigitte said, "I remember little from after the Darkness took possession of me but I remember Derek trying to stop me. I knew in a distant corner of my mind that I was supposed to return to the Queen. I had been flooded with the Darkness but the ritual wasn't complete yet. I still had no soul. I knew I needed to return to her and she would remove it. She had commanded me. It was like an annoying voice in the background. But I was able to force it down. Just like the command to not hurt Derek.

"I remember shoving my hand into the knife wound I had given him so I could get away to seek my vengeance on the world and then it all went black. The next thing I remembered was being trapped underground. I couldn't breathe. I was running out of air and I clawed above me, hoping it was the right way. I gasped air and I felt... different. The Darkness was gone and I felt good and whole for the first time in my entire life.

"When I died, the Darkness fled my body. While I lay dead, a small voice said that I was forgiven. The Goodness filled me and I breathed again. I was given a second chance. My first time around I had chosen bitterness and anger. It had consumed me since I'd been a small child after bad things had happened to me. I had carried it like a sword and a shield. No one could get close except Derek but he was so broken he could never have fixed me no matter how hard he tried.

"I was alone but I felt a calling to use my power so I just waited for the Goodness to show me an opportunity. On accident one day, I found a refugee nomad. Then another and then I started searching for them. My ability grew and grew as more were added to our numbers. I've stretched my ability to its limit protecting this Glen. Don't go beyond the line of stones. The Darkness waits. My power forces the Darkness away. It is like a Goodness bubble that covers the whole camp. Can't you feel the light?" she asked closing her eyes and extending her hands.

Elinor was nodding. The absence of the Darkness around them was the greatest feeling on Morland. It made her feel like everything might really be all right, like there was a presence for good here.

"What about her?" Peter asked nodding his head to Emmaline.

"Her story is her own, boy," Jol bit back.

"Emmaline…" Brigitte said ignoring Jol, "is a dream made flesh. I didn't know if we would ever meet. She is like a half-sister. The Queen made each of us daughters, of a sort, but our fathers are not the same… It's very confusing."

Emmaline's eyes met Jol as she said "It is a night for truth and it is time for some of my story. Mother tried to make more children after the older siblings were gone," Emmaline said. "But she had used all her life magic on the seven. On her own she could only wield fire and Darkness and to make children one needs light and life. But that didn't stop her from trying. She wielded her fire like a sword and tried very, very hard." Emmaline said holding out her arms and legs.

It finally hit Elinor what all those scars meant. When one of Derek's siblings had given themselves to the Darkness they had had to cut themselves to let the Darkness in. Jermaine had cut his arm and Brigitte had sliced her palm. Elinor looked over and saw the scar that Brigitte wasn't hiding.

So, Elinor thought in horror as she put the pieces together, *every scar on Emmaline's body was the Queen trying to force the Darkness inside her. Emmaline was cut with a fire sword over and over as the forces of Darkness slammed into her trying to fill her. It was a miracle she was alive. It was a miracle that the Darkness attacking her hadn't broken her, or broken her more.*

"But I couldn't be made fully into one of hers," Emmaline continued. "When the Queen spilled my blood on the sacred ground and forced her magic in me, the Goodness poured in to save my life. But it was still a little too late for me. The Queen had not been able to fill me with the Darkness but her magic had mingled with mine and I was none the less marked as her child. And because of her limited success, she would never let me go. My magic became different after that day. It came out in visions and prophecies. She locked me away and had her guards write down what I said. I can't stop it. The words just flow out. I didn't mean to tell her that Derek was coming. I don't know exactly what I am or how I can see things before they come. I'm different. But you are different too, Elinor."

Elinor didn't want to be different. Especially not Emmaline's kind of different. Elinor wanted to be a regular normal girl but she guessed that that ship had long sailed.

"You can enter the spirit world without aid," Emmaline continued, "You do not need *that* plant. The spula vine is dangerous and the nomad children shouldn't play with it. The spirit world is not a place to enter using tricks. It is our battlefield and haven and not a game," Emmaline said giving a wide disapproving glance to the crowd. "But you can enter the spirit world without the plant. You see all of Morland. What is visible and invisible. You are the link to the spirit world we have been waiting for," Emmaline said taking Elinor's hand. Brigitte looked at Elinor like she was seeing her for the first time.

"Thank the Goodness," Brigitte whispered with her eyes closed. "Thank you." The listening crowd murmured along and Elinor felt chills rise up her spine.

"The link to the spirit world?" Elinor asked.

"Yes," Emmaline said. When she spoke she suddenly looked well, whole. Emmaline's eyes shined with intensity. "Your gift is not simply seeing Morland. You are joining with the spirit world. And you can heal it. The Darkness floods the world and the Goodness is pushed back and back. But you can clear it out."

"How?" Elinor said.

"I… I don't know yet. Sister will help."

"Yes, I will. Of course. Alone you can do little," Brigitte said. "But the Goodness is with you. I can see it. And with help you could do amazing things but we'll make a plan later." Brigitte nodded her head to a woman with black hair who stood to address the large crowd that had been slowly gathering around the bonfire.

"My name is Lina. Tonight is a night of celebrating. Two sisters have returned and they bring with them someone very special. Tonight is my night to lead the bonfire and I want to tell our story. I can't help but think of our beginning when we are on the eve of something new." She smiled and began.

"When the world was new and young, we were born from the wind. But winds do not only blow from one direction and we were scattered. Some were pulled by the south wind that swept in from the sea," she said looking at the South nomads.

The South nomads were the fewest in number. The Queen had burned and razed the South Coast without warning and few escaped. Elinor could see why Derek had thought Brigitte was a Southie. They all shared her dark skin and Scottish accents. "They learned to harness the sea's storms and built great ships that let them tame and befriend it," she continued as several of the south nomads turned their gazes south.

"A cold north wind blew down and pulled some of them with it. They stayed as long as it howled but when the snow and ice stopped they were released and wandered the length and breadth of the land. But every winter when the ice woke up it pulled its children home to the forest below the mountain," Lina said.

The North nomads were beautiful. They were dark and pale and looked like what Elinor thought elves would look like in real life. They had opened their land to Brigitte and together they had turned it into a sanctuary for all nomads.

"The harshest wind took many and drove them deep into the West Plains. It howled and roared and smoothed the land. But it could not break its people. They learned to howl back. They rode the wind on horses who could almost fly. Neither horse nor man feared the gale or anything the land could throw at them," Lina said nodding to the small group of tan men and woman.

Elinor knew little of the West nomads. She tried to remember what she'd learned from Derek and Peter. She knew they raised horses and lived in the West Plains but that was all. And that Jermaine had been a Westie. Their tan skin spoke of the sun and living outside.

"The people who had not been claimed by the North, South, or West wind got caught between the three of them. Their home was nowhere and everywhere. They learned how to mend and keep the balance as they traveled between the other three clans."

There were many other East nomads like Winter and River, women with pink hair and men with white blond hair. Before things had gotten bad with the Queen, they had traveled the whole land in their wagons or on horseback.

"We are one people. We have been hunted and she has tried to break us but she does not understand that we cannot be broken because we stand strongest together!" Lina yelled and the clans yelled back with her.

Derek

His soul came back later and Derek had still not been able to pry his door open. It must have been magic that kept it closed. He'd always been able to lock-pick any door in the castle the last time he'd lived there. Why was he trapped in his room? She obviously didn't trust him this time around and he couldn't blame her. He had murdered all of his siblings and she was still sensitive about it, he guessed.

"No luck?" his soul said nodding towards the door and Derek rolled his eyes. Derek was about to ask his soul what he'd found when he heard a knock at his door and it opened wide the next moment to reveal the Queen.

"Since we are both awake there is something I want to show you. I was going to wait until tomorrow but I see there is no time to lose. Come," she said. When Derek didn't move with her out the door, the Queen's fingers sparked with flames. Derek followed.

"The castle has certain aspects that are more beautiful in the night. Don't you think?" the Queen said as she led him down a dark hallway. It was eerie and he had to remind himself that there was nothing scary about the castle. He'd walked these exact hallways in the dark a hundred times. But not alone, with his mother.

"I've made a few new additions that I think you'll appreciate," she said and he didn't notice anything at first. Derek followed behind her in a trance he couldn't shake. She stopped in the middle of the hallway and was looking at a glass case in an alcove.

Derek's heart stopped. In the case was *his* flower. The soft red petals shone like rubies in the candlelight.

"You must have figured I would eventually find another of that flower of yours. Eating it in front of me was not the smartest thing you ever did," she said laughing softly. "You could have done it in the woods and I would have never known. I've had several soldiers eat the flower, and it sends each of them to their birthplace... after it has taken its price. I would very much like to know where it sent you that you were able to evade me for six years while barely aging. I tried very hard to torture it out of Jol. Can I even express to you what a betrayal it was to find out you'd been to him *after* the warrant was on your head? He paid for it." she said smiling.

Derek stopped to look at the flower and wished with all his heart the glass case wasn't locked. It was so like her. She loved to dangle unreachable hope before people. She was the worst sort of cat. Playing was her favorite part, right after the kill. But he wasn't the man he had been last time. He was stronger. He was harder. And he had two weeks to find her weakness and destroy her. He would enjoy killing her very much.

135

She was a fool to show him this. Did she think that a glass case and a lock would keep him out? This was his escape. When he was on Earth again she wouldn't be able to get to him. But despite his glee a chill settled over him because she was not a fool.

"Maybe I should change this display," she said tracing her finger over the glass case. "I think this would lose most of its value when, just for example, a door was to be found."

Derek tried not to react to her statement. He knew she hadn't found it yet, this door to somewhere else she sought single-mindedly. If she had, Garrison would know and she would have already been through it. So he only allowed himself one deep shaky breath before he followed behind her as she moved past the flower as if it were nothing. She had something bigger to show him then? The flower wasn't her pièce de résistance? He was suddenly very tired of her games.

"What is it? What more are you hiding from me? I'm tired of this," Derek said. He didn't move to follow her. She turned slowly to face him.

"I am not hiding anything from you, my son. You just choose not to see," she said with a bite of coldness. "You do not see what is in front of your very eyes. You never have. You only think of yourself. But there is so much more. So much I want to share with you. The stars are just waiting for you to accept the mantle of your birthright. Can you at least try to believe that what I want for you is for your good?" she sighed exasperatedly then she took two steps closer to him and he walked back until he was pressed against a wall.

"You will not speak to me again in such a tone, do you understand?" she said resting a hand on his shoulder. He felt his skin getting warm. "I am your mother and your Queen," she continued as his shirt started to melt into his skin. He set his face to keep from crying out. "Your six years away seem to have made you forget your place." He was breaking out into a sweat as his skin was burning. "Apologize to me," she ordered. He did not hesitate. He would bear the scar from tonight forever.

"I'm sorry, Mother. Forgive me," he said bowing his head.

In an instant the flames were gone and the cold air rushing at his burn was excruciating. He lived to fight another day. Yielding was the only option when she was like that. He'd seen the damage stubbornness could do. Another day…

"I'm done with you for the night. Will you return to your room on your own or must I walk you there myself?" she said as she headed to her own room. "Oh and if you send your little spy to my room again without my permission I will burn *all* the flesh from your bones," she said, her voice booming in the empty hallway.

She turned to look between Derek and Derek's soul who had been watching from down the hall. "As long as you are alive I'll be able to complete the ritual. You decide what state you will live in for the next two weeks. The spirit world cannot hide secrets from me any longer," she said fingering the large green stone in her necklace. He'd noticed that necklace the moment he'd seen her again but he had thought it was nothing.

Derek's head was spinning. *No. No. No. No.* He made himself lock it down. He couldn't let her know what this did to him. He somehow had to find the strength to keep fighting. He had to keep fighting her. *It isn't over yet. It isn't over yet,* he told himself. Derek bowed his head toward his mother and returned to his room in a haze. *No. No. No.* She could see his soul. *No, it was impossible.* Once he entered his room, his soul found him. He had fled as soon as the Queen had seen him.

"I'm sorry," his soul said slipping silently into the room. "I messed this up for us, didn't I?"

"No," Derek said. "How could we know that she'd found a way to see you. It's not your fault. But it does explain why she changed so much. She was guarding herself from you. I'd never thought of you as so scary."

"That's where you were always wrong," his soul said smiling softly. "I should go and I… I don't think I should come back."

"I know. She knows that we are separated and I'd guess that she's known for a while. I think she's known long enough that she already has a solution. You need to go. Get as far away as you can."

"Am I the one leaving you behind this time?" his soul said sadly.

"Yep. This time you get to live. Go to Elinor. Tell her what's happened and... Tell her not to come here! Don't let her scry into the castle. What if the Queen can see her too? The Queen can't know about her. She can't already, I'm sure. And we need to keep it that way," Derek said.

"I agree. I was going to go check on Elinor soon anyway. She's been traveling with Jol and a couple other people. I have no idea where they are going and neither did Elinor. And she needs to know about the Queen. Then I'll get as far from you as possible. Maybe that will stop it... And Derek I think there is more to Elinor's gift. I don't know what but don't lose hope. We'll think of something. We always do. Every day you don't see me know that I'm working on a plan. You need to be thinking too. So when we are together again our two half stupid plans will come together to be one awesome plan to get us out of this mess okay? Goodnight. Try to get some sleep," his soul said and was gone.

Derek fought sleep. He knew a new dream was coming and his mind was already too full. He couldn't unlearn what he'd already learned tonight and he couldn't handle any more secrets. He just needed the world to stay the same level of awful for a couple hours. In the morning he'd figure something out. He wished he wouldn't dream. But of course he did, that was just how Morland played him.

Derek's Papers: Full moon in 13 days

The dreams are harder to fight now that my soul is gone... It doesn't help that they are _more_ now. More real. Just... They aren't just dreams.

At first it was only snapshots. The fire. The hate. The smoke. The same three things over and over but then it grew more detailed. I started seeing and feeling different things. And it has now turned into a story. I am always her. I don't know her. She feels like a stranger. And last night, I finally got to see what this phantom woman hated: a baby in the snow.

The baby cried in the snow. But what I was seeing was second to what I was feeling. Hate. Such poignant hate even I had never felt before. Who could hate a baby so much? Who are these eyes I am dreaming from? I can't see myself and I can't decide what is happening in the dream. I am watching and entranced.

The small cabin was close by but the baby cried in the snow. The snow melted around her and hissed into steam. The snow was such a stark contrast to the fire already burning through her veins.

The baby hadn't meant to kill her mother. She'd killed her mother before she was able to breathe her first breath of air. Her father threw her out into the snow and said a prayer over the locked door as his only backward glance. I knew this, like I knew the hate. I also knew it was the winter solstice, the coldest, darkest, emptiest day of the year.

The child could never have frozen to death but even creatures of the flame must eat.

Then there is an old man. He doesn't pick up the baby at first. He stares and he must not have liked what he saw. His brows furrowed but he picked the baby up all the same. When she set her bed of hay on fire later that night bearing no burns or singed hair, he only lit a pipe, leaned back in his chair, and whispered a name "Ash."

The dream ends.

Ash. I've never met a girl named Ash in Morland. Who is she and why am I dreaming about her? Is she even real? Who dreams about real things? I'm no prophet. I am probably really narcissistic to even pretend the dreams are more than my subconscious's desperate attempt to distract myself from the ever-shortening time between the full moon and myself. But I have a feeling this girl, Ash, is important. I wish I could find her. Not that another fire mage would do me any good. I've already got two of those.

Chapter 13

Brigitte

It still felt an unsteady yoke, the yoke of leadership. It had fallen suddenly on her shoulders like a sprung trap. Brigitte was able to forget it sometimes, in the tide of all the work she had to do but earlier when she'd seen Elinor's face in clear awe it had made Brigitte uncomfortable. She was no wise woman. If Elinor indeed knew her story, then how in the world could she still look at her that way?

Elinor's words had shaken the core of Brigitte's world. She replayed what she'd been told over and over in her head. Derek was from another planet, another world. And he'd spent every moment on Morland trying to return. It explained a lot. It was the reason why he was always going away and would never tell her where or let her go with him. He was looking for the way back to his home. She hadn't found it strange that he never talked about his past, she sure never did except the once. He'd been odd but not so odd that she would have ever thought in a million years that he hadn't been born on Morland.

But she couldn't find the reason for why he never told her. Maybe it had all been a game, playing prince. Maybe he'd never really considered her a sister so why tell her anything. Did he think she would betray him? She had loved no one and nothing so much as she had loved him and couldn't she have helped him? Two sets of eyes were better than one and then she could have gone with him.

When he escaped and left her, maybe she could have found a way to be on Earth with him. Instead Jol had abandoned her and told her that Derek was busy and then she heard rumors that he was gone, vanished out of thin air. She worried that he was dead because it wasn't even a possibility that he had left her.

She had so wrongly assumed that Jol had told Derek and that Derek would come when he was done with whatever new mysterious task he had been doing. But Jol had never told him. She'd known that in her heart. That the Mage could never be trusted and yet here he was in her hidden sanctuary. It sent familiar waves of anger coursing through her. So much of what had gone wrong was his fault.

It's not all his fault, she told herself. She had made her own choices. She had chosen the Darkness and even now it still searched for a foothold. Anger was one of the easiest ways to surrender to the Darkness. It was such a small step, almost unnoticeable.

Brigitte made herself take a deep breath. The Mage had done wrong in this story but so had she. And so had Derek. But Derek was alive and he was here. They'd find some way to mend what had broken between them. No matter why he hadn't told her, she knew that he loved her. She remembered the torment in his eyes before she'd let the Darkness in. He had been devastated and heartbroken. No matter how this great battle ended, the only thing Brigitte was certain of was that she wouldn't stop until she got her brother back. No matter what.

Learning of James's existence had been nearly as big a shock as hearing Derek was from another planet. A piece of Derek separated from himself. A piece that had been here in Morland all this time. To another, it would have explained Derek's detachment, his cold apathy, and tightly locked feelings but to Brigitte it felt like a slap in the face. Had she not been his emotionless twin? Had she not felt a kinship with him partly because of those things, because he was broken and lost? To know that he had been missing his soul while he'd done all that and she had had her soul while she...

Derek had killed her without his soul. He'd killed her, Felix, Gabriel, Riley, Jermaine, and Milena without his soul. But Brigitte had watched a man die before her eyes without blinking. She had watched him die from the poison she had given him. She had killed a man and watched him die with her soul tucked neatly inside letting it all happen. *What kind of monster am I?*

She did not deserve the second chance she'd been given. She deserved the Darkness and being soulless. Derek should have left her to her choices. She remembered so clearly a moment of panic in the middle of the ceremony, a moment where she realized what had happened and she screamed for it to stop. It was not what she wanted. It was a fate worse than death but it kept barreling towards her. And she had chosen it. She had chosen that horrible clawing and burning Darkness. She'd screamed in wordless terror but her mind said 'Please. Someone make this stop."

But when the pain did stop, it was too late and she did not care anymore. She didn't remember much until she woke up in the ground, forgiven and new, with her beautiful gift of light. But what she did remember of the Darkness made her wake up with nightmares and feel such deep shame and regret.

How could the Goodness give *her* this gift? She had spat in Its face. She had chosen the Darkness every time there had been a choice: bitterness or acceptance, anger or joy, rage or peace, jealousy or contentment, murder or forgiveness. But Derek's sacrifice, his love for her, had saved her. No matter what other feelings she was struggling with regarding Derek's true identity she was so grateful that he had done it. Even though she didn't deserve it. He had saved her when he'd killed her. And she thanked the Goodness every day.

The council assembled at dawn and Brigitte was one of the last to arrive. The Mage met her eyes instantly trying to read her. They had not spoken after his confession the previous night. She had nothing to say to him and he had said enough. Emmaline walked in yawning with Winter on her heels and looking around Brigitte saw all were now present. She still found herself waiting for someone else to start and then remembered that she was in charge. This whole Glen had been initiated by her and she hadn't been able to shake the leadership.

"Good morning, council," Brigitte said meeting the eyes of the men and women sitting in a circle in the largest wagon the Glen possessed. The leaders of each clan were there: Wolf of the East, Calla of the South, Victor of the North, and Joseph of the West. As well as Jol, Winter, and Emmaline. Elinor was left out of this first meeting for a couple reasons. First, she was too close to Jol for the questions that needed to be asked and second, she needed rest. Elinor hadn't even stirred when Brigitte had gotten ready that morning. Elinor would have no rest during the coming weeks and Brigitte just wanted to give her a couple more hours.

"I'm sure you all know Jol, the Mage," Brigitte said inclining her head to him. There were no warm welcomes and greetings. Everyone in the wagon knew his reputation and were not glad he was there.

"The first thing we need to say is that we *know* you, Jol the Mage. We know how many have been killed at your hand and by your word. More nomads than not," Brigitte said watching as Jol's eyes turned a cool steel and she watched his hands for signs of flame. "But we cannot deny that it must be some work of the Goodness that has led you here of all places with Emmaline of all people as your guide. But I still must ask you some questions. Be advised that there are those among us who can see lies. Do you mean us harm?"

"No," Jol said. Brigitte looked to Joseph. His eyes flickered quickly between brown and gold. The sign that he was using his magic. He nodded his head. The truth.

"Does anyone know you are here?"

"No, they will know I was rescued from the prison but they do not know where I went."

Truth.

"Are you still the Queen's man?"

Jol hesitated. There was stirring among the leaders.

"She was the one who has had me locked in that cell for five years." Brigitte lifted her eyebrows to tell him 'and...' The prison was not a pleasant place but few survived the Queen's displeasure long enough to arrive there.

"There is much I cannot change but I wish her dead just as you do. I would have every trace of her erased from the land. Why else would I have had Derek kill his siblings? She needed to be weakened and Derek was the only one capable of the task. I am no longer the Queen's man," Jol seemed to hold his breath at the last sentence, she wondered if he wasn't sure if it was true or not but Joseph nodded and almost everyone exhaled.

"No," Victor said. "His word does not mean anything. He *cannot* be trusted."

144

"He speaks truth," Joseph said. He kept his voice neutral but Victor was all but calling him a liar, implying that Joseph either lied about what his magic was showing him or was too foolish to see the truth. Joseph's magic allowed him to *see* the truth. When he activated his gift, his eyes shifted color from brown to gold. He'd once explained his magic was like seeing wind that flowed through a person. The wind changed color and speed. It faltered in deception and shown bright in truth. There was no deceiving him. No matter the skilled liar, the winds of the spirit could only speak truth.

"Have you a question you wish to ask, Victor?" Brigitte said trying to pull the council meeting back around.

"So many. Why have you let him cross the barrier?" Victor said turning on Brigitte and she had to try very hard not to roll her eyes. She would have given her leadership to any clan leader but him. He lived for strife and dissension. The land the Glen resided on was his and he somehow resented the presence of so many. Even though they were his kin and they had nowhere else to go.

"Do you side with the Darkness?" Brigitte asked Jol. Ignoring Victor. There was only one way to win this. She was in charge. It was her council and her way.

"No," he replied. Joseph nodded.

"Do you seek to aid those who serve the Goodness?"

"Yes." And Joseph nodded.

"Do you regret the lives you have destroyed in the name of the Queen?"

He said yes but had to turn his eyes away. She wondered if he doubted his own answer but Joseph nodded.

"So you will aid us in our battle against the Queen?" Brigitte said.

"Yes, in what I can. But I can do little from here. Derek will be at the castle already and he is a top priority. If she is allowed to complete the ritual, there will be no stopping her. I'll ride tomorrow morning, if a horse can be made ready."

"Not so quick. You talk like a man with a plan. We will know what it is. You have offered your aid and we accept it. You will stay a week. Long enough for us to finalize the best plan and long enough for the council to trust you enough to let you go," Brigitte said.

Jol smiled a small smile and nodded his head. "Of course, council."

"Do you have any further questions, Victor of the North?" Brigitte asked. If he fought her again and doubted the veracity of Jol's answers then he would be challenging half the council. It would send a rift down the whole Glen and would shatter their tentative unity. Victor wisely bowed his head. *It's not like you could leave*, Brigitte thought. *You hate how much you need me but you need me all the same.* If Victor kicked them all off his land, he would be exposed to the Darkness and would be at risk of discovery from the Queen's soldiers.

"Now to discuss Elinor and her ability," Brigitte said and was glad to see the eagerness among the leaders. It was good they saw hope and she was glad for the help they each promised to prepare Elinor for what was to come.

After the meeting, Brigitte sought out Emmaline and tried to get some information out of her. She asked her where she was born and how she came to be a target for the Queen but Emmaline had no answers. Instead she paced and sang under her breath. It was enough to drive Brigitte a little crazy herself. Emmaline wouldn't talk about it but something was bothering her. Something she couldn't or wouldn't talk about. Her movements were nonchalant but her eyes were full of things, deep things.

Brigitte knew almost nothing of Emmaline. She'd first dreamed of her a year or so ago. She'd heard Emmaline calling and didn't understand what it meant but Brigitte waited. She had hoped one day Emmaline would find her way home. Brigitte knew little more than what she'd gathered upon first seeing her. Emmaline had walked through the barrier into the Glen and it was like seeing an old photograph of herself, which was the strangest way to think of it because they were physically opposites. But Brigitte knew who Emmaline was and what she was.

Emmaline had enough of Brigitte's old self about her that she was instantly recognizable. Fear and horror should have been her first responses. But the realization that the Queen had made more children didn't come until later. Her first thought had been joy. She had a sister and she was safe. That had seemed all she needed to know.

But Emmaline was different from her and her siblings. Emmaline didn't have the Darkness inside her, she only had the Queen's blood and the Goodness. And something bad had happened to her. It was putting it mildly to say that Emmaline was a little broken. She looked like a delicate porcelain doll. Her skin was alabaster and her dark hair curled softly at the ends. If someone simply looked at her, she might just seem detached, like her mind was just somewhere else.

But when she spoke and when Brigitte studied her she saw the cracks and the flaws. Something had happened to Emmaline. It wasn't just the network of scars that crisscrossed her body. It was the skittishness that would overtake her and her eyes that saw beyond. Brigitte stopped pushing. She wasn't even sure if Emmaline would be able to speak about it and who knew if talking would even help. Brigitte decided that her job was to love her, to listen to her, and to protect her.

Elinor

Elinor moved silently out of the wagon, careful not to wake the other women but she saw she was the last one up. Each of their beds were packed away into the side cupboards to make room for daytime use and Elinor copied them before leaving.

She stepped out into the sunlight and her head didn't hurt and tears fell free from her eyes. She was crying out of sheer incredulity and relief. It hadn't really sunk in that her headaches were gone. Being on the run and constantly wounded had distracted her. And in the back of her mind she had been keeping watch, waiting for their return on the horizon. But they were really gone. She couldn't believe it and she wasn't quite sure why she was crying.

Is it really over? she dared to think. *Are my headaches really gone?*

She was alone in the early morning and even in her happiness she felt alone. It was like she'd finally allowed herself to look in the mirror and she had no idea who the girl was looking back to her. *My head doesn't hurt.* It felt like missing limb syndrome or getting a new limb where one had been lost. It was alien and exciting and scary.

Over a year ago Elinor had woken up with a horrible headache that never went away. It didn't go away at doctor's offices or with prayer. It didn't go away as the weeks turned into months and then into a year. At her last doctor's appointment, they'd told her that she had a headache disorder called New Daily Persistent Headache. And that basically meant her headaches might never ever go away. She'd been trying to accept it with grace and not bitterness. She'd been failing. It hadn't helped that her headaches brought hallucinations of grandeur. She would see a forest whose only inhabitant seemed to be a young man. And that young man was the mirror image of a horrible boy at her college, Derek.

She now knew the identity of the man she'd been seeing in the forest. He was James and he was Derek's soul. Derek and his soul were two separate people and she kind of felt like that herself. Old Elinor's life had been built around her pain and now that that was gone she felt like her life was built on nothing. It was like the foundation had been ripped away and the whole house was shaking and swaying.

There was a song she'd learned as a child that explained exactly how she felt:

"The foolish man built his house upon the sand.

The foolish man built his house upon the sand.

The foolish man built his house upon the sand and the rain came tumbling down.

The rain came down and the floods came up.

The rain came down and the floods came up.

The rain came down and the floods came up and the house on the sand went *splat*."

The song then talked about the wise man who built his house on the rock. It didn't go splat but stood firm. The rock was God. The man whose life was built on Him could withstand any rain or flood.

It hit Elinor suddenly that she was going to have to start all over. She was going to have to rebuild her life on something real. She wouldn't fall into the trap of building her identity on herself. God was the only thing that didn't change.

But she was still going to have to figure out who she was now. She definitely wasn't the Elinor she was before the pain started. That girl felt a million miles away. And she wasn't the Elinor whose life was one horrible headache either.

I have no idea who I am.

It was scary and exciting. She wondered if this was what was supposed to happen at college. The famous reinvention that happened once a kid was away from home and it is just them and the world really meeting each other for the first time.

She chuckled at herself. Who but she would look this gift horse in the mouth? Who cared who she was? Her head didn't hurt and she didn't care why or how. She smiled and breathed in Morland's healing air. She was free and she was hungry and that was enough for now. She followed the flow of people as they led her to a large bonfire in the center of the Glen. Breakfast was, wonderfully, still being served.

Ryan

The nomad camp was strange. It was so full of life but also peaceful, especially in contrast to every other second he had spent on this stupid planet. Ryan couldn't quite believe he was still in Morland. Morland had been horrible since the moment he'd climbed over that dumb tree. It had been a dangerous and anxiety-filled journey every single step of the way. It would have been so much easier if Morland would just stop trying to kill his sister.

First the slash marks on Elinor's stomach from the strange creature and then the wounds had to been sewn up which made Elinor scream which made Derek punch her in the face which led to them being captured. Ryan had nearly killed Derek then and there. He still might. Then they'd escaped and been on the run and Derek's sew-job failed and Winter had cauterized it which had been traumatizing for everyone involved, except Peter who'd looked pretty smug for whatever reason. But that wasn't enough, no, then Elinor gets an arrow through the leg and had to walk on it for days.

She'd received some sort of medical treatment yesterday and seeing her asleep had finally allowed him to exhale the breath he'd been holding for a long, long time. *Maybe she won't die here.* Their family would kill him if he didn't bring her back in one piece. He'd promised them. Of course they probably still thought he and Elinor were in Boone at Derek's parent's cabin. He could hardly remember that stupid weekend that had landed them here.

They were only going to Boone to look around. Ryan had been told nothing specific, only that Elinor had something weird going on and he wasn't going to like it. That had been enough. He had felt pretty capable of protecting her from whatever could happened. *Idiot.*

They were taking a weekend vacation in Boone. What could possibly happen? Everything. Everything bad happened. He learned all of Elinor's truths in one horrible dump as she lay unconscious with Derek looking at her bare stomach. Ryan didn't want to believe them, either of them. But Peter was so earnest and Derek looked like death, and Ryan found he couldn't doubt them.

Elinor's headaches were letting her see another world and that world had attacked her somehow across space. Three white lines had appeared like magic markers across her stomach. Claw marks from a strange creature apparently. And the rest was just a continuation of a series of horrible events. Ryan was exhausted.

He had wanted to stay by Elinor yesterday as she rested but Winter had dragged him away and told him to just let Elinor sleep. And he followed her.

Winter was absolutely transformed. The knowledge that she was not the last East nomad had changed her whole demeanor. She had been a stoic warrior girl with a consuming need for vengeance and yesterday afternoon he had seen her laugh. It was beautiful and strange. It was like meeting her for the first time.

They'd talked all day as Winter had explored the Glen with him and later they'd all sat down by the fire. Winter had ended up sitting next to him and he'd felt the dumbest smile creep up his face. He forced it down and told himself to pull it together. So what she was the most beautiful kick-ass woman he'd ever met? She lived in Morland and he was going back to Earth with Elinor as soon as he could manage it. It was the most impossible long-distance relationship that could ever happen. So he pushed it down.

He'd spent the night under the stars with the other single young men, Peter included, in the North nomad section of the Glen surrounding a small campfire. Elinor and the girls were in a wagon in the East section and he didn't envy them. There was something comforting about seeing a sky full of stars instead of a ceiling, as long as the weather was nice, which it was. He could feel his burden of worry being lifted a little. They might finally be safe. Even if it was temporary, he was relieved.

He didn't realize what a huge stress load he'd been carrying all day every day until it dissipated. They were not being hunted. They were not on the run. They were hidden by some crazy magic shield and the Goodness was all around them as a palpable essence. And Elinor was around other people with magic who might be able to help her understand her ability. He hoped that they would know of a way to make it go away. The worry that when they went back to Earth her headaches would come back was never far from his mind. But that was worry for another day. That was future Ryan's problems.

The morning was bright and crisp and there was bustle around him as everyone prepared for the day. He followed his nose towards the smell of breakfast and saw that Winter was sitting close to a large fire warming herself in the sunlight. Her pink hair wasn't braided for the first time he'd seen and it fell around her face as it trailed down her back. She looked different, softer. It stopped him in his tracks. He'd seen her kill three people with stone arrows and he couldn't believe that that Winter was the same Winter that was closing her eyes as the wind blew her hair back from her face. He might have stood there all day trying to make sense of it but she looked up sensing his attention and motioned him over to sit.

"Good morning," Winter said as he sat down next to her.

"Good morning. Did you sleep well?" he asked and mentally shook himself. What a strange question to ask someone. It felt too personal and intimate but she answered with a smile.

"Hmm. Yes, and no," she said. "I woke up several times and felt nervous that I couldn't see the stars and then I'd remember where I was and the joy of it kept me awake a little while longer. So I don't know that I slept well. But I am well."

"I'm so happy for you," Ryan said. "You are safe and among your own people."

"Yes. For now," she said.

"What do you mean 'for now'?"

"Well this can't last forever, can it? It's only a temporary haven. What happens when Brigitte dies and her magic is gone with her? No, this is only a place to catch one's breath. That doesn't mean I'm not thrilled. I still... I still can't believe it. There are so many of my clan. It fills my heart and gives me chills," she smiled up at him and pulled her hair to one side. Her fingers started to braid it but them she stopped herself. "Anyway, things are starting. I don't know what the Mage has planned but the council will get it out of him. Something is happening and I'm going to be in the middle of it."

And like that the pieces clicked. There wasn't the old Winter and the new Winter. She was at heart the girl he already knew. She wasn't really the soft, free-haired young woman she looked like this morning. She was the warrior and the avenger. She was sharp and quick. But she was able to enjoy the wind and to *look* relaxed, whether she was capable of true relaxation or not, who knew.

Being in the middle of things was not his idea of fun. And he worried that Elinor would be pulled into things no matter what he tried to do. Thinking about his sister seemed to summon her. She was walking through the wagons toward Winter and him. Her smile spread wide across her face. He hadn't seen her smile like that in a long time. She came right up to him and hugged him.

"Isn't it a beautiful day?" she said beaming up at him. She nearly skipped, despite her injuries, over to the women serving breakfast and they started chatting amiably. Ryan just stared after her. He'd felt a little guilty leaving her yesterday to explore with Winter. Elinor had been unconscious but their bond had deepened to a place where he felt uncomfortable and nervous being away from her. But seeing her prance around the Glen with a song almost on his lips, he exhaled from somewhere deep inside.

"Good morning," Elinor said to Winter. Elinor awkwardly held out her arms that were laden with tea and rolls. Winter took a roll and just smelled it.

"Does it smell like home?" Elinor asked. Winter nodded and Elinor smiled wider.

Peter came walking up with two young men who looked like twins despite the several years between them. Peter was talking and laughing and the older of the men nodded at Peter's conversation but his eyes dove straight to Elinor.

"Hey guys, you have to meet my friends," Peter said smiling. "Elinor, Ryan, Winter, this is Ian and his brother, Bo. They are training me in the blacksmith shop," Peter said beaming. Ryan shook each of their hands and noticed when the taller man's eyes lingered on Elinor. Ryan picked back up the yoke of older brother and settled it comfortably over his shoulders again. He'd felt weird without it anyway.

The taller boy, Ian, introduced himself formally to Elinor and asked if she'd toured the Glen yet. Before Elinor could answer, Brigitte was at her shoulder. "Oh good. You've already eaten. We need to start training. No time to lose. You'll meet the council today," Brigitte said helping Elinor to stand. Winter followed behind Elinor and gave Ryan a flash of a smile before she was gone. Ryan couldn't help but smirk at Ian's dejected face. Thankfully, Elinor didn't even give a backwards glance.

Elinor

Elinor followed Brigitte and wondered what her training would look like. She'd never trained for anything in her life. She had played one year of soccer in elementary school and had never danced or played any instruments. She didn't think she had any skills that had involved training of any sort. She had good study skills but that was it.

Brigitte led her into the largest wagon she'd seen so far. It was filled with a half dozen people and they studied her when she came in. Emmaline and Winter smiled at her and she guessed they were there because they each had magic. Elinor copied Brigitte's pose and sat on her knees with her head slightly bowed.

"It's true," a man said whose white blond hair and accent marked him an Eastie. There was no arguing his statement as nods made their way around the group. Elinor almost hoped one of them would have doubts and realize maybe she was just a regular girl and not the long awaited key to saving Morland. *It's already overwhelming and we haven't even started yet,* Elinor thought trying to muffle her sigh.

"We don't have much time until the full moon. Do you understand what is required of you, spirit child?" he asked her.

Elinor supposed 'spirit child' was her and she answered. "Um. No, I don't really understand. So I'm a link to the spirit world and you think I'll be able to stop the Darkness somehow?" Elinor asked.

"Not exactly," he continued. "You will need to become one with the Goodness. You will need to empty yourself and bond with it. You will become only a mirror for the Goodness to reflect into the world. We will teach you to embrace the Goodness and to fight the Darkness inside yourself."

"The Darkness is inside me?" Elinor said looking to Brigitte with fear she couldn't keep down. Elinor's hand went instinctively over her stomach. The claws marks were still a fresh memory. Is that how the Darkness had gotten into her or had it always been there?

"Everyone has some Darkness in them," Brigitte said. "Did I not already have the Darkness in me when I chose to live a life of hate and distrust even before the Queen chose me? It wars inside of everyone and we must choose who our master will be. You must fight and conquer the Darkness within yourself. You must face it and name it and choose the path of the Goodness. Only then can you bond with the Goodness to flood the world with light."

"But it's more than that," a West nomad man said. He had short dark hair, tan skin, beautiful brown or maybe golden eyes, and a kind smile. "You must *understand* the Goodness," he said. "That is the source of your power. Because power must come from somewhere. Ours comes from the Goodness and *hers* comes from the Darkness. When you trust and bond with the Goodness it will be a cord not easily broken."

"How does my bonding with the Goodness save the world? How is that even accomplished? Why can't *you* bond with the Goodness?" Elinor asked Brigitte. Brigitte literally projected a bubble of Darkness-free air wherever she went. She expanded it to fill the whole Glen. She was much more qualified than Elinor was. It would be nice if Brigitte could just handle this and Elinor could just pretend to be a nomad in her fancy new nomad clothes until this was all over and she could go home.

"What you feel," Brigitte said motioning her hands around herself, "is the extent of my ability. I can push the Darkness back but I cannot set the Goodness free. And I could not expand my reach to cover the whole planet. My gift is the gift of reprieve and safety. It isn't a gift of saving."

"Brigitte has not defeated the Darkness that was residing over this place," the East nomad man said. "She has only pushed it away. She is a bubble on an ocean. If the bubble spread to fill the whole ocean would the water go away? No. And the bigger the bubble is, the less stable it becomes and the easier it is to pop. Brigitte has kept this bubble small and because of that it's undetectable and impenetrable. If the Darkness knew we were here, I don't think she could maintain our shield for very long. It taxes her. As small as this is it's a constant struggle to keep it up. Brigitte's gift is not a fighting gift. It can never be what it isn't. Yours though..."

"Don't be afraid or disheartened, spirit child," an elderly South nomad woman said, her accent was even thicker than Brigitte's and Elinor had to focus on her mouth to understand her. Her gray hair was in one long braid at her back and she had a strand of blue beads woven into it. "We are here to help you and to train you. We do not force you out into battle alone and unarmed. Will you accept our instructions?"

"Oh yes. Please," Elinor said nodding.

"It won't be easy," the North nomad man said. He had dark black hair that was long and tied with a black cord. He wore mostly black as well. When he looked Elinor up and down, he sighed.

"I'm not afraid of hard work," Elinor said.

"We'll see," he replied.

"We will begin one at a time," the East nomad man said. "The people in this room are the elders. Among them is our last mage, not including the children," he said looking at Winter, Brigitte, and Emmaline. "We should introduce ourselves. You'll have thought us uncivilized," he said smiling and his full beard made him look kind and jolly. He wore a pale blue shirt and tan pants. She noticed that his shirt had some embroidery on it as well.

156

"I'm Wolf, leader of the East nomads. That grumpy man is Victor of the North. Joseph is the leader of the West nomads and our lovely Calla leads the South. We have little time to prepare you. The full moon with be here soon and that will be our only chance to strike. We will each get three days with you to impart and teach all we know. It will be hard work but it is necessary work. On the thirteenth day you will meditate and prepare for the full moon that night. It is not ideal. But we will take what the Goodness has given us and it will be enough. We start now. I will go first. Come with me." When Elinor cast a glance at her friends, Wolf said "You will train with them during your free time." But Elinor had a feeling she wouldn't be having much of that.

Elinor hurried to follow after Wolf. He slowed to talk with her as they walked. "I am the leader of the East nomads. I have no living family but those that have found refuge here. Every Eastie that comes here is my long lost child." He turned to look at her and said "Thank you for bringing Winter home."

They were stopped at the entrance of a large garden. There were patches of herbs and flowers she recognized but many more she'd never seen. Wolf found a spot among the plants and motioned for Elinor to sit across from him. "East nomads are wanderers but no less connected to Morland than the other clans. We will learn of the land today."

Elinor had been terrified to begin training but it was starting easier than she would have thought. Wolf told her all the names of the plants growing in the large garden behind their wagons. He quizzed her on them and then he told her to enter the spirit world and just lie among the flowers.

The spirit world was the realm just removed from the visual, physical world. It was where the Goodness lived and it was a place most people couldn't visit unaided. Elinor was not most people. Anyone else who wanted to go into the spirit world needed to use spula vine, a plant that separated a person's consciousness from their body. Elinor had used it before and the feeling was strange. It made everything look white and fuzzy like she was walking the clouds.

Things were different when Elinor went into the spirit world on her own. Then she saw things like they were but more so. She could see *everywhere*. By only a thought she could see anywhere on Morland she wanted.

She'd used her ability to be a lookout to find the men who shot arrows willy-nilly into people's legs. When she went into the spirit world she could zoom to look at places like she was a telescope or something. But while she could look all over Morland her physical body stayed put. It was always weird at first to see her body just sitting there while her spirit moved. Each time she'd gone into the spirit world she was never really alone. The Goodness had been there but just out of reach.

Elinor took a deep breath and felt her spirit slide into the other realm, the spirit world. And the difference was like a tidal wave slamming her in the face. She felt the Goodness instantly and fully. It felt like being surrounded in warm sunlight. The presence of the Goodness was like a sigh after a good day's work. It was like a blanket fresh out of the dryer. It was like the yellow brick road making her path crystal clear.

Elinor suddenly *really* understood. It had felt lovely coming into the Glen and being free of the Darkness. But being free from the Darkness was different that being in true communion with the Goodness. The whole world was connected to the Goodness, not just humans. Every plant and blade of grass was a part of the same system. She felt like a potted plant that had lived its whole life alone in the small soil of the pot but was then suddenly replanted in a forest. Her roots were spreading out and finding fellowship and new depth. *This might be the greatest moment of my life,* Elinor thought.

Wolf sat next to her, a world apart but his still presence was reassuring. It would not be hard to join with the Goodness when the time came. It was natural. It was life. It was everywhere and everything. Elinor was able to stay in the spirit world longer than she ever had before. She wasn't forced back into her body like the previous times, instead she was aware her time was up and she chose to come back. She realized one of the big things she'd have to work on was her strength and endurance. Elinor didn't think she'd be able to complete whatever she had to do in the course of an hour.

158

When she came back, Wolf was still meditating with his eyes closed. Elinor didn't know if she should speak so she settled for copying him. She closed her eyes and sat among the flowers. It was intoxicating to be still and quiet and safe after so much time of danger and fear. The stillness enveloped her.

I wish I could live right here. Here in this perfect moment. In this peaceful garden. With only the sound of my breath and feel of the breeze and the smell of flowers.

Elinor was surprised out of her relaxation when Wolf moved to stand. "You did very well today," he said giving Elinor a hand to help her up. She stretched her arms and felt so sore. She realized why when she saw the sun was low in the sky. How long had she been sitting in this garden? She hadn't moved an inch in hours!

"Tomorrow will be harder. Rest tonight. But after tonight you will train with the children until you are asleep. We have no time and so much to teach you. Thirteen days until the full moon. So rest while you can and get some food at the fire." He set a hand on her shoulder for a moment and then led the way to food. Elinor's stomach was rumbling. Being in the nomad camp was safe and nice but she did feel like she was always hungry.

Thankfully there was plenty of food to go around. She'd have to ask Peter where all the food was coming from. She was sure he already knew everything there was to learn about the nomad camp. It hit her how similar he was to Colton, her little brother, and she felt a pang. She suddenly wished her whole family was with her. It would be so much easier if they were together but Morland was the last place she ever wanted them to come, especially the little ones. But even so, Colton would have loved it.

James

She was sleeping so peacefully, James forgot everything else for a moment. Everything but his name. He was no longer just 'Derek's soul'. He had a name. James. That was him.

He had traveled long and hard to reach Elinor. He moved much faster than running but he couldn't teleport. He'd followed her trail like a bloodhound. He didn't know how he did it but he'd found her.

"Hello," he said hovering above her. He had too much to tell her to let her sleep.

She woke suddenly and jerked away when she saw him. "Derek!" He didn't like how the sight of him looking like Derek made her so upset. What had Derek been like on Earth to make this sweet girl look afraid?

Anything, James thought. *Derek was capable of anything.* Derek and James were two pieces of the same person. Most peoples' souls stayed nicely packed inside but James had been pulled free when Derek crashed into Morland so long ago. Then when Derek had escaped back to Earth, James had been left behind. Alone and unseen. No one but Derek had ever been able to see him. Until Elinor.

"Shh. It's me, James," he said and when she smiled it sent a jolt straight to the core of him. No one had ever smiled at him like that.

"You found me," Elinor said yawning.

"I can find you anywhere. What is this place?" he said looking around at the sleeping women on either side of Elinor.

"It's a nomad safe haven. Oh, James," she said turning to look at the sleeping figure to her left and James followed her eyes and saw a woman. And then he really saw her. *How? How? It can't be. How?*

"Brigitte?" he said standing in front of her. "Elinor, what is this?" he said his eyes pleading.

"She is alive. When Derek thought he killed her, he only killed the Darkness in her. Her soul hadn't been taken yet and she came back to life. She woke up later that night."

"Wake her up, please," he asked. Elinor nudged Brigitte.

"I'm sorry to wake you but someone needs to talk to you," Elinor said. Brigitte sat up and Elinor said, "Remember how I told you that Derek's soul was outside his body?"

Brigitte nodded her head sleepily.

"Well he's here to see you," Elinor said.

Brigitte looked around the room and Elinor patted the ground in front of her. James sat where Elinor motioned, transfixed. Brigitte lit a lantern and looked for him. James wanted to shout and wave his arms, "I'm here! I'm over here!" But he knew she wouldn't be able to see him.

"Tell her I'm sorry, Elinor," James said. "Tell B I love her."

"He says he's sorry. He says he loves you, B," Elinor said.

Brigitte's face softened and tears fell silently from her eyes.

"Hello, little brother," she said to the air. "It's been too long."

"Are you really okay?" Elinor translated for him. "I'm so sorry. Oh B, I'm so so sorry."

"Yes, Derek. I'm really okay. I'm the best I've ever been. I forgive you."

James felt something inside himself buckle. He couldn't believe he'd just heard those words from her. He never expected to receive absolution for the things Derek and he had done. He made no allusion that it was Derek's sin only. They were one and the same even if they were separate.

"Do you really mean it?" James asked.

"Yes. You saved me from the greatest mistake I ever made. Thank you for loving me enough to do it. I can't imagine how hard it was for you. Thank you. I love you, little brother. Someday soon we'll be properly reunited. But first we need to keep you safe. What are they planning up at the castle?"

"Oh that's why I came. She can see me. The Queen. She has this necklace that we think lets her see the spirit world. Or it has nothing to do with a necklace and she might be trying to put us on the wrong trail. Somehow she can see me. Elinor, you can't go to see Derek. It's too dangerous. I can't go back either," James said. He felt a chill thinking about Derek alone in the castle, waiting and not daring to hope.

"Yes, you'll need to stay here with us and help Elinor. She's our greatest hope," said a pale little woman yawning as she sat up.

James turned to her and he felt it. The kinship. It was strong and pulled him to her. He didn't even feel that with Brigitte now that she was reborn into whatever she was now.

"Hello, little sister," he said smiling. "I'm going to guess that I'm not the last born anymore."

When Elinor translated, Emmaline beamed under his invisible attention.

"This is Emmaline," Elinor said introducing them.

"I don't know how I never felt it. I watched the Queen when she tried to make more children. I know I didn't watch her every second but... You are different than us," James said studying her.

"Yes. I'm technically only your half sibling. I don't have any of the Darkness in me only Mother and the Goodness. It wars inside of me. *She* knows there is something inside me but she doesn't know the Goodness well enough to see it when she's faced with it. She only kept me alive because of my *sight*. She had someone transcribe what I said. I couldn't help it. I sometimes feel so lost inside myself." As if to prove her point, she wrapped her arms around herself but only for a moment then she turned to look at Elinor.

"There is a way to save Derek and the whole world. The Darkness cannot abide the light. Something is coming for you," Emmaline said taking Elinor's hands. "I see it in the stars. I see it in your eyes. But you aren't ready." Emmaline's eyes were huge with worry as she turned to look at Brigitte. "She isn't ready. She isn't shining."

"We can help her, little sister. She's only trained one day. We have time. Don't worry. We'll polish her up like a new mirror, you'll see," Brigitte said pulling one of Elinor's hands inside her own.

"Yes, make her a mirror," Emmaline said. "And do it now. She'll need to be ready for the full moon. So few days."

"I'm here to help, too," James said. "You can count on me."

Derek's papers: Twelve days to full moon.

Another dream…

The hate is always the first thing I notice when the dream starts now. It is overpowering and so strong I still taste it once I'm awake. It lingers. But this dream was different. Before it had been just snapshots that I had to piece together and feelings that bombarded me on all sides. But this dream ran so smoothly, like a film. I have to write it while it's fresh and I can still see it and remember what everyone said, even though I hate to relive it. She is such a wretched little creature, Ash. Maybe the antipathy and dislike I feel for her are after-effects of the dream, that I'm feeling whoever's thoughts these are too strongly. Because Ash is so alone and unloved and I should not despise her. But the old man despises her too.

Killing her mother haunted Ash. She muttered about it in her sleep and it was written all over her face if anyone cared to read. The uncontrollable furnace inside herself was her constant reminder that she was a monster. The old man spared her no pain in the telling of her origins.

"Your father threw you out into the snow because you killed your mother. He would have let you die," he told her. Ash is little, maybe five years old. That's such a horrible thing to tell a child but it must not be the first time she's heard it because the dark haired little girl doesn't even flinch.

"Why?" she asked. And the why asked so much. Why was she this way? Why couldn't her father forgive her? Why had she killed her mother? Why hadn't she died that night like she was supposed to? Her thoughts ring so loudly in the dreams. It's like she's shouting but her lips never move. The old man must not hear her thoughts or her words for that matter because he doesn't answer her.

She stalked her father's house and left flowers on the ross of her mother's grave. Her father must have known her. There were not so many foundlings in town that he wouldn't recognize the one that looked like his dead wife. But he never looked at her. She didn't blame him. She felt her mother's murder all over herself. The old man told her that she looked like her mother, the same dark hair and keen eyes. Ash never looked at herself.

The old man had visions. He saw death. He courted it. But he could not see Ash's death. He asked her over and over where her death was. She did not know when he asked her and she did not know when he beat her. She would escape to town whenever she could. He was not welcome in town. People did not like to know their deaths.

She became his ambassador to the world. She bought his food and did odd jobs in the village to pay for it. She cleaned his house and fed his livestock. She grew into a pretty young woman, dark and curved. She was quiet which the townsfolk equated to mysterious. As long as the old man lived she was granted a modicum of protection. But the old man died in his sleep when she was twenty years old just as he told her he would and she was alone. And a beautiful woman all alone was too much temptation for some.

Three men came in the dead of night and thought they could have her but they had no idea what they were stepping into. She had until then managed to keep her fire a secret. It was a constant struggle to keep it quiet and inside herself. Her fingers always itched with it and she finally let it out.

She burned the bravest man alive with a snap of her fingers and as always the flames caused her no pain or damage. The fire was as much a part of her as her own skin. The other two men fled with only the smell of smoke to remember her by and she foolishly thought that was the end of it.

But in the morning came the law man with his iron shackles and a stone prison with a view of the gallows meant just for her. And the stone prison wouldn't burn. And then the dream ends and I feel more claustrophobic in this dumb castle than ever before.

Chapter 14

Derek

Derek stared up at the ceiling and wished the day would just start already so it would be closer to being over. The mornings were the hardest, when the dreams were still thick in his mouth. When they felt real and strange. Derek tried to forget about them during the day. He'd write them down and then forget it, as best as he could anyway. His mind had enough rattling around in it and he couldn't waste time wondering about Ash and the narrator woman who hated her so much. He was mostly sure that the dreams were trying to tell him something. He didn't know what it meant or who was sending the messages but it didn't feel friendly.

He exhaled loudly and climbed out of bed. He looked around his prison room. The door stayed locked. There had been some water and rations in his room when he'd arrived two days ago but he knew it wouldn't last until the full moon. So she either wanted him weak or she would be back. He wasn't sure which was worse.

Derek only had to last another twelve days. Twelve days at the most, surely they'd come for him or he'd think of something before then. He tried to reassure himself but twelve days waiting in lonely anticipation of having his soul devoured by the Darkness felt like a long, long time. His soul hadn't come back. Derek was relieved with every moment that passed and his soul stayed away and kept Elinor away. But he couldn't deny that he didn't wait all day for any sign of him.

Derek was not built for solitude. He wished he was. He had tried so hard after being home on Earth to just *be alone*. He didn't deserve company and he should spare the world himself. But if Derek stayed away from everyone then he'd only be with himself and that was a big problem. Because in the solitude lurked his demons and he couldn't endure his own thoughts and condemnations even if he considered it a form of penance. So he sought the company of others and hated that he needed it and hated himself for his weakness.

His parents had been poor company for so many reasons. Mostly because they were always on guard for another 'break'. They were waiting for him to rave about being a prince on Morland and the evil queen that reigned there.

When he'd come home after five years of being trapped on Morland, he'd been shocked to find that no time had passed on Earth. So when he'd told his parents that he had been gone for five years when in *their* reality they had seen him that morning, they were... concerned.

They couldn't or wouldn't believe him. Whichever it was, he had trouble being around them for long periods of time. He wasn't sure if it was his bitterness at their disbelief or just the concerted effort it took to pretend to be as young as his body looked that made it hard to be in the same room as them. So it was a gift he didn't deserve when he found Peter.

Peter would not take 'no' for an answer. He had decided he was going to be Derek's best friend and that was all there was to it. Derek had tried to fight it. Peter was a good kid and he didn't deserve to be friends with a murderer but he'd caved under Peter's relentlessness. Derek hadn't ever planned to tell Peter the truth about himself. He'd seen how well that had gone with his parents but Peter had known something was off.

Derek hadn't done a great job hiding his hunt for Morland. He was sure that someone had been there before him and he was always searching for some piece of evidence or some knowledge that would help him when he went back. And he knew he would have to go back.

One day, Peter had asked what he was looking for and when Derek had told him the truth, Peter had somehow believed him.

Pacing his locked bedroom, Derek wished he'd never told Peter anything because Peter was the one who'd told Elinor. And Elinor was the one that had dragged them all back here. If he hadn't told Peter, then none of them would be in Morland. Derek would not be trapped waiting for the full moon to devour his soul. Peter would not be who knows where in who knows what kind of danger and Elinor... Elinor would probably be dead.

168

Derek couldn't change the past and he felt like a monster for wanting to. This was what solitude did to him. It made him face the horrible man he was. He was a creature of red-rage and no sympathy. But his soul wasn't. His soul was outside his body somewhere with Elinor and they were making a plan. He knew it. His soul had promised and Derek believed him. They had twelve days. He could last that long. He had to.

Elinor

Elinor learned the meaning of meditation. She also learned the meaning of boredom. It appeared that there was a very fine line between the two. Wolf had picked her up outside her wagon as the sun rose, fed her a roll, and then they'd meditated. She'd then spend as long as she could in the spirit world and then meditate in nature and then go back into the spirit world and then meditate. Elinor had a strong feeling she'd be doing the same thing tomorrow.

It wasn't as new age-y and weird as she'd imagined it would be. It wasn't chanting affirmations or visualizing what she hoped would happen. It was only opening herself up and letting the Goodness in. It was letting her spirit commune with the world, kind of like wordless prayer. Because Morland wasn't a dead rock with dead plants growing and dead animals. Everything was a part of the same beautiful puzzle and she just had to settle into her place. And Elinor couldn't argue with the results. Instead of lasting twenty minutes in the spirit world, she could now last for hours.

Elinor was released as the sun set and she hadn't taken two steps out of the garden when she saw Peter's grinning face. It was such a big grin, so joyful, like it was just barely keeping a laugh in. Despite her sore muscles, hungry belly, and tired body she grinned back. It would have been impossible not to grin back.

Peter

"Hi!" Peter said giving Elinor a hug. "I thought you'd never get done." Her smile was the greatest thing he'd accomplished so far that day and he'd accomplished some super awesome stuff.

"I have so much to tell you, El! But you first," Peter said.

"No. Food first," Elinor said leading them towards the central fire.

"Okay food first. But tell me as we walk, was today good?" he said. Even though he'd had a great day, even though he was on a magic planet, even though he was safe and alive… He couldn't shake the last tendrils of jealousy that it was Elinor getting magic training and not him. He didn't wish that she *wasn't* the chosen one or whatever, he just wished that he was too.

"Yes. I'm definitely getting stronger. I'm not sure exactly how my being able to meditate for a couple hours defeats the Darkness but I get that I'm on day two of twelve. And that I'm getting the super Spark Notes version of *Magic 101*. So today was a good day. I feel good about it."

Peter reached over and gave her shoulder a hug. Elinor had been so sad and hopeless for a long time. And now, finally, she was learning and growing and changing. And so was he. He just hoped that the people they ended up as when this is all over were compatible. Although he couldn't imagine a version of Elinor that wouldn't be just right for him.

"My day was great, by the way," Peter said as they waited in line for food. The central fire had several smaller fires with cauldrons or grills over them that fed the whole Glen. The food consisted of many of the same ingredients but the spices and flavors were way different.

Tonight was their third dinner at the Glen and it looked like the options were: stew with potatoes and green leaves that almost smelled like curry, grilled lamb with grilled asparagus with a red gravy, and chicken soup in a large bread bowl. Elinor went with the chicken soup but Peter always tried the most Morlandish dish, a.k.a. the weirdest one so he chose the one that smelled like curry.

"This does not taste like curry," Peter said grinning. He'd chosen the right dish. It was earthy and spicy and he felt like one of those kids at the table in the movie Hook. He was eating food on another planet. He wasn't sure when that thought wouldn't be weird but he'd been on Morland for a while now and it was still a dream come true. Except when it was all a nightmare, of course. But that was life.

"You are so funny," Elinor said grinning back. "You are really happy here, aren't you?"

Peter looked at her for a moment. Was she happy here? Why was she asking him? Even if she hated Morland and the Glen and everything they'd seen, Peter would always tell her his truth.

"I don't know if I've ever been this happy."

Elinor just smiled and ate. He was okay to just sit and be. Peter noticed Winter and Ryan sitting next to each other across the fire. They were sitting quietly as well. Sitting close and quiet.

Peter smiled but didn't feel the need to mention it to Elinor. The entertainment was starting anyways. Each night one nomad clan took the center and did a little something. Their first night had been a nomad clan origins recap which had been super helpful and last night the West nomads had set out a tea tasting table led by a man named Tiny, which was an interesting name since he was tall, thin, and sporting a long auburn beard and mustache. Peter bet he did know a lot about tea.

Tonight a group of pink haired women and white haired men came out into the center with white lanterns and four large tapestries held up by wooden frames.

"Welcome and good evening family and new friends," said a woman with short pink hair cropped tight to her neck. "Tonight we will show you the completion of our great catalogue. In each of these beautiful tapestries depicting one of the four seasons we have woven hundreds of seeds. We have a seed from every known plant but they aren't just tossed on. Bring your attention to the summer tapestry."

The summer tapestry was done in a gradient from bright green to yellow to orange. Peter noticed that each quilt was of a similar style but in different colors. And each quilt complimented the one next to it. The summer one ended in orange and that was the first color of the autumn one. Each started or ended with the color of the one before and after. It was clever. Summer: green to yellow to orange. Autumn: orange to red to brown. Winter: brown to white to blue. Spring: blue to pink to green.

"Those are so cool," Peter said. Elinor just nodded as if she was still just taking them in.

"The summer tapestry has seeds for every plants that grow in the summer. You could take this tapestry and bury it anywhere and have a small garden of everything you'd need. The same is true of each seasonal tapestry. Each one is filled with the seeds needed to grow plant in that season. It is our goal to provide these tapestries for all who wants them. So when…"

Peter and Elinor were distracted by Victor and several other North nomads grumbling behind them.

"They just can't wait to leave. It's not good enough for them here. And they want everyone gone. I bet you'll only get one of those tapestries when you agree to leave. Not that I don't want all the Easties gone but I find their eagerness to leave insulting to my hospitality. Not that anyone is going anywhere. It would be just my luck for the Queen to live forever. The girl will never win."

Elinor and Peter both decided they were done eating and started ambling through the wagons.

"He's the worst, right?" Peter said once they were out of ear shot.

"Yeah. I am not looking forward to training with him. I hope all North nomads aren't like him."

"They aren't. Bo and Ian are great. Oh, you haven't met them. Wait, yeah you did yesterday morning. Sorry it's been a busy couple of days for me. You too, I guess," he said chuckling. "But really I've got so much to tell you! Okay so I don't have a badge or anything. They should have badges but I'm part of the council now!" Peter said grinning at her surprise.

"What? How? I thought only mages and leaders of the clan were allowed in the council meetings," Elinor said.

"Yeah that's how they'd like to keep it but I'm surprisingly stubborn when people are deciding the fate of my friends without asking me or them about it. You should have heard how they talked about Derek, like he's not worth saving, like he's a liability."

During the first full day at the Glen, Peter had spent a little while with Ian and his brother at the smithy and then he'd wandered around, hoping to catch Elinor on a break. That was before he'd known that she didn't get breaks. She just trained until she was asleep on her feet, hungry, and spent.

So Peter had needed to fill his time on his own. It wasn't hard. He started to really commit himself to learning blacksmithing. It helped that he loved every single second. He felt like he was visiting colonial Williamsburg except it was real and he wasn't just in the audience. Ian taught him the basics quickly and had no scruples about working him to the bone. Peter would have been content to spend his full day there, even if it was exhausting, if he hadn't found another venue that needed him more.

He'd stumbled into the council meeting while looking for Brigitte this morning after lunch. He had wanted to ask her a question about supplies and had heard raised voices from a large wagon in the North nomad sector.

"He has made his choices and they have led him to where he is. Our only goal is to protect ourselves! We don't disagree that the Queen needs to be removed but we are not going to jeopardize the plan by an impossible rescue mission for someone who may not even want to be rescued," a loud male voice had said.

173

"Derek is non-negotiable," Brigitte had said. "Besides the fact that he is my brother, he is an invaluable resource."

"He is a fool and a liability," the man had said.

Peter had walked in without knocking and faced the assembly with barely concealed anger. "What's this about? I was led to believe that you were going to help us save Derek. Is that not unanimous?"

"This is a council meeting, boy. It's closed," an older North nomad man had said.

"If you think I'll be leaving Derek's fate to you all another second they you really don't know anything. I'd just assumed that you weren't all normal humans only concerned with their own interests. I forgot for a while that altruism is not a natural state. But I see the way of things now," he had said sitting down. "If you don't mind would you tell me your plan, from the beginning?"

Peter had been shocked at his own boldness. It had come over him in a rush. He couldn't believe that Derek's fate had been discussed without him or Elinor present. He did concede that Brigitte would fight for him but she was only one vote. But Peter wasn't going anywhere. Not anymore. He didn't have anything better to do. He could just go work at the smithy in the afternoon or evening. He was pretty sure if the meetings stayed like they were today he'd very much want to hit something after.

"The council, huh?" Elinor said. "Anything I need to know or are you sworn to secrecy?"

"It's mostly arguing. On how or when or if to rescue Derek and how or when or if to have you go after the Queen," he said.

"Go after the Queen?" she asked. "Like it's that easy? All I've done is meditate. All I can do is go into the spirit world. Do they say how I'm supposed to 'go after the Queen'?" She was getting worked up. Her face was turning red and her eyes were smarting a little.

"Hey, it's okay. You are tired. You've had a long day," he said rubbing her back.

"I'm not a child who needs a nap. I asked a reasonable question," Elinor said as she stopped walking and pulled her shoulders straight as if getting ready for a fight.

"El, I'm sorry. I didn't mean to patronize you. I think you are amazing and brave and strong and beautiful. I'll go with you to Mordor. I'll carry you if I have to. I'm on your side. I don't know what you are supposed to do. But I'm on the council for *you*. To be *your* champion and for Derek. You'll know what I know. I've got your best interest at heart."

She huffed a little and brought her shoulders down. "I'm sorry. I am really tired," she said laughing. Peter chuckled and pulled her into a hug.

"Alright. I'll walk you back," Peter said with an arm around her shoulder. "You are doing great by the way. Absolutely crushing it."

Elinor turned out of his arm and smiled wide. "Hi!" she said.

"What is it?" Peter asked trying to see who Elinor was looking at.

"Oh, I forgot. Sorry guys. Peter, James is here. James, this is Peter. Derek's best friend. James showed up last night."

Peter knew better but he looked around.

"Hi?" he said.

"He says 'hi' back," Elinor said turning to look into the night, presumably at James, Derek's soul.

"What news does he have on Derek? Is he okay?"

"He's okay for now," Elinor said. "He's at the castle but safe. James can't go back because the Queen can somehow see him. So he's here with us. We have no way of knowing how Derek is doing now. No," Elinor said to James, "It's not your fault. You had to leave him. He'll be fine. He's been without you for years." Elinor yawned for about ten seconds and then nodded and waved.

"He's gone. He said 'good night'. I'm really sorry you can't talk to him," Elinor said. "You'd really like to get to know him. Maybe one day. But," Elinor yawned again, "good night from me too. You are a good friend," she said as she walked into her wagon.

"Night, El," Peter said biting his check as he turned to leave. *A good friend. Two steps forward one step back.* He was getting showed up by an invisible man. Peter sighed. *Always second fiddle to Derek.* But Peter shook it off. It didn't matter. And he didn't want to add even a single drop of negativity to his new life. Because that's what the Glen was, a new life for Peter.

He never wanted to leave. He had found his purpose and his place. He wanted to help these people and serve the Goodness. Because the Goodness was real. It seemed crazy that Derek hadn't believed in the Goodness because the Goodness was the most real thing Peter had ever felt. It was so real that everything else felt fake. His abusive dad. His runaway mom. His empty boring life. They all belonged to someone else. He hadn't thought about them once since coming to Morland. He'd seen enough Darkness and evil in his life that it felt so right and simple to dedicate himself to the only good thing he'd ever found, the Goodness. Morland was a lot of things but she absolutely positively wasn't 'the worst.'

Elinor

"How can I be so exhausted? All I've done is sit on my butt with my eyes closed," Elinor said yawning when Brigitte finally called it a night after a couple more hours' worth of mediating. Elinor had wondered if they would go all night.

"Meditation is an extremely difficult practice to master. Few are capable of that kind of stillness of mind and body," Brigitte said yawning and smiling as she arranged their sleeping mats. She pulled them out from one of the clever cupboards that lined the wall. The bedding was tucked away during the day to make room for sitting and eating.

But in the evening all the blankets were pulled out and daytime equipment was tucked back into its cubby. Winter had decided to stay with her people but Elinor and Emmaline had opted to stay in Brigitte's wagon. It wasn't really in any clan's quarter. It was close to the main fire and faced the sunrise.

Elinor had studied it during the day for any personalization Brigitte had made but there wasn't much. On the outside it was stained a dark brown with green painted accents. Inside, during the day, there were a dozen multicolored cushions, a teapot and a small stove with a chimney and a desk for writing. No drawings or decorations. It was pretty but utilitarian.

"I'm certainly not made for it," Brigitte said yawning again as she stretched. "But I'm glad for the practice. I forget to calm myself. It's so important."

Elinor had worried that it might be uncomfortable living with them. She'd never had to share a room before and she had only met Emmaline a week ago and Brigitte only a couple of days ago. But it wasn't strange.

For the first part, she felt like she'd known Brigitte for a long time. She was a fairy-tale made real and Elinor knew her whole story. Also it was nice to meet someone that Derek had loved so much. It was like getting a secret glance into who he really was. And secondly, Elinor didn't really want to be alone. Morland wasn't that nice to her and she wasn't quite ready to visit it one-on-one yet. She felt safe sleeping between the two women.

The only caveat was Emmaline's crying.

Sometimes Elinor would stroke her hair or hold her hand. Emmaline didn't wake up but Elinor felt better for it and she thought that maybe she cried a little quieter. Brigitte did not like it and the first night she had demanded that Elinor explain. But she couldn't explain. All she knew was what Jol had told her, that it was every night and that she shouldn't be woken. So Brigitte had just watched and in the morning she had not asked Emmaline for an explanation.

"Yes. But everyone should learn to mediate," Emmaline said as she brushed her dark hair in long strokes. "It is integral to being alive. Being still is an essential piece. People think life is always moving and moving. But life is also sitting and waiting. You must learn to do both. People should probably all be locked in a prison cell for a couple years to teach them. It's the best way. That's why I'm so good at it."

"Yes. That's one option," Elinor said turning away to hide her smile. "Or they could just have Wolf teach them."

"Yes, but well we only have one Wolf and many people..."

"Oh well. You can't save the whole world," Elinor said burrowing under her blankets waiting for Emmaline to blow out her candle.

"No. I can't. But maybe you can," she said in a whisper before blowing out the flame. Elinor felt chills rise all over her body. She kept forgetting that the point of her training was to prepare herself to fight the Darkness. People really thought she could save Morland. But all she knew how to do was meditate and close her eyes. But despite her worries, sleep came quickly and before she knew it she had one last day of meditation awaiting her.

Chapter 15

Elinor

The first two days of meditation had been relaxing. Elinor had needed it. She'd needed to be in silence and stillness and let her weary soul rest. But the third day she found it harder to sit still. She wanted to do things. She wanted to get stronger and be a boss. But Wolf made her sit. He would notice immediately when her mind would wander and her worries would creep in.

"Seek the stillness. Calm yourself."

Then she'd take a deep breath and try again. But her mind kept tormenting her. She wondered if this was throwbacks from her headaches. She'd often felt worthless spending so much time sitting and doing nothing. Sitting in the dark and waiting. She'd wished that she could be contributing to society and her family but instead she'd been stuck in the prison of her mind.

Elinor reminded herself that those were lies. She had been doing something while she laid in the dark. She had been resting. She'd been trying to pull together the strings of strength so she could join the world. It had been essential. Resting was not laziness. And she knew that but... it was hard to stop the voice that made her feel like she was worthless.

So as Elinor tried to clear her mind, she told herself the truth. That this training and meditating was doing something. It was the first step in the process of getting stronger in her magic. It was important and it was worthwhile. And she finally felt it snap in. The waves of peace washed over her and she gave in to the stillness.

"You've progressed very far," Wolf said as the sun set and they sat across from each other to discuss what Elinor had learned. "You are impressive for a non-nomad. Had you meditated before coming here?"

"No," Elinor said stretching. "Well maybe. You've heard that I used to have horrible headaches? Every day, all day?" Wolf nodded. "Well I spent a lot of quiet time in the dark. I learned to entertain myself without thinking or moving. I just made the hours pass by and hoped that at the end of it I felt better. I usually didn't and so I'd sit in the dark silently again and try not to be angry or sad and eventually one of the times I'd come out of it a little better and spend some time in the lit, loud world. Maybe it *was* a kind of meditation," Elinor mused.

"The Goodness aligns each person with their purpose and grants them the strength they each need. I do not doubt that your trials have strengthened you for the large task that lies ahead of you."

Elinor mused at that thought. She'd really come to believe that her headaches meant nothing, that they were the product of a fragile body in a broken world. She had never thought it was some kind of trial or punishment. But maybe it did mean something.

Maybe I had headaches for a reason. The thought was comforting and unsettling at the same time. It would be nice that it wasn't in vain, that it didn't all happen for no reason. But if there was a reason then God had given her headaches on purpose. She didn't really like that thought either. Even if the end purpose was to save a world, it still stung. Maybe she was just a horrible selfish creature. She should just be grateful that all her suffering might bring some good.

"Tonight you will stay up until the sun rises," Wolf told Elinor jarring her from her thoughts by that sentence.

"Wait, what?" Elinor said.

"Emmaline will join you. But we will now conclude our training together. You have done very well and I wish I had more time with you. You remind me of my granddaughter. She died two years ago. She shared your still flame. My advice as you progress through your training is to mediate each morning and night. Calm yourself and seek the Goodness. Those two practices will aid you in all you do." Wolf rose and rested a hand on the top of her head for a moment before helping her up and leading her to the main bonfire.

Elinor's stomach grumbled and she hurried to eat as much food as she could before Emmaline came for her. Elinor knew that Emmaline was probably going to be very excited about their all night mediation and she was not disappointed. Emmaline appeared at her side like a wraith.

"I will teach you the true nature of mediation," Emmaline said grinning from ear to ear. Elinor always felt a little disconcerted to see her smile *so* wide. It wasn't that Emmaline's face was made for a frown, it was just that she was usually such a solemn, ethereal creature with her big deep eyes and to see a Cheshire cat grin spread across her face straightened Elinor's spine. It didn't help that Emmaline did not share the world's sense of humor. Her smiles came from strange and unexpected things.

Peter had actually made her burst out laughing one night at the fire when he'd sang a children's song about a frog and Elinor had nearly jumped out of her skin at the sound. And then she'd started laughing and everyone was laughing. For all her strangeness, Elinor really did adore Emmaline. Elinor felt a strange kinship with her. They were both viewed by others as being a little broken and fragile.

"All night, huh?" Elinor said standing as Emmaline paced impatiently while Elinor scarfed down the last of her dinner.

"Yes."

Elinor started walking back to their wagon but Emmaline pulled her the opposite way.

"Nope. If we do it in our wagon, you'll just want to fall asleep. So we are going to do it in the stables. The horses will keep us company."

Elinor followed behind and found herself smiling. She loved horses. They were so powerful and beautiful. She respected them very much. She'd only been riding a couple times in her life but it was thrilling. There was no a chance to ride one at the Glen. They weren't allowed to leave but maybe she could just sit on one for a while.

Emmaline greeted each horse and then said a name under her breath that Elinor didn't quite catch. She pulled down two saddle blankets and motioned for Elinor to sit across from her.

"How long can you stay in the spirit world?" Emmaline asked her.

"Umm I haven't really timed it but a couple hours. Four maybe."

"False."

Elinor just raised her eyebrows and waited.

"You put those limits on yourself. You decide that it can only be done for a couple hours. You could live in the spirit world if you wanted. It does not throw you out, you get scared and leave. You pull yourself out. Stop doing that. Tonight you'll stay all night. Don't come out and mediate and rest. You don't need to. Stay all night until the sun rises and then some. Stay until someone comes looking for us."

"I don't know, Emmaline..." Elinor said.

"Ugh!" Emmaline said grabbing the sides of Elinor's face. "Did you hear what I just said?" she nodded Elinor's face with her hands. "Your only limits are the ones you give yourself. You are a strong woman. Now prove it."

Elinor took a deep breath, felt the peace of the spirit world wash over her, and heard a knock on the door. She looked up annoyed and saw morning sunlight filtering through the stable windows.

Whaaaaat? Elinor thought. The whole night had passed in a blink. *Wow.* This time when Emmaline smiled, Elinor smiled right back at her.

"That was awesome," Elinor said. "But I am going to go take an amazing nap. Coming?"

Emmaline smiled. "Not just yet. You've got a bigger day ahead of you than me. I can nap whenever I want."

"Lucky," Elinor said winking. "And thank you."

Ryan

Ryan yawned as he prepared for another terrible day in the Glen. He passed Elinor but she just nodded and yawned. She'd been up all night with that strange Emmaline. Maybe she was having a harder time than him. Emmaline had a way of changing things for the worse. Well at least for him. Ryan rolled his shoulders to loosen up. He did not want to be covered in bruises again today.

The first day Elinor had started training with Wolf, Ryan had been at a loss as to what he was supposed to do. He would only get in the way of her training, having no magic himself and a dislike for people who pushed Elinor too far. So he'd gone looking for Winter and instead had found Emmaline. Or she had found him, which was probably more the truth since the first thing she had said to him was "Why aren't you training?"

"Training?" Ryan had asked. "Elinor is the one in training not me, Emmaline."

Emmaline had rolled her eyes and grabbed Ryan by the sleeve. He had indulged her and allowed himself to be lead to an empty horse corral.

"What are you doing, Emmaline?" Ryan had asked but she'd already turned her back to him and walked into a small stable. She had come out a couple minutes later with a middle aged man with tan skin and dark brown hair. She also had him by the sleeve.

"So you want to be trained?" the man had asked looking between Emmaline and Ryan.

"I'm sorry, sir. But I have no idea what I'm doing here. She dragged me along. I'm sorry to waste your time," Ryan had said as he had turned to walk out.

"No. No. No," Emmaline had said moving swiftly to block his way. "The creatures of the Darkness are coming for Elinor. Will you stand against them? They will come with tooth and claw. They hunger to taste her blood again. Will you stand against them?"

Ryan had felt his face pale. He'd been a fool to think they were safe here.

"When do we need to leave?" he had asked Emmaline. "Now? How close are they?"

"No. No more running. The fight will be here and as you stand now, you will be able to do nothing to stop them. They will tear her to ribbons if you do not stop them. So?" Emmaline had said shifting her eyes between Ryan and the man. "So get to it. Pick up that sword and learn how to defend your sister," she had said in a huff and had then turned on her heels and walked away muttering something about how he was a thick-brained man-child.

"Alright, I think I see the way of things. You are the new lad who came with the Mage?" the man had asked Ryan.

"Yes, my name is Ryan. I'm sorry this came about so strangely but... would you teach me how to fight?" Ryan had asked finally noticing the swords that hung at each side of the man's belt.

"Yes. I try not to doubt when a wise woman has a premonition about something. I'll teach you what I can. My name is Damon. I am a Westie and I mostly work with the horses. Or I try to. There are too many Westies for too few horses. We are not so good at sharing," he said with laughter in his eyes.

"But in my last life, before the Glen, I was a trainer of horses and men. There is much to fight against in the plains and everyone was trained before they were allowed to step a foot outside their doors. And I have a feeling once that little woman's warning is heard by more than the two of us, you will not be alone in your training. Which is good. Sparing is essential to mastering the skills. But you won't have time to master anything. Our first lesson is how to hold a sword without harming yourself or an innocent by accident."

Damon had pulled both of his swords free and handed one of them to Ryan. Ryan had turned the sword in his wrist and life had felt more like a dream than ever. Never in a million years had he ever imagined that he would be holding a real sword that he would have to learn to use.

"How does it feel?" Damon had asked as he watched Ryan swing it slowly.

"It's heavier than I thought it would be. But it feels good."

"Alright we begin," Damon had said as he moved his arms and the sword in a slow deliberate pattern that Ryan copied. Ryan's arms had grown tired quickly but he hadn't let himself stop. The next time someone came to hurt Elinor he didn't want to have to rely on a pink-haired girl to protect her.

Each morning when Ryan arrived another man or woman had joined their training. Everyone had been at a different level but Damon had moved around easily giving a dozen different tasks and instructions. Damon led with such ease. Ryan wondered why Peter didn't come. This seemed like the exact kind of thing he would love but Peter probably loved everything about the nomad camp.

Ryan had decided *not* to tell Elinor. It wasn't that he was ashamed or embarrassed, he just didn't want to worry her. She had enough going on without having to worry about an imminent attack of those horrible creatures that had clawed her stomach. And thankfully, she had been busy enough that she didn't notice Ryan's complete exhaustion every evening when they'd meet up for dinner and festivities at the bonfire.

Usually someone told a story or put on a little presentation in the evenings at the bonfire. It was a small affair and it usually carried on in the background while everyone ate and conversed at the end of another day. But Ryan always looked forward to it. And he told himself that it had nothing to do with the fact that Winter always sat beside him.

She'd come over without asking if the seat was available and she'd dive into the politics of the East nomads and how it was amazing and irritating to be around her kin again. Ryan would tell her about training and she would threaten him that she was going to stop by and test his skills. He *really* hoped she wouldn't. He was nowhere near the swift assassin that Winter was and he was loath to embarrass himself in front of her.

Winter was the one bright spot in his days but he wouldn't let her distract him. He was training to protect Elinor. Morland was the worst and it was coming for her. He shouldn't get too cozy. He needed to stay focused and get her home safe.

Familiarity and routine did not ease his training but just made him sore at the start and end of the day instead of just the end. *This nomad camp is the worst.* Ryan thought that thought over and over as he ducked and barely avoided taking a hit to the side of the head. It was the worst.

He wished for the millionth time that they were all home and that he would wake up in the morning and find this all to be a strange horrible dream. But it wasn't. And he had the bruises to prove it. Although they were fading quickly from the salve Winter gave him, he just added new ones on top.

His mind went blank for a moment remembering how she'd rubbed it into his back. In an instant his feet were kicked out from under him and he landed hard on his butt.

"Focus, Ryan," Damon said with a grin. "Where is your head this morning?"

Chapter 16

Derek

His dream last night had been vague, nothing to write down. There hadn't been a story and he was relived. It hadn't been a progression of Ash's story. It had just been a flashing repeat of fire and hate but dulled somehow. It was like the signal had been dampened and he was only getting snapshots again. And he didn't mind at all. He might even smile if tomorrow morning he woke up with no dreams.

Derek jumped when he heard a knock at his door.

Who would knock? he thought.

And then he saw a scarred stupid face grinning at him with a tray. Derek had to stop his relieved laugh when he saw that Garrison was not alone.

"Your late," Derek said. "I ordered breakfast an hour ago,"

"Yes, my prince," Garrison said bowing and grinning. "I'm only a poor cripple and I do my best." Derek made himself keep a straight face for the four guards that waited outside his room. He'd bet they were there all day. Maybe she wasn't so sure about her magic lock.

Garrison closed the door behind him with his foot and set the food down in front of Derek on the floor.

"What the?" Derek asked pulling Garrison aside and ignoring the food. "What are you doing here? How did she let you?"

"I brought you here. Practically bound and gagged. She has complete faith in me," Garrison said in a hushed voice. When Derek moved to grab his things to follow Garrison out, Garrison put a hand on his shoulder and stopped Derek.

"Not yet," Garrison said. "Things aren't in place."

"It doesn't matter. The flower is here. The one that sent me home. I need you to get it for me. It's my only way out of here."

Garrison seemed to really think about it.

"Okay. So you hightail it out of here and the rest of us are stuck in this horrible mess *you've* made again. Is that the gist of it?" Garrison said with steel eyes.

"What do you imagine I can do?" Derek said. "I've been here for four days and I haven't even been able to pick that stupid lock. I'm trapped and useless. If I stay here and let her destroy my soul and make me a slave to the Darkness would that be better? Let's just make her a little stronger, shall we? I'll be dead and she'll be stronger. Is that your idea of a good plan?"

"You know it's not. But there has to be another way. She cannot live forever and you are the bloody Rebel Prince. Do you not think people would fight in your name?"

"What people?" Derek scoffed. "The battered and broken peasants without magic. Every man of strength and wit is already her solider. Oh, that's it isn't it?" Derek said sarcastically. "You really think you can turn her army against her. You would have to get all of them or she'd be onto it and she'd burn us all alive. Don't you remember the last time someone tried?"

"You know I remember," Garrison said touching his scar. "But it will be different this time. And I think this is a much better plan than your idiotic one. Do you think you are the only one who wants to escape this hell? Do you think you are the only one who has suffered at her hand? You are a selfish bastard. You'd take the easy escape again. Just go back home and forget about us. Pretend we aren't real. Pretend our people aren't being murdered every day for a magical birthright they can't even help.

"Thank the Goodness that fewer and fewer are born with the gift. I'm tired of seeing their blood on the ground. But you don't care about that. This isn't your home. These aren't your people. You are just their bloody prince after all and that means nothing to you," Garrison spat.

Garrison was a madman and an absolute lunatic to think that anyone would rebel because of his words, because of which side Derek was standing on. It was laughable. But Garrison wasn't laughing.

"Where are you going?" Derek asked. Garrison had his pack beside him and his extra swords were wrapped at his back.

"She may trust me but she's already sent me on another mission. There is chatter in the North. I'm not sure what but it's enough that she's sending me and my men to investigate. I wonder if she's sending me to keep me away from you. Any idea what she's so worried about it? Or is this just a wild goose chase and I haven't fooled her at all?"

"No, I have reason to believe there is something there..." Derek said. "I have some other friends here. They came with me from my home and they were with Jol heading North. I don't know why they were going that way but they were being led by a woman I've never met."

"Your friends broke the Mage and the little seer out of the prison?" Garrison asked barely keeping his voice down. "Who did you bring with you? It is not such an easy feat to accomplish."

"I don't know how they did it but they did and who is the seer?"

"I don't know much but she is the only other magic user allowed to live besides the Queen and the Mage. She sees things. All anyone knows is that she and Jol were broken out of the prison together with no leads as to who had done it. That must be why she's sending me North. She must have some indication that they went that way.

"Well that's good that she's sending me, I'll intercept the Mage and see what he's planning. Maybe *he's* not afraid. I'll drop off your flower before I go. It'll brand me a traitor but at least you'll get to go home. If I bring you the flower and you return to your home world would you swear to come back with men and weapons? Maybe there is something in your world that could aid us."

"None would come. It would take time to convince them Morland was real and even then none would come."

"Ah I see you are the poster child for your world as well as ours. I'm sure they are missing you," Garrison said with a sneer and a shake of his head as he turned to leave.

"Garrison, wait."

Derek couldn't make the words come out. How could he tell Garrison to forget about the flower, to go after Jol and to make a plan with him and the rest of the soldiers? This was Derek's chance. So what Garrison would be outed as a traitor? That was going to happen anyway and he'd probably make it to Jol before she caught him...

Derek couldn't do it. Because what did his life matter anyway? What did his life matter if he abandoned every friend he'd ever made? He wouldn't just be leaving Garrison in a fix, he'd also be leaving Elinor, Peter, and Ryan. He wasn't *that* big of a bastard. His life would mean nothing if everyone he cared about was trapped in Morland.

"Leave the stupid flower. How can I help you?" Derek said.

"I knew it," Garrison laughed clapping Derek on the shoulders. "I knew it. You couldn't have changed so much. That baby face of yours could never do such an asshole move. I don't need much. More information. Tell me everything that will turn her men from her and I'll need time, Derek. I'll have to leave you here. I'll be back in time I swear. I'll be back and we'll win this thing. Don't you feel it?" Garrison said. "Things are going to be different this time. I know it. She won't live to see another full moon."

Elinor

After Elinor's short nap, Brigitte was waiting and ready to escort Elinor to her new trainer.

"You should change first," Brigitte said setting down a pile of clothes. Elinor didn't argue. She had been wearing the same outfit for a couple days and a fresh set sounded nice. But the outfit Brigitte had with her was very different from her current set. Instead of a shirt and embroidered skirt, her new outfit was three pieces: loose blousy pants, a tight tank top, and a snug jacket with beads accenting it. Everything was in shades of blue, black, and white. It was really flattering.

Do I get new clothes every time I get a new teacher? That was the first exciting thought she'd had since coming to Morland.

"Can we eat first?" Elinor asked as Brigitte led her presumably to her new instructor for the next three days.

"Oh she'll feed you and you'll be glad for it," Brigitte said. "You'll be training with Calla, the leader of the South nomads. She's very sweet and a good cook." Brigitte led her through the South quarter of wagons to a small blue one with painted black waves on the lower half. It didn't have wheels and all the windows were rounded like the portholes on a boat.

"This is it. Good luck," Brigitte winked as she left Elinor to enter on her own. She had no idea what to expect but she was glad there would be breakfast. The worst part about meditation was that she missed all the meals. Elinor knocked.

"Come in," said a thick brogue and Elinor walked in to find the dark-skinned woman from the council meeting sitting cross-legged on a pile of pillows. The walls were painted a dark blue and the cushions were white but the blue of the walls seemed to leak into the white and made them look almost blue. There was a single large conch shell on display on a small table. It was a stunning environment, elegant in its simplicity.

"Welcome to my home. I'm Calla," the woman said. Her black hair was streaked with white that seemed to shine against the strands of beads woven in her hair. She wore black flowing pants and a snug blue jacket. She also had wrinkles that creased when she smiled.

Elinor nodded her head. "I'm Elinor and it's nice to meet you."

"I've heard about your ability from the Wolf but I want to hear from you. Now how much scrying have you done, lass?" Calla asked as Elinor sat across from her and faced a mountain of food. Brigitte had not been lying when she said that there would be breakfast. The tray was laden with what appeared to be every kind of biscuit as well as jams and sausage and tea. Elinor smiled wide and tried to *slowly* stuff her face.

"Not much. I've scried to Derek once and to look around the area but I think that's it. I've been into the spirit world many times and when I was home I'd *see* Morland but I wasn't scrying exactly, I don't think."

"You need to *know* Morland if you are going to save it. You need to understand her. You need to memorize every mountain and valley. You need to know the sea and the land. I know you've connected with the ground and you understand that *everything* is connected. Now you need to expand that knowledge beyond an Easties' small herb garden. I'll guide you," she said pulling a small vial from a cupboard. Elinor guessed by the green color that it was spula vine extract. "We will not visit the castle or the capital. Do you understand? Don't even think about it. Let *me* guide us." Only when Elinor nodded did the woman inhale the contents of the vial.

Elinor closed her eyes and sent herself into the spirit world. It was so easy. All of it. It was as natural as breathing. Maybe she was always meant to come to Morland and learn this. It felt right. Calla was waiting for her.

"I am no mage and I cannot scry. The spula vine can only take me this far and you cannot take me with you. I'll describe where I want you to go. You'll go there and come straight back, yes?"

"No need," said a voice from behind Elinor. "I can take her. I can't exactly scry but I can travel fast." James said taking Elinor's hand. He smiled widely and Elinor chucked.

Calla's eyes grew wide.

"This is James, Derek's soul," Elinor explained. "James, this is Calla she'll be my mentor for the next couple of days."

"You look so like him," Calla said.

"Well I am him. Part of him," James said.

"You can guide her safely in the spirit world?" Calla asked

"Yes, I'll keep her safe as houses," he said patting his sword. "And we'll stay far away from the castle and anywhere the Queen might be."

"It is probably best to have a guide. See the land and know the land. We will discuss everything when you get back. We only have three days so make the most of them," Calla nodded to Elinor and Elinor bowed her head as Calla faded away.

James whispered close to her ear, "I want to take you to the sea first."

"Okay. But how will this work? I've only done it once. So I'll just think of the sea and I'll be there? How will you get there? Will you have to walk?" Elinor asked.

"No. I move fast but I've been wondering... I think I can hitch a ride on your scrying. Try it. Think of the South sea and don't let go of my hand. If it doesn't work, just stay where you are and I'll find you, okay?"

"Okay," Elinor closed her eyes, focused, and in a breath she was suddenly there. James was grinning like an imp beside her. He swung her around once in his arms and then held her hand tightly as they walked along the shore and stared out into the sea. She didn't pull her hand away. He was affectionate but in a friendly way, she told herself. He'd been alone so long and she couldn't begrudge him his only human contact.

"It's beautiful," Elinor said pulling her eyes from their locked hands and out onto the sea. She'd always loved the ocean. It was probably impossible to hate it. The sand was white and looked like powder. There were several islands off the coast and the water glittered endlessly around her reflecting the sun.

"I come here a lot," James said. "But it can be depressing because I'm the only one who gets to come here," he said turning around to face away from the water. Elinor copied him and her mouth opened. When everyone said the South Coast was 'ash', she'd assume that there had been a fire and that it would look run down but the reality was horrible.

There was nothing left.

Nothing.

The whole town was dark ashes that danced in the breeze. It was slowly making its way to the shore and she wondered if in another couple years the sand wouldn't be white anymore.

It was a devastating site. That ash was all that was left of a whole city. There wasn't a wall left standing. She didn't wonder anymore at there being so few South nomads at the Glen, she now wondered on how there were any.

The Queen had wrecked *total* devastation. Her hand was swift and efficient. No one would have risen against her again after that show of power. Tears fell from Elinor's eyes as she thought of how many people there had been and how no one could come here to pay their respects.

She knelt down and rested her hands on the ground. She wished she had words but she didn't. She didn't know any of the people who had died but she felt their loss keenly. She felt the presence of the Goodness fall on her and she felt sorrow there too. Elinor realized that joining with the Goodness wasn't only happiness and fun. It meant taking on the ugly, hard side of life and facing it dead on. James kneeled beside her and they sat silently for a long while. Elinor finally remembered that she had a lot to see and she stood.

"Show me the rest of the coast. I want to see it all," Elinor said.

"There isn't much. Well there is a deserted harbor to the east a way, you should probably see it." He took her hand again and didn't let go as they walked along the abandoned docks. It was massive. There had been a serious shipping industry there. The layers of uninhabited wooden walkways looked like a haunted roller coaster, jagged and broken in places. Elinor smiled darkly, the Queen probably regretted her anger now that she didn't have access to whatever they imported or fished.

"What was it like before?" Elinor asked James. "Did you ever come here with Derek?"

"Oh yeah. We came here a bunch at first. The Queen was always concerned about the South Coast and she liked to send her men to rough things up and cause trouble. It was... so full of life then. It was so loud sometimes that I'd have to leave Derek for a couple hours. It was full of fish and men and woman and children. Every free inch of the docks were covered with booths of things someone was selling.

"There are islands out there. I wonder if they were burned just like the coast. Probably. Or maybe they are just trapped, shipless, unable to come home. That sounds like her too. She brooks no disobedience or rebellion. That's why the nomad glen is so precious. I didn't think there was a free inch on this planet but... It fills my heart. If I have one..."

"Of course you have a heart," Elinor said reflexively but even holding his hand tightly she didn't know. She didn't understand the dynamic and division of body and soul. James felt so different from Derek. If they didn't share the same face she would never have thought they were the same person. She wondered if people would think the same thing about her if her soul got pulled to the outside.

"We should probably get back," James said. "I don't want to keep you out too late on our first outing together."

"Thank you for taking me here. I'm glad I saw it," Elinor said sliding into his arms for a hug without a thought. "Even though it was hard to see. You were a great guide." She blinked and they were back at the Glen. "So I'll see you tomorrow?" she asked before she returned to her body.

"Wouldn't miss it for the world. I'm so happy to be involved. I felt like I'd be in the way while you were training with Wolf but now we can work together and you'll be seeing a lot more of me. I won't be so scarce."

"Good," Elinor said squeezing his hand once before she was gone.

"Tell me where you went," Calla said handing over a plate of sandwiches and peppermint tea. The sandwiches turned out to be cream, jam, and chives which were delicious. Elinor liked Calla very much, even more after what she'd seen today.

"I went to the sea," Elinor said after she'd eaten a small sandwich. She hoped it wouldn't be torture for Calla to hear.

"The sea?" she said with eyes full of longing.

"It was so beautiful."

Elinor told Calla about the ocean in as many details as she could muster. Calla soaked it in like a sponge. The ash coast was as much a part of Morland now as the sea was. Calla's brimming tears fell freely and quietly.

"What did you learn?" Calla asked with a tear or two still clinging to her cheeks.

"I'm not sure. I learned that I'd never experienced the kind of sadness and loss I saw today. I've lived a very sheltered life."

"Yes but there is so much more that the South Coast has to teach. The ocean, does it remember the fire? Does it feel pain? Is it altered because of what happened?"

"No. It's probably the same it's been since Morland was born."

"Yes. Exactly. You may think that we only love the sea because it is our home and birthright. But that is not it at all. The sea is our teacher and mother. Our friend and tormentor. The sea is ever-present and enduring. The sea does not change as we do.

196

South nomads spend their lives studying the constant sea. But it is not frozen like land. It is alive just as much as we are. It has moods and fancies. It rises and crashes and is shaken by stormy winds and yet at the end of the storm it is the same. It does not allow the forces of the world to alter its essence.

"It ebbs and flows and returns to what it is. That is what you should learn from the sea. Ride the waves that life throws at you and do not break. Be fluid in the storms but do not lose the way back to yourself. You have given me as much today as I have given you. Your assignment tonight is to think of the sea. I want to lend you something until our fight is done. I wasn't sure it would be right for you but I know now that it is."

Calla reached for a grey box she had at her side. But the box was not really grey. It was a dozen shades of black and white and blue that flowed into each other in a beautiful chaotic cohesion. She pulled out a small ring and placed it on Elinor's thumb. Elinor looked down and her breath caught.

At first it had looked like a silver ring bearing a blue stone, like a sapphire but like the box it was more than it appeared. The stone in the ring changed. The color swirled flowing from blue to black then back to blue then to white then to blue again. She watched it several times before she realized. It was the tide. High tide was the blue to black. Then the regular blue again which was normal tide and then the white of low tide as the water receded back into the ocean. Blue, black, blue, white and it repeated over and over. It was mesmerizing and beautiful and obviously magic.

"Did you make this? I thought you said you were not a mage," Elinor said.

"I have no magic. But my grandmother did. She made jewelry. I want you to wear this until our fight is done. I want you to have a constant reminder of the sea. It is so strong that it could break down a sea wall and yet soft enough to protect the coral in its depth. Find that place within yourself. Find your ability for strength and gentleness. Calm and storm. Cold depths and warm shallows. A mage must find and harness both sides."

197

"Thank you. This is so beautiful. Thank you. I've never seen anything so gorgeous. I will take good care of it until I return it to you. I understand what a treasure this is."

"Study it and yourself. Use this as the aid when you meditate tonight. You should show it to Brigitte. Even though she is not a nomad, she also is a child of the sea."

"Oh one thing I just thought of," Elinor said as she rose to leave. "I left the safety of the Glen today but I didn't feel the Darkness while I was out in the spirit world. Do you think it just wasn't at the coast?"

"Oh it's still at the coast," Calla said. "It's everywhere but here. But the Darkness cannot be where you are when you are in the spirit world with the Goodness. Your bond with the Goodness leaves no room for the Darkness. This is how we win. This is how the Queen is defeated. The power of the Goodness is stronger than the Darkness."

Elinor nodded and smiled and then walked back to her wagon with a full belly, a beautiful magic ring on her finger, and a mind filled with everything she'd learned and needed to remember.

Emmaline was already asleep which was rare and unfortunate since she'd be crying shortly. So Elinor took her time getting ready for bed. She removed her pants, tank top, and vest and put on her soft linen nightgown. She decided to sit up and wait for Brigitte. Elinor stared down at the ring and meditated. It was strange at first to do it with her eyes opened. She'd always had her eyes closed when she mediated with Wolf but the ring was a great aid.

She had spent a lot of time at the ocean during her life. Atlanta was five hours away from the ocean and they went often for family vacations. The South Coast as not so different from the Atlantic Ocean. An ocean was an ocean. There was definitely something hypnotic about the waves coming in and out.

Elinor thought back to what Calla said and hoped she'd be able to find the kinds of balances that she'd spoken of. Elinor had a feeling that it took a life of practice not just three days. But she liked a task and she was a dedicated worker. So she stared into the ring and tried to settle her soul into being as constant and flexible as the sea. Strength and gentleness. Calm and storm. Cold depths and warm shallows. Elinor repeated it as a mantra to her mediation. Strength and gentleness. Calm and storm. Cold depths and warm shallows.

"Elinor, Elinor," Brigitte whispered as she lightly shook Elinor's shoulder.

"Oh sorry. Meditating. Occupational hazard of being the chosen one to save the world. Did you have a good day?" Elinor asked.

"I did. Things are getting so busy around here. Everyone has an idea about what our next step should be. It's difficult to find the right choice among the throng."

"Calm and storm," Elinor said rolling her shoulders. Meditation was relaxing but it also made her stiff.

Brigitte's eyes lit up and she smiled. "Exactly. You sound like a sea-girl. I take it things went well with Calla."

"Oh yes. I like her very much."

"Not just because she fed you?" Brigitte said laughing as she dressed for bed.

"Nope that's only a small piece of it. I feel like I need to write down everything she said and study it every day. She is very wise. Oh B, she told me that you'd like to see my ring," Elinor said extending her hand.

Brigitte actually gasped. It was barely audible over Emmaline's starting sob.

"Do you know what this is?" Brigitte asked pulling her eyes away from Emmaline to look back at the ring.

"I know that it's magic and very precious. Calla's grandmother made it."

"Her grandmother was the greatest mage of the South nomads. That is why Calla is the South Elder. She is practically royalty. That ring is her birthright and proof of her heritage."

"I'm only borrowing it," Elinor said. "It's just a part of my training. I'm giving it back when the fight is done."

"When the fight is done?" Brigitte asked leaning forward for clarification. "Did she say 'until the fight is done.'"

"Yes. I don't know the exact words but she said something like 'I'm lending this to you until our fight is done.' What does it mean?" Elinor asked nervous.

"That ring is not just a beautiful magic item," Brigitte said taking Elinor's hand as she stared into its blue ever-changing depths. "It is how the leadership is passed between South nomads."

"But I'm only borrowing it," Elinor clarified. Brigitte was not understanding that.

"Yes. You are 'borrowing' it until our fight is done. Do you know what our fight is? The fight is against Darkness and not just the presence of Darkness that is covering our world. Our fight is against all Darkness everywhere. The 'fight' is not over until the Goodness wins and Darkness is destroyed forever. You have just been made leader of the South nomads." Brigitte said with wide eyes as she leaned back into her mat.

"What?!" Elinor said and then lowered her voice seeing Emmaline had finally fallen into true deep sleep. "What? How could she do that without telling me? That's such a huge responsibility. I've never been in charge of anyone, well except my little brother and sister. What am I supposed to do? I'll just give it back. I'm not even a nomad."

"You can't," Brigitte said shaking her head and laughing under her voice. "This is your responsibility now, little sister. Or are you my aunt now? Màithrean, that's what we all called Calla."

"Not funny, Brigitte," Elinor said. "What am I supposed to do?" Somehow this felt like way more responsibility than saving the world.

"First, you need to go to sleep. But you should probably mediate first. Calla would not have given you that ring if she wasn't sure. You can ask her yourself tomorrow. But please don't worry tonight. Your only job now is to train. Learn everything you can. But now that you are a leader I'd like your official advice on what you think our next tactical step should be. But that can wait until tomorrow," Brigitte said kissing the top of Elinor's head.

"Now close your eyes, lay down, and calm yourself. This is a great honor and you should feel only proud and happy. You have been found to be exceptional and you are now a nomad. What better way to be joined to Morland than to be one of her people in both blood and tribe? Sleep now, Elinor. All things work for the good for those who trust the Goodness," Brigitte said as she blew out the last candle.

Elinor was extremely sure that she would never sleep again. What had Calla been thinking? She felt like she was barely more than a child. She was only eighteen. She had very few life skills and had spent the last year and a half of her life in some weird partial invalidic state. But before fear and self-doubt could completely take over, she made herself close her eyes and mediate. Strength and gentleness. Calm and storm. Cold depths and warm shallows. She emptied her mind and felt the Goodness and sleep steal in like thieves.

Brigitte

Brigitte couldn't sleep. She slipped out of the wagon as soon as Elinor's breathing steadied. Elinor's news replayed in her mind. She was the Màithrean. It wasn't that Elinor didn't deserve it for all she was giving to fight for them and it definitely wasn't that Brigitte had wanted it for herself but it was still such a shock.

Brigitte did not *hate* the South nomads but she avoided them. Part of it was that she still found it jarring to hear her own accent coming for others. She'd lived so far away from the shore for most of her life and had encountered few South folk, nomads or other. They did not often venture far inland. But Brigitte had stopped caring for the sea. It had taken so much from her and given absolutely *nothing* in return.

She'd never understood its allure. She'd taken its measure and run as far north as she could. Because the sea had killed her father in one seamless gulp. Or at least that was what the other fishing boat reported. It had just swallowed him, boat and all. It had been a stormy sea. The kind of sea that summons hurricanes. But her father had sailed rougher seas and loaded his boat. She had been ten.

The sea had killed her father and left her defenseless. Her 'mother'... She couldn't even call her that in her own thoughts. That woman was a monster. Brigitte made herself take a deep breath. She didn't know why she tortured herself thinking about *her*. She was probably a pile of ash and could do Brigitte no further harm. But even fifteen years later Brigitte still felt the sting of anger and fear. She wished that the knowledge that her mother was dead would erase all the things she'd done but it didn't. That woman had set her on the path she'd taken and landed her where she was for better or for worse.

That woman hadn't mourned her husband a single day. The ocean had taken him and she had *shrugged*. She'd had little patience for the hardworking plain man and was probably relieved to be free of him. She had no problem or shortage filling her bed that hadn't even had a chance to grow cold. That wouldn't have mattered if they'd only stayed there. But they had wandered to the next room and her *mother* had done nothing to stop them. Her grandmother had been the only one who had spoken for Brigitte but it had been too little, too late.

Brigitte found that she'd been washing her hands in a small basin for several minutes and her hands were raw. It would be awhile until she felt clean again. She didn't often let her mind walk such dark corridors. *All things work for the good for those who trust the Goodness,* Brigitte repeated to herself with a wry smile. She'd said that same line to so many lost and broken nomads who had wandered into her glen. And they took the cliché line as well as she did herself. It was a bitter draft to swallow. But she did and she made herself dive into the chain of events and face it all.

If her father hadn't died, Brigitte would never have gone more than a mile away from him. He was an anchor. He was a place of protection and happiness. He was a good, simple man and Brigitte would have been a good, simple girl living on the South Coast and she'd most likely be a pile of ash right now.

If her mother had been a good mother, Brigitte might have still left the seaside but she would not have fled it like the ground was on fire. She might have found a nice town and settled down. She never would have travelled as vast as she did. She never would have made it as far inland as the castle. She wouldn't have had the overpowering need to find a new life as anything or anyone different than what she was. A princess would do as well as anything, she'd decided. She never would have found Derek. She never would have been filled with the Darkness and then freed from it. She wouldn't have her gift that could save people.

If she had been protected then, she would be ash like her mother and all the nomads around her would be dead.

That realization struck her like a punch in the chest. She hadn't expected to find a reason for her suffering when she had started the mental exercise. But she saw now how her pain had led her to a place where she could help so many people but she would have traded anything to have made it to the Glen any other way. She would have paid any other price.

Her journey had been long and hard and cruel. But when she looked around at the life pulsing inside her protective shield, it didn't seem *such* a heavy cost to pay and it felt like such a long time ago. Almost like it happened to another version of herself. At least for now, at least while the lanterns were shining bright and the mood was high, it felt worth it. If there had been no other way to end up here, then it was what it was.

She knew she wouldn't be able to sleep so instead she walked the corridors of the Glen and studied the stone barrier that marked the edge of her spell. She wished it was bigger. She wished there was more land for farming and livestock, more room to spread out. Any number of people started to feel like too many when they were all trapped together under a bubble. The clan leaders did their best to keep things calm and to quickly put to rest fighting and arguing but it was inevitable. The four clans had not met like this in over a seventy years. They had joined together with the men of the land to fight the Queen and when they had failed they each fell away from the other and had tried to return to their lives.

That had been impossible, of course.

The Queen hadn't focused too hard on the nomads at first, part of it was probably that they were the hardest to catch. They moved around and did it well. But when the towns had been purged of magic and able-bodied young men for her army, she'd started hunting the nomad clans down.

Brigitte remembered when she'd first heard the news about the South Coast, she had retched for a good hour. The word they had used, *ash*, was a nightmare realized. She felt like she had made it happen by laying the plan years ago. She felt like her desire to burn it down had filtered back to the Queen. Brigitte could not help but feel that it was all her fault somehow.

Even now with some time between the event, she still felt a sickness in her stomach and a responsibility because if Derek hadn't stopped her that night she might have done this exact thing. She hadn't had any magic at the time but fire was an easy trick for any human.

The knowledge of what the Queen had done and what Brigitte had almost done was one of the biggest catalysts for the creation of the Glen. She could never fully assuage her guilt but each saved nomad made her breath a little easier. And now they were all together again and something was coming. She hoped they'd be able to figure out what they were supposed to do and how they could help Elinor. Because Elinor was instrumental to everything. And becoming Màithrean was one tiny puzzle piece of the plan.

Peter

The cool night breeze helped clear Peter's head. He'd had another long day in the council room and he knew it would be another long day tomorrow. Elinor's magic was growing and that made the leaders restless, nervous, and excited. Elinor was able to slide in and out of the spirit world with ease. She could view anywhere on Morland. Those two things were cool but the key to everything was that when Elinor was in the spirit world she was there with the Goodness. The more often and longer she stayed in the spirit world the stronger the bond became. It would become strong enough that wherever she went while in the spirit world she would bring the Goodness with her. She was like a dirty bomb laced with radioactive Goodness. It would spread and consume the Darkness.

But there was more that Brigitte and some of the leaders guessed because they seemed wary and were hesitant to act. Peter wanted them to act now, to storm the castle and save Derek now. But Elinor's task must be bigger than Peter could see right now. He wanted to save Derek and defeat the Darkness but he needed Elinor to be ready. So he'd wait. He'd give her the time to train. It just gave him more time to pretend he was a blacksmith. The warmth of the coals and the cold of the night were a calming combination. It helped his brain to be able to focus on a physical task to try and blank his mind.

But it always came back to Elinor.

Elinor had been as hard to tie down as a summer breeze since they'd come to the Glen. It was strange to see her so little after having been each other's constant companions for so many days while on the road. Now she was so busy. Training from sun up to sun down. He usually only saw her for a while at dinner and then exhausted, she'd go to sleep. He never knew when he would see her or talk to her. He didn't want to be in the way but it was hard to be apart from her.

So Peter stayed busy. He spent the mornings and afternoons in the council meeting every day, then after that he'd spend the rest of the day at the smithy. This was for the best because after a couple hours in the meeting he usually *really* needed to hit something. Then if he was lucky he'd have dinner with Elinor and then collapse on his mat under the stars and try to rest enough to start it all over again the next day.

But he hadn't seen Elinor all day or the day before. He had hoped her training was not starving her and he found he felt a little restless if he didn't get to see her at least once a day. He just liked to reassure himself that she was okay.

He'd grown accustomed to her company, addicted was probably closer to the mark. He'd had a crush on her on Earth and coming to Morland had somehow strengthened it to something he wouldn't name. Because if she had been too busy and overwhelmed to think about having a boyfriend on Earth she was definitely too busy and overwhelmed now.

So he would wait and enjoy the time he was given. In all their discussions they had never talked about 'the kiss'. It had hung in the air between them for the first couple days after it happened. Or he'd thought it had hung there. She'd only just had her stomach cauterized and to be fair she probably hadn't been thinking of anything but walking and not dying. He'd supported her with an arm wrapped around her for most of the day, switching with Ryan sometimes. She would lean on his shoulder at night when they sat at the fire and she'd slept not a foot away from him.

But all of that was just friendship.

But the kiss had definitely not been *just* friendship. He remembered the heady moment when her arms had wrapped around his neck and she'd clung to him as though she might drown. It still quickened his pulse to remember it. But she hadn't mentioned it. She hadn't said a thing about it and she acted the same as she did pre-kiss. It was infuriating. Maybe what happened in the cloud spirit world, stayed in the cloud spirit world but Peter had felt something and he knew Elinor had too.

So he'd wait, as long as it took. When things were calm and they were safe. And it made sense. He always hated it in action movies when the couple would stop to make out with bullets flying and a bomb to diffuse. They just needed to wait a few days, escape the danger and then they could kiss as long as they liked.

Even though Elinor was busy, she was never really alone. He knew James was around. And he would see her talking to herself but really to the invisible man. James was always there, unseen and taking her attention. Peter had no idea how he felt having Derek's soul as Elinor's new constant companion.

It sent a strange pang of jealously through him and he made himself shake it off. James was a spirit, an invisible soul. It wasn't his fault he couldn't talk to anyone but Elinor. And that gave Peter an idea and it filled his mind. He should go see James sometime. Why hadn't he thought of it before? Who cared if Emmaline told everyone the spula vine wasn't good? He'd already used it once. And talking to Derek's soul would be really cool.

He made himself blank his mind when he almost hammered his thumb. Ian yelled at him and Peter put the thoughts of Elinor and James back in the tight box in the back of his mind. When they were home. He'd think about it again when they were home.

Chapter 17

Elinor

Elinor was up like a shot as soon as the sun crept in through the windows. If she still had headaches she would have hated it here, the sun was everywhere. But she didn't have headaches. It still amazed her that this was her new reality. This new reality had its own issues, of course, but anything was easier to bear than the weight she'd carried for the past year, maybe even this ring…Maybe. She went straight to Calla's wagon and knocked as she entered the wagon.

"What is this ring?" Elinor asked barely stopping herself from taking another sniff of the fragrant breakfast scents emanating from a large tray in front of Calla.

"My grandmother's ring," Calla said with a wry smile creeping up her face. Elinor raised her eyebrows and Calla continued. "I would not have given you that ring if I wasn't sure. You are bonded to Morland as surely as if it was the only air you'd ever breathed. Your fate is tied to that of our people. I gave you that ring because I trust you. But that is not what we'll be learning today. You've seen the sea but that is only one part of Morland. We'll talk more about your role as Màithrean when you return."

"That word again," Elinor said. "What does it mean?"

"It means the aunt of your mother's side. But in this case it means sister of Morland and aunt to her children. An aunt is someone who looks after the children in their mother's stead. Someone who loves them like a mother but is able to see the truth of things without the blinders of motherhood. That is your title now. Màithrean. But as I said, don't focus on that now. We have such little time and so much to accomplish. Where is he?"

And as if to answer her call James came strolling into the wagon without the convention of doors or windows.

"He's here," Elinor said sharper than she would have liked. She did like Calla. She was *pretty sure* she still liked her but she did feel like she'd been tricked and it sat awkward on her shoulders.

"Good morning, sunshine," James said offering a hand and inviting her into the spirit world.

"One minute," Elinor said grabbing several baked treats and chasing it with tea that was a bit too hot. Whatever being 'aunt' of the nomads meant she was going to make sure it didn't include missing meals. "Okay let's go," Elinor said trying to slide into the spirit world but it felt like she was walking through tar. She looked up at Calla for an explanation.

"I see we are going to have to discuss this now. You fear and anger are making it difficult to join the Goodness in the spirit world. Tell me what exactly is troubling you about the ring," Calla said.

"Okay first. Why didn't you tell me? You told me to show it to Brigitte. Did you just not want to tell me yourself because you knew I wasn't going to be happy about it?" Elinor said.

Calla didn't rise to Elinor's tone but remained steady and unmoved, *like the sea,* Elinor thought bitterly.

"I was not consulted before the ring was given to me. I was the first Màithrean that did not possess magic. I was an ordinary girl. I was not prepared for the task, to say the least. But does the ring not fit already? It is an easy burden to bear at first and you will grow into the rest of it. It will shape itself around you. I am still *a* Màithrean, but you are the rising Màithrean. I will still perform many of the duties while your training takes all your time. Do you love Morland?"

"Yes," Elinor said and was surprised that she meant it. For all the ways that Morland had done her wrong since she'd arrived she did love it. It was beautiful and different and worth saving.

"Do you love the people of Morland?" Calla asked.

"Yes."

"That is all that is required of you. Love Morland and love her children. That is what being an aunt means. The South nomads will do as they will do and you will advise them when you feel they need advising. You do not dictate their lives or rule them. You are simply to be there when they need you and to love them. Is that so impossible?" Calla asked with raised eyebrows.

No, Elinor thought. *It was as easy as being a sister.* She didn't tell her siblings what to do unless they were in danger or if her mom told her to help them with something. She wasn't their boss or their mother. She was their friend and protector.

"I think I could do that. I am sure there is some other young woman, who was born a south nomad who would be more suited to the task. I wish you had just told me all this yesterday," Elinor said.

Calla smiled and let out a breath that Elinor hadn't known she'd been holding. "Yes, I see now that I might have. But I needed the bond to set and seal. And I wasn't sure how you would respond but I should have known. I knew you were the one and I should have trusted the Goodness and known you would accept your destiny. But all is explained now. Is your fear and anger gone?"

"Yes," Elinor said grudgingly, feeling more like a rebuked child than a great and powerful aunt but it was something she'd grow into, she guessed, hoped. She turned to look at James and he was smiling so rottenly that Elinor was in the spirit world and hitting him playfully before she even took a breath.

"You liked that, huh?" she said trying to get him. James might be incorporeal sometimes but when he wasn't he was still over six feet tall and easily evaded her wrath.

"Yes, I enjoyed that very much. I almost thought you were going to stomp your feet at one point but alas. Maybe next time," James said smiling widely.

"Uh huh. You are so funny, aren't you? Maybe I'll just head up the mountain without you and you can walk," she said taking a couple steps away from him.

"Hey, I'm sorry," he said grabbing her and holding her tight until she gave up. "I was just messing with you."

"I know. I was just playing too," Elinor said looking at up him with her chin resting on his chest. "So where to?"

"Ladies choice, take us to the top of the North Mountains."

Elinor had done zero hiking in her life. She'd lived in the city of Atlanta and hadn't done a lot of outdoorsy things. They had went to the beach and amusement parks as vacations. Boone had been the first mountain cabin she'd ever stayed in and they hadn't had a chance to hike. Elinor hadn't even seen the view in the daylight. So she had nothing with which to compare the grand splendor she saw before her.

The mountains were not so tall as the Rockies or the Himalayans but it was dizzyingly high up. There was snow at the peak and the view was absolutely stunning. Elinor felt her breath slip out in a gasp as she turned to take in the panorama of the world.

"This is..." she said to James unable to find the right word.

"Yes. It is, isn't it? The North Mountains are beautiful. I've never been up this high" he said edging closer to the center of the peak.

"Are you afraid of heights," Elinor laughed taking his hand.

"Maybe. It's really high up here," James said not allowing her to pull him back to the edge.

"But we aren't really here and you are just..." she stopped when she saw his face fall. She wished she could take her words back but it was the truth. James was *just* a soul. He was *just* a spirit. But it didn't feel that way most of the time. When she was here with him he felt more real than the Derek locked far away in a castle.

"I'm sorry," she said hugging him as his arms stayed at his side. "You aren't a *just*. I don't know exactly what you are but you have every right to be afraid of a mountain cliff."

"No. I'm sorry," he said finally hugging her back. "I guess I'm a little sensitive about my 'justness'. I know I'm not a whole person. But I guess I don't like to hear you say it."

"Let's go somewhere else. Take me somewhere with people. With people and life and flat ground. Oh can we go to... Alentar. That's Jol's birthplace, right?"

"I don't know where Jol was born. But we can go to Alentar. It's a big enough town. It will give you the feel of Morlanders without being too near the castle."

James

Just. Just. Just. The word hung around his shoulders long after he told Elinor he was over it. He'd been playing a dangerous game with himself. Touching her and holding her and pretending that all of it was normal. When it wasn't normal for so many reasons. He was intoxicated with her company. Maybe she could have been anyone. Anyone who could hear and see and touch him. But he liked to think that Elinor was special, that he'd have felt drawn to her even if she couldn't see him. Not for the first time he wondered what Derek thought about her.

Elinor's wide eyes and excitement made him laugh softly. She was pulling his hand and running from shop to shop and pointing at things she'd never seen while James explained. He was glad they'd come here. Alentar was a good choice. It was a far enough way from the castle and big enough without being overwhelming.

It was still mind-blowing to James that Jol was Elinor's grandfather, that Jol had been to Earth, and had been absolutely zero help to Derek on that front. He'd made Derek think he only barely believed him. The fury rising in James was a rare occurrence for him. He couldn't wait till Derek knew but truthfully Derek's anger was not something James ever really wanted to awaken.

"My grandfather was born here," Elinor said turning to him. "I wish I could bring my dad here. He thought Jol was from the United Kingdom somewhere. But this place is really neat."

Alentar was like most medium sized cities in Morland. The main street was packed with two story stone buildings on both side of the main road and there were several side roads that led to the farms and mills. There were bakeries and blacksmiths, clothiers and dressmakers, pubs and inn, stables and butchers. Like most cities in Morland it felt more like the past than it did a city on another planet but James supposed seventy years of oppression was enough to shake the magic out of a place.

Many traveled to the city only to sell their goods before journeying home along one of the roads that led out of town. He tried to see it as Elinor was seeing it. It made him smile a cruel little smile that he was so used to Morland he couldn't quite tell what she would find so different. He didn't think about going home, or he hadn't before... Before Derek returned and wasted James's sacrifice. What had been the point of James staying behind in Morland if Derek was back at the castle waiting for the full moon again? Maybe this was all inevitable, maybe he'd only bought Derek time. But now they had Elinor. That had to mean something...

The sun was getting low in the sky and it gave James an idea. There was really only one place to be for a sunset.

"Hold my hand, I know where we should go next," James said smiling. "Take us to the West Plains."

Elinor

The West Plains were never ending. That was the only way to describe it. They'd appeared in the middle of it and she could not see it's edges. There was not a single tree on the horizon. It was flat and wide and she could *see* the wind. She'd never *seen* a wind before. She'd only ever seen the effect of it, the leaves blowing or the rain being swept around. But the West Wind was a thing. It was the incarnation of 'a force of nature'.

She wished she was there for real so she could feel it. Scrying was amazing but wherever she went she was only a ghost, a silent invisible observer, unable to touch things or change anything. And that was how James felt all the time. Poor James.

"Has Derek ever been here?" Elinor asked.

"No. He never went this far west. Nobody comes this far except Westies."

"Where do they live? What do they eat?" she asked and James chuckled.

"I have no idea. You'll have to ask one. Come on let's just walk a bit and soak it in,"

The West Plains were beautiful in a unique way. It was like those dreams where she'd run and run and end up exactly where she started. It was just hard ground with tall grass endlessly spanning in all directions. There were no trees or rivers. She couldn't even see the North mountains.

"It's really incredible, isn't it?" Elinor said turning around in circles. The sun made the grass look like fire. It was red, orange, and almost purple. She wished she was an artsy type and could paint what she saw. But no one would ever believe that her work was based on a true place.

"It is," James said. Then his hand stiffened in hers as he looked behind her. "What the...?" James said. Elinor turned and saw a large black mass moving swiftly towards them. James pulled her behind him in an instant and held her there with his left hand while his right drew his sword. Elinor peered around him and saw a herd of black things charging towards them, gaining distance in impossible strides. James held her tightly against him and said "Think of the Glen. Now!" Elinor obliged him and they were back in an instant.

"What was that?" Elinor asked. James had been so serious and intense. He almost always had a wry smile waiting on his lips and his serious tone had been startling. James didn't say anything but he tapped her stomach. Elinor paled.

"It was those creatures?" Elinor wasn't afraid of much. But those things... She never wanted to see another one of them again. They were creatures of the Darkness, inky black with every surface made for scratching and clawing.

"I don't know what they were doing out there and I hope they weren't looking for us... Don't scry without me, okay?" he said pulling her to his chest. "I don't know what I'd do if..."

Calla cleared her throat and Elinor pulled back. Calla must have taken spula vine because she was in the spirit world with them. Elinor was so comfortable with James and he was very physical that she forgot how it must look. He was a man, a handsome man and he couldn't quite keep his hands off her. It made her blush and it didn't make sense. James wasn't a person really. He was Derek's soul. But that didn't stop her blush.

"I should go. Bye, James," she said.

"Bye, my little mist girl," James said walking out of the wagon.

"I did not come into the spirit world to spy on you but I felt a surge of unease come off your body and I decided to come in. What happened?" Calla asked.

"We were in the plains and all of the sudden a great black mass was coming towards us. It was those creatures of the Darkness. The ones with claws," Elinor said putting a protective arm across her stomach.

"Brigitte told me that that was what caused your wounds but I have never seen one. We did not know they existed until you encountered one. Are they not so common? I would think that she would have the whole land covered in them."

"I don't know how common they are but these were the first I'd seen since coming here. I should have asked James. I know he's seen them before."

"But you are unharmed this time," Calla said brushing Elinor's hair away from her face.

"Yes, I think so," Elinor said doing a body scan.

"Good. Alright. Now tell me about the plains. What did you learn?"

Elinor took a deep breath as she calmed herself. She was okay. She wasn't hurt. "I learned that Morland is still really dangerous. As a whole it's not as nice as it is here in the Glen. And I wish I could go home."

"Part of that is very true," Calla said. "The Darkness fills the land and Morland is its prisoner. Not only the people need to be saved but the land as well. But do you think this battle isn't also going on in your home world? Do you not think that the Goodness and Darkness are not also battling on your world as well as every other?"

Elinor paled. She didn't like to think that this was going on invisibly on Earth but Calla was right. Running home to Earth was not the answer. Just because the Darkness was invisible didn't mean it wasn't there. And she believed the Devil was real. She'd just forgotten that forces of evil have many names and shapes. What Calla said was true, everywhere there was light there was a darkness trying to put it out.

"You are right," Elinor said. "I'm not going to run away and leave Morland."

"What else did you learn?" Calla said nodding and changing the subject.

"Well, the Plains are endless and beautiful in their own way. But they are also wild and empty. I don't know. The plains are strange. I have no idea how anyone can live there. Not that its horrible there but I just mean logistically. Where is their food and shelter? And the wind. It's amazing. It is its own being. It looked so powerful. It has shaped the whole West Plains hasn't it? Flattening it out and running over the whole surface until it's as flat as glass."

"You are almost there," Calla said. "I'll help you. The West Plains are home to the West nomads. It is a perfect example of the diversity and ingenuity of man. They are not trapped there. They chose to make that place their home. They have learned its ways and they flourish under its whirlwind and tempest. There are many things to learn of the West and their plains and winds. But one of them is to make the most of where you are.

"They have made that barren landscape their home and retreat. The how and why is their story to tell. The second is that sometimes things are beyond our strength to control. There is no mastering or taming that wind. It gives gifts and takes away but at its own discretion. The West nomads know this and accept peace in their uncertainty. They live differently from all other nomads. Their bond with the land gives them what they need and nothing more. It is the ultimate acceptance to know that man cannot control the world. That man cannot really control anything. There is nothing man can make that will calm that wind but it can be harnessed to aid them in small things. They farm the wind. They have made inventions that harness some of the wind's power. They do not own the wind but they work together."

"So the moral is that the world is a hard place with Darkness and strong winds and there is nothing we can do about it," Elinor sulked.

"No. Man has a great misunderstanding that if he is not in charge then something is wrong but Morland and the wind live in harmony and so do the Westies and the wind. The moral is to live in symbiosis with the forces of good and like you did earlier to protect ourselves from the forces that seek to destroy us. The great lesson of life is distinguishing between the two. Knowing that which can aid us and that which can kill us."

Elinor nodded. That was true enough. Even on Earth people tried to control the world. They wanted to master the sea, sky, and land but they didn't own or control any of them. And most people struggled finding what was good for them and what would destroy them. It shouldn't be hard to distinguish but it was. The Darkness was tricksier on Earth. It didn't look like a giant black cloud of clawing monsters. It looked more like a lie or a wrong step. Elinor did agree that the lesson of life was distinguishing between the two and then choosing the right one. She was just getting hit with one truth bomb after another with Calla.

"You did well today. I think we will change our training tomorrow. We do not know where those creatures may be and I think we'd best stop scrying until we know more. Take the rest of the day off. I'll see you tomorrow. You did well."

Elinor stretched as she walked but was too restless to head straight to dinner. And the sun had about an hour until it would completely set so dinner might not even be ready yet. She decided to go check on Ryan and Peter. She hadn't seen much of them which she took to be a good thing. They must each be finding their place at the Glen.

Ryan

As the days progressed Damon had started pairing him with others for sparing. That had been when the bruises and soreness really started. He didn't *really* hate Morland but his mind would tell him that if he had been on Earth he wouldn't have be getting his ass handed to him by a scrawny man who barely came up to his chest. Strength was not all there was. So much of it was technique and speed. Ryan had assumed that if he was the bigger of the two he would win but that hadn't always been the case.

Sparing was perfect for guys like him. He was competitive and it made training a game and a challenge. No man liked to lose to a group of his peers. Especially as his little sister walked up with wide eyes and a wider smile seeing him get tossed to his back as his surprise left him wide open.

Elinor walked over laughing so hard she clutched her side. "Is this what you've been up to?" she said still giggling, "I love it. This is a good look for you. I wish our family could see you flinging a sword like a fantasy hero. I'm getting a musketeer vibe or maybe like a crusader. I'm so glad I came to find you today. What if I had missed this?"

Ryan started laughing and told her that she was sworn to secrecy. She shook her head and said no way.

"So when did you decide to become a sword-wielding knight?" Elinor asked leaning against the fence next to Ryan. He hesitated a moment wondering what he should say. He settled on a bit of the truth.

"I know something is coming, El. The full moon gets closer every day and I won't stand aside helpless when things start up. But don't worry about me. How have you been? Why were you released before dinner? Your instructors usually work you until the moon comes up."

Elinor

She decided not to tell him about her encounter with the creatures. He'd only worry and she was fine anyway.

"Umm, we did enough for today. I'm supposed to be resting but I wanted to see what you were up to and I was not disappointed," Elinor said grinning at her big brother.

"Yeah, this was not something I planned to be doing. But Emmaline corralled me and you may not know this," he said smiling. "But it's very hard to say no to her." Elinor smiled back. She sure knew it.

"Are you okay?" Elinor asked. "I mean this is not something I ever thought I'd see you do."

"El," Ryan said with raised eyebrows. "Don't you dare add my wellbeing to the giant list of things you need to be concerned about. I'm fine. Totally fine. Yes, this is so weird. Yes, I just want to go home. But I'm here and since I've got nothing better to do." He shrugged. "Why not, right?"

"Ryan, back to it. That's enough resting," a man called out and Ryan waved as he walked back into the confusing fray. Elinor was so glad that Ryan was busy with a purpose. If she'd had a free moment to think she would have been worried how he'd been adjusting.

Now it was time to check on Peter. Elinor meandered through the wagons and started to give up on finding Peter when she found him yelling with a hammer in his hand.

Peter was covered in sweat, from the top of his head to his black pants. His blond hair was partially pulled back and she realized it had grown out since they'd been in Morland. He was looking more and more like a native. His muscles were working as he hammered down on a bit of metal, turned it and hammered again. He was yelling at Ian who came over and showed him how to do something. Elinor could have watched him all day. He looked like a blacksmith from a novel.

Ian saw her first and yelled at Peter who wiped his brow and turned. His face lit up when he saw it was her. Elinor smiled back and realized how much she'd been missing Peter. It hit her all at once and she was so glad she had found him.

"You don't have to stop," Elinor said when Peter started to put his things away.

"Okay, just another minute and I'll be at a stopping point," Peter said grinning as he flexed making Elinor blush and roll her eyes.

"He's doing very well," Ian said from behind her and Elinor turned startled. He moved like a cat.

"I'm glad. I'm sure he's loving it," Elinor said.

"How is your training going?" Ian asked. He stood too close and Elinor was starting to feel a little warm herself. Ian was handsome in the way Derek was: dangerous and good looking and very aware of those two facts. His black hair was tied back at his neck and his pale skin was flushed from the fire and the exercise. His eyes were intense and locked onto Elinor's eyes. It made her take a step back especially as Ian took a step forward.

"It's going very well. I'm training with Calla now. I like her a..." Elinor said stopping suddenly as Ian grabbed her hand.

"It's true then," he said holding her hand softly in his as he ran his thumb over the ring. "You are the talk of the Glen, auntie," Ian said softly with humor in his eyes.

"Yeah, we are still figuring all that out," Elinor said sliding her hand out of Ian's grasp. Peter had not missed the display and was at her side with a hand on her back in an instant.

"Dinner?" he said leading her out as he grabbed his jacket from a peg on the wall.

"Goodbye, Elinor," Ian said. "I'm sure I'll see you soon."

"Yeah. Bye, Ian," Elinor said without turning back.

"I'm glad you came to find me," Peter said smiling.

"Yeah I decided I needed to check on everyone. I just got back from seeing Ryan. Do you know what he is doing?" Elinor asked.

"Yes," Peter said smiling wider. "It's so stinking cool. Everything is. This whole nomad camp is unbelievably awesome."

"I was surprised you weren't there with him. It seemed like something you'd love," Elinor said.

"Yeah. I'd be lying if I said I haven't gone over to train with Damon a night or two after dinner but honestly I just don't have the time. And I tell myself that blacksmithing is cooler than sword fighting, even though it probably isn't," he said winking. "But only so many hours in a day, right?"

"That is very true. I'd kill for another six hours. I'd use every one of them to sleep though. I wish I could borrow the hours from a couple months from now and just have extra short days then. Because I need the time way more now than I will when we are home again but alas I cannot control the time space continuum," she said smiling and it felt good. *Smiling with Peter is my favorite thing,* Elinor thought.

"Yeah. I'm sorry I didn't tell you sooner that you aren't a Time Lord. I kind of thought you knew."

Elinor laughed and poked him in the ribs. "Ha. Ha. Now you promised dinner."

Peter acquired the said dinner but they carried it to the edge of the border overlooking the forest.

222

"I'm so glad you came to see me today," Peter said again dividing up the bowls of stew and bread. "It's a rare treat to get time with the chosen one," he said elbowing her in the ribs.

"Ha. Yeah, it's not so fun as the books make it," Elinor said pulling at the edges of her bread.

"What's going on? I know you, Elinor. Tell me what it is. Is it about that ring?" Peter said with a hand on her knee.

"You know about the ring?" Elinor said.

"Oh yeah. Everyone knows about the ring. Sorry Ian was all over you about it but that ring is big news."

"I never asked for this. Any of this," Elinor said motioning the ring and the whole stupid Morland.

"I know. But life has a way of giving more than we'd ever hoped for. Elinor, you are living the life of my dreams. You have magic. You are the only hope to save a whole planet and destroy the Darkness. You have the ability to actually help Derek. Don't you think I'd kill to be you? I know you didn't ask for it but it's an amazing gift, Elinor. And you get to use it without the cost of headaches, where is the problem?"

She shouldn't have been surprised that Peter couldn't understand. She had a sudden empathy for Derek as he tried to endlessly explain to Peter that Morland was actually the worst. But Peter couldn't really hear it.

"If I could give it all to you, I would. I wish you could do all this. I'd let you in an instant," she said clutching her forehead.

"Is your head hurting again?" Peter said worried.

"No. It's habit I guess. I just...Have you ever looked in the mirror and had no idea who you were? Like I know I should be so happy my headaches are gone but it's like the bullet got removed but the skin and muscles are still all angry and bitter over getting shot. I don't know how to be the old Elinor again. The Elinor before this started." Tears were welling and she took a couple deep breaths to keep them in. Peter opened his arms and she leaned in with a weak smile.

Every morning Elinor would wake up and stare into the sun and think "Who am I?" She has no idea who she was. She wasn't headache girl and she wasn't who she was before. She was trying to figure it out when suddenly everyone was expecting everything from her. She didn't want to be the chosen one. No one really did. It was the worst.

The goal is to be the random kid at magic school who is happy that exams got cancelled because the warrior children saved them or did something stupid, no one knew the whole story. She didn't want to be the one who had to give up everything and fight really hard every day. She'd always imagined that the day her headaches ended everything would be perfect and calm and she'd finally be a normal girl.

"Some things don't change, I guess," she said chuckling softly in Peter's chest as a tear or two slid free. "I'm sorry," she said without pulling free.

"El, you don't need to be the old you. You need to find the new you. I have a feeling that *this* you is going to be the most awesome version yet. Don't be afraid or overwhelmed. Just take it a day at a time. Maybe you are everything they say and maybe you aren't. But what if you can help get Derek back? Isn't that worth working for? Even if you aren't this crazy savior, maybe you can just help free Derek and get us home. That's all I'm hoping for. And El, I'm going to try everything I can to help too. We are in this together. No one is hanging all their hope on you. You are a piece of the puzzle. I think you owe it to yourself to see what you can do."

Elinor looked up at him and nodded. Peter gave her one last squeeze and then let her go. But he took her hand and they stared in silence at the trees. James arrived just as quiet as ever and sat at her other side. He smiled and she smiled back. She wondered if Peter noticed when James was around.

"He's right, you know," James said. "You get to pick who this new Elinor is and having only met this version of you, you probably won't believe me but I'm pretty sure this one is the best."

"Thanks," she said softly.

Peter

He could feel it. The moment Elinor finally stopped worrying and just gave in. It was like a strong wind had finally blown passed. The stillness and calm were restoring. They talked for another couple minutes but her yawns were increasing in frequency and he held her hand as they walked back to her wagon.

"Good night, El," he said only letting himself hold her for two breaths.

"Good night, Peter," she said.

When Elinor didn't let go he smiled and said, "Are you asleep already?"

When he looked down, he saw her closed eyes and then she went completely limp. He laughed and scrambled to hold her upright. She laughed and let herself be helped up.

"You are super comfy," Elinor said. "But I think your weary blacksmith arms might not be able to hold me upright all night."

"You underestimate the guns," Peter said flexing. "I could carry you to the moon and back."

Elinor laughed again. "Maybe next fall break. This one is a bit overbooked." Still smiling she waved one last wave and went into her cabin.

Peter took a deep breath. That rare silly moment with Elinor had been so good for his soul. He had been starting to feel weird because being around Elinor was kind of stressful and he'd would be lying if he said he wasn't a little frustrated with her. Was it really so terrible? Was it such a burden to have magic and be able to use that magic to help everyone?

He felt guilty for the ugly thoughts and jealousy that flickered through his mind. Because that was really all it was, jealousy. It wasn't her fault. It was just infuriating to be one person removed again. So close to being important. So close to having the secret and the power. But he was only the best friend, again.

He *was* busy and he was doing things that mattered. The council was critical and he was a council member but he'd rather be the hero. Instead he was the paper-pusher, the behind the scenes producer. But all that was changing now.

Things were finally happening. Peter felt bad for not telling Elinor, especially when he'd kind of promised to keep her in the loop. But he was taking care of it. She had so much going on. She was overwhelmed and exhausted. He was just lightening the load. And she was not going to be happy that he was leaving…

But he had to. The council had finally come up with a plan. The bare bones but they had all agreed. It was a small miracle. And Peter had one last task before he started packing. He needed to get some spula vine.

James

It was nice to have some quiet time after Elinor was asleep. James had grown so accustomed to spending all his time alone that he found he still liked to have some time to himself while she slept. It recharged him. Being around too many people for too long always drained him.

226

Maybe it was the feeling of being invisible that he didn't like but either way the Glen was *very* nice at night. James was so content and at peace sitting watch outside of Elinor's wagon that he didn't notice when someone started calling him.

"Um James?" he heard a voice say.

James turned around to see Peter.

"Hello," James said walking over to meet his physical body's best friend. "Spula vine?" James guessed. Peter nodded as he looked around and at James.

Peter wouldn't be able to travel or really walk around the spirit world like Elinor could. When someone took spula vine to glimpse the spirit world James was told that everything looked white and cloud-like. James didn't see it that way. He saw everything like he was really there. And it was strange to think that Peter couldn't see that they were sitting outside of Elinor's wagon, Peter would only see white. But James liked to think that maybe he just had the ability to see Elinor more clearly than others did.

"Wow. You look just like him. You are his soul and not Derek right?" Peter asked. James smiled wryly.

"Everyone says that. But no, sorry to disappoint. I am not Derek or not exactly. Elinor has named me James and it fits."

"It's nice to meet you," Peter said extending his hand. James tried to smile.

"Sorry," James said waving his hand right through Peter.

"But I thought you and Elinor could touch?"

"She and I can. Elinor fully crosses into the spirit world. At that point the two of us are in the same plane. You aren't really here. You are only... It's like you are looking through a window. You and I are still on other sides. But it's nice to meet you, none the less."

"I've heard so much about you, from Derek," Peter clarified.

227

"I'm sorry but I've heard very little about you. I haven't had a ton of time with Derek. But he told me that you were a good friend to him when he needed one. Thank you."

"Yeah. He's a good guy, sometimes," Peter said smiling.

"Yeah, that's pretty true," James said. "He was a good guy to come back here to save Elinor. I was really shocked when he told me."

"Things went bad so fast. I don't think he really had a choice."

James laughed. "Peter, you know very well that Derek doesn't do things he doesn't want to do. Everything is a decision, a calculated choice. I'm just still surprised that she was able to get to him, enough that he decided she was worth saving at the cost of himself."

"Of course Elinor is worth saving," Peter said his voice raising and his hands clenching. James realized that he should have been paying better attention. Peter wasn't *just* a friend to Elinor. And his words only confirmed it. "Elinor is good and kind and sweet. Derek isn't great sometimes, a lot of the time. But he's not a monster and Elinor is worth it," Peter said.

"I know," James said with raised hands. "I'm sorry for implying she wasn't. Elinor really is something special. She's absolutely changed my life. I'd seen her spirit projecting into Morland as a misty figure and I knew it was something different. And now having someone to talk to… It's really amazing. She is amazing. She's something rare and bewitching. Derek's choice to save Elinor is the greatest thing he has ever done."

Peter

Talking with Derek's soul hadn't been as weird as Peter imagined it would be. James was a lot like Derek but with that extra bit. The good stuff.

228

Peter was glad he'd come. He had decided to visit James mostly as a whim. Sitting with Elinor earlier had given him an unsettling idea. She'd looked over suddenly and had whispered a word and smiled a shy smile and he'd realized neither were for him. And since he hadn't seen anyone there he realized it must have been James. James was Derek soul. It was really cool and strange and he should have met him sooner but six days at the Glen had passed really fast.

Peter had had to do some major convincing of Wolf to be given a small vine of the green plant. It helped that Wolf and Peter were often on the same side of things at the council meetings. Peter had told him it was vitally important that he enter the spirit world. Eventually Wolf had agreed but not before confiding that someone had been stealing the spula vine and to be on guard while in the spirit world.

The spirit world had been just as cloudy and strange as the first time he entered it. He'd found James quickly after calling for him, he'd just appeared in front of him.

Peter hadn't thought through what he'd wanted to talk to James about. He'd just been seized by the idea that he should talk to him and he'd went. And Peter had not been prepared for what he would find. James's adoration of Elinor was *very clear*. It confirmed a weird jealousy he'd been harboring under the surface. James was in love with her. And what the hell did that mean? And more importantly did she know? Peter wondered what he was supposed to say and settled on the thought that made him feel the best.

"I know you will anyway but I'll feel better if I ask you. Will you keep an eye on Elinor? I'll be leaving the day after tomorrow. I'm going with the Mage and Winter and a bunch of warriors."

"You are going to help Derek?" James asked intently.

"Yes," Peter said.

"Oh I am so glad to hear that. I've popped my head into the council meetings a couple times but they are so infuriating it makes me want to blow my brains out so I never figured out where all the arguing landed. You are going to the castle?"

"Yes. Jol has a plan but he's not telling us what it is and Winter has a plan but it just entails killing everyone. So I'm hoping that in between the two of them is the remnants of a useable plan. We should get there in time. Hopefully we'll have a day to spare but we'll be there by the full moon for sure. Do you know how to use that sword?" Peter nodded to his waist. "And how can you have a sword by the way?"

James chuckled. "I woke up with it when I separated from Derek. Some strange conversion system left me with the sword and not Derek. But yes I can use it but only in the spirit world." James took a deep breath before he spoke again. "Thank you, Peter. Thank you from both of us. You are a good friend. I'm sorry I didn't get more time to know you but I am so grateful. You always defend Derek in the council meetings. I'd been putting all my eggs in Elinor's basket but I feel a million times better having a second plan in motion. I wish I could go with you but she needs me more here. And of course I'll look after her. I'll guard her with my life. You can count on me."

Peter was struck dumb. He'd kind of expected for James to be as confrontational as Derek, to guess his intentions and jump down his throat. So his open gratitude was off putting. And he felt his jealously melt away a little. What better guard over Elinor than someone who was a little in love with her?

"You are welcome. I'd do anything for Derek. He's my best friend. And I'll rest better knowing you are looking after Elinor. Thanks, man," Peter said extending his hand and then remembered and just nodded his head. James nodded and smiled back. It was so bizarre to see this smiling, jovial creature wearing Derek's face.

Chapter 18

Elinor

Elinor wasn't quite sure what to expect from Calla on their third and last day together. She didn't imagine that Calla would want her to scry again when those creatures might be out there. And when she walked into the wagon and saw it absolutely full of South nomads she wished she had walked into the wrong wagon.

"Calm down," Calla said reading Elinor like a book. "Sit, Màithrean. Here have a biscuit." She really must know Elinor because that was the only thing that could make amends after ambushing her with Màithrean duties first thing in the morning.

"Elinor, these are some of your nieces and nephews. You will meet them and all the others. You will learn every name and face of the nomads that live in this glen. Know Morland and know her children. You must know both to accomplish your task," Calla said nudging a young woman next to her. Her hair was a dozen small braids braided into one long braid with ribbon woven through it.

She sat before Elinor and bowed her head slightly. Elinor did the same.

"I am Belle," the young woman said. "It is so good to meet you, Màithrean. I was born on my father's fishing boat," she said resting a hand on an older man who was sitting beside her. "We were trading on the border of the West Plains when the fire came to the coast. We travelled and hid for a year before Brigitte found us. I am glad to know you and to tell you my story. May the Goodness shine upon you." Belle nodded her head and rose to leave with her father.

Two more nomads took their place in the wagon and slowly Elinor met them all as they shuffled alone or in groups to sit in front of her. Calla had told her to learn their names and faces and Elinor had a sinking suspicion that there was going to be a test at the end. So she pulled out every pneumonic device she'd learned in school. Belle, braids, boat. She could remember that. Now she only had to do that a few hundred more times. Whenever Elinor's eyes grew too wide at the task ahead of her, a new teapot full of tea would appear at her side and the Màithrean was temporarily appeased.

After she met every South nomad and they each wished that 'the Goodness would shine upon her', the East nomads started trickling in. Elinor pulled out her mind palace and tried to remember everything she'd learned from Sherlock on how that actually worked. She recalled little but Benedict Cumberbatch's eyes like the ocean and that did nothing to help.

It was such a nice surprise to see Winter's wonderful face that it took her a moment to follow when Winter went into her life story and how she ended up at the Glen.

"My family were healers, not with magic but with herbs and lore. We traveled all over this land helping and healing. There was no town we weren't welcome in until suddenly we weren't. It wasn't just that our skills felt too close to magic, it was that the Queen had marked all nomads as rebels and insurrectionists. My family died when I was thirteen. I had left camp to bring a draft to a family with a sick child and by the time I returned they had been attacked. I... I didn't make it in time to save anyone. My mother and father. My sisters. My aunts and grandmother...

"After that I kept my hair covered. I stopped using the plants to dye my hair but it held fast always marking me for what I was. There were still enough sick people that I could make a living and being only myself I could skip town after I was paid and before the soldiers arrived.

I learned to fight from a young soldier who was injured and left for dead in a rock collapse. I held his healing ransom for his instructions. My blood yearned for vengeance and when I never saw another human with pink hair I knew I had to live to make sure the Queen was ended. After that I journeyed to the West Plains. I'd always heard that they had the best fighters... It was a dark time for me. I received training but it cost me.

"I'd lost hope when I was finally captured last month until a battered young woman was thrust into my rolling prison. I knew something was different about her. My magic called to her. I helped her escape and we broke into a prison cell to free the Mage. Then a strange little creature led us on a merry chase that landed me home. Thank you, Elinor. I am in your debt and I will be on your side until our battle is won," she said taking Elinor's ring hand in hers and pressing her forehead into it. "I know you are a Southie now but you are also my sister. May the Goodness shine upon you."

"No, thank you, Winter," Elinor said with a hand on her shoulder to keep her seated. "You saved my life at least three times. I never could have escaped from that wagon. I would be dead in that wagon with an infected stomach. I would not have made it one step of this journey without you. You've patched up every part of me. I thank the Goodness every day that it brought me to you. Maybe we were each captured so we would find each other." The thought hit Elinor like a ton of bricks as she said it. Things work out for the good...

At the time being captured had seemed like the first of a horrible series of events that led to her almost dying all the time but instead maybe it was the first step on a path laid before her that was for her good and for the good of Morland. If Winter hadn't been captured... Elinor didn't know where she would be. And if Elinor had never been captured then Winter never would have found her way here to the Glen. It wasn't just coincidence. It was the fingerprints of a carefully laid plan.

"Thank you, Winter," Elinor said resting her forehead on Winter's hands. "I am with you until our battle is done. May the Goodness shine upon you, my sister." Both girls were a little tearful when the next nomad took her place.

Ian and Bo came late in the day and side by side they told their story. Both of their parents were dead and it was just the two of them. They'd found the nomad camp almost on accident when they'd been hunting. They'd only been at the Glen for four months. Bo was younger than he looked and was still in nomad school while Ian was two years older than Elinor and worked in his late father's trade as a blacksmith. The each kissed her hand and Elinor thought they were gone until she heard Ian's voice in her ear. "I'd like you to come over for tea or coffee some night this week. Peter will be there, of course. I've already asked him. Stop by anytime."

When Elinor waited five minutes and no more nomads came through the door she laid back on the floor yawning.

"What a day, Calla," Elinor said. "What a day."

"What did you learn?" Calla asked.

"I knew you were going to say that," Elinor said still not getting up. "I learned so so much. It was amazing to hear everyone's stories. In the places I've lived I only knew bits and piece of people's stories or none at all. But to know so much about my community, to know everyone's names... This place is really something special, isn't it?" Elinor said.

She'd thought that when she was done, she'd be grumpy and exhausted but instead she felt filled. She'd learned three hundred plus reasons to keep fighting, to keep trying and training. She was being given the opportunity to help and just felt humbled and grateful. Every story she'd heard was from someone who'd had it worse than her. There wasn't anyone who hadn't lost a family member or all of them. The nomad camp was a surrogate family. Few had actual blood relatives alive and it made Elinor feel so blessed and it gave her new drive and motivation to help.

"I have a request to make of you, Elinor," Calla said. "Tonight at the bonfire I want you to speak. Don't look so frightened. I want you to tell everyone what you scried. Tell them of the oceans and the plains, share that gift with them."

"I think I can do that," Elinor said smiling. She stretched and followed Calla out into the Glen.

234

Winter

The council meeting was running longer than normal because it was the last one, well the last one she'd be attending. The week had been moving at both a snail's pace and a lightning strike. Winter wanted it to be over. She needed it to be *then* already but there was still so much to do. It was getting late and still they sat and talked and talked and talked. Winter's skin was itching and she wasn't sure how many more minutes she'd be able to talk to these people.

"Ten is not enough!" Winter said eying the Mage down. He too was itching for the week to end when he could leave but he was doing nothing to speed up their discussions.

"We'll need a force that can slip behind her defenses. We could never get enough men to attack her head on."

"Forty," Winter countered. They needed to have enough men to counter whatever they came against.

"Twenty-five," Jol said. "Twenty-five well trained men would do far better than fifty overeager youths."

"Thirty. And I agree that we only take the best. If thirty cannot be found that I approve of, then we'll take fewer. I'll check every man who wants to accompany us myself."

Jol rolled his eyes and Winter grinned. He wasn't so bad, even if his hands had a thousand times more blood on them than hers did. But a drop of blood covered just as thoroughly as a bucket. She wondered when she'd ceased to count the drops. Was she then any better than the Mage? Yes, because she did not keep secrets. She did not hide her plan deep away from the light.

"Alright, we are agreed then. A group of no more than thirty men will accompany Jol to the castle when the week is up," Brigitte said.

"Jol *and I*, will accompany them you mean," Winter said meeting Brigitte's eyes with all the frost her name gave her.

"I had wanted to discuss that with you in private but I think you should stay here. Just listen," Brigitte said with a raised hand as Winter stood. "Your gift could protect everyone here when the battle comes. And I know it will come, Emmaline has warned us."

Winter shook her head. She needed to go. She wouldn't be any help if she stayed in the Glen. Her magic had been... unreliable at best and missing at worst. Brigitte didn't need to know any of that. Winter had to get out of the Glen. Everything would be better then. Something about the Goodness barrier was altering Winter's magic.

"What did Emmaline say?" asked Victor with raised eyebrows. He was a hard man and had not been "given" the leadership of the North so much as he "effectively seized" it. Emmaline was not there to defend herself because she had stopped attending the council meetings after they became more arguing than planning, which had been very near the beginning.

"She has mentioned to several individuals," Brigitte said, "that something is coming and that we need to prepare. She is vague and cryptic but I think it would be ultimate foolishness to doubt her."

"Could she not be an agent of the Queen or the Darkness? Can she truly be trusted?" Victor said.

"Yes," Jol said surprising Winter at the feeling in his eyes. Peter looked surprised also. Jol was as cold as they came except towards Elinor and Emmaline. "Emmaline is no agent of the Queen," he said. "She is a forgotten plaything, a failed experiment. And every one of her prophecies that I have heard has come to pass. You had all best prepare as much as you can."

"If a fight is coming here then why are we sending forces away? What is there to gain at the castle? Elinor will be able to do everything from here, correct?" Joseph, the West leader, asked Brigitte.

"Yes, she does not need to be physically near the Queen and she will do better starting from here where the Goodness is so concentrated. I wonder the same question, Joseph. Why must a fighting force be at the castle? What is there to gain when there is so much to be lost here? So much that needs to be protected," Brigitte asked looking between Jol and Winter. Winter noticed that Peter was keeping quiet which was unusual for him.

Winter tried to keep her face flat. She trusted Elinor. She really did. But whatever her spiritual, invisible weapon was it would not be as satisfying as cupped hands filled with the Queen's blood. Winter had a vow to remember and she did. The Queen would face her judgement and Winter was to ensure that happened. If Elinor failed, there must be forces ready to finish the job. But Jol spoke before Winter could find the words she wanted.

"There is a piece of the plan that must be done there, for Derek's sake," Jol said.

"And what is your plan, Mage, that must be done in secret away from our watching eyes?" Victor said angrily.

Winter didn't really care what his plan was. He was coming at the Queen with sharp blades and arrows and Winter would add her stone ones to the mix. The rebel prince could live or die for all the difference it made to her. He'd lived a charmed life as prince and if it wasn't for his kinship with Brigitte and Emmaline then Winter might think worse of him. As it was, she'd probably make sure he lived, after she'd gotten her revenge.

"I've told you that it is safer the fewer who know. And as I've said over and over it is a plan that aims to defeat the Queen and save Derek. Can that not be enough?" Jol said getting angry. Peter growled under his breath. He himself had also asked the question Victor had just asked. Why must Jol's plan be secret? But Jol never gave a real reason.

"Your word will never be enough, nomad-slayer. But somehow it must be," Wolf said. "For we have not the time to babysit you and maybe it is best you are not here when the fighting starts and your allegiance would be tested further. Go but do not take every warrior with you." Wolf's eyes turned to Winter and she lowered her head. Even though she'd only known Wolf a few days, he was her clan leader and she tried to heed him. Fifteen warriors or maybe twenty, just enough. Enough to do the job. And there would be two mages, her and Jol. She'd get her magic back and all would be well.

Her fingers called to the stones beneath the wagon and... they didn't move. She found herself testing it every couple minutes. She was exhausting herself but she just wanted to know the second her magic came back. She had to be able to shake it off, whatever it was that was dampening her magic. It had started to fade the day they arrived at the Glen. It was probably just the nomad camp, something was off about Brigitte's barrier. *It would be fine.* She told herself she wasn't worried but her brow creased as the stones stayed unresponsive. And when River brought her a bag of pink seeds yesterday Winter knew that her hair was no longer growing in pink.

Something was wrong. She thought she'd been the one, the first to not need the seeds but that honor was no longer hers which should have been fine because she'd never deserved it. But their disappointment in her made her stomach turn. She only had to last another couple days among her people and then she'd be free. It was a bitter horror to think that thought when all she'd ever wanted was to be home again. But that wasn't true, all she'd ever wanted was vengeance.

The East nomads wanted more from her. Ryan wanted more from her. He didn't say it but she read it in his eyes when they sat together at dinner. She'd thought she'd be able to forget him when she got settled with her clan and he got settled wherever he ended up. But then she had seen him with a sword in his hands and had been lost all over again.

She watched without being seen. His clumsy attempts should have made her lose interest but his determination and strength made her glare with inner frustration. Winter was very glad that the week was almost up. She was not as strong as she'd imagined she was and she couldn't stop smiling at him.

Ryan

The sweat was rolling off him. Damon was relentless. Ryan knew he could leave at any time, that he owed Damon nothing, and had made him no time commitment but still he found he couldn't leave. The challenge and the exertion were addictive. And the intense mental and physical demands left him no room to think about anything else.

He didn't think about the looming threat and if he'd be able to protect his sister this time. He didn't think about Winter and her strength and contradictory gentleness. He only thought about what his arms and legs were doing and what his opponent was going to do. When Damon tapped his shoulder with his blade to signify that the match was over Ryan nodded his head and turned to leave when he heard a soft applause.

"Well done. We'll make a solider of you after all," Winter said with a kind laugh in her eyes.

"Ha, I know better. I'm a novice who only just stopped stabbing himself on accident and I have no taste for real fighting," Ryan said walking towards her.

"Maybe that's because you haven't tasted it yet," Winter said winking.

His mind stuttered and took a moment to remember words. "I doubt that would change anything but you are the expert. I can't be in your company as smelly as I am. I'm gonna go rinse in the river. I'll come find you after?" he asked.

"I'll come with you," she said. "I need to wash off the council meeting and it will probably be a while until I'll be able to take a long rinse."

"Why is that?" Ryan asked not wanting to know the answer as they walked west. The river was at the end of the fields and there was a foot path that lead between the crops.

"I'll be leaving tomorrow," Winter said. "Off to the castle."

"What will you be doing there?" Ryan asked running his fingers against the wheat to distract himself.

"I'll be killing the Queen," she said.

"Oh great. I was worried it would be dangerous," he said and he couldn't stop the bite in his words. "Sorry. I'm sure you'll be safe. I mean you have your magic and no one could get close to you anyway."

The sound of water stopped her reply. The river was about thirty feet wide and just deep enough in the middle to get completely covered if he sat down. The magic border extended about fifty feet beyond the bank.

Ryan didn't say anything as he unfastened his sword and took off his shirt and boots as he waded into the water. It took all of his control not to turn around as he heard the sound of clothing rustling. But he was still a man and when she joined him in the water he had to turn to look. She was wearing a sleeveless shirt and a pair of small shorts and the idea of her leaving tomorrow became unbearable. Her smile and swaying hips didn't help either.

"Don't go," Ryan said. The stones at the bottom of the river were smooth and the cold water instantly cooled his sore muscles but looking at Winter was making him warm right back up.

"I have to," she said meeting his gaze steadily as she took a step closer.

"No, you don't."

"Yes, I do. It is the only thing in the world that I *have* to do," Winter said with a fierce nonchalance as she leaned her head back and soaked her hair. It turned a dark rose color. She looked like a freaking water nymph and Ryan's words flew out of his mouth without his consent.

"There is more to you than blood and vengeance. I've seen it, Winter. Don't go. Stay," Ryan said taking her hand in the water.

"There is *nothing* more than blood and vengeance. You don't know me, Ryan. What else do I have but this?" she said.

"You aren't the only East nomad anymore. You have so many people here who care about you."

Winter rolled her eyes. "My family is dead. All of my family. These people... they mean well and they are my kin but they're not my family. I don't belong here anymore than you do. I am nothing but the promise I made."

What promise, Ryan wondered. *Was she bound by some oath of retribution?* "So what happens when you kill her? What happens when the Queen is dead?"

And she finally looked away. Her eyes flickering to their interlocked fingers. "I don't pretend I'll survive it," she said as she pulled her hand away and moved to leave the water.

"No," Ryan growled taking her hand back before she could walk away. "I don't buy it. You are so much more than this! Your family would want you to live. They would want you to live your life. There is so much more to life than blood and pain."

Her eyes were huge in the dim light and they asked him, *what else is there?* They begged him. He held her hand tight but it didn't squeeze the words out. They were there on the tip of his tongue, words he could never take back. Words that would change everything and nothing... Because he couldn't stay in Morland and she wouldn't come to Earth.

What life would she have on Earth? She had no skills that could be used for income. She had very little traditional education. She would be helpless and unprepared, which she would hate. He could never make her come with him. And she could never make him stay. He would never leave his family and even if he didn't hate Morland anymore, this was not the world he would choose for himself.

So he bit back the words.

She nodded.

And he let her go.

Winter

What had she been thinking? He could never have understood her. And more importantly he never really wanted her. She'd seen it in his eyes tonight. He was tired of her already and he just let her walk away. A pox on him! She didn't need him anyway.

She'd been playing a dangerous game with that handsome boy. But that's all he was, a boy. What did he know of the depths of suffering? Nothing. He'd lived a charmed and protected life. They were as different as a moonbeam and ray of sunshine. She'd let herself wonder for a moment if he might be her lochien. Her soulmate. Her match. She berated herself. She'd forgotten that she didn't get one of those. Her mate was vengeance. It could never have been this boy.

He had to be the reason she was losing her magic. He was distracting her. She wasn't focused. She'd been filled with happiness and hope. She needed to refocus and remember. Her gift was for vengeance and stone arrows caked with the Queen's blood. The Queen surely wouldn't be able to stop them with her flames.

Winter found a quiet spot in the woods close to the border, but not over, and called on the stones around her. They quavered and quivered but didn't rise. She clenched her fists and closed her eyes, willing the pebbles at her feet to rise. One rose up and then fell to the ground with a small tap. She pounded her fists on the deaf stones.

No! No! she yelled in her mind. *Not now! Not when I'm so close. Not when we leave for the castle tomorrow! No!* She'd never felt so alone and helpless. She'd thought she knew loneliness and helplessness like the back of her hand. They were her least favorite things in the whole world, even considering snakes. And she hated snakes. But the loneliness and helplessness she felt right now was so bitter and heavy, she felt like she was drowning.

A frustrated moan slipped out of her lips. What was she without her magic? How would she ever avenge her family? And if she couldn't avenge her family then what was the point of being alive?

242

Emmaline's words flew back to her and chilled her blood. She'd told Winter that she was painted in invisible blood and that she needed to wash it off or the stones would stop listening. How was Winter supposed to wash off invisible blood? Had Emmaline done this? Had she made the stones stop listening?

Elinor

Elinor felt a little nervous. She wasn't afraid of public speaking, per say, and she now knew everyone's name but it was just a little scary to stand up and speak. Thankfully, Calla started.

"Màithrean, has something she wants to share with us. You know that she has the ability to travel the land with her spirit. She has agreed to tell us what she saw."

Elinor stood up and looked around at all the faces she knew and spoke.

"I know all of your names and stories but few of you know mine. I want to tell you that before I tell you what I saw. My name is Elinor Marie Lirdin. I was born on Earth but I am a quarter Morlander. My grandfather is Jol, the Mage. My Morland blood gave me the ability to see across space and view Morland when I lived on Earth but it also gave me horrible headaches everyday as my soul was traveling between two worlds.

"While trying to learn more of my power I was attacked by a creature of the Darkness. My soul was terribly wounded and we had to come to Morland to fix it. We were captured by the Queen's men and that's where I met Winter. She saved me. Over and over," Elinor said looking for Winter but she couldn't find her in the crowd.

"Then we made our way to the prison to rescue Jol and we got the lovely bonus of Emmaline," she said winking at her. "Emmaline led us here to the Glen and through some trickery I became Màithrean. That is my story and that is who I am. I am glad to be a Morlander and South nomad. Now let me tell you of your homes."

She told them first of the South sea. She used every descriptive detail she could think of. She told them about the sky and the waves and the sand. She told them how it looked like a peaceful dream. She didn't mention the town of ash. They knew all about that. What they wanted to hear about was their home. They couldn't go there so she brought it to them. They South nomads hung on her every word. Drinking it up as though she was the first fresh water they'd had in years. Some cried. She felt like she was finally paying tribute and respect to the many who were killed there.

Elinor then spoke of the plains. She told them of her first impressions of amazement and smallness when faced with the overwhelming vastness of the West Plains. She told them about meeting the West wind and how she could see it, really see it. She told them of how the sun seemed like fire as it set across the sand.

Next Elinor described Alentar. Her grandfather's face lifted suddenly to meet her eyes. She told him about the streets and the shops and how it was full of people living their lives despite the Darkness. They were as safe as they could be and they were thriving despite the danger. She wondered when Jol had been their last but his attention made her feel like it had been a while.

Last she told them about the view from the top of the world. She told them how the North Mountains were intense and vast and gave her the most beautiful perspective of their stunning country. How everything looked perfect and clean and peaceful from so high a vantage. Long after the fire died, she was still talking and shaking hands with nomads. They were so grateful and Elinor's heart was so full. It was an honor to help these people in any way she could.

Emmaline

Blue, red, green. Blue, red, green. What does it mean? Emmaline mused as she walked between the brightly painted wagons. *The colors mean something. Blue is water and sky. Red is blood. It can only ever mean blood. But this time it is four bloods. Morland blood. Royal blood. Light blood. Dark blood. But green...* She put it out of her mind, locked it away to pull out later.

There were many things she locked away that she never pulled out, *never ever*. But this Glen full of people was a good place and good places helped keep the bad things locked away. It was still a good place even though Jol was there. He was not good. He might of been or might still be good but it was impossible to tell which.

He paced the Glen like a caged animal and she should know. She'd heard him walk the perimeter of his small cell over and over. She would count the steps sometimes. One, two, three, four, five, six, seven, eight, nine, turn. One, two, three, four, five, six, turn. He was doing the same thing here but she didn't know how many steps it was, maybe she should count them.

But not even counting kept her visions away. Visions of colors and faces. Visions of pain and coming clouds. She could never make herself see what she wanted or what other people wanted. The Queen had wanted to know certain things but Emmaline couldn't tell her. So Emmaline was locked away, deep and far away and listened. Emmaline rarely liked what she listened to. No one ever did. Brigitte did not like what she heard at nights. After Elinor spoke at the fire, Brigitte finally asked it. Emmaline was proud of her for waiting so long. She must have felt it, the rising tide. The *thing* was going to happen soon.

"Emmaline," Brigitte said as they walked back to their wagon. "Why do you cry at night? Every night?"

Emmaline studied her. She wanted to be able to tell her. But Emmaline felt like her thoughts were bottles adrift in the sea of her mind. It was hard to pull the right one out at the right time.

"I'm haunted," Emmaline said and it felt right. It was the right bottle.

"By who?" she asked.

"A dead woman. Or a woman who never was or is yet to be. She haunts my sleep and I can't protect him from it anymore. I was able to at first but his link with her gets stronger and stronger every day. I can't close the door and it has spread to him. I can't stop it. He'll feel the whole force of it soon. But maybe he can make some good of them."

"Who can use them? What's going on, Emmaline." Brigitte held her hand and Emmaline wished that she could just tell her. She wanted to help her sister. She loved Brigitte. She'd sent her dreams as well, but only good dreams. When Emmaline had known that it was starting she had introduced herself to Brigitte through dreams.

Thankfully Brigitte only shared the Goodness with her now so she'd be spared what was coming. He wouldn't be. Emmaline wasn't sure who, sometimes she knew. Sometimes she knew his face and his name even though they had never met but she couldn't remember just then.

"How can I help you?" Brigitte asked. But the bottles had all drifted away and so Emmaline walked away singing to herself.

"Maybe the shadow knows," Emmaline said over her shoulder. He might know and he might not. Maybe he wasn't even real. She tucked that thought away while she sang. Singing was her only comfort. It had helped her hold together the bits of herself when she'd been locked away. And singing helped her find the words to things. It helped her fit the pieces together. But it wouldn't help yet, she needed more pieces. She needed a bigger moon. And thankfully this one was getting bigger by the day.

She went to the stables and smelled the air. It smelled like home or what she thought it had smelled like. She liked that they had their names above their heads. She wished everyone did that. *Rosebud. Buckwheat. Opal. Jules. Sandstorm. Hazel.* They each turned their heads when she passed them and stroked their noses. She'd had a horse once. His name had been Joshua. She made herself repeat his name often. She'd drawn it over and over into her cell. It was important. She forgot it all the time but she always remembered it quickly. "Joshua," she said running her hand over the wooden doors. "His name was Joshua."

James

James was not expecting much. Elinor had gone to sleep and he had another quiet night ahead of him. Not sleeping was the worst. He complained to Derek that the not eating was worse but not sleeping... No down time, ever. No time where he was allowed to obliviously forget his life.

246

But no, part of his curse was not being allowed to escape it. Twenty-four hours a day, seven days a week alone with himself. But that was before Elinor. So when he heard a sound, he thought it was Elinor unable to sleep. He did not expect to see his sister, Brigitte. And he did not expect her to smile at him. She could see him.

"Brigitte." Her name came out as some broken whisper. She turned her head and saw him.

"Hello, little brother," she said walking over slowly, cautiously. He should have followed her lead but he couldn't stop himself from rushing over and grabbing her into a hug. She slipped through his arms and he thought that might be the final piece that destroyed him. He couldn't even hold her. He sank to his knees and said with a shuddering breath "Don't ever do that again."

"Which part?" she said chuckling as she sank down across from him.

"Any of it. All of it," James said lifting his head to look at her, really look at her. His hands were over his mouth and he couldn't stop shaking his head. It wasn't that he hadn't believed she was alive. He'd seen her with his own eyes for almost a week now. But not being able to talk to her made it seem more like watching old family videos than being in the same room with a real person. And here she was in the same room, alive, and smiling. He just couldn't believe it.

"Sounds good to me," she said. "The same goes with you." And then her smile faltered and fell. She'd been treating him like he was Derek but James knew very well that he wasn't. He wasn't much of anything.

"Are you disappointed that Derek isn't here?" James asked.

"Derek is here,"

"No, Brigitte. I'm only James, Derek's soul." *Only.*

"Are you not two piece of a whole only split up? Are you not both my brother? Are you two different creatures? No. You are my brother and so is Derek. You are both Derek and you are both James."

James only looked at her.

"Why didn't you tell me?" Brigitte asked. She knew. She knew where they were from.

"We wanted to tell you. A thousand times. A million times but..."

She waited watching. She wasn't going to let him off the hook. So James tried to gather his courage. He'd hoped that this task would fall to Derek. That they'd talk about this later when everyone was safe and Derek would be the one who'd have to see her face and deal with her feelings of abandonment. But it was James's lot to have the feelings, so he squared his shoulders and spoke.

"We weren't born on Morland. I know you know but want to tell you. Earth is so different from here, as a rule I don't like to think about it since I can never go back but B, you'd love it. You'd absolutely love it there. There is no magic and so no evil witch queen. There is still evil but nothing that wouldn't survive a physical attack, just mortal men.

"There is technology like you couldn't imagine and I couldn't possibly explain. I lived a safe and happy life and then I came here. We fell through a portal and found Jol within days. He was traveling with a band of soldiers as they searched for Garrison. And Derek told him everything, he told Jol and Jol said nothing," James spat.

Jol had said nothing. James wondered now why Jol didn't make Derek look for the portal then and there but maybe Jol didn't ever really want to go back to Earth.

"Jol took Derek in and explained the rules of the world. He told Derek to never tell anyone our secret and we soon discovered enough reasons to keep it to ourselves. We didn't want any of the people we'd met to find their way to Earth. It needed to be protected from this garbage world so Derek told no one. Not Garrison. Not you... It wasn't that we didn't trust you. It was that we'd been keeping the secret for years before we'd met you and it was second nature."

"So every time you guys left you were looking for the portal?" Brigitte asked.

"Yes. All we wanted was to find the way home. Before our siblings started turning, we almost stopped looking. Brigitte, we loved our life with you. Becoming your brother was the best thing that ever happened to us. I wished every day that we had stopped looking, that we had been there when... When you needed us. B, I'm so sorry. We are so sorry. Leaving you that day destroyed all of our lives. Our selfishness ruined everything. It has tortured each of us every day since then. We can never make it up to you but giving you the truth is a start." James waited, unsure what she would say. He expected her to turn around and leave. She owed him nothing and he deserved nothing from her.

"I'll never understand why I wasn't told. Never. But I forgive you. Both of you. I meant it when I said it earlier. I've had a long time to think about what went wrong and I'm so grateful that you did what needed to be done when the time came. And we'll have plenty of time for each of us to make amends."

"Plenty of time? What do you mean? Are you going to come visit me more?" James said hopefully. Elinor was great company but there was nothing like family and he had so much to say to Brigitte and so much he needed to know. Elinor had told him the bare bones of her story but he needed to hear it from her.

"No... I don't think it's safe to come here too often. The spula vine is addictive and Emmaline doesn't like people using it. And I listen when Emmaline gives a warning. I mean that we'll have time when you are reunited with the rest of you and we'll have the rest of our lives to catch up."

What did she mean? James thought. *Derek and I will always be like this. It's the only way.* He didn't realize he hadn't spoken out loud until Brigitte's brows furrowed.

"Derek and I..." he said trying to find the words. "This is just how it is. I don't know if I can ever go back to Earth and Derek will never come back here again after he's free. It's just the way things are. I know that both of us would give anything for the life you talked about. But... It just can't be."

"What if the Queen is destroyed? There would be no danger in you being whole then. There has to be a way," Brigitte said fiercely, her eyes glinting. "I won't give up until we find a way. I'll find a way to join you and Derek together again into one whole person."

James smiled, there she was. She'd been so bogged down by responsibility and troubles but he'd found her. Brigitte was a fierce creature and maybe she'd forgotten but there was was.

"Who could stand against you?" James said. "It will surely be as you say," he said bowing and chuckling.

"Do you talk to Elinor much?" Brigitte asked and James tried to read her face to see more into her sudden topic change.

"Yes. She is the only one who can see me. And she needed my help when she trained with Calla. Why do you ask?"

"I ask because things are going to get difficult with Elinor's training and I think it would be best if you gave her a little space."

"What do you mean 'difficult'?" James asked unhappily. "What is going to happen?"

"Tomorrow she starts training with Victor and I have a feeling you are going to want to intervene very much. But don't, please. She needs to learn."

"I'll try my best," James said giving as much of a promise as he could. He did not like the sound of any of that.

"It will be alright, don't worry," Brigitte said. "Oh, I have a question... Emmaline said something earlier and it made me think."

"Emmaline is a rare bird. I have absolutely no idea what to make of her though. What did she say?"

"She says she's being haunted and that that's why she cries at night. She said maybe the shadow would know. I thought that might be you."

James bit back a smart reply. "Yeah, it probably fits. But this is the first I've ever heard of someone really haunting anyone. I wish I could help."

"Worth a try," Brigitte said shrugging. "I should probably go. Until we see each other face to face," she said blowing him a kiss as she vanished.

The dreams are back. Full force. Maybe stronger than before. Whatever was holding the tide back is gone and they are pouring down on me again.

Hate. Fire. Fear. This one is good and strange and ... I don't know what it all means but it's powerful and sad.

The stone walls of the prison were as unyielding as the fire that wouldn't stop pouring out of her. She would be hanged for killing the man who had tried to attack her. The fury radiated from her. She hated that she was a woman. She hated that she was helpless. The rage rolled off her in tidal waves. And just as the injustice was suffocating her, he came in.

He told her she was free.

He told her the truth had come out and she was found innocent. His kind words did what nothing had ever been able to do, they calmed the firestorm inside her. She took his hand without burning him and without looking back.

His kindness baffled her. The town people had considered her an oddity to be endured. But he saw beauty in her fire. His father had been able to find water for a well anywhere in town. Some had thought he'd just had a knack for guessing but he knew his father was something more. She stayed with him for several weeks and his soft ease and quiet words drew her in. She had never imagined that people could be this kind. When he told her he loved her she gasped and fell back. Love.

It was strange feeling Ash's love in sync with the hate radiating from whoever's view I'm watching from. Even before the dream was finished I knew it could not end well. Poor Ash.

They married quickly and they were happy for a while as most are but then they became unhappy as all do. She'd thought about children often. She wanted them in a way she'd thought could never be realized. She used to dream that maybe if she had a child she wouldn't be so alone. Maybe she'd even die in the process and her debt would be paid.

But just as she began to really hope, it was dashed. Something about the fire inside her made her womb unable to keep a baby. She tried to hold the fire back but it inevitably flew from her and the babies were instantly lost. She cursed her weakness and inability to control her flames.

When she lost the third baby in a year, she become obsessed and angry. It consumed her. Though he assured her that he loved her none the less for her inability to bear him children, she couldn't believe him. She knew he was lying and her failure to give him what she wanted drove a deep, deep wedge. He could not reach across to her and she didn't want him to. She was a failure and a mistake. She was nothing.

One night after coming home from his good friend's house where the wife had just given birth to their fourth child, Ash flew into her darkest, reddest rage. The look on his face had told her everything she'd needed to know. He'd held the new baby and his longing was still all over him. Her temper, which had always been hard to keep in check, boiled over.

"You hate me for not being able to have children," she yelled as the fire poured from her skin. "I know it. You are going to leave me!"

"I love you. Please calm down. Look at me, Ash. Look at me. I'm here," he said over the roar. But she just shook her fire mane at him. He continued speaking and she looked up at him with tortured eyes. "I don't need children. I wish you could hear me. I wish you could believe me. Your fire is a gift. It's something beautiful. I wouldn't wish for children if it meant you weren't you anymore. I could never hate you. Do you hear me? Never."

She didn't hear his words but was instead fueled by the words she heard in her head. He was going to leave. He surely already had a mistress in town. He could never love a barren woman like her. She was a monster and an abomination. She had killed her own mother. She was twice over a murderer. He deserved more. If she loved him she would leave. But she couldn't.

She just stared at him as the pain rolled off her in waves. He was going to leave her. What would she be without him? Alone again. A woman in a world where women were things and victims. He reached for her, trusting that his love would save him from the flames as it had before, that his touch would calm the red fury and bring her back to him.

But before she could stop it, the fire rose hotter and faster than it ever had and it burst from her. It burned him to ash as he tried to hold her in his arms. The full moon shone down on her through the new hole in the roof as she howled with despair, screaming into the night as she breathed in her husband and felt his ashes in her clenched fists. Tears poured from her eyes and sizzled on her cheeks as they evaporated leaving no proof of her pain. She didn't realize that she had been calling out into the dark night until something answered her.

...

I don't. I don't even know. What is this? What does it mean? I don't want these dreams anymore. It can't mean anything. They are just dreams. Maybe if I say it enough I'll believe it. Because if it's true I do not want to dream again... Because I have a horrible feeling I know what comes next.

Chapter 19

Brigitte

She should've known that they'd want to leave at first light. They'd technically given her a week and not a second more. But a week had not been enough time. It sat ill with her letting Jol go to do who knows what he thought was best. Brigitte had been on the tail end of what he thought was best before and she was relieved to see Peter silently and unobtrusively join the party. Peter would help keep things above bar. She wished she felt the same way about Winter.

"You know I wish you were staying," Brigitte said to Winter as the pink-haired woman packed several short swords into a bundle.

"Yes, I know," Winter said her eyes fixing on Emmaline. She seemed to be deciding if she was going to speak with her. But the words just bubbled out, whatever was on her heart was on her lips.

"Give it back," Winter said locking eyes with Emmaline. "Make it come back."

"Wash it off," Emmaline said with raised eyebrows as her only inflection.

"Emmaline, there is nothing to wash off. Will it come back when I leave here?"

"Will what come back?" Brigitte asked looking between the two of them. They looked like two boulders having a staring contest. "What is going on with you two?"

Winter blinked first. "My magic is gone. It's been leaving me since I first walked into this stupid camp," Winter whispered kicking the rocks are her feet. "And she won't tell me how to get it back."

"Your magic is gone?" Brigitte asked shocked. She had never heard of anyone losing magic. It just didn't happen. The only thing that muted abilities was being exposed to the Darkness for long periods of time but Winter had been in the Glen. For Winter's magic to lessen when exposed to the Goodness was strange and Brigitte didn't like it. She did not like the knowledge that their abilities could just go away. What if hers did? Her power was protecting so many people.

"Winter, you need to tell me more. Maybe I can help you? Did something happen when you came her? Please think," Brigitte asked.

"Nothing happened," she said flicking her eyes to Ryan for a moment. "Nothing happened. Emmaline made this happen. She told me my magic would leave after I first met her."

"Wash it off," Emmaline said. "I told you to wash off the blood or the stones would stop listening."

"What blood!?" Winter yelled, showing Emmaline her clean hands.

"It's time to go," Jol said without looking at any of them.

"Fine," Winter said leaving in a huff. "Bloody fine."

"Winter, if you don't have your magic, you should stay here. Maybe we can figure something out," Brigitte said.

"No. I'll probably be fine once I leave here."

"Your ability is linked to the Goodness. All of ours are. If there is something wrong it can be fixed here. The Darkness will only further suppress your ability."

"Maybe the Goodness is suppressing my ability," Winter said turning to leave.

"If that is the case then you should heed Emmaline's warning. You will not right things with the Goodness by running away."

"We'll see about that," Winter said giving Emmaline one last glare.

"Wash it off!" Emmaline yelled after her. "Let it go! Hate can never make. It can only destroy. Wash. It. Off!"

Jol

Jol was *very* ready to leave. The week could not have passed soon enough for him. Brigitte had asked him for a week and he'd given her one. There had been debates and planning each day and Jol spoke little, preferring to keep his plans to himself. He would have preferred to leave alone but he was not in charge here. Winter was coming with a small band of nomad warriors. Ryan had been following Winter around like a puppy and Jol hoped he wouldn't be laced with too many incompetent fighters.

Jol wished he could feel the peace and calm that the nomads felt in their protected haven but all Jol could feel was the coming storm. They would not be safe here forever. There was a timer on it and he didn't want to be anywhere near here when the Queen discovered what had been hidden from her.

And he had things to do… He needed to make things right with Derek and that started by freeing him. Jol was glad their fighting force would be small. It would be easier to maneuver and sneak. Because there was no way they could win a head on battle. But he only needed to bide his time. He only had to hold them off long enough.

"I'm sorry, Elinor. But I need to go," Jol said trying not to notice Elinor's lip as it started to quiver. She'd been surprised when she'd seen him packing his bag in the early morning light. She had tried to convince him to stay. She must really have been busy this past week to not have known what was coming. It filled him with a strange pang of regret that he'd potentially wasted his last week with her. But it was too late now. Later, if they got a later, he'd choose her.

"What? Since when? You only just got here" she said. "Why do you need to be at the castle? What is your plan?"

"It's only one week to the full moon and I need to leave now if I'm going to make it to the castle in time." He stilled his hands from packing and said "I can't tell you my plan."

"Why?"

"I don't think you will fail. I believe that you'll be able to use your powers to fight the Darkness but… we need a back-up plan and I think it's safer if no one else knows what it is. If you do fail… I can't let the Queen know my plan. She can't know that Brigitte lives and that… Can you trust me?" Jol said.

"Does your plan kill the Queen and save Derek?"

"I hope so."

"Then I can let you go," she said giving him a hug goodbye.

Peter

"I'm coming with you," Peter said running and out of breath. "If you are going to help Derek then I'm coming." He slung the sword and dagger he'd made with Ian's help through the side holsters as he followed Jol. He had purposely not suggested his joining the party during council meeting. He didn't want it to be voted down. They could debate if it was the right choice after he was on the road but that also meant he hadn't been able to tell Elinor.

"Fine," Jol said. "Winter! Are you ready?"

Peter had overheard bits of Winter's heated debate with Emmaline earlier and she was still looked angry about it. Emmaline had been cryptic about something and Winter had yelled at her which had done nothing. "Let it go. Wash it off!" Emmaline had said in a huff before walking away. Peter only chuckled. That was exactly Emmaline.

"Yes, I'm right here. You don't need to yell, Mage," Winter said.

"Peter, you are leaving, too?" Elinor asked moving swiftly towards him. It was his turn now. "Who else is leaving? Are you leaving?" she asked Ryan. Ryan only rolled his eyes and shook his head.

"Was anyone going to tell me?" Elinor said turning her full force on Peter. She shook her nomad ring at him and said "I'm the bloody Màithrean. Does that mean nothing anymore?" Her eyes were wide and her hands were somehow suddenly full of his shirt. She didn't seem aware of it.

Ryan stood to the side watching with a silent brood and Peter was a little pleased that he wasn't the only one in deep water. Ryan and Winter were not making eye contact.

"Elinor," Peter said. "I'm sorry but I have to go. I'm not helping anyone here."

"Were you even going to tell me?" she asked.

"Yes. I... I was afraid the council wouldn't let me go. I needed to make it look like a spur of the moment choice. I was going to tell you," Peter said. "I'm sorry. I promise I wasn't going to sneak away."

She exhaled a huff and studied his eyes. He didn't know what she was looking to find but eventually he saw resignation enter her eyes. "What will you be doing?" she said. "I don't want to be away from you. It fills me with a terrible feeling. What if..."

"I have to go, Elinor. If there is anything I can do to help Derek it will be there."

"I understand, I guess. You need to go where you can do the most good. But I don't like it," she said. "It just feels strange to be away from you. I'm sorry we haven't seen each other much since we came to the Glen."

"You've been busy trying to save the world," he said pulling her into a hug. Elinor was right, it would be strange to be separated and he didn't like it. When she didn't pull away right away he just went on holding her. "Be careful. Be safe," he said kissing the top of her head, "I'll see you when we win. Do your best. Don't doubt yourself. I believe in you and I will see you soon, Okay? Everyone here will keep you safe. I have asked a couple people to look after you." Peter said pulling away to look her in the eyes. "We are both coming out of this. Whatever is coming I'll see you soon. I promise." She pressed in for one last embrace and then let him go.

Peter nodded to Ian and Bo. He'd asked them to keep an eye on Elinor. He knew that Ryan was staying but Morland had a habit of going after Elinor no matter who was in the way and it sent a jolt of terror down his spine to leave her. But Derek needed him more. Elinor was safe and protected in the Glen. She could do everything she needed to do from here and James was around somewhere to guard her as well, well as well as he could.

Emmaline pulled his sleeve and couldn't quite meet his eyes. "It won't be your fault. None of it is your fault. Remember that," she said finally lifting her gaze. Her eyes shone and he saw through her strangeness to how beautiful she was. It took a minute to look past her words to the young woman who spoke to them.

"Can you tell me more? What do you mean Emmaline? What is going to happen?"

She bit her lip and grabbed his hand. "Morland waits for you to finish your task. It needs you," she squeezed his hand once and walked away. He shook his head but he couldn't quite shake the chill her words gave him. But the idea of Morland needing him was kind of what he'd always dreamed.

Peter wasn't thrilled to be going with Jol. Little had changed to repair Peter's first impression of the man. Derek was going to be so upset when he learned the truth about how Jol having been to Earth but as mind-blowing as that was, it wasn't even his worst secret.

Peter could imagine what Jol might say about keeping his first secret from Derek. Jol himself hadn't found a way back to Earth so he couldn't have really helped him anyway. Also Jol didn't know Derek. If Derek had gotten tortured or something he could have revealed Jol's secret. Sure they were dumb reasons but Peter could slightly understand why Jol would have held his tongue. But his second secret...

There was no purpose except to hurt Derek. Except to keep him suffering for his sins. Peter could not think of a single reason, no matter how far-fetched for keeping it from Derek that Brigitte was alive. But what was done was done. Maybe Jol would find some way to fix it, to atone.

Elinor

They were really gone. Peter and Winter and her grandfather. She hoped that she was right to trust him. She hoped that they wouldn't need his plan, whatever is was. There was only one week until the full moon and she was excited for her first day of training with the North nomad elder, Victor.

He was an elegant looking man with pale skin and dark brown hair. He also looked like someone best left alone. She'd only really talked to him yesterday when he came to Calla's wagon but knowing that someone's family was murdered by the Queen didn't tell her much about him.

Her new pile of clothes was waiting for her when she woke up and she excitedly put on a pair of dark pants that almost touched the floor and a blood red top. The clothes were loud but plain. Nothing frilly or extra. Just expertly made and made to be noticed. It was stunning but she bet it made her look a little pale, which she was so she couldn't be mad at the outfit.

"You are late," Victor said the moment Elinor turned onto the row and saw his wagon. It had taken her a little while to find it. There were so many more North nomads than all the others combined and that equated to a lot of wagons.

"I'm sorry. I wasn't sure where your wagon was," Elinor said bowing her head.

"That is an excuse. You are linked to the spirit world. You could have used that to find me and been ten minutes early as I expected. Now you are a total of twenty minutes late and we have only three days together. I asked Joseph to give me one of his days but he refused. What that Westie thinks he can teach you that I can't, I cannot imagine. I have spoken extensively with Wolf and Calla to get a view of where your biggest deficiencies are. There are several but with only three days... Well we shall begin."

Elinor moved to go into his wagon but he stopped her with a loud sniff.

"No, we train out here. Join with the Goodness."

Elinor sat down and obliged him. She closed her eyes and relaxed in the spirit world. But she was only there for a moment before she was pulled back forcefully.

"What the?" Elinor said. But she put the pieces together quickly. She instantly learned four things. She was freezing, soaking wet, Victor was holding a bucket over her head, and it was going to be a long three days.

"Pitiful. Just as I suspected. You can only hold onto the Goodness during calm, serene meditation. I can assure you that battle is nothing like that. It is yelling and screaming and blood and so much worse than water being poured onto your head. Again."

Elinor had no words but she went back into the spirit world and was thrust out again.

"Are you even trying? Are you a secret agent of the Darkness? Again."

Elinor had no idea how to do the thing Victor was asking her to do. She wasn't choosing to leave. Her body was responding to some innate fight or flight response. She calmed her breath and her temper. She told herself that he was probably doing this to help her and not to torture her. *Probably.* This time she watched as Victor dumped the ice water on her head but the shock her physical body felt pulled her spirit back in.

"Ugh!" Elinor said standing and pacing as she tried to dispel the lake that was saturating her clothes, skin, and surrounding ground.

"You give up already? Ha," Victor said.

"I'm trying!" Elinor said. "Can you help me? Can you tell me how to do it?"

"I have no magic. I cannot tell you how to be stronger and better. You will learn or you will not but it will not be because I give up on you. You need to try, Elinor. Really try. Go into the spirit world and do not let anything pull you out. Again."

When Elinor finally mastered it *hours* later, she was clinging to the Goodness with tooth and nail. She wrapped herself through it like needle and thread. She felt a moment of relief when he'd dumped the bucket on her head and she hadn't been pulled back to her body. She'd thought she'd won. Until she saw her body tip over and her whole face was thrust into the bucket. She came to coughing and choking.

"What was that?" she yelled couching and spitting out water. "Are you trying to kill me? I passed your test. I stayed in the spirit world but then you had to go and cheat and try to drown me!" Elinor said huffing and feeling very unamused at the gathering that had developed to watch her water-boarding.

"Oh I'm sorry. Would the Darkness only sprinkle you with rain, would it only pour a cup of tea on your head? No. The Darkness is coming at you with all the forces of evil that it can muster. You must learn to stay under the water as long as I keep you there. Do not let your physical worries concern you. Thank Goodness," he said looking beyond her, "the sun has set. Go. I am done with you for today. Be better tomorrow. Be stronger. Good night."

Elinor could not leave fast enough. She was so angry that she didn't even want dinner. She wanted a warm bath and to sleep for six more days. She exhaled loudly unable to keep it inside. She thought she might explode. Victor was unfair and impossible. He was making her do things that a human could never do. Was she supposed to develop gills? Was that the purpose? Because she couldn't actually stop breathing without dying. Unless that was his goal. He was obviously, probably, an agent of the Darkness. Infiltrating the Glen to sabotage her. It felt like the only reasonable explanation.

She walked straight into Ian while she was stomping in her blind rage. She hit him hard. Elinor flew back and would have fallen on her butt if he hadn't have grabbed her wrists and pulled her up and very close to him.

"I'm sorry. I wasn't looking where I was going. Thank you," she said still inches from his face. She tried to pull her arm free but he held fast for a moment.

"Is everything okay? Your face is all flushed and you are," he said letting her go, "soaking wet and freezing." He laughed a little and at Elinor's unsmiling face he toned it down. "What happened? Oh you started training with Victor, didn't you?" Ian said with all amusement gone from his face. "Yes. It's that horrible with everyone. I know it feels like it's just you but I promise it's not. You will survive it. What can I do to help you?"

Elinor blushed and then said "I would kill for a hot bath. Can that be done?" Elinor had only taken lukewarm baths and only after several other women had already used the water. She had had to turn off her germ worries because she'd needed very much to be clean. But a hot bath, a true hot bath all to herself, sounded like Christmas.

"Come with me," Ian said pulling her swiftly to the blacksmith building. "You mustn't tell anyone. This has to be our secret. If they knew, I'd never have any peace and quiet." Elinor nodded her consent solemnly and followed him behind the building and past a barricade of chopped wood. It was a little oasis. There was a metal tub attached to the back wall of the building and Elinor could feel that it was hot from a foot away.

"I had the great idea of stealing some of the excess heat from the kiln. It's on the other side of the wall and the heat pours out of it on all sides. Don't touch it until we fill it with water. It won't burn you once it's filled but it stays pretty hot."

Elinor helped Ian carry the water over from the well. There was one dug near the smithy for all the water they used so it didn't take too long. Elinor stuck her finger into the water and a wide smile filled her face.

"Thank you, Ian. Thank you," Elinor said touching his arm.

"No problem at all. Peter asked me to keep an eye on you. I think making sure you don't die of hypothermia falls neatly under that category. Take your time the water will stay warm for as long as you need it."

Ian walked away before Elinor felt awkward and she quickly undressed with only the woods watching and plunged into the tub. She rolled her shoulders and let the water soak into her bones warming where she had been freezing cold. She looked up at the sky as the sunset was fading quickly into a black starry night.

Only two more days with Victor. She could survive two more days. It would be much easier knowing she could have this waiting for her at the end of a day of having half an arctic ocean dumped on her head. Ian was very kind to share this with her. After an hour, she made herself get out and dress. She didn't want to still be in the tub when he returned.

She walked around to the front of the blacksmith building wanting to thank Ian again but he wasn't there. She noticed that the door to the wagon nearly touching the shop was wide open and she peeked her head in.

"So are you a new woman?" Ian called out from inside as he a sipped the mug he held in his hands. He'd changed out of his working clothes and was wearing dark pants and a white top. His dark hair was braided down his neck and his eyes were intent upon her.

"Oh yes. And thank you. I really appreciate it," she said turning to leave.

"No, please come in. I've made enough coffee for the both of us. This will warm your inside and then I'll have completely defrosted you."

"Thank you, again," Elinor said sitting next to him and accepting the steaming cup he placed in her hands. His wagon was small and the only seats were side by side in a small window seat. "Where is your brother?" Elinor asked looking around for Ian's mini-me, Bo.

"Oh he's off making trouble I'm sure. Blacksmithing is not his calling like it is mine."

"I'm sure my brother is off causing trouble as well. He spends most of his time training with Damon."

Ian smiled. "Oh he does? Well Damon is a good man. He'll train your brother well. I sure do miss having Peter around. He was a very quick study."

"Me too. I wish he was here. But we all have to play our parts to help the Goodness."

"Yes. We all have parts to play, that is for sure."

Elinor finished her coffee and handed him the mug. "Thanks again."

"No problem, again. You could stay for a bit. We could... go for a walk," Ian said.

Elinor smiled a small smile and said "No, thank you. I have another horrible day ahead of me and I need my rest. Good night."

"Good night."

Peter

The long day of traveling reminded Peter just how great the nomads were. Their band of warriors was a total of fifteen men and a couple women. But they traveled fast. It surprised Peter how fast traveling could be when no one in the party was injured.

Once they stopped for the night, Peter stretched. It felt good to exercise after a week of working over an anvil. His sword felt good in his hands. He was a natural at blacksmithing and he wished... Plenty of time to consider the future when it was safe, when they were definitely all going to live to see it.

Peter jumped when the forest rustled and then filled with a couple dozen men, one of them had a mean scar down the side of his face and he spoke first "Lost?" he asked.

"Who are you?" Peter asked standing as he reached for his weapons. Their leader was wearing a uniform. He looked familiar.

"I'm the Mage's nephew, Garrison," he said with a smile tugging at his lips as he winked, actually winked at Jol. "And who are you all?" he said taking in the group.

"*The* Garrison?" Peter asked. Peter had seen him from afar when they'd first been captured but he hadn't known it was *Garrison*. Peter had heard so much about him. It was a little bit like meeting a celebrity. That explained how Garrison been able to sneak so close to their group without anyone hearing them. He was an amazing solider.

Garrison raised his eyebrows and then bowed. "The one and only. Whatever you heard about me... double it and it's probably true."

"How did you find us?" Peter asked.

"I've got my ways," he said winking at Winter who rolled her eyes then he became serious. "Cutting it kind of close, aren't we?" Garrison asked looking up at the half moon above him. "What is the plan, Mage? How do we save him?"

"First off, how did you find us?" Winter said eyeing him down. She was half his size but Peter had seen her fight. It would be very interesting to see who would win between the two of them.

"Derek sent me. In a roundabout way. I've been looking for you while I've been doing other tasks."

"What tasks," Jol said interested.

"Let's just say," Garrison said turning over the cuff of his jacket to reveal a small flower sewn on in red thread. "That you'll have a hard time finding a solider without this stitched on his sleeve and that would be because we have them all tied up and captured." His grin went all the way up as everyone's jaw dropped.

Jol

"No..." Jol said taking a step back. He couldn't believe it. He'd toyed with the idea of a military coup for years and he'd always shut it down. Her magic was too strong for a frontal assault. Dividing her army and pitting half of it against the other would be disastrous. Jol could probably hold his own against the Queen for a little while but she had the endless reservoir of Darkness to fuel her energies. She would win.

But a secret attack... Changing all her loyal soldiers with enemy troops under her noise was breathtaking in its stupidity. It only took one man to turn. One man's fear to overtake him and all was lost. Garrison was taking a huge gamble and Jol almost felt himself smile. Almost. "That is an overwhelmingly idiotic plan, Garrison. There are too many soldiers to turn or capture without tipping her off."

"That's part of what makes the plan so great. It's so dumb she'll never see it coming. And we weren't able to get to everyone in time. There are still soldiers at the castle. Soldiers who have no idea about our revolution. And when things go south they will side with the Queen. I don't doubt it. That's why I have my men waiting at the castle. They will be our backup. Things are different this time," Garrison said. "Now it's your turn. What's your plan?"

"We are going to kill the Queen," Jol said.

"And how will we succeed where everyone else has failed?" Winter asked. It still surprised him that he'd gotten her and her warriors to follow him without a word being told as to what he'd planned. That would have to change, he supposed. They probably needed to know...

"Because we are going to kill Derek first," Jol said.

Two voices spoke at once yelling and accusing. Jol sighed. This was exactly why he hadn't told Elinor. Saying the plan out loud made him look like a villain. But he was sure. He was sure that killing Derek would weaken the Queen enough so that she could be killed. And he was mostly sure he could kill Derek for a little while without making him dead forever.

If they killed Derek right after he'd been possessed by the Darkness but before his soul was taken he would come back like Brigitte. It had happened once. It would happen again. Then the Queen would be weak at last. She wasn't indestructible, only very powerful and long lived. And she could and would die on the full moon. He told Peter and the others that the plan was foolproof, that Derek *would* come back. But secretly he doubted himself. What if he killed Derek and he stayed dead? Would it still be worth it if the whole world was saved?

The only other person who knew was Emmaline. He'd hoped that her prophetic ability could tell him if it would work but she'd only nodded and said "He'll probably come back. If he wants to." *That was enough*, he told himself. It was almost an endorsement. If it was doomed to fail she would have told him, right? He had to trust that.

Chapter 20

Elinor

"This has stopped being fun," Elinor announced to Emmaline and Brigitte as they were getting ready for bed. Elinor had spent another day being tortured by Victor and she had made little progress.

"Sorry, which parts were the fun parts?" Emmaline asked. "The scratchy parts," she said making claw marks at Elinor's stomach "Or the shooting parts?" She pulled her arms into an invisible bow and arrow and fired at Elinor's leg.

Elinor squirmed away from Emmaline's imaginary weapons and said, "You are right. What was I thinking? Morland can never be fun. I'd forgotten," Elinor said sighing as she fell back on her mat.

"Was it very hard today?" Brigitte asked. "I know Victor can be difficult sometimes."

"'Difficult?' 'Sometimes?'" Elinor said incredulously. Her training over the first week had been challenging but pleasant. Everyone had been nice and focused on helping her connect to the Goodness and Morland. But now things were… not fun. She hadn't complained to Brigitte and Emmaline yesterday because the hot bath had melted away her anger but it had been dark when she'd stopped training today and she felt weird sneaking behind the smithy to bathe.

"Do you know he tried to drown me?" Elinor asked.

"Did he really?" Emmaline asked with shining eyes.

"Yes. But that was bad Emmaline," Elinor said shaking her head.

"Why?" Brigitte asked.

"Why was being drowned bad?" Elinor asked incredulously.

"No. Why did he do it? What was he trying to teach you?"

Elinor huffed. She knew what he was trying to teach her and she'd failed over and over. "He was teaching me how to hold onto the Goodness. He was trying to teach me that mortal issues like being able to breathe should not distract me from my connection with the Goodness. But I'm pretty sure if I had died my connection with the Goodness would be severed anyway…"

"No, it wouldn't," Emmaline interrupted matter-of-factly. "When our bodies die, we do not die. Our spirits are eternal. They will always exist in one form or another. It would probably be easier to complete your mission if you were dead."

At Elinor's face, Brigitte spoke up while laying a hand on Emmaline's shoulder. "What my sister means to say is that you are able to join with the Goodness but you aren't trusting. You keep holding a part of your consciousness back. You are protecting yourself. And if you were no longer living, which we do not want to happen," she said looking at Emmaline, "you would not have that fear holding you back. Your training will not progress from this until you learn it."

"The Darkness will not be so nice as to drown you. You must let us make you a warrior," Emmaline said closing her eyes. Elinor closed her eyes sighing but she didn't go to sleep. She knew she needed to meditate and calm herself.

Calm and storm.

She knew they were right but it was so frustrating. She thought that she'd finally found her thing. The thing she was destined to be good at. She'd never had a unique talent and when the training had started so easily, she'd thought this was it. But it was so hard now it was impossible not to be discouraged. She took a deep breath and went looking for James in the spirit world. She'd meditate later when she didn't feel so wired and keyed up.

James

James had thought he might die. Not that he could. But watching Elinor being nearly drowned over and over and being able to do nothing to stop it felt like dying. He had left a dozen times but each time he was pulled back, like her suffering was some sort of magnet pulling him in every time she was in distress. She never saw him in the small crowd that gathered like vultures to watch her *suffer*. He thought about making himself known a hundred times but Brigitte's instructions were in his mind. She needed this. Even if it was killing him, he couldn't interfere.

She had to learn this skill, even he could admit that. But there had to be a million different ways it could be taught. James felt the anger and helplessness of being a ghost flare stronger than ever. He could do nothing to help her but be there. Even if she couldn't see him through the tears that covered her face. He made himself bear it with her. He'd be waiting for her at the end.

Tonight she hadn't stopped until late and he followed her as she walked oblivious. He thought about calling out to her but it was dark and he'd probably scare her. And maybe she just wanted to go to sleep. He was glad she didn't go to Ian again, he worried James. Not just because of his marked interest in Elinor that she ignored, or was oblivious to, but there was something wrong, a vague wrongness that James couldn't articulate.

He followed Ian sometimes, waiting for him to do something that he could tell Elinor about but he just went about his day doing normal and appropriate stuff. James tried to tell himself that maybe it was jealousy. Ian was a man with a soul and a body that could be there for Elinor in a way he couldn't but it really wasn't just that. It was something more. He'd find it.

James was ready to give up on Elinor for the night when she came storming out of her wagon. He could tell that it was just her spirit and that her body was tucked up for the night in her bed.

"Well hello there," James said smiling brightly. Elinor turned to look at him but did not smile. He came behind her and wrapped his arms around her.

"I'm sorry I couldn't help," he said shyly resting his chin on the top of her head. She huffed and pulled away. "I wanted to. It was torture to watch but Brigitte made me promise to stay out of your training."

"Brigitte did what?" Elinor asked.

"She came to see me. Just the once. It was so good to see her. To really talk to her. I can't wait until Derek finds out. He'll be a new man once he knows she's alive. She only wants what's best for you and I didn't want to get in the way of your training. I didn't want to distract you."

Elinor gave in and walked into his waiting hug. "Where do you want to go?" Elinor asked as James led her.

"I think we should stay here. I know we haven't seen those creatures since that time in the plains but we have less than a week to go and I'm not risking you. Let's just sit right at the edge."

In the spirit world, James could see the edge of the Goodness field that Brigitte projected even in her sleep. Elinor and James sat with their toes a few feet away from the stone markers that circled the camp. It made James feel a little more alive to be so close to danger.

"I know you can do it," James said stroking the back of her hand with his thumb. "All of it. I *know* you can do all of it."

Elinor squeezed his hand and said "Enough pep talks for one day. Can we just sit and watch the stars for a bit or tell me a story?" She started to lay down and James joined getting to the ground moments before her so she was pillowed on his chest as they both stared up at the sky.

"Anything for you," he said. He did not release her hand. "A story... Do you see that group of stars there?"

"The ones that looks like a circle?"

"Yup. Those. Garrison used to tell Derek the myths around the constellations. He knew all of them. So the circle of stars is a ring. If you look to the left there is a string of stars that kind of looks like a tear drop, do you see it?" he asked and then took her hand and pointed her finger at the stars he was talking about.

"Well, that is Leila," he said. "She was the most beautiful woman in Morland and was admired by all who saw her. Her father was very poor and when wealthy merchant started to take notice of his daughter he encouraged her to consider him but she only had eyes for her father's servant. But her father did not approve and promised her to the older cloth merchant against her wishes. The man had six children and Leila would be his third wife.

"The night before her wedding she ran away with her love, the servant. They ran from one hiding place to the next with the wealthy merchant always on their heels. After four years, Leila grew sick and became too tired to run. Her love knew that if she couldn't run, the merchant would find them and his large band of men would kill him and Leila would be helpless and forced to marry the awful man.

"So one night while Leila slept, her love went to find a mage. He begged her for a way to protect and be with his love forever and to keep her out of the merchant's grasp. The mage was a trickster and she gave him his wish but not in the way he wanted.

"Leila woke up in the sunshine and saw a small golden ring on a pillow of leaves and flowers. She knew it must be from her love and she put the ring on without a thought. She was instantly transported to the heavens and transformed into eternal lights. She looked down on Morland and felt such joy that she was free and that she could finally rest with her love.

She looked across the sky but she couldn't find him. She called to him but he didn't answer. Suddenly she felt her ring grow hot and she looked down and saw that there were engravings on the ring. It said "My love, this ring is my final protection for you. When you wear it we are always together. There is nowhere I'd rather spend eternity than on your finger." The mage had turned her love into a magic ring that would protect her in the heavens. She technically granted his two requests: that he could protect and be with her forever and that she was safe from the merchant.

"Leila cried one large tear and couldn't cry anymore as she was frozen in place in the eternal sky." James stroked Elinor's hair with his free hand. "It's really a pitiful story but I don't think Leila should have cried because I don't think he minded being a ring on her finger. He gave his life to protect her. No man would regret that choice."

Elinor rolled over to look into James's face. She giggled when a tear splashed onto his chest. "It was a pitiful story but really beautiful. Thank you, James."

He couldn't stop himself from running a hand through the curtain of her long hair as it hung over him. "You are so beautiful. I'd turn into a ring to protect you from an evil merchant." Elinor sat up and wiped her face on her sleeve.

"That's too much to ask and I can't imagine having a suitor chase me all over Morland for four years. So I can't imagine that ever being necessary. But that's a sweet thing to say."

James pulled an arm across her and pulled her head back to lay on his chest again. "Now I'll tell you a funny one," he said. If it was up to him this night would never end, she'd never return to her body and they'd always be there in that precious moment. He played with the ring on her finger as he spoke and her hair spread across his chest was the most beautiful thing he'd ever seen.

While he told the story of a magic frog that could only speak the truth she ran her thumb along the scar on his wrist. It was his only scar, one of the big differences between James' soul body and Derek's physical body. Derek had a zillion scars while James just had the one. In the darkest moment, the moment after Brigitte's death James had wanted an escape from the crippling, excruciating grief. But when James had drawn his sword against his wrist it had made a mirror mark on Derek's. James realized he couldn't hurt himself without hurting Derek too. He was trapped but also saved.

"I'm so glad you are here with me," Elinor said after the story was finished.

"So am I," he said. The pain of the past was worth it to get to live this moment.

Derek

His new plan was working really great. Derek was feeling really good about it. He wasn't tired. Nope. Not one bit at all. He was going to stay awake forever or for the next five days at least. That was a completely reasonable goal. Doctors at hospitals or people being tortured stayed awake for days at a time. And he'd pulled his share of all-nighters. He just needed to do it all in a row. But if he needed to take a nap that would be fine. People didn't dream during naps, he was sure.

His last dream had been horrible enough that its nonstop repeat going through his brain was really helping him to stay awake. Seeing a man being burned into a pile of ash had a way of keeping a person alert and watchful. Ever since Garrison had come, he'd received a morning tray with food for the day, fresh baked food, water, and a pot of coffee. He decided that he'd ration the coffee to last the whole day, giving himself a shot of it when he felt his eyelids start to close.

Five days to go. He could do it. He just had to keep thinking of things to busy his mind with. But all he could think about were the women of his nightmare. Ash and the woman who hated her. Which one was which? And where was the other one? One of them was good and one was bad. One of them was an ally and one of them was...

Derek jerked his head up; he'd fallen asleep standing up. He was only two days into his plan to never sleep again and he was struggling. He made himself jump up and do thirty burpees and then thirty push-ups and then he decided that he should break one of his bookshelves to make a pull up bar. That would keep him awake. Bookshelves. Books. He should be reading. He enjoyed to read; he was pretty sure. In all honestly, Derek hadn't read a book for only pleasure for a long time.

Everything was a mission. Part of the mission. A task to be checked off and completed. That's what he needed to do. He needed to make a stay awake checklist, an endless list of things to do. He could sleep when he was done with them. Five days' worth of tasks.

Derek hoped Elinor and Peter were okay. They were probably asleep. They had no dedication to the mission. He wondered where they were and he hoped so much that they were safe. *They have to be all right*, he told himself. *It will have to be okay in the end.* Wasn't there some pact that life made with humans to only be so horrible for so long? He actually didn't think that was true. Life got to do whatever it bloody well pleased. But a checklist was what he needed. *The ground should probably be lava*, he wrote.

Chapter 21

Elinor

It was Elinor's last day with Victor and she should have been thrilled to be almost free of him but she was furious with herself because she was failing. Her frustration grew hour by hour and her despair and irritation at herself were hard to check. But Elinor took a deep breath. Victor wasn't going to stop trying to drown her until she stopped letting it bother her. It all came back to the disturbing truth that her life wasn't worth more than everyone in Morland. It wasn't. And if the cost of winning was her life then she felt like a selfish monster for denying it.

She'd forgotten that in every book she'd read that involved a chosen one the ending was always the same, their blood spilled on the ground. No one besides Victor had made any allusion to it. No one had told her that doing the task before her might kill her. She understood. She wouldn't have told herself either. No one likes to be the sacrifice.

Elinor entered the spirit world and prepared herself. Victor was going to hold her head underwater until she came up for air and then he was going to yell at her. But that wouldn't happen this time. She did trust the Goodness and with that thought she closed her eyes and wove the two of them tight together. She wasn't going to let her mortal needs pull her away. When she started to fade back into her body, she held on tighter. Nothing in this world would tear her from the Goodness. But then everything went black.

Someone was pounding on her chest and then there was fire in her throat. She coughed up a gallon on water and someone pulled her into a tight hug. She was shocked when she realized it was Victor and that he was smiling.

"You did it! I knew you could do it! You released your fear and trusted that the Goodness would protect you. I knew you could do it," he said, laughing pulling her into another tight hug.

When she started coughing again he released her and all of the onlookers started to cheer. She saw that James was not looking too happy. He nodded a weak smile and then faded into the crowd. She didn't blame him. She wouldn't have liked watching him drown, even if it was only for a minute. A warm blanket was wrapped around her shoulders and she was carried/dragged to the bonfire.

"Ha," Victor said jokingly pushing Joseph in the chest. "She is all yours, Westie. But she has nothing left to learn. I have done the impossible."

Elinor was still reeling from the fact that Victor had actually let her drown and that now he was completely transformed. He was proud of her and he told everyone who walked by that Elinor would save them all. But she was too tired to really care at the moment. All she wanted was a bath.

She was relieved when Ian wasn't there and she filled the tub herself. Sliding into the hot water was absolutely divine. She didn't ever want to ever be drowned again and she didn't want to ever leave the tub. *I can probably save Morland from right here.*

"I thought I heard something," Ian said coming around the corner. Elinor tried to cover herself but he laughed and turned his back to her. "Sorry, I just wanted to make sure it wasn't someone else and my secret had been discovered. Take your time. I'll have coffee ready if you decide you want some. Well done today. I'm sorry that I can't say you are the first that Victor has technically killed but you are definitely the prettiest," Ian said with a half look over his shoulder.

Elinor splashed water at his back and he raised his hands in defeat as he went back to his wagon chuckling. Elinor was alone with her hot water and turbulent thoughts. She should be proud of herself like Victor was. She'd defied her physical needs and done her duty but she just felt really sore and tired. Elinor braided her hair once it was scrubbed clean and fastened it at the back of her head. But once she finished the task her mind found something else to weave and wind through.

So she'd learned that she could let herself die for the cause and it wasn't really a nice thought. Ryan was going to be really mad if she died in four days. He would not agree that 'the needs of the many outweigh the needs of the few' as Spock would say. But if it was his life that would settle the debt, she knew he'd do it.

But thinking it through she didn't think she could let Katie or Colton sacrifice themselves. It was an unavoidable hypocrisy. And she really just had to make sure that Ryan didn't know. But the fact that he spent every day training with weapons was a tip off that he knew something was amiss and something was coming.

She wasn't going to stop by Ian's wagon. She shouldn't. Elinor had been trying to ignore his intentions and his lingering gazes. But she felt like the cost of using his bath was at least coffee. She wasn't leading him on; she was just being friendly. It would be rude to just leave.

It would have been easier to be his friend if he wasn't so handsome. His good looks reminded her of Derek and that raised her guard but it also reminded her of James which confused her very much. It would just be easier to keep her life Ian-free but he was determined. She shook those thoughts away and walked towards his wagon.

But when she got to his door, he was walking out quickly. He grabbed her hand and said "Change of plans. Go change into a dress. I'll see you at the bonfire. Oh and I like your hair like that." Elinor didn't have a second to ask for clarification because Ian was off like a flash with only a sly smile to explain himself.

Elinor found a royal blue dress in Brigitte's chest of clothes and figured that Brigitte wouldn't mind. It was a soft material with a wide belt that wrapped around her waist a couple times. The dress came to the middle of her calf and would have probably been a little short on Brigitte, Elinor thought smiling. She didn't know everything about Brigitte, after all.

Everyone was at the bonfire, which rarely happened. Most of the time people came and went, eating in shifts and moseying around before heading to bed early. But everyone was there now. Elinor found a spot to stand and waited to find out what all the fuss was about.

Ian came to stand next to her. "Now that is a dress," he said grinning.

"Thanks. It's Brigitte's. What is going on?" Elinor asked. Ian didn't answer but he nodded his head towards the center.

The crowd died down as a North nomad woman named Ophelia stood up and walked to the middle.

"Tonight is our turn and we decided that we are long overdue for a celebration. We have forgotten that we are safe and alive in these woods and there is much to thank the Goodness for. Especially since it brought this young lady to us," Ophelia said motioning to Elinor who blushed crimson. "She has survived Victor's training!" she said raising her hand like it was a victory.

Several "barely"s and "not technically"s were called from the audience. Everyone laughed.

"So tonight my family," she said sweeping her arms wide as several other North nomads came to join her carrying instruments. "Tonight, we dance!" The music started and Ian pulled Elinor to her feet before she knew what was happening. It was a fast dance and Elinor worried for a moment that she would look like a fool for not knowing the steps but Ian's sure hands led her flawlessly through the song.

When it was done, Elinor was laughing and smiling. "You look beautiful when you laugh," Ian said not releasing her hand as the band prepared to begin another song.

"It feels like a million years since I laughed," she said with shining eyes. She tried to pull away but Ian led her into the second dance and then a third. Elinor had never had such a fun night in her whole life.

She felt one with the beautiful nomad community and she was really happy after such a long, long time of sadness. She drank it in. It didn't matter that it was Ian she was dancing with. It could have been anyone and many of the dances had her swapping hands with other people.

Everything went smoothly until she found herself partnered with Ryan for a dance step. And with neither of them knowing the way, they ended up laughing and muddling it up. But then a moment later the dance shifted again and Ryan paired back with his partner and Elinor with Ian.

She tried to release Ian from the obligation of dancing with her a couple times after she noticed that there were few men who danced so well as him but he held fast to her hand. She wondered if he considered this part of keeping his word to Peter. But his dark eyes drew her in and issued a challenge at the same time. She stopped trying to pull away and instead found that she was holding on.

They danced and danced. Slow and close. Fast and flying. Dancing with Ian was effortless. She didn't have to think about it at all. His hands led her swift and sure and she found that following his lead was natural. She never would have guessed how much she would love dancing.

She wondered if this was how it was supposed to be. Boy meets girl. They dance. They laugh and that's it. No one is trying to kill anyone or save anyone. It is just a man and woman dancing. Nothing broken. Nothing missing. She stopped herself from overthinking, not wanting anything to ruin the night.

As the band began to die down and fewer and fewer people were dancing there came a slow and deep song. Elinor and Ian had established an unspoken rhythm and flow. He pulled her close and she settled against him without either of them saying a word. Elinor didn't know the words to the song but it spoke to her.

She found herself humming along and when the words repeated she sang softly.

"I'd know you anywhere.

I'd find you anywhere.

I'd meet your eyes amidst the throng.

I'd hear your voice above the song.

Come run with me.

Come take a chance.

Come take my hand.

Come take my future.

Take my hopes and dreams.

They're all for you.

I am yours.

As I stand.

All I'm lacking.

All I am."

"It's a beautiful song, isn't it?" Ian said over her head. She nodded without moving away from him. "It's about the moment when your ayai becomes your lochien," he said.

"Your what becomes your what?" Elinor asked pulling back slightly to look at him.

"Is that not a word you use? Um… an ayai is the term for the one you court to find your lochien."

"Is lochien like a spouse?" Elinor asked.

"Not exactly. It's deeper than that. Anyone may marry anyone but only your true love may be your lochien. You will only ever find one and you often go through many ayais until you find your lochien."

Elinor thought that was a perfect way of thinking about love. Dating with the sole purpose of finding your mate. People on Earth didn't do that. They dated for fun and they dated people they would never want to marry.

"Have you found your lochien?" Elinor asked him. She noticed that the music had ended and that everyone was dispersing as the night wanted to turn into morning.

"No," he said not releasing her yet. "I search on." He reached into his pocket and pulled out a necklace. The chain was small and delicate and hanging in the middle was a black stone. It literally shone in the moonlight, the bonfire flickered off it making it look like something magic.

"I... It's beautiful," Elinor found herself saying. She couldn't take it. It would mean something to him. But in an instant he was behind her pulling her hair off her neck. She found herself standing very still. He clasped the small chain and released her hair.

"Goodnight. Thank you for the honor," he said. He bent in half and pulled her hand quickly towards him before she escaped. His lips were soft on her wrist and she was sure he could feel her heart pounding.

"Goodnight Ian," she said when he released her and she hurried back to her wagon.

James

James had thought that once he'd found Elinor, he would never feel ignored again. That she would always see and hear him and he'd feel less like a ghost. But she hadn't seen him all night. She wasn't even looking for him. She'd spent every second dancing with *him*. It had been a unique brand of torture to watch her leaning into Ian chest as he held her close and spun her around the fire. James hadn't been able to make himself stop looking. He hadn't been able to leave.

Elinor was humming to herself as she walked down the deserted streets to her wagon. That stupid necklace that Ian had given her hung at her collarbone. The sun would be up soon and she didn't seem to care. A small smile was hiding at the corner of her lips.

"What was that? What were you doing with him?" James asked. Elinor jumped and turned to look for him. He grabbed her hand and fell right through it. "Please meet me," he asked hating that he couldn't touch her, hating that he had to beg her to come to his land because he was insubstantial in hers. Elinor nodded and once she was settled in bed she came to him.

"So?" James said taking her hand. "Let's go somewhere. Anywhere. Go north above the mountains." He had to get away from this Glen.

"James, I don't know. I don't think it's a good idea to scry," Elinor said staring at his hand holding hers.

"It'll be fine. I've spent some time there and it should be clear. Please, let's go. The place is called Mirror Lake."

Elinor obliged him and she didn't even look at her surroundings before she responded.

"So what? I was just dancing," Elinor said pulling her hand away as he reached for her again. "You are not my keeper."

"If you wanted to dance you should have come to see me. I wish you'd spend more time here," he said humming softly as he pulled her into a slow dance.

"I spend every waking hour in the spirit world."

"But not with me," James whispered onto the top of her head. She exhaled and held him a little tighter. They swayed and he felt a lock release deep inside his chest. Everything was okay again. "Let's come back here tomorrow night and the next, too. Things are going to get really crazy and I want as much time with you as I can. I've missed you so much these past few days."

She stilled and he pulled back to see what was wrong. And he saw it pass over her face, some horrible realization. He wanted to go back in time and make it where she didn't ever have that look. It could only mean something bad. She released his hand.

"This isn't real," she said covering her face with her hands. "This isn't real. This might as well be a dream." He pulled her hands away. He had to see her face. She was wearing a horrible mix of pity and grief. He shouldn't have looked.

"I've been escaping to this dream with you and it isn't real, James. This is not real life," she said motioning to their surroundings. He was shaking his head and he wanted to shake her.

"Where are we?" she asked. They were on the side of a beautiful misty lake. The trees on the far shore looked like black sentinels and the moon was shining a bright gold over the water. It looked like a haunted fairy land.

"This is Mirror Lake. They call this part of the world the Misty Shore. It's very north, on the other side of the mountains. The water would be freezing if we could touch it. But isn't being able to touch something what makes it real?" he asked resting a hand on her cheek. "I'm real, Elinor."

"I'm a fool," she said leaning into his hand miserably. "You are not Derek and Derek is not you. What future is there, James? I am going back to Earth and you are here. But even if I wasn't leaving what then?"

"Oh and you have a future with Ian?" James said hotly.

"No. Maybe. I don't know. I haven't even thought about it."

"He isn't good, Elinor. Something is off about him. I can't put my finger on it but... I don't like him."

She raised her eyebrows. "Have you been watching him?"

"Yes," James said unembarrassed. He had no concept of privacy and secrets. It was his only perk.

"And? What have you seen him do?"

"Nothing concrete but…"

She broke him off with harsh laugh as she tried to run her fingers through her long hair but got snagged in the braid. She pulled it free hastily and her wavy hair shone in the faint light.

"What am I doing? I should be focusing on mastering my magic and saving Derek but instead I'm playing house with you and forgetting myself with Ian. I'm not a girl who can just dance with a boy. I have expectations and so much pressure on me. It's almost the full moon and I can't believe I'm having this conversation with I spirit I thought was my… Never mind what I thought."

"Oh no!" James said. "You don't get to stop there. What did you think I was, Elinor? Because you cannot lie to my face and tell me this doesn't mean something," he said pulling her into an embrace. "I see how you look at me. I can feel your heart pounding. Tell me I'm not real."

She whispered the words softly into his chest. He didn't hear it but he felt it.

"No, I don't believe you. Tell me I'm not real now," he said pulling her lips up to his. He wrapped his hand through her hair and felt her hand open on his chest. She didn't pull away. He brought his other arm to her low back and pressed her against him. Her free arm grabbed his side. But he pulled away when he felt a drop of water hit his face.

"You are not real," she said as tears rolled down her face. His hands fell away from her.

"If I'm not with you, I'm alone. Can you even imagine that? There is no one else who can see me at the Glen. You are everything to me," James said.

"I know," she said nodding. "I know. But I can't make you real, James. I need some space," Elinor said softly. She hadn't moved. She was still inches from his chest and if he hadn't let go they still be holding each other. "I need you to give me some space." Her actions contradicted her words as she took his hand but in an instant he learned her meaning. They were back at the Glen.

"You shouldn't leave the Glen." Elinor said. "I think it's safest here but I need some time. I need to focus. You are too much."

Too little and then too much. James felt anger flash in his eyes a moment and then it was gone. He nodded and walked away from the girl he loved. They were both fools.

I fell asleep and...

Fire. Hate. Ashes and then... No. Write it down, Derek. Make yourself write it down. Write it down, dammit!

She is covered in the ashes of her husband. The sky is visible through the charred roof and a voice answered her pleas. It was more... feelings than words.

I wish I'd never heard it. I wish I didn't know it.

Finish it, Derek.

It told her that it wouldn't bring her husband back and it could make the pain stop. So nothing would ever hurt again. And it swore to give her the children she'd never be able to have. She consented without a thought. In a moment.

And then a dark cloud was encompassing her. So thick it choked her and pain racked her body.

It was exactly like... I'd never wanted to see that ever again. She realized who had heard her call and who had answered her and what it had cost. It was the Darkness and he'd given her power and he'd taken her soul. Her face registered a moment of doubt, a moment of full knowledge and...

I want to throw up. I want to un-see it. It was so like Brigitte and I can't have these feelings about her too. She doesn't deserve them.

Then in an eternity and a second it was over. Her black eyes gleamed in the moonlight. She brushed the ashes off her hands and stepped into the embrace of her new lover, the Darkness. It filled her and then she became my Queen and my mother. And knowing this, knowing how it started does nothing. It gives me nothing. I was such a fool. I thought that my mother was the watcher in the dream, that I was seeing her hate someone. Seeing her hate some poor young girl.

I thought it was a weakness. I though this girl, Ash, would be some kind of key or leverage. But all that hate was ... I should have recognized it. After all my self-hate is stronger than most. She hates who she was. The Queen hates that she was Ash. She hates that she was weak. I was right that she wouldn't have wanted me to see it because it was no gift from my mother. It must be a gift from... from the Darkness? But that didn't make any sense either.

Why didn't I recognize her? Because these are two different women. It's not just the black eyes. It was... seeing both of them... Ash is unrecognizable as my mother. No one seeing Ash could know her. There are so many thin, tall women with dark hair in Morland. And their generalized descriptive points are the only thing they have in common. If I hadn't seen it with my own eyes... But I had.

I'd wondered obsessively who Ash really was. It would have been nice to have someone hate her as much as I did. I thought what an ally, all that hate. But that hate can't help me. Because Ash is the Queen and the Queen is Ash. And I have nothing and no one to help. Those dreams gave me nothing but oh God let this have been the last one.

Chapter 22

Derek

Derek was sure she was coming for him even before he heard his door unlock. He still wasn't sure if she knew of his dreams but if she did, she'd want to see his face. She'd want to gloat after he knew it all. He didn't think she would want him to know about Ash but maybe she did. Or maybe it was just a torture device of the Darkness. And if she didn't know about the dreams, she would want to make sure he was living in anxious agony of what waited only days away. Either way when his door opened Derek was not surprised.

"Let me show you the conservatory. I think you'll love the view," the Queen said without preamble as he stepped into the hallway to follow her. The conservatory was placed where the gardens had been. She had completely demolished everything that had been there before. The gazebo was gone as were all the hedges and bushes. It was now an immaculate room filled with exotic potted plants. Some he recognized and some, scarily, he didn't. He knew very well that Morland had unending secrets and new unknown things made him nervous.

The room was like a hothouse museum. White. Crisp. The perimeter walls were stone that had been whitewashed bright white. One wall backed the kitchen, two backed the dining room, and one was the outer wall of the castle. But it was the glass roof that drew his attention. There was a small white table and chairs to the side like it was a fancy tea house. *Who did she sit here with?*

He might not have recognized it was the garden except for... the blood patch. It was in the center of the room. The dirt was stained a deep rusty red. The Queen saw him staring at it and she smiled. "So you know what it is. Did Jol tell you about it?"

"Yes, Jol told me but not until I'd already seen it. I was watching when you killed that cook's daughter who had magic. You slit her throat over the ground and the whole garden shook with Darkness," Derek said.

He also remembered watching Jermaine and Brigitte offering their blood over the spot but he didn't want to mention them to her. The Queen bent down and ran her fingers lovingly over the dirt with a touch as soft as a feather. It made him feel sick. How many people had she killed over that spot? Hundreds? Thousands? Everyone she could find who had magic.

"So you know then that this is my secret, all that magic blood pouring back into the ground. It gave off its life magic which weakened the Goodness. And it gave me all that I needed to make you seven. Oh don't look too hopeful. I can see it shining in your eyes. I can see your mind working for a way to escape. But there is no escape. The full moon is four days away.

"But were it in two years, there would still be no escaping it," she said pointing up. "In four days it will be full." There was a ghost of the waxing moon out in the morning sky and he guessed it would shine directly over the red ground.

"Then, you'll be the perfect son again. I'll remove that pesky soul that's been filling your head with poison." She smiled a cool dark smile as if she could read Derek's mind. Derek's soul was far away with Elinor. He told himself over and over that he was protected. She wouldn't be able to find a way to get his soul. Derek knew it.

"You haven't complimented my new necklace," she said lifting the large green stone hanging around her neck. Derek hated looking at it but he couldn't stop. Things would have been so different if she didn't have it. If she didn't have that necklace that let her see the spirit world. "I never would have found this if I wasn't looking for your flower. It made me curious what else was growing in my woods. I thought magic had abandoned that land but it had only gone deep into the ground.

"This is a very rare crystal that grows when a field of spula vine has been trampled underfoot. This," she said running her fingers over the stone, "does many clever things. It allows one to have communion with the spirit world. I thought I would only see the Darkness but imagine my surprise when I saw *him*." Derek looked around but his soul hadn't returned. She hadn't missed his search and smiled.

"At first I wondered why there was a ghost who looked like you in the spirit realm but I've stolen enough souls to know what one looks like. You know it has really all worked out for the best. Because I didn't know last time that your soul wasn't still inside you. The ritual would not have worked. But don't worry. I've worked all that out. Soon your soul will be destroyed and you'll finally start to take after your father."

"I know who my father is. His name is Nathan Jensen," Derek said. *Nathan. My dad is Nathan Jensen,* he repeated to himself.

"What a dreadfully common name," she mused. "But no. He is no more your father than that whore is your mother. Can't you feel it?" she said plucking at the air like she was playing an invisible harp. He shook his head, not sure if it was a good thing or a bad thing that she'd finally gone insane. But then Derek went still. He felt it. A pulsing. A vibration that resonated inside him.

"Ah," she said. "You finally hear his call. Did you never wonder if I was your mother, who was your father?"

A coldness settled inside him. A horrible realization dawned on him. He whispered it. "The Darkness."

"Yes," she said just a quietly, walking towards him as she flashed a dagger and pricked his finger. She wove the drops of blood in the air and started to spread it apart. "When I chose you that day, you were reborn as ours. Mine and the Darkness's. He would give me the children I wanted and the power I craved and I'd give him your souls and willing soldiers for our plans. The fairest of trades. In your other home did you still feel his pull? Was it far enough to get away from him?"

His face must have said it all because that smile slid across her face again. "Soon there will be nowhere that is free of us. The universe is wide and we have so much to do. You should have known that you could never escape us. We are in your blood," she said and he saw it. Woven in with his blood was a strain of Darkness, black as ink threading through the red.

"I don't believe you," he said.

297

"Try it yourself. It's no trick," she said handing him the dagger.

He sliced through his forearm without hesitation. He wiped the blood on his hand and worked it between his fingers. His hand began to shake. He could see it, the dark shimmer that filled his blood cells. It was inside him. He had to get it out. His mind was frantic with that thought. He raised the dagger again.

"Oh no. You must save it," she said laughing pulling the dagger from him. "I wish you could accept that I do this for your ultimate happiness. You'll be at peace and you'll be with me forever. You won't have to play whatever trick you did to keep your youth. I would enjoy it more, if I didn't have to force you," she said flicking her hand open as she sent a trail of fire that wrapped around his neck, just licking him but not burning him.

"I could burn you alive. I could melt your skin from your bones," she sighed. "But I see your eyes. I see that you would rather burn than bend. That's part of why I chose you. Your total disregard for the competition and the fiery passion inside you that you use all your energy to squash. You know I'll break you, if I have to," she said wrapping the fire tighter around his neck and allowing it to burn and then just as suddenly to release him. She walked from the room and left Derek to his dark despair. Two thoughts filled his mind: He had to get away and she didn't know about his dreams.

Elinor

Elinor had walked into her training session with Joseph feeling tired. The training and the dancing and the fight with James had emptied her. The full moon was only four sunsets away. Even though she was drained and weighted down she knew she'd be ready. Well pretty ready. And it helped that she felt pretty. Her new clothes included a full cream dress with a white sash and strappy sandals. She loved dresses. Thinking about dresses reminded her of last night with Ian and James and... She touched the necklace at her neck. Why couldn't she just forget about them both?

298

She met Joseph in the stables and he had a brush in her hands before he even said a word. She loved horses. Elinor thought that these would probably be her most enjoyable three days until Joseph said "Why do you despise the Goodness?"

"I don't despise the Goodness," she stuttered out surprised. "I mean I've only been in Morland a couple weeks but I think the Goodness is great."

"No, I can feel your bitterness and … it's like a grudge," he said looking her up and down.

"I don't know about that. I mean Morland as a whole has dealt me a crappy hand but I don't really blame the Goodness for that."

"Oh then maybe it happened before you came here, when you were on your home world. I heard you had terrible head pain when you were there."

"The Goodness was not on Earth. I would have noticed this," Elinor said breathing deeply. "And yes I was a little bitter and resentful towards God but…"

"Did you think your God was so small He only resided on Earth? That your little planet was his only home?"

"I don't know," Elinor said a little hotly. "I guess I never really wondered if God was hanging out on Mars or not. They are the same then? How can you know?"

"The Goodness or God, as you like, created every star in the sky and every planet that circles them. He was there when they were each born and He will be there when each is destroyed. I'm sure His relationship with each world is different but He does not change. If you resent your God from Earth then you resent the Goodness, they are the same. There is only the one. There is only one God. Only here we call it 'Goodness'."

Elinor let herself really think about it. It made sense. It was small thinking to think that God would only have business on Earth. But it felt so different here. The struggle for light and dark was as clear as day. It was obvious who the good guys were and who the bad guys were and the Goodness felt real and the Darkness was a visible, palpable force that everyone believed was real and struggled against.

It was so different on Earth. Most people didn't believe in God or the Devil. They liked to think that what they could see with their naked eyes was all there was. And it was harder to feel them there. Maybe the Darkness on Earth didn't turn everything sepia hued but it was still everywhere covering everything. It was almost worse not being able to see it.

Elinor didn't want her God to be the Goodness, she realized with a horrible pang. She wanted the Goodness to be a new god who would treat her better and who had different rules. She'd never understood how people could just invent a deity and then worship the thing they just made but she'd almost done it. She'd been ready to toss God over and give the Goodness a go at protecting her. But now that she knew the truth she couldn't continue her blind eye.

Her God was here and He was reaching out for her just like He'd always done. If anyone deserved a second chance it was Him. Knowing now that her headaches were a birthright of sort, the genetic mutation of having a grandfather with magic, it was a little easier to lay her armor down. It wasn't like she just had migraines and God chose not to fix her. She was a quarter Morlander. It was in her DNA and her body had been calling out to Morland for a year. It was a part of who she was. It was impossibly easy to shrug it off when she was able to see the big picture.

Her body had been having headaches because her soul had been hopping across to Morland every time she blinked. Her headaches and vision brought her to Derek who was able to bring her to Morland. And now that she was here, she was one of the only people who could help save Morland. Her gift, the strange genetic throwback was exactly what Morland needed. She'd always heard that God's plans were for her good but it had been hard to swallow when she'd had an endless horrible headache stretched in front her as her only future. Instead now she saw that her suffering had been terrible but it had led her here, to her purpose.

If she'd never had her headaches or her ability, then she would be helpless to save Morland and Derek. God still wanted to use her even after she had railed against Him for over a year. She was the one who didn't deserve a second chance. She remembered the first time she had gone over to the spirit world when Winter had been cauterizing her stomach and she'd felt such overpowering peace and love. That was from her God. Even after all she'd done and the hard bitterness that had filled her, He loved her.

She needed to forgive Him and forgive herself and lift up the yoke of her duty. Morland needed her. Derek needed her. God had prepared her for this. And she knew that if she said no, if she couldn't let it go, if her wounded pride and entitlement wouldn't let her do what was required, hope would arise from somewhere else. God was going to save Morland and she needed to decide if she was going to be involved. She could sit it out. She could decline the kind offer of battling the Darkness. But the Darkness would be battled and God didn't need her.

How long would it be before someone was born with her ability? How could she possibly be so horrible and selfish? She couldn't and she wouldn't. She somehow kept forgetting that all this training was for real. It was to prepare her to fight the Darkness and she had so few days left. And another couldn't pass without her starting this one on her knees.

"Very good," Joseph said kneeling beside her outside of the stall. "Release your bitterness. The Goodness is not only good. It is just and merciful and strong and vengeful and forgiving." They sat there for a couple minutes and then Joseph helped her up. "We have dealt with one of your problems. We will deal with the next tomorrow. But today we will care for the horses. Let the mindless chores release your mind. Wander to a place of meditation and prayer."

Later in the day, Joseph brought out a horse blanket and laid it between them. It had tassels on each end and a zigzag pattern of triangles in red, blue, and green.

"This is you," he said separating one green thread from the tassels on the end closest to him. "Where does this thread come out on your side?"

Elinor tried to trace the thread from start to finish but she couldn't. It wasn't a simple braided patterns she could follow or vertical stripes. The green thread wasn't always visible and she had no idea which tassel on her side contained that exact green thread. "I couldn't guess," Elinor said shrugging.

"Yes. Since you didn't make this blanket you can only guess. The journey of this thread is not straight or simple. It is often hidden and twisted with other threads. It is the same in our life. While we are being woven through the tapestry of life we can only see where we have been and guess where we will go next. Other people's threads run parallel or suddenly cross ours making knots and braids.

"We don't always get to see the final piece but sometimes we get a glimpse. Sometimes when we look back we can see the pattern start to make a little sense. But sometimes we just weave up and down and it seems like we are accomplishing nothing. But each thread plays a piece. With only one thread the blanket would never keep a horse warm. But the Goodness is the weaver with the pattern and design in mind. When our time ends and we reach the tassel on the other side we will finally get to see the glorious design and our little but important part in making something so beautiful."

Elinor ran her fingers along the blanket and looked how the path of the threads didn't always go the easiest path, how it seemed to be taking the long way to the bottom. But she couldn't argue with the end result. It was beautiful in its simplicity and function. *Everyone plays a part.* Elinor thought. *I'm just one thread. One thread who needs to trust the only One who can see what's actually going on.*

Ryan

Ryan had not been on his A-game when he went to training that morning. He'd been up late dancing with every pretty nomad girl who could wrangle him but his heart had not been in it. He couldn't stop thinking about Winter.

She filled his mind and wouldn't let him have peace. He had wished so many times last night that she had been there. But she was on her 'vengeance quest' with Peter and they were probably getting really close. Dangerous situations breed intimacy. He knew that. And what did it matter because he wasn't staying. There was no scenario that ended with him staying in Morland. He was taking Elinor back. His life was on Earth.

His mind argued back that he felt more alive here. He remembered the moment when he'd crossed over and it felt like his fading batteries had been replaced with overclocked ones. He'd felt like a million bucks. But he told himself that it was the adrenaline. It was the constant fear and danger that bred that. If he lived in Morland he would get tired and bored just like he used to do on Earth. And what about his family? No woman was worth abandoning his family. So he was glad Winter hadn't been there last night because it would have just made the inevitable harder.

And he was still mad at her. She was so blind. She couldn't see how life was just waiting for her. The Glen and the other East nomads were just waiting to love her but she couldn't see it. All she could see was her vengeance. And the word felt like a joke. Who pursued vengeance? It was something only heroes and villains in movies did. But vengeance wasn't something that could be found, bought, or sold. It wasn't even really something. It was emptiness and he wished he had told her that. He wished she was still there. He needed to make her listen. But what did it matter to him what she did? He was leaving soon, hopefully.

But it did matter. Winter mattered so much to him and he hoped she would live long enough for him to yell at her again. But Ryan pushed Winter to the back of his mind. He had enough to worry about with Elinor.

The full moon was coming and he didn't know if he had learned enough to protect her. Also he'd seen her dancing last night with Ian and *only* Ian. That girl was a boy magnet. It was like every male she spent any time with fell in love with her. It was ridiculous. But the knowledge that they were both going back to Earth removed Ian from his mind. That boy could dream but in a couple days they'd be lightyears apart.

At the end of a long day sparring with Damon and many others, Ryan sank down at the bottom of a post and took a couple deep breaths to calm his pounding heart.

"You did well today," Damon said sitting next to him.

"Thanks. I just hope it will be enough," Ryan said. He so hoped it would be enough. These long days could not have been in vain. It would make a difference.

"Enough for what?"

"Enough to protect my sister."

"To protect her from what's coming?" At Ryan's raised eyebrows Damon just motioned to the full corral full of men and women wrapping up from a day of training. "We all know something is coming. But you alone can never be *enough*. Your sister's fate is not in your hands. It never was and it never will be. Her fate rests with the Goodness. As do all of ours. You can train to get stronger, to become more disciplined but you cannot protect your sister from the Goodness's plan. I'm sure this is hard to hear."

Ryan stiffened, angry. What was the point of this, if not to protect Elinor? He was her older brother. Protecting her was his first job. But Damon was right. Ryan was so out of his league. A lifetime of training with a sword could never protect Elinor from the Darkness waiting just outside the barrier of the Glen. But maybe the Goodness could use him. Ryan knew he was a piece of the puzzle. He nodded to Damon.

"You are right. I just wish you weren't. It's so hard to trust anyone else with her wellbeing," Ryan chuckled.

"Who better to trust than the Goodness? Who could possibly love her more?" Damon said standing and extending a hand to Ryan. He nodded again and took his teacher's hand.

"Thanks. See you tomorrow."

Brigitte

Brigitte found herself pacing around the fire and she made herself stop. *The Goodness works things out for the good,* she told herself. It was a constant effort to calm her worries about trusting Derek's welfare to Jol, the traitor, Winter, the warrior, and Peter, the clueless. If Derek made it out alive it would be because of divine intervention from the Goodness.

It wasn't that she herself would fare better at the impossible task of defeating the Queen but it was infuriating to be so far away. To be in the Glen with only one job: holding a bubble in place while others fought, while others got to charge into the castle with swords and magic. She just held a bubble. It was a *special* bubble, at least, and she knew that without it everyone at the Glen would be in danger from the Queen and the Darkness and Elinor would never have been able to train so diligently. But with the battle coming closer it felt like such a small thing.

At least the council was a more bearable task now that there was nothing left to plan. They still met as they had done every morning since there had been more than one kind of nomad in the Glen. But there was little to say. They worried the same old bones and prayed that Elinor would be ready.

Brigitte was so proud of her. She felt it bursting from her skin. Derek was right to bring her to Morland. It was divine planning that brought them here. Elinor was so brave and strong. She'd learned to meditate in a shocking amount of time. Brigitte flushed to recall that it took her two years to be able to sit still all day and pray to the Goodness. Her mind was not always a place she could bear to be for that long.

And Elinor was Màithrean, the south nomad leader. Most south nomads had dark skin like Brigitte's but she had learned long ago that family had nothing to do with skin color or accent or birthplace. That red-headed swordsman had been her brother in truth if not by birth. Elinor was born of Morland blood and her temperament was very like the Southies. She was quiet and calm and she too *yearned*. She ached for things profoundly. First, to be healed from her headaches. And then for peace and strength to do the task ahead.

Elinor had also survived Victor. Brigitte heard what people whispered after Elinor had finished training with him. They said that she wouldn't survive it. They said that that was why Victor had tried (more like succeeded) to drown her. It worried Brigitte. She had come to care for Elinor. They shared a wagon along with their strange, dear Emmaline and the three of them had naturally formed a bond.

Yet another thing she could do nothing about. If Elinor failed or succeeded, if she lived or died, were all things that Brigitte had no control of.

Sweet Goodness, she prayed, *please watch over Derek. Protect him please. Guard Elinor and let her complete the task ahead of her. But let her live. Calm my heart and my worries. Remind me that your will is good and you are enough for me. Amen.*

When she returned to the wagon, Elinor and Emmaline were asleep and she breathed a deep breath. While she was in control of so little it was a great comfort to have two loved ones under the same roof. To hear their steady breathing and to count at least two safe and sound. But trouble was coming to the Glen and all those who lived there and Derek was in the gravest danger of all. But she made herself undress and get ready for bed. She closed her eyes and meditated. Strength and gentleness. Calm and storm. Cold depths and warm shallows. Goodness help her. *It's going to take forever to fall asleep.*

'Derek's papers: Full moon in three days

I told myself that the last dream would be the last... But of course the story doesn't end with the Darkness. That's only the beginning.... That's the day the woman I called 'Mother' was born. So there had to be more. The dreams want me to know how I was made. They want to show me how the Darkness got inside my blood.

The hate is a subplot now in the dreams. It's not as strong and it's now aimed at the world. And the world changed overnight. There was no coronation ceremony or election. She made herself Queen in the space of a breath. And with her rule came the Darkness.

I had wondered why the Darkness had spread _then_. They said it came out of the blue and covered everything with no warning and no explanation. I had wondered why not before? Why not the moment Morland was formed out of space dust? But feeling my mother's thoughts I knew why... It had needed her. She thought that it needed her and only her but I knew better. It just needed someone. It just needed a vessel.

The killings and the battles flashed like snapshots across my vision. Everyone with magic was slaughtered before my eyes over and over and over. So many. So much blood spilled over that red earth. The Goodness in them was sapped out and poured into the ground. And I felt her joy as the presence of the Goodness grew less and less with each death. It wasn't enough for her that the Goodness was covered in the blanket of Darkness. She wanted the Goodness gone and she needed the life magic that people with magic possessed in their blood.

The red stained ground grew and grew and then one day bursting through the soil came a stone. It was black and looked like obsidian or onyx but for the sparkling red vein that wove through it. It had been what she'd been waiting for. It had been the point of her whole damn life.

I saw my siblings appear one by one into the picture. Each was kissed on the cheek by mother after drinking a sip of wine. Only now I know it wasn't just wine and it wasn't just a kiss. The wine had a seventh of that blood stone mixed into it and the kiss finished the bonding. I'd figured out there was some sort of spell that linked me with her. I'd felt her pull and seal with that kiss. But worse than knowing the mechanics, was knowing the specifics.

It took an enormous toll on her to bind each of us. Even with the Darkness's borrowed power it near exhausted her. But when my siblings completed their rituals it was as if her deposit was returned tenfold. The sheer volume and depth of her power was staggering to feel. I'd been right to kill them. At least I finally know that for sure.

But I also know that their power isn't gone it's still linked... to me. If she takes my soul, she'll get it all back. It will all have been for nothing and she will never be able to be stopped by anyone. The amount of power that is waiting on me is indescribable. It's almost like I'm at the top of a roller coaster. I'm still and motionless but when I move there will be more power and speed than I've ever know.

And there is one more thing... My dream told me something I'd wanted to know for a long, long time. I finally received the answer to my most haunting question. "Why me?"

I could hear her thoughts or memories of thoughts when I saw myself battling below in the competition. She picked me the moment I'd walked in. She'd known. She'd known with all of us. It was only ever the seven of us. It couldn't have been six or eight. It couldn't have been Garrison or anyone else. We were as destined to be hers as we were destined to die soulless at her feet. But she'd seen something inside me. Some part of me _called_ to her. But I didn't have the Darkness yet. I was just a man without a soul. She'd seen her kind when she saw me and she'd known I was the seventh. She'd known I was her son. A child of bitterness and hate.

I was always meant to be this. To be here. I cannot be saved from what I am. It is destiny's cruelest joke that after all my running and fighting and training, I am trapped in this bloody room and the full moon rises in three nights. What was the point of anything I ever did? What was the point of my life? Why was I ever born?

Chapter 23

Elinor

Only two more days of training. Today, tomorrow, and then the next day was the full moon. Her mind went racing from excitement to terror. What had she really learned in the two weeks since being here? She kind of wished that her lessons had included using a sword or offensive magic like a fireball or something. She felt so inadequate. No amount of training would make her a warrior. Elinor's mind was running in a million different directions and the horses noticed. The stables were filled with loud exhales and stomping hooves.

"You are upsetting the horses. They can sense when your spirit is troubled. Tell me what is bothering you. Your training?" he asked and Elinor was impressed. She'd forgotten that one of the elders did have magic. Joseph had some magic but she didn't know the specifics.

"You've just met me," she said, "and I seem really healthy and normal but back home I was a broken pitiful mess. Bitterness and anger were my constant attackers. Even if my headaches are gone, for now, I am still that girl. I just ... I just feel like I'll never be enough. That I won't be able to do what everyone needs from me. I let people down and I'm not there when it's important. I feel like an empty girl. What's in my spirit that could save anyone?"

Joseph stared at her and tapped the horse's side and motioned to his ear. Elinor leaned over and listened to the horse's heartbeat. She closed her eyes and just listened.

"Do you know what my gift is?" he asked when Elinor eventually moved away from the horse.

"No," she said. She watched as his eyes shifted from brown to gold and back again. "I see what's inside a person's soul. I can see Darkness spread when someone lies. I can see the Goodness glow when someone is around a person they love. Your heart, Elinor, shines like the sun. Your struggles and difficulties have shaped your heart into an armored lantern. The Darkness cannot reach it and hope shines out of you for all to see. Elinor, the light inside you can save the world. All you need to do to master your ability is to believe that the Goodness's plan for you is for your good and that you are worthy of your brave heart. The Goodness will do the rest."

Elinor's eyes welled and Joseph nodded and left her alone. She placed a hand over her own heart and finally gave in. She had tomorrow and the day after was the full moon. Maybe she would be ready. No, she *would* be ready for it. Whatever it ended up looking like.

She knew the basics. She would merge with the Goodness and destroy the Darkness and also save Derek somehow. She wished she could practice it or do it in small pieces every day. But she knew that she would have one chance. The Queen couldn't know that Elinor existed yet. It needed to be a surprise attack and Elinor trusted the Goodness. Things would work for the good and she assumed when the time came there would be one clear path to follow. She tried not to worry about it too much.

Training with Jeremey was not a lengthy event. But she found herself mulling over what they talked about for the rest of the day. His truths were as heavy as Calla's ring.

Ian was waiting for her outside of the stables. His eyes were bold and sharp. She'd kind of hoped that she could just avoid him until the full moon and then just say goodbye as she went home to Earth. But seeing him now... She knew that would be wrong.

"I looked for you yesterday," Ian said moving closer.

"Yeah, I'm really busy training. I don't have a lot of free time," Elinor said.

"I know. I already have the bath ready. Come over and rest. You'll wear yourself out."

"Thank you, that's very kind of you but I think I'll just grab some food and eat in my wagon. I have a lot to think about and not much time. Thank you, though," Elinor said moving past time.

"Should I apologize?" Ian said sticking out an arm to halt her pass. "Was the dancing too presumptuous? I thought we were just having a fun night." His fingers traced her necklace and Elinor felt something. Why was she avoiding him? Ian was only being kind. He was only being a good friend.

"No. You don't need to apologize. It was a really great night. It's good to see you..." she had started to lean closer to him and shook herself a little. "I just don't have time for whatever this is," she said motioning between the two of them. "For whatever you hope this can be. Nothing is more important than what I have to do."

"I'm sorry for the misunderstanding. I only mean to extend friendship to you. Maybe you read more into things. Peter asked me to look after you that's all. Don't make things awkward," Ian said getting a little red in the face.

Elinor felt like an idiot. She was so narcissistic to assume that every man she met was in love with her. Ian just wanted to be her friend and she was forcing him away, just like James... No, things had been more with James. There had been something special and strange and impossible. He had obeyed her wishes and was staying out of sight but she still found herself looking for him.

"So, a nice hot bath?" Ian said leading the way. She hadn't even realized she had started following him. He was only being a friend. It would be weird to keep making a big deal so she let herself be led.

Chapter 24

Derek

The full moon is tomorrow. Derek carved into the walls of his bedroom with the broken leg of a table. *Tomorrow. Tomorrow. Tomorrow.* But the walls only scratched. He'd tried ramming the leg through the wall, the door, the ceiling, and the floor but nothing budged.

Where was Peter? Where was his soul? Why hadn't they come for him? Why had they let so many days slip away? He reminded himself what his soul had said: No news was good news. His soul was with Peter and Elinor making a plan. There was a plan. But what would it be? They couldn't know how tightly the Queen was bound with the Darkness. She could not be killed until they were separated. Derek made himself stop stabbing the wall and sat down to pretend to talk to James.

"The facts," Derek said to the empty air.

"The Queen is Ash," his soul would say. "She is bound to the Darkness in some tripped up wedding ritual. But she wasn't always this. She used to be just a girl."

"And the Darkness is in us. It has been since we were made prince."

His soul would nod silently for a moment. Maybe it should have made him feel a little better, that the Darkness had still been with him even when he'd went home. Maybe it could have annulled all the things he'd done. Because that was surely where his red rage was from. It was from the Darkness that flowed through his veins.

If that was all he had learned he might have felt relief but he'd learned more, of course. She'd seen something inside of him, something that called to her. She'd seen her own dark kind and she'd picked him instantly among of the throng. Was that more lies? Because if it was true then it didn't matter that he was trapped in Morland. It didn't matter that he'd lost his soul. Because if that was true, then he was always destined to become the monster he became even if he'd lived every bloody day of his life on Earth.

It was better not to know.

He wished he'd never had a single blasted dream. They replayed in his mind. He told himself that it was better before. That it was better before he knew. He couldn't unlearn it and he could do absolutely nothing to change it. Derek pulled out the sheets of paper that detailed his dreams. He reread his words with a strange detachment. It didn't make it easier or worse to replay his dream. It was just the same level of horrible and he was finding that he was just getting used to it and developing an immunity or something. They meant something and nothing and it almost didn't matter which. But a thought struck him. There was something about it that didn't make sense.

"Okay. Why does the Darkness pick her? Why then?" Derek asked his absentee soul.

"Because it needed her," he would say. "It needed a vessel. Maybe there was something about her that allowed the bonding."

"The Queen is the weak link. The Darkness cannot exist in this form without her. And she's at her weakest. The weakest she's been since before she destroyed Felix's soul. If there was ever going to be a time it's now," Derek said.

"But that leads us right back around. So what she's a weak vessel? We don't know how to unbind them and she can't be destroyed until then. She may be weak but the Darkness isn't. What weapon is there to sever a person from the Darkness?" his soul would ask.

"There is only one weapon that can be used against the Darkness." And Derek knew no one who could wield it. He certainly couldn't. Only weeks ago he'd told Elinor there was no Goodness and there was no God. And now they were his only hope.

Please be real, he prayed. *Please be real.* Because from the Queen's not so subtle comments he knew that this wasn't just about Morland anymore. She had said "the universe is wide and we have so much to do." She was going to spread from world to world like a cancer, killing everyone with magic and covering each world with Darkness. And if things didn't go well tomorrow, if he was turned into a soulless minion of the Darkness then Earth might be their next conquest and he knew where the bloody portal was. *Please,* he prayed, *Oh Goodness, please be real.*

Emmaline

The morning light was bright and crisp and they were coming. Tomorrow. The dark things. The things from her dreams. The things that make her cry and everyone cry. Emmaline sang *the* song as she walked. It was the only one.

"His blood will flood the veins of the world. His blood will burst the dam."

"What?" Brigitte said.

Emmaline turned around. She hadn't known anyone was there. Sometimes it seemed like the world only existed inside the dark silky curtain of her hair.

"Emmaline, what did you just sing? Were you singing about Derek? Is he in danger?"

"Of course he is," Emmaline said gripping handfuls of her own hair. It had been right there. A thing she needed to know. "What's the next line of the song?" Emmaline asked her sister. Her sister would know.

"Which song?" Brigitte asked.

"THE SONG," Emmaline yelled. She flinched at her own voice. She hated how loud it had gotten. The force it took to open the locks around her mind made her legs stop working and she had to sit down. She opened the door just a tiny, tiny bit. It wouldn't make a difference so close. It would be okay. He'd be okay. The words came and Emmaline sighed.

"The Darkness cannot abide the light. It makes the Darkness flee," Emmaline sang smiling. She grabbed Brigitte's hand and started walking and then started running. "I know how to save Derek. We must tell Elinor. Oh no. Is it tomorrow?" Emmaline asked slamming her feet down and looking around frantically. Maybe she'd lost today. Maybe opening the door had pushed it away. "Hurry tomorrow is today!" She yelled but didn't flinch. There was no flinching tomorrow, only fighting.

Elinor

Tomorrow. Tomorrow is the full moon, Elinor repeated it to herself as she left her wagon. She was the last to leave. She'd indulged and let herself sleep in this last time. She wondered what secret inner truth she'd be facing today with Joseph at the stables. But it was Ian waiting for her when she opened the door.

"Good morning," Ian said. "Want to grab some coffee before you start?"

"I should get going," Elinor said smiling. "Maybe later?"

"No," Ian said taking a step closer. "How about now?"

She nodded and followed him without even thinking about it. It seemed like overnight Ian had just become a staple in her life. He was always there and it felt right.

She held the warm mug in her hands and studied Ian and his wagon. It was a simple bachelor pad but he was anything but simple. North nomads looked so like elves. They were tall and graceful, handsome and regal. It was really a dangerous combination.

Ian reached between them and tapped her necklace. "I'm glad you are wearing this. It makes me happy," he said.

"I..." she hadn't worn it on purpose. Every time she was aware of it and what it meant to be wearing a necklace a man had given her the thought just kind of slipped to the back of her mind and she forgot about it. For all of Ian's talk of just being friends, his gaze seemed to promise other things. Elinor watched with frozen fascination as he moved closer. With one hand on the necklace and another wrapped around her neck, he pulled her close and kissed her lips.

Elinor melted instantly. *Ian. Ian. Ian.* Her mind repeated his name like a mantra as she pulled him closer and deepened the kiss. Images of dancing with him flashed through her mind. It had only ever been Ian. She'd been fighting what she knew, fighting what she felt. When he'd held her and spun her, she'd felt whole and right. *Yes,* she told herself. *Yes, it's Ian.* His hand slid from her neck to her low back and she was pressed tight against him. A moan escaped her lips as he pulled her onto his lap.

"There we go," Ian said breaking their kiss. "Finally. You fought me so hard, little mage. Let's go for a walk."

"No," Elinor purred. "I think we need to stay here, Ian. Ian. Ian." Her essence was filled with only his name. He smiled wide and kissed her hard once before pulling back again.

"Let's see if you are really ready," he said tracing his fingers on her necklace. "What do you want, Elinor?" he asked

The words came unbidden from somewhere outside herself but they were none the less true. "You. To please you," she said.

"How long have you wanted me?" Ian asked pulling his fingers back to hover over her skin.

"I... Just now. What is happening?" Elinor said looking down to see that she was holding Ian with arms and legs wrapped tight around him. She couldn't remember how she had gotten there and what had led her there. She couldn't remember the last moment she remembered. Something was wrong. She tried to pull away but Ian placed his palm on her chest covering the necklace.

"Let's try that again. How long?"

"Always. Forever," she said. Everything was alright. Everything was clear. She had forgotten for a second that Ian was all that mattered. Ian was all there was. Just her and Ian in this moment. She never wanted this moment to end. There was a buzzing in the back of her mind but she intended to drown it out with Ian's moans.

He chuckled deeply when she ran her fingers through his hair and grabbed tight as she removed the space that had somehow arisen between them.

"There she is," he said moving away after a moment, pulling her arms free from his neck as he ran his fingers down the full length of the chain giving her delicious chills. "If only I'd been able to finish this necklace sooner, we could have been having so much fun but alas time is running out. I think we need to go for a walk," he said dancing his fingers up her collarbone along the thin chain. "Come, on," he said pulling her up.

She saw nothing in her surroundings but him. Where was he taking her? It didn't matter. She only wanted to be wherever he was. She would follow him to the ends of the world. She didn't notice anything until Ian led her right over the border of the barrier.

It hit her hard and sent her to her knees. A thousand thoughts poured into her mind, like a door had been swung opened. Why had she let Ian lead her across the barrier? What was she doing with Ian? Why had she been kissing Ian? It didn't make any sense but those thoughts jumped to the back of her mind as the Darkness poured in around her. She'd forgotten what an awful force the Darkness was. She felt like she was suffocating and drowning and being crushed into a singularity. It was hard to breath, hard to think.

"Ah," Ian said taking deep breaths. "I hate it in there. But we each have our parts to play don't we, my sweet? I had worried that you were too strong but I shouldn't have. You are just a girl, after all, and you could never have resisted me," he said running a hand along her chin to make her look up at him. She jerked her head away. She wasn't sure what was going on but Ian was not on her side. She reached to unclasp the necklace, it suddenly felt like it weighed a hundred pounds.

"Oh, no," Ian said crushing her hands in his. "I spent nearly weeks making that bloody necklace and you are going to wear it. It was very difficult to bring a little of the Darkness inside her barrier. Peter almost caught me a dozen times but I was able to sneak into the forest to charge up the stone, a little every night. I managed somehow. You liked it didn't you, my dark whispers." Elinor's eyes flashed as she struggled to pull away from him. "But enough of this, let's go."

At his command the forest came alive. The creatures of the Darkness appeared out of nowhere and flooded the forest. Elinor recoiled as far as she could in Ian's grasp. They were the stuff of nightmares. They oozed like smoke and oil but their claws very very solid. They waited for his second command. He simply nodded and the creatures dove on her and against her will Elinor was pulled into the spirit world. She watched as her body slumped to the ground and her soul was caught between the creature's claws.

"Ian! Please," Elinor yelled but his face was transformed. James had been right. Ian was not good. Dark tendrils pooled around him and Elinor wondered how no one in the Glen had noticed their double agent. How had she not noticed? Maybe the elders hadn't even checked the young generation for magic. Because now that Elinor was in the spirit world she could see that Ian's dark magic was radiating off in pulsing waves that knocked the breath out of her.

"Won't I be rewarded for bringing you to the Queen? She has no idea what a weapon these hidden nomads possess."

"You'll never bring me there in time. The full moon is tomorrow. The Queen will be dead by the time you take me to her and then Derek will kill you," Elinor spat.

Ian laughed a deep laugh. "You have such faith, you little fool. You think your friends left to save Derek? I spied on the Mage while he was here and he told the crazy one that he's going to kill Derek. You thought you were sending Derek hope but you've only sent him the country's greatest assassin."

"No!" Elinor yelled. "I don't believe you."

"It doesn't matter if you believe me," Ian said pulling her chin up as he commanded the Darkness to pool under her to force her even higher.

When they were eye to eye he said "There is a whole camp full of the Queen's men not far from here and when I tell them that I found hundreds of nomads they will come running to destroy this stupid Glen. And I don't need to bring your body to the Queen. What would she want with this?" he said running his fingers though Elinor's hair and sliding his hand down her back. But he wasn't touching her physical body that lay on the ground, he was touching her spirit. How had he brought himself into the spirit world without spula vine?

"You are going to scry the both of us into the castle and she'll sacrifice your soul to the Darkness."

"You can't make me," Elinor said with more courage than she felt.

"Oh yes I can," he purred into her ear as his creatures drove their claws in deep and Elinor screamed. It was so much worse being able to feel their attack. The last time they had brought their claws to her she had only watched, a world away from the violence. But being fully present while it happened was almost unendurable.

Somehow over her own scream she heard a small voice. "Elinor. Find the Goodness." But Elinor couldn't. She'd never felt weaker and farther from the Goodness. When the creatures released her for a moment, Ian was close by crooning in her ear, "Elinor, you don't have to die today, you know. You need to accept the truth that you have been lied to, brainwashed.

"The Goodness has no real power. It is the residue of the old age. It is dying, if not dead. The Goodness is for those who are too weak to face the Darkness inside themselves. They all have this," he said motioning to the Darkness around them. "They all have this inside themselves but they are afraid. Afraid of true power. They prefer to pretend that the Goodness has the power so they don't ever have to get off their asses.

"But you like this power. I saw how it sang to you through the necklace. Just give into it," he said running a hand down her neck. "Choose the Darkness. I can see it in you. I know how you've struggled so just let go. Let it all go and come with me. You can serve the Queen without dying and who knows what could come between us. I know you've felt something. I saw it in your eyes when we danced. And I felt your desire for me in the wagon. No one has made you feel as alive as I do. Choose me and I'll present you to the Queen as my prize and woman." He stared into Elinor's eyes and she spat right in his face.

"So be it. Die then," he said and the claws where back. She thought it would never end and she could see nothing but the blood running in her eyes. But then she heard something and the claws released. She turned her head. Ian was looking around, listening for something. And then she saw him, James with his sword drawn and his eyes full of rage.

He burst through the trees and was fighting with Ian. Ian sent the creatures at James but James easily slashed through them. He moved like a cobra striking one after the other and he spoke to Elinor the whole time. "Fight it, Ell!" he shouted. "Seek the Goodness. Don't give up!"

And when the creatures thinned under James's sword, he moved on to Ian. Ian may very well know how to make swords but James had watched and trained with Derek for years. Ian would fall to James's rage and skill.

But Elinor's pain blinded her to everything else as one creature found its way to her and this time she felt something acidic seeping under her skin. *No!* She cried in her mind. She felt the Darkness trying to take hold of her and she fought back. She called to the Goodness and *instantly* she felt her heart open and the light filled her.

As soon as Elinor was filled, the light poured out of her like an explosion, filling the dark woods with the Goodness. The creature holding her exploded. Ian hissed and disappeared into the woods. Elinor slid down and saw that James was holding her.

"James," she whispered. "You came."

"Of course, El. Always. But honey, I know you are tired," he said wiping the blood from her face. "I know it hurts but you need to listen to me. You need to return to your body and cross back into the Glen." Elinor felt her eyes growing heavy and her bodies felt sticky with blood. She had to hold on. That was what she had learned. Stay in the spirit world no matter what happened to her body.

"Hey! No, stay with me. El! Please!" James said stroking her face. "Please go back to your body. Please."

Elinor nodded weakly and slid back into her physical body that had fallen like a rock when she'd been forced into the spirit world. The wounds inflicted to her spirit were mirrored on her body and she felt pain everywhere.

"There you go. Okay now take off the necklace. Now, El. Then you have to make it across the barrier. Please. I know it's hard."

She listened to James as if he was the only sound in the world. She reached a hand up and tore the necklace from her neck. The thin chain snapped like a string. And then with shaking legs and arms she crawled across the barrier.

"Good job, my girl. Good job. Now I need you to yell. Really loud. Please, honey."

Elinor's scream ripped through the Glen as she started to fade in and out of consciousness.

The last thing she remembered was Emmaline cold hands on her brows as she sang to her. *Maybe that was death*, Elinor thought, *a cold hand and a soft song.*

Ryan

"What happened? Where is Elinor?" Ryan said scanning his eyes for Elinor who was usually involved in any upheaval happening on Morland. And of course she was in the center of it. *Of course.* He'd been a fool. He'd thought she was safe. He'd let his guard down.

Elinor had thick gashes oozing blood all over her body and her breathing was unsteady. There was a flurry of East nomads washing and treating her wounds.

"What happened?" Ryan repeated as he grabbed Brigitte shoulders. She shook him off and he saw the sweat dripping from her brow. And then he felt it. There was a dark aura coming off of Elinor. A spider web of black veins was spreading from her chest. He sat down at Elinor's feet, the only part of her that seemed unharmed and he waited.

It took all day and as the sun set, Ryan knew the worst was over. Brigitte had finally sat down and the air in the room felt better. The black poison looking stuff that had been spreading under Elinor's skin was now a network of light pink scars. Elinor's other wounds were bandaged and a strong herbal scent hung in the air. He wished there was a healing mage or something like that but he was pretty sure there wasn't. He just wished he knew what had happened.

Answers finally came in the form of Bo. He came into the room looking drawn and pale. "I didn't know," he said suddenly, the words pooling out of his mouth. "I knew something was wrong but I didn't know he'd hurt her."

Ryan was up in a flash, all fatigue forgotten. "Who did this?"

Bo lowered his head. "Ian." A north nomad woman jerked her head up sharply.

"No," she said. "It cannot be."

"Come," Brigitte said moving to leave the wagon. "Bo, you can tell us the whole story out here. We won't bring anymore bad energy into the sick room. We'll talk outside." Brigitte nodded to Emmaline who remained and held Elinor's hand. Ryan caught a line of Emmaline's song and he was glad to be gone. Something about blood flooding the veins of the world. He shook it off and followed Brigitte.

"Ian kept saying that the Goodness was keeping us blind and that there was more to the world. I thought he was just talking," Bo said shaking. "He liked to talk. I thought that's all it was. He'd leave the Glen sometimes... He saw me following him and told me to stay away. He'd been sneaking spula vine, too. He was using it every day. I stopped coming to the blacksmith shop but I shouldn't have just let him keep going. I should have told someone but he's my brother..." Bo looked in agony but Ryan spared him no sympathy. Even though he knew that he would keep any secret Elinor asked him to.

"Well," Bo continued, "Ian was acting extra strange tonight and I followed him and Elinor. He led her past the barrier and then they disappeared."

"We were fools to not look more closely at the children. Not all power comes from the light," the North nomad woman said with tears in her eyes.

"Was he like the Queen?" Ryan said. "Did she make him one of her children?"

"No," Brigitte said sitting down exhausted, "I don't believe so. We all have the capacity for Goodness and Darkness inside of us. We each must choose our master. Whether Ian was searching for the Darkness while using the spula vine or if it *found* him, I can't guess. The spula vine opens a person to the spirit world. The Goodness is not the only thing waiting there.

"Ian made the choice to follow the Darkness as anyone may do. He *chose* the Darkness without help from the Queen. He *chose* the wrong path. He will not make it past this barrier again. But he will surely alert our enemies. We must prepare for an attack. We know that they have a camp not far from here. They will probably be here right when Elinor is needed. Hopefully she'll wake in time. If she doesn't… this may well be our end."

Ryan walked back to Elinor's sleeping form and prayed. He didn't have words but his silent plea dripped from every pore of his being. *God, help us.*

Chapter 25

Elinor

Elinor awoke covered in a cool breeze. Her body felt like the old days when she was always coated in Bengay. But as her consciousness awoke she felt it, the pain. She sucked in air through gritted teeth as she tried to sit up.

"Oh thank God," Ryan said helping her up. "How are you feeling?"

"Sore. Everything. All the things are sore and hurt. What happened?" Elinor asked and then she remembered. "Ian." The horror washed over her and her eyes were searching for the other man involved. And there he was sitting in the furthest part of the wagon from her, James. His eyes were uncertain and he watched her without coming closer.

"James," she said as tears filled her eyes. "I'm so sorry I didn't trust you." He was at her side in a moment.

"I'm sorry, Elinor. I should have gotten to you sooner. I should have been able to stop him." James said with his head in his hands. Elinor reached out to touch him even though she knew she couldn't. He looked up and smiled at her.

"You saved my life. Thank you, James."

"I don't know about that," he said wryly. "I only helped you save yourself."

"It was more than that. If you hadn't have been there..." she said and wished to say a hundred more things but she could see that the sun was sinking past noon and she took a deep breath.

"It's tonight, isn't it?" she asked Ryan. "I slept yesterday away, right?"

"Yes. It's tonight. You sure know how to pick 'em, huh?" Ryan said with strained eyes. She appreciated that he was handling this calmly. She tried to smile back but she wasn't sure if her face did or not.

"Ha, you have no idea. Am I in the clear?" she asked River, who had been tending to her wounds.

"Clear enough. You'll be sore like the dead for a while but you are well enough for what's to come."

"And it comes fast," Emmaline said taking Elinor's hand. "Can you do it?"

Elinor nodded. She was so tired and in pain everywhere but she'd never felt more determined to fight the Darkness than she did then. She would free this stupid planet from the stupid Darkness if it killed her. And she felt like fighting. Ian had been a successful test. When he'd pulled her into the spirit world and the creatures were attacking her she hadn't returned to her body. She was as ready as she would ever be.

Elinor spent the little day she had left in mediation and trance. She didn't enter the spirit world but she was ready. James sat silently with her.

As the sun was beginning to set, Emmaline told her the missing part of the plan. She wasn't just going to bond with the Goodness and clear the planet of Darkness she was also going to bond to Derek's soul.

Brigitte explained Emmaline's vague instructions. "The Queen's ritual will be in three parts. The first is that she'll have to get Derek's soul somehow. And he is here… But we are assuming she has a plan to reunite them. The Queen can't destroy Derek's soul if it's not near her and she needs it as a sacrifice. But again we have to prepare for the worst.

"Next she will flood Derek and his newly reunited soul with the Darkness. Then the last part of the ritual is removing and destroying Derek's soul for good leaving him with only the Darkness inside him. But before that happens you and the Goodness will have bonded to Derek. So when the Queen tries to take Derek's soul she'll be flooded with the Goodness instead. That would, according to Emmaline, destroy the Queen and break her bond with the Darkness freeing the world and flooding it with Goodness."

"Easy peasy," Elinor said trying to smile.

As the sun set, Emmaline said, "It's time."

Emmaline closed her eyes and when they opened they were clear and bright. "They will be here soon and you should start your journey. The moon won't be fully risen for an hour. But our adventure starts now. You will be so beautiful. You'll fly through the castle as a ball of light but they won't be able to see you." Emmaline smiled so sweetly as she rested her head on Elinor's shoulder. "And I'll guard your body," Emmaline said.

"Oh thank you..." Elinor said. "Um what will you be guarding my body from?"

"The Darkness," Emmaline said. "The Darkness cannot abide the light. It will try to consume you. But I won't let it. Sister will help too and your warrior brother."

A horn sounded. The Queen's army was here. She hoped that this meant there were less at the castle for Jol to contend with. Jol... Elinor remembered what Ian had said.

"Emmaline," Elinor said. "Is Jol going to kill Derek?"

"Somebody will die," Emmaline said solemnly. "I can't tell who. There is too much Darkness and it is colliding with the light. Do you still want to go?"

"Do you know Jol's plan?" Elinor asked. She had been worrying over it since he had left. She trusted that Peter would protect Derek but she still felt uneasy.

Emmaline didn't respond at first then she said "Whatever happens this day, the Darkness will leave Derek. Is that enough?"

Elinor nodded and took a breath. She didn't really have a choice but she was not comforted. Elinor looked up and saw true dark settling fast. She needed to hurry. The Queen wanted Derek's soul and Elinor was the only thing standing in her way. Derek was in terrible danger.

"Not as much danger as you," Emmaline said softly to her.

"Um. What?" Elinor said

"One more time, why does it have to be Elinor?" Ryan asked.

"The Goodness is constricted. The Darkness borders it on all sides. When Elinor fully enters the spirit world, she will pull the Goodness towards herself and in the process expel the Darkness everywhere she goes," Brigitte explained. "Then she will go to the castle and bond with Derek."

"How exactly am I supposed to do that?" Elinor said.

"You'll know," Emmaline said. "The Darkness cannot abide the light."

Elinor groaned at Emmaline's cryptic response. James moved close and whispered, "I'll see you on the other side. I wish I could go with you but I need to get as far away from Derek as I can. I'm going to try to put some miles between us. Just in case…"

"I'll find you. When it's over. When we win. I'll find you," she said passing a hand through his chest.

Elinor took a deep breath about to start when Brigitte said, "Oh and tell Derek that I forgive him."

Elinor nodded and closed her eyes. She was distracted for a moment by the pain of her body but Victor had trained her well indeed. She took breath and focused as she fell into the spirit world. She felt the Goodness all around them. Elinor felt whole.

"Before I go…" James said trying to find the words as he pulled her into an embrace. "Oh Elinor," he said into her hair. "My little mist girl."

"It will be okay somehow, James. I know it."

He pulled back and looked into her eyes. He leaned in and kissed her on the lips once, softly.

"I know it will," he said and was gone.

Elinor wished she had been given clearer instructions. Elinor prayed out to the Goodness she couldn't see. *I'm here. Please let me do something to help. Use me.* And she felt herself join with the Goodness more tightly than ever before as they fused as one.

Ryan

Elinor's body fell lifeless to the ground. Ryan could see a light glowing from her chest and then rising from her mouth as one last gasp escaped and her body stopped breathing. Ryan grabbed her body, shaking her as he turned to vent his rage.

"Why isn't she breathing? This has never happened before when she went into the spirit world. What have you done to my sister."

"Be quiet," Emmaline hissed. "She is safe with the Goodness. You are needed here. The Darkness will sense what has happened and come for her. Protect your sister. Pick up your sword." Emmaline herself pulled two daggers from a wooden box and crouched low waiting. "It begins," she said with gleaming eyes.

Derek

Derek was escorted from his room with fifteen armed guards. He was wearing the uniform she had sent to his room. It was the uniform of a general minus the sword, of course. He hoped it didn't mean that Garrison was dead.

Derek hadn't seen his soul since his first night at the castle and entering the conservatory without knowing 'the plan' was making him crazy. He told himself that nothing had happened yet because his soul was being careful. He was keeping away to guard 'the plan'. Because there had to be a plan. But they sure were cutting it close.

She was dressed in a red gown that made her look even more stunning and horrible than normal. The red fabric seemed to move and shimmer like fire. The combo of black hair, red dress, and pale skin made her look like death incarnate. Somehow Derek steadied his breathing. His panic would only increase her pleasure. But he had trouble hiding it when he noticed that the walls were lined with soldiers.

"Mother," he said bowing before her.

"Oh Derek, are you going to be amenable?" she asked studying his face.

"Yes of course," Derek said. *There is a plan. I just have to wait. There has to be a plan.* But before he could start another repetition. The glass door to the conservatory started to melt.

"How upsetting," the Queen said pursing her lips. In another second each guard in the room had a noose made of fire around his neck. Derek scanned the room frantically and all show of coolness left him when Jol walked in.

Jol was alone and Derek exhaled the breath he had been holding. The Mage had come to save him. His soul had found him and everything was going to be okay. But when Jol wouldn't look at him Derek began to worry that something was terribly wrong.

"I'm very hurt I wasn't brought in for this festive occasion," Jol said without releasing her guards. Derek knew that she couldn't negate another fire mage's power she could only add to it. She herself was immune which was the reason Jol was probably still alive. He was no threat to her.

"And you wonder why you weren't invited? This is why," she said motioning around. "You've ruined the celebration."

334

"I mean you no harm," Jol said. "I only want to be back in your good graces. I wanted to make amends."

"This looks a lot like an act of war," the Queen said.

"I'll release them as soon as I have your word that they won't kill me. I know you can never trust me again but if you see how I'll stand by and let you take him. It will be a start. I made one mistake six years ago. Let me try and correct it."

The Queen tilted her head like a snake evaluating if the prey in front of her was worth the effort of killing. She turned to study Derek. He knew the betrayal he felt must have been written all over his face.

This has to be part of the plan, Derek told himself. He should blank his face but he couldn't. Maybe Jol's years in the dungeon had removed any ties of 'friendship' between the two of them. Derek *had* ruined his life and just left. *This can't be real,* Derek thought as he closed his eyes.

Jol

Jol thought Derek's face might kill him. The boy's hope had flared to life upon seeing him and then Jol had watched as it turned to confusion then despair then emptiness. The Queen had loved every second of it.

"Alright. We'll give you a chance. Check him for weapons and restrain him," the Queen said. Derek stared ahead, his face finally a mask, as Jol released the guards. It was good she'd called his bluff so quickly. He couldn't have held so many guards for long.

"It's almost time," she said pulling Derek into the moonlight that shone down from the glass roof. Derek's hands were bound and she forced him to kneel in front of the red stained dirt. She lifted his chin to force him to look at her and said, "Join me willingly. You could rule by my side, my son. What do you say?"

Derek spat in her face and she hissed as she slapped him with enough force to send his head reeling back.

335

"You can't take my soul. He is safe from you," Derek said.

"No one is safe from me," she said. "I know your little shadow isn't here. But it doesn't matter how far he runs. What do you think will happen to you," she said as she unclasped her necklace, "if you were in communion with the spirit world? That's where your soul is. Do you not think that there is a force that has been trying to unite your two broken pieces into one? But you've been in different realms with no way for the other to cross over. Until now," she said with glittering eyes as she slid the necklace over Derek's head. "Don't you want to be whole?" she purred as Derek was knocked back to the ground gasping.

Derek

Derek hadn't truly believed he would ever be whole again. Being in Morland and being able to see his soul had felt like enough. He hadn't really needed more. When the necklace had been placed over his neck he had felt his soul rocket like a cannonball into his chest. It had felt like he was pulling the whole universe into himself and it was amazing.

How could he have ever thought that he didn't need this? It was pure contentment. It was joy. He was all the good parts of himself again. He breathed. It felt like a very long time. But after what was really only a moment, the horror of the situation hit him. He had his soul and that meant she could take it.

Derek struggled against his binding. He tried to stand up but she forced a hand on his shoulder and he felt the fire just under the surface. He stopped fighting for a moment. He had his soul, there had to be a way out. Maybe if he took the necklace off but then... He be might alone again. But he'd be alive.

"I can't wait until your soul is destroyed. He has somehow caused me even more trouble than you have," she said sighing. "Well no point delaying the process. Let's give your soul some company in there shall we."

"No wait," Derek said begging, pleading. "Please, Mother. You don't have to do this. I'll stay with you but just not like that."

"No dear," she said. "This is the only way. I need a son I can count on in the coming wars. The Darkness and I need a loyal son and general. You are what you are and you will become what you will become. You are a murderer and a liar. You are nothing without us."

"Maybe... Maybe I am nothing now but I used to be something just like you, Ash," Derek said watching her closely. He had no doubt that his dreams were true. And he just hoped there was something in them that could buy him time.

She hissed and slapped him hard across the face again. That confirmed his theory that she had not sent the dreams.

"How do you know that name?" she asked.

"I know a lot more than that name. I've seen your whole life, Ash. I saw you abandoned in the snow. I saw the old man and your husband. I saw..." He was interrupted by another slap. His face felt like it was on fire but maybe there had been a little flame in that last slap. And it took him a moment for his vision to stop spinning.

"You will not speak of him," she said softly with ice running through every syllable.

"Why? Because a part of you still loves him? Because you regret what you did? Then don't do it to me. Spare me. Make the right choice this time. Please." He thought he saw something, a flicker, a movement at the side of her lips. But then it spread into a cold sneer.

"If you have indeed seen it all then you know that what I am now is superior. That creature," she spat, "did not deserve the breath in her lungs. She was nothing. And I am everything. I regret nothing and neither will you. It would have been so much better if you had been willing. Do you know what will happen to you?" she said grinning broadly. "The Darkness will flood every part of you. Every tiny unseen bit. You will know true communion with your father. Then once the Darkness fills you, I will take out your soul because you won't need it anymore. The Darkness will be your soul. I could have made this less painful but you've made me angry."

"The Darkness didn't choose you because it wanted you, Ash," Derek said. "It just needed someone, *anyone*. You were just the most pitiful, the one most willing to throw away everything to escape your garbage life. It needed a vessel and you were just dumb enough and desperate enough to do it. It would have taken *anyone*. You think you are special. You think it loves you. You are a fool, Mother. You are the weak link and I will find a way to break you. And when you are broken so will your precious Darkness."

He saw it again, that unnamable emotion that ran past her eyes but it was quickly followed by the rage and hate he knew so well. He braced himself for what he knew was coming. But he was glad he'd said it. Maybe he'd planted a little seed of doubt and it would sprout someday. For now, she knew the truth and didn't like it. That made him smile which made her yell as she sent the Darkness towards him. He noticed too late that her slaps had left an open cut on his cheek and the Darkness rushed in.

Jol

A dark mass fell on Derek and he screamed. It made every hair on the back of Jol's neck stand up. Jol had had men tortured and he'd heard their screams. Those were children's laughs compared to the sound coming out of Derek's mouth. It lasted a long time and Jol almost wavered. But this was part of the plan. Derek needed to be filled with the Darkness. So that when they killed him only the Darkness would die and Derek would be free. And she would be weakened. Garrison's army was waiting down the hall and he hoped they had the sense to wait and stay hidden until they were needed. Jol couldn't believe he was just standing there as the Queen filled Derek with the Darkness. Maybe his plan was flawed.

Chapter 26

Derek

Pain. Pain. All the blood in his body was boiling. His whole body was on fire. His skin was being flayed off and the raw wounds splashed with acid. He screamed. Everything that had been inside of him was being pushed to the side as poisonous tar flooded in. His screams started to sound like they were from someone else but there wasn't anyone else left in the world. All there was this pain and a couple broken pieces of a prince.

And then after what felt like a thousand years it was over. Derek felt different. He felt like a dying man having received miracle healing.

He smiled.

His mother stood above him. He fell down at her feet and kissed her shoes.

"There, there, my son. All is well now," she said patting his head. "Rise. Let me see you."

Derek saw his black eyes mirrored in his mother's and felt... nothing. No joy. No worry. Just loyalty to her. Derek turned to see the world with his new eyes and then he saw *him*. The betrayer. A darker redder rage filled Derek than he had ever known in his life. It pounded at his temples and he strode foreword to release it.

Jol had betrayed the Queen when he'd sent Derek away with the flower and Jol had stood by and let Derek become this. But no... that wasn't the betrayal. That was a good thing he'd done. Derek's mind was fuzzy but he moved to kill Jol all the same. His blood sang for it. His hands were still bound but that would not stop him. He growled as the ropes snapped free under his flex.

"Wait a moment, lamb," the Queen said and Derek stopped. "There. Finally! Your siblings were not so obedient. We'll decide Jol's fate later. He did prove himself. So let's get that soul out, shall we." But she stopped speaking as Jol smiled a wide deep smile.

"Not so fast," Jol said.

Derek attention was drawn to the melted doors as he saw soldiers pouring in but not just from there. The whole conservatory was surrounded. Jol *was* a betrayer.

The Queen tutted and shook her finger at Jol. "You haven't changed at all," she said. "What a disappointment."

Derek looked to the door as countless armed men and women filed into the conservatory. A snarl escaped his lips as Garrison walked in already swinging a sword. Derek elbowed the guard nearest him in the face and took the sword that dropped from his hands and he walked to meet the General. Derek's blood sang with the promised violence before him.

"Hello, General," the Queen said. "You weren't invited. As you see, I have a new general."

"I'm not here for the show," Garrison said keeping his eyes on Derek as they walked towards each other. "I'm here for your head, Majesty. Now if you'll excuse me I need to kill your son." Garrison nodded his head to the Queen in mock-respect and smiled wide at Derek. Derek smiled a dark smile back.

Winter

Winter hummed with excitement and anticipation. The conservatory was filling with soldiers but Winter had eyes for only one person. The Queen stood before her and today would be the day. Today would be the day for vengeance and retribution and blood. Winter knew that the blood spilt today was the only thing that could remove the invisible blood of her family that coated her skin.

340

Winter took a deep breath and called for the stones. They would hear her now. They would answer now that the enemy was within her grasp.

Winter called.

And waited.

But the stones stayed silent. Had she had the ability to pause time she would have taken that moment to howl an unholy roar that would shatter the stones with its volume. But she didn't have that power either. So she shoved her rage back inside and used it as fuel for her twin swords that hung at her sides. There were many ways to make a person bleed after all.

Peter

Peter walked in and stared. It was more horrible than he had prepared himself for. Derek was *gone*. It was an alien wearing his skin. Everything had changed, how he carried himself, how his face rested, his black eyes. It was like looking at Derek's evil twin. Peter was looking at a stranger and the Queen hadn't even finished the ceremony yet. Peter knew that Derek's soul was still inside there, only locked down by the flood of the Darkness. There was still time. There was still hope.

Everything happened so fast. The Queen motioned for soldiers to attack and all of them moved but not in the same direction. Peter couldn't see their sleeves but it was pretty obvious which men had been turned and which had no idea what was going on. To each side's credit, they believed in their cause enough that they were willing to fight their brothers over it. Men were pouring in and the few loyal to the Queen were becoming outnumbered as they closed their ranks.

Garrison's men were moving with precision and skill. It was like watching a choreographed fight scene from a movie. It was easy to watch from Peter's instantly capture position on the sidelines. His shock at seeing Derek had left him open and his lack of skill had made it too easy to ambush him. They'd taken his sword but his dagger was still hidden.

Derek had made a beeline for Garrison and they were locked in a fierce battle. "Long time no see," Garrison said ducking Derek's blade. "Is there something different about you? A new haircut?" Derek glared but didn't answer as he increased his speed. Garrison was not holding back either but maybe that was because Derek was a creature of rage and violence and he wasn't going to stop until he chopped off Garrison's head.

Winter was fighting three at once, her swords striking like vipers. He wondered why she wasn't using her magic. Her nomad warriors fought like feral animals, moving like lightning and slashing everything in their wake.

But even still the battle was over in minutes. And it was all Jol's fault.

Jol had said that the only way they wouldn't die would be if he was able to keep the Queen's attention long enough. So the moment the commotion started, he was in a battle with the Queen. Each of them was layering their magic on top of the other one to protect who each wanted to protect and attack who they each wanted attacked. Peter could see it happening. It was so much subtler than if they were in a movie. He'd see the Queen send fire at a rebel solider and then Jol would encase her fire in his fire which wouldn't hurt that solider but at the same time he was trying to attack some of her men and she'd protect them.

It was more like an intense game of chess than a battle. They were both sweating and getting sloppy as a solider or two started to fall on each side. The Queen staggered for a moment and Peter felt hope. Then he felt like a fool because Jol failed to notice when one of her soldiers crept behind him and the fire proof sleeve was snapped over his arm rendering him useless. It was the same sleeve she'd used to trap him last time and Winter wasn't near him to break it free again. It was over.

The Darkness coalesced behind the Queen, visible for a moment before she yelled and every solider had a flame collar tightly wrapping around their throats. She then released five of them who had been defending her. Peter did not imagine that this was how anyone had seen the battle ending. Having Garrison trapped did not release him from Derek's wrath. But the Queen called him off with only an inch between Derek's sword and Garrison's throat.

"You," the Queen said meeting Garrison's eyes with as much loathing as he was giving her. "You betrayed me. I will make you suffer for years. You will beg for death. How did you imagine this ending? Did you think numbers were enough to end me? I can't even look at you."

Garrison opened his mouth to release a snarky comment but Derek was faster and punched him hard in the face before a syllable came out. The Queen ignored it.

"And who do we have here?" the Queen said examining Winter. "Where have you been hiding, little nomad rat? I can taste your magic, weak as it is. We will fix that," she said as the guards began leading Winter to the side with the other survivors. They were not hampered by Winter's violent attack to free herself. "And you are?" she asked Peter motioning for the solider holding him to bring Peter closer.

"He is Peter. He was a friend of mine," Derek said.

"Where did you meet such a pitiful fighter? I trust he is not a solider of mine."

"No, Mother. I knew him from my birth planet, Earth."

Peter felt his face pale and he didn't dare look at Jol. Peter then knew for certain that his friend, Derek, was not in control of that body. Because never in a million years would Derek tell the Queen about Earth but Peter watched in horror as Derek did exactly that.

"Ah yes. I did wonder its name. Earth," she said tasting it and Peter wanted to scream, to fight, to do something.

"Can you take me there?" the Queen asked.

Derek nodded. "Whenever you wish."

"Imagine the worlds we could have conquered with all seven of you," she said smiling sadly.

"I'm sorry, Mother," Derek said.

"I know you are now. But all will yet be well. Just a couple things to handle before we leave. Did you come all the way here to save him, Peter?" the Queen asked running a nail down Peter's cheek. "He is saved now. But let's test it, shall we?" she said in a conspiratorial whisper. "My son, kill this boy," she said tossing Derek a dagger from her belt.

Derek dropped his sword and caught the dagger in his hand as he walked toward Peter without hesitation. Peter stared into those black eyes and wondered if he could make it to his own dagger in time. The guard holding him had released him, eager to get out of Derek's way. Peter would only have to contend with Derek but he was a real fighter and Peter was just a Boy Scout. Derek raised the dagger to Peter's heart and Peter said, "Derek. I know you are in there. Please stop."

"What are you to me?" said a cold voice from Derek's lips. "What have you ever done but use me? Are you happy? I finally brought you here. Is it everything you hoped for? Is Morland your perfect magic planet?" he said pressing the dagger closer, drawing blood. The Queen's eyes lit up and Peter's stomach dropped impossibly further. "You don't know me. You've only seen the mask. This is who I really am," Derek said drawing a red line with Peter's blood.

Peter took a sharp inhale but continued, "Derek, this isn't you. You are good. I know it. You need to fight it. You need to listen to your soul. It's still in there, just waiting. Fight the Darkness. You are not the Darkness! You think you can only do wrong. You think you are evil but you aren't." Peter hesitated but decided to take the risk, "Brigitte is alive."

Derek stared at him like a robot whose power source was suddenly unplugged, sagging a little. Peter continued quickly, "She is alive. I've seen her. You didn't kill your sister. Derek, you can fight this. I know you can. I am your best friend and I love you, man. You don't have to kill me. You choose. Your soul is still inside you. Fight it!" The dagger shook in his hand. Peter heard the Queen's growl.

She whispered in Derek's ear, "You need to kill this lying boy. Brigitte is dead. You killed her yourself. Kill this boy. He is nothing to you."

The dagger clattered to the ground.

"You fight me even now," the Queen hissed through closed teeth. "I would never have let you keep your soul even if you were completely obedient but I never imagined that it would stand up to the unending Darkness I've filled you with. What makes your soul so strong? Maybe I'll be able to tell when I destroy it," she said as she moved to slam her hand into Derek's chest.

Elinor

The spirit world was different. She'd thought she had known it like the back of her hand but it was different now. It was now made up of only two colors. Black and White. Light and Dark. Elinor flew through the woods and into the castle, bodiless and free. She could feel something was happening. The Darkness pooled and rushed, clearing out of her way before she even reached it.

She was with the Goodness. This presence filling her, around her, was God. She couldn't believe she'd ever doubted His love for her. The certain pure love filled her. It was impossible to doubt such peace. An assurance filled her that everything would work out for the good. Her thoughts were and weren't her own but the peace radiating inside herself was something she hoped she got to keep. She flew into the castle ignoring walls and pathways. She went to the epicenter. She prayed that she wasn't too late.

The Queen didn't see her. Elinor saw that her necklace was around Derek's neck and that he had James tucked deep inside. But she also saw the great sea of Darkness that was inside him. And at the Queen's command the Darkness would force Derek's soul out and destroy it completely leaving him as only a husk for the Darkness to control. Elinor flew faster than the Queen's outstretched arm and time stopped as she crashed into Derek.

It was quiet and dim.

Derek's soul was so tiny. It was hardly even there. She whispered to him but he didn't stir. She caressed him to wake up.

"Elinor?" he thought weakly.

"Yes. I am here. The Goodness and I are here to save you."

"I cannot be saved. It is too late. I am almost gone."

"It is never too late, Derek."

"It's too late for me. I deserve this for what I've done. She chose me for this and she was right. I was weak enough to let the Darkness in."

"Yes. You deserve such a fate but you can be spared it."

"How?" he asked.

"Let the Goodness in. All will be well."

"There is no Goodness, Elinor. The Goodness isn't real."

"How can you say that? Can't you feel this?"

"All I feel is the Darkness and you."

"Derek, you need to forgive yourself for what you've done and forgive the Goodness for letting it happen."

"No one can forgive me. Not myself. Not a deity that doesn't exist."

"I can forgive you, Derek. And so does Brigitte." Elinor sent him the memory. Sent him the words Brigitte had said and repeated them over and over. *Tell my brother I forgive him. Tell my brother I forgive him. Tell my brother I forgive him.*

And Elinor focused all the love and peace she was feeling and pushed it towards Derek's soul. She sent her own feelings of forgiveness and the one thing he really needed.

"Hope," Derek said softly. "I never thought I'd feel that again. I don't deserve it."

"Take my hand, Derek. Please let the light fill you. Accept the mercy. God's grace is sufficient, even for you. You can have a new life."

"I want a new life."

Jol

Jol watched as every hope failed. Their idiotic team had each failed in their own spectacular way. Jol had never really thought it would work. He'd hoped. He'd be lying if that fool Garrison hadn't given him a *seed* of hope. But being right back where he'd started three weeks ago with his own bloody hand locked in a fire proof sleeve was a horrible poetic justice to his inadequate attempt at doing the right thing for the first time in his life. *I should have known better. A man like me cannot do good, no matter my intentions,* Jol thought.

Now they were all going to die. There would be no rotting in jail this time. It would be a horrible violent death for the lot of them. At least Elinor was safe. That was one thing. Maybe she'd make it to the portal in time. All that was left now was to watch Derek's soul get ripped out of his body. It would be the perfect horrible ending for this fool's errand.

But before the Queen's fingers reached his chest, Derek fell lifeless to the ground. The Queen cradled him looking frantic and Jol found himself crying to anything that could hear him to save this boy. *Goodness?* Jol thought. *Please. Please save Derek.*

As the Queen stared at Derek, oblivious to everything else, Peter shot forward and sliced Derek's throat with his dagger in one quick movement.

"No!" The Queen yelled, slamming Peter against a stone pillar with a wave of Darkness. She grabbed the blood like she could force it back in but it flowed free and fast. Derek didn't move as he lay dying. Jol held his breath. What if he'd been wrong?

"There is still time," she said to herself as she slammed both of her hands on Derek's chest.

They all waited.

Then the world exploded in a flash of light.

Chapter 27

Ryan

The moment Elinor had gone, Brigitte had said she was raising a stronger shield. But to make it last the onslaught, not Ryan's favorite word choice, she could only cover herself and Elinor. Ryan hadn't liked the sound of any of that and he'd felt it when he was no longer protected by Brigitte's Goodness shield. He'd staggered but righted himself as he had exhaled a sharp loud breath. Emmaline had nodded to the sword at his belt and mouthed "good luck". Then *they* had descended, black creatures made of mist and shadows but real enough to claw and real enough to bleed.

Ryan had woven through the steps and skills he'd learned from Damon and it had barely kept the onslaught of monsters at bay. The creatures had poured in from the shattered windows and climbed over the broken door remnants.

Emmaline had been fighting like a ninja. She had moved fast and floated through one monster and then had flown over the corpse as it had disintegrated into foul black slime. Ryan hadn't had time to watch her. The monsters had poured in endlessly. He'd had no concept of time and his only goal had been to keep them away from Elinor's unmoving, not breathing body. But a few got through and were killed but not before a new gash or two had been added to Elinor's impressive collection.

Then after an hour or a year, Ryan had no idea but his limbs had felt like jelly, it had been over and all the creatures had disappeared. The Queen's soliders had looked around confused but they were very outnumbered and were soon captured.

The creatures were gone but Elinor hadn't woken up.

Ryan had tried yelling at Brigitte and Emmaline but it hadn't made Elinor's chest rise with breath. Ryan had pulled back her closed eyelids and her eyes had been freaking out like they did when she was scrying. He hadn't known if that a good sign or not?

"Calm down. I can still see a web of magic around her. Her body will keep. She isn't dead yet," Brigitte had said.

"Dead yet? Why did I listen to you!" he had yelled. He had then just stared at Elinor and waited for her to breath.

It took forty-five excruciating minutes for Elinor to wake up.

Elinor

Once Elinor had convinced Derek to take the Goodness inside himself, she had been ejected from Derek's soul and pulled towards her own body. The last thing she had seen was Peter slicing Derek's neck open and then she was back at the Glen.

Elinor opened her eyes and took a shuddering, gasping breath. She could tell without looking that she had fresh cuts covering some of her body. Brigitte, Emmaline, and Ryan were watching her. Ryan face was locked into a mask of despair and rage.

"Ryan, what's wrong?" she asked.

"Oh thank God! Thank God! I thought you were dead," he said holding her as he took deep breaths into her shoulder. "You didn't wake up. I thought you were dead."

"Get up. We need to hurry. Please," Elinor said pushing Ryan off as she rose on shaky feet. She stumbled as she headed to the stable to find a horse. She had to get to Derek, to the castle. But she had to stop when her head swam and she looked down at the drops of blood that marked her path. She wondered how much blood she'd lost over the past month. *It's like I have a vampire boyfriend,* she thought and almost smiled at her own cleverness. But no she couldn't find her own blood trail humorous because Derek's blood pouring from his neck kept replaying in her mind like a horror movie. Would she ever smile again?

"No. Wait. Is it over?" Ryan asked. He was covered in sweat, black tar, and deep gashes oozing blood.

"Yes," said Brigitte closing her eyes. "I can feel it. The Darkness is gone. My shield isn't even up."

"Elinor, what happened?" Emmaline asked, sweat shining on her face as well.

Elinor told them what she remembered.

"But I'm not sure how it ended," she said. "The last thing I saw was Derek being filled with light, the Queen's Darkness leaking from her hands to devour his soul, and Peter slicing Derek's neck open."

"Then what?" Ryan asked.

"Then I don't know. I got shot across space and woke up with a shock in my own body. That's why we need to go now. Derek might still be in danger."

"So you are telling me you don't know if the Queen is dead or if Derek is even alive?" Ryan said.

"I'm sure that *something* happened to the Darkness," Brigitte said. "I mean they are gone aren't they?"

"Who is gone? What happened here?" Elinor asked looking around to see that the Glen was wrecked. Wagons were destroyed, debris was everywhere and it seemed everything was splashed with black, foul smelling liquid. Wounded men and women were being treated and the whole placed reeked of a sewage smell.

"Your scratchy friends came to finish the job," Emmaline said wiping the black blood off her daggers. "But I guarded your body, so did you brother."

Elinor looked down at her dozen fresh cuts with raised eyebrows and Brigitte said, "You didn't see what they fought. They saved your life. You are lucky to come out with only cuts." Elinor hadn't noticed that she'd been sliced while she'd been gone. She supposed that meant that she should send Victor a thank-you card.

"Thank you. Thank you all for protecting me. But we have to hurry," Elinor said. "I need to know what happened."

"I know you do, Elinor," Brigitte said. "I do, too. We all do. But it will take us at least a week to travel to the castle. You'll have to be patient until we can know. Or you could scry over and tell us what you see."

"No," Elinor said. "Something is different." She rolled her shoulders and felt it. The Goodness was still with her even though she wasn't in the spirit world. Their bond was still intact and she had an idea. "No, we go now. I'm going to teleport us there."

"What? How?" Ryan said with wide eyes.

"I see the Goodness on you like a fine silver thread. Can you really carry us over?" Brigitte asked.

Elinor thought about it and felt pretty certain. She had transported James while she had traveled. And this was only impossibly more complicated than that but she felt a certainty and the power rocketing through her veins made her feel like she could fly to the moon if she wanted to. "Yes, take my hand."

Brigitte, Emmaline, and Ryan were the only ones who joined her. She was sure she could take more but she agreed that the fewer the better for her first try. In the span of a breath, they arrived in the hallway of the castle and Elinor walked quickly towards the conservatory.

All the guards are gone. That must be a good sign, Elinor thought. But then she saw the prone figure in the center of the room and ran.

Derek wasn't moving. His throat had indeed been cut and his blood was all over the floor. So much blood. She skidded to a stop and knelt by him.

"Derek," she said brushing his hair back from his face. "Please wake up." Elinor hadn't cleaned up after her latest wounds and his blood covered her own like the newest coat on a macabre painting. Her first aid training took over and she did what she had done to Derek many times. She looked for breathing. None. She looked for a pulse. None. She laid a hand on his chest and brought her cheek close to his mouth to feel for breath. No movement. No breath.

"Derek," she said pulling him up into her arms. He was still warm. "Please. This can't be real. Please, Derek." Her body heaved aa a sob started to build. *This isn't real. I'm not really here. Morland isn't real. The Queen isn't real. Please, let me be crazy. Oh God don't let this be real.*

Ryan

Ryan's feet wouldn't move past the door. Elinor was holding Derek's body and sobbing. The Queen was gone. Maybe she had fled. Maybe she was dead but she wasn't in the room now. Emmaline moved past him singing a song softly. Brigitte stopped next to him as her hands rose to her trembling lips. Tears fell instantly from her eyes like a faucet had been turned all the way on. Peter had thrown up in the corner and was sobbing into his hands. Winter stood with blank eyes surveying the room. Her nomads nursed their wounds and waited. Garrison sat with his back to the wall and his men sat silent beside him. Jol stood alone and stared off into nothing. It was the most pitiful thing Ryan had ever seen.

"Everything was supposed to be okay," Elinor cried into Derek's shirt. But then she jerked up like she'd been struck by lighting and she began to look frantically around the room. "James?" she cried out. "James? Where are you? No. No. No," she said shaking her head and resting it onto Derek's chest gripping his shirt with both hands as if she was trying to wash away his blood with her tears.

Ryan finally came to and moved into action.

"Elinor. Hey, Elinor," he said trying to pull her back from the abyss she was sliding into. She let him hold her and she cried. The remnants of a golden necklace lay severed on the ground.

Chapter 28

Peter

Peter sat unmoving against the pillar the Queen had thrown him against. He couldn't even look at Elinor as she cried over Derek's dead body. Dead. He was dead. Derek was dead. Peter had killed his best friend. His mind was stuck with that thought on repeat, *I killed my best friend. I killed my best friend.* It didn't matter that the Queen had screamed as she disappeared into an explosion of light. It wasn't worth it. What did he care that a Witch Queen on a different planet was dead? It didn't matter. Morland meant nothing to him and Derek's life wasn't worth saving a whole world. It just wasn't.

Peter made himself keep taking deep breaths so he wouldn't throw up again. He had tried to wipe all of Derek's blood off of himself but it was in his clothes and on his face and under his nails. The old man had lied. Derek was never coming back. He never could have. It was all a lie to save this stupid world. Jol had just wanted his tyrant gone. He had never cared for Derek. Peter was glad to see that Jol was upset. Maybe the price he'd paid was making him feel even a tenth of the horror that Peter was feeling.

Peter looked at the broken necklace. Maybe that had been the final straw. Maybe if it hadn't have broken he wouldn't be dead. Peter couldn't do anything right because Derek was dead.

Emmaline came to sit next to him and she took his hand. He tried to shake her off. He didn't deserve comforting. He was a murderer. But she pulled his arm sharply when he tried to get free and he gave up. He hardly noticed that she was singing under her breath. But something about it made him lean closer to listen to the words.

"His death has set the magic free.

His death has freed the land.

His blood has flood the veins of the world.

His blood has burst the dam.

The Darkness cannot abide the light.

It makes the Darkness flee.

The Queen is gone.

His soul awaits.

The girl has set him free."

She sang the song over and over and Peter turned to her, "Wait. What does this mean? Is this one of your prophecies?" She didn't stop singing. Peter stood up and moved to Derek. Emmaline had said that his soul awaits. Peter grabbed Elinor's shoulder.

"Elinor, can you see his soul?"

Her face was empty like everything living inside her had been sucked out. She just shook her head.

"His soul awaits, Elinor. We need to find it," Peter said trying to pull her from her trance. Maybe there was a chance. But she just stared past him.

"Brigitte," Peter said. "How long were you dead?" She just stared at him not hearing his words. Peter yelled at Jol, "How long was she dead?"

"Maybe an hour. I came later that night and she was already out of the grave and waiting for me."

"Okay we wait an hour. I know it's been a while. But we wait another hour," Peter said sitting next to Derek's body.

"How long was I away from my body after the Darkness was gone?" Elinor said looking at Ryan.

"Forty-five minutes or so. It could have been longer," Ryan said.

Everyone's hope was a palpable thing. They all stared and waited. But an hour passed and then another. Brigitte was the first to move as the sun started to rise. She kissed Derek's forehead and then pulled back sharply.

"There is magic still in him," she said. "I can feel it. A small trace. Like the web that was over you, Elinor. Don't you feel it?"

Elinor laid her hand on Derek's forehead and it almost seemed to glow along with her hand. She pulled it back as she ran a finger across her skin thinking about something.

"Then why isn't he back yet," Elinor said.

Emmaline's song rang clear through the glass room.

"His death has set the magic free.

His death has freed the land.

His blood will flood the veins of the world.

His blood has burst the dam.

The Darkness cannot abide the light.

It makes the Darkness flee.

The Queen is gone.

His soul awaits.

The girl has set him free."

"His soul awaits. We just need to find his soul," Elinor said.

"Where is it?" Peter asked.

"It is where it should be," Emmaline said walking over to Derek's body. She laid a hand on his chest.

"His soul is in there?" Elinor asked moving quickly to kneel on the other side of Derek's body.

"Then why doesn't he wake?" Brigitte asked.

"I'm not sure," Emmaline said. "His soul is inside but it waits. Something is blocking it. It could be... I think he just wants to go home. He is so tired. Can't you all feel it? It radiates out of him. His soul is calling for Earth. He will not wake up in Morland. He wants to go home."

Elinor

"Alright, We'll need to gather supplies, wagon, horses," Brigitte said moving to leave the conservatory to prepare their trip back to the portal but they just didn't have time. That trip would take weeks. The wagon bearing Derek's dead body would slow them down. No, they needed to be at the portal now.

"No," Elinor said grabbing Brigitte's arm. "We aren't riding there. I'm going to teleport us there. Now. Derek needs to be home now."

"Elinor, I don't know if you should tax yourself. You've had a long couple of days," Ryan said eyeing her stomach that was still in the first stages of healing from her cauterization not to mention the many, many injuries she'd had since that first one. Her numerous bandages made her looked like mummy.

Elinor took stock of herself and even though she was tired and hurting, the limitless power of the Goodness was still at her fingertips. She knew she could do it. They were still linked. She still had a web of Goodness over her just like Derek did now. Hers hadn't dissipated when she'd woken up. Maybe that was how she was still linked to the Goodness. But however it was possible she knew she could take them to the portal.

"I can do it and we should go now. I can't imagine I'll be able to keep all this power forever. So grab a hand," Elinor said. Peter looked at her like she was a total stranger. But that was fair. She was a completely different creature than she'd been when he'd left.

When Brigitte, Winter, Emmaline, Garrison, Jol, Peter, Derek, and Ryan were all touching her or each other, Elinor closed her eyes and they were gone from the cursed conservatory and within sight of a glittering shining portal. Elinor exhaled, more than a little relived that it had worked a second time. What if she could do this forever?

As the group started towards the tree, some of their party stayed back.

"I only came to escort the ladies home. When Derek wakes up, tell him that I'm glad I got to see him again," Garrison said smiling.

"You are coming, right?" Elinor asked Jol. She had to bring him back. Her dad needed to know that he had been loved and wanted. He needed to know that Jol had not left him on purpose.

"I... I don't know, Elinor. Maybe it would be better if I stayed gone. Could I ever fix things with him? Could he ever forgive me? No. And with the little we have guessed about how travelling between worlds work I could be young again. I'd be the same age I was when I left him. We'd be close to the same age. I think it's best if I stay," Jol said.

"No. My father is a good, kind man who deserves the chance to know his father. I want you to come."

"Then I'll come," he said.

Emmaline

Emmaline loved when things feel into place. They so very rarely did. They had heard her song and listened and she knew now what the colors meant. Blue. Red. Green. Blue was the sky, the night sky. Red for was the four bloods: Derek's, Elinor's, Darkness's, Light's. Green was new life, which was so obvious now.

Derek's soul was planted inside his chest like a little seed. Derek, his name was Derek. Her brother. She remembered his name now too. She hadn't been able to find his name when she'd been fighting the dreams. Her bond with their mother had been so strong, too strong. It had been flooding her veins with constant poison and her mind with a dense fog. But Emmaline felt different now.

She'd known the moment Derek came to Morland and the Queen had heard her. Emmaline usually dreamed of her mother and the dreams had become so much worse after Derek had returned. Emmaline didn't always remember them when she awoke in the morning but she could feel the soot on her fingers. And when she couldn't hold them back they flooded through her bond and into Derek. But the dreams had worked. The dreams had helped. Derek had used them to chisel a small crack, a tiny seam and the Goodness had wiggled in.

Everything was going to be okay, well everything except for that portal. It was not well. It was a dim light. It was blinking and sputtering and it needed to go to sleep. She held her thumb up to measure it and then counted on her fingers. She grabbed her sister's hand.

"It's dying," she said nodding to the tree. "And then the portal will sleep." She counted on her fingers again and said "Yes. Eight trips. There or back. But the tree can only carry a person eight more times. It's done such a good job." She said nodding at it in gratitude.

"Really?" Brigitte said her shoulders sagged. "Well I think the two of us should stay then. We shouldn't waste them."

"No. Please, Brigitte, you need to come," Elinor said walking over. "When he wakes up he is going to need to see you."

"I'll see my brother again someday. I know it. But the portal is weak and fading. And I have a feeling we will need every bit of energy it has left. We will be waiting here."

"Don't you want to know that he wakes up," Elinor said.

"If she is sure, I am sure," she said motioning to Emmaline. Emmaline nodded. She was *pretty* sure. Everything was working out great and she felt like it would keep going good. Good liked to add to itself. Of course, all the bad wasn't gone so maybe it would stack on top of itself instead. But there was time. She didn't know how much. More if Peter stayed. But she didn't know what he would do. She couldn't read his face even if she could read one of his futures. It looked like a good one.

Emmaline went still and suddenly turned to the East. It was open. "About time," Emmaline said scoldingly. It had missed all the excitement and Emmaline almost wanted to ignore it. But it was singing so loudly and persistently that she forgave it.

"What?" Brigitte asked.

"The door is open," Emmaline said.

"Which door?" Brigitte asked.

"*The* door," Emmaline said. She didn't understand the confusion. There was only the one.

"The door in the mines?" Garrison asked.

Emmaline beamed and nodded.

"Where does it go?" Brigitte asked.

"Somewhere else, of course," Emmaline said.

Peter

Peter overheard their conversation in rapt attention. Everything was already bad but hearing that the portal was weakening was one too many blows. He had to take one of those three spots back. Because if Derek was really dead then he had nothing on Earth. He glanced at Elinor who hadn't even been able to meet his eyes. Yeah, he had nothing and no one if Derek didn't wake up.

361

Why not come back to Morland? Or to the somewhere else of Emmaline's crazy door. Could he possibly do more harm than he'd already done? Then at least Elinor would be safe from him. He'd go back to Earth now but he'd be taking one of those spots back. It was a relief, an escape plan. A way out he didn't deserve.

Emmaline grabbed Peter's hand and said, "You could come back you know? You'd have a place here."

Peter couldn't think of what to say to her. It was eerie how close her words were to his thoughts. Because with Derek's lifeless body on the ground in front of him, all he could think about was running away. Peter couldn't even stir excitement that he had just been teleported somewhere.

"You could come back. Back to me," Emmaline whispered as she kissed his cheek in farewell. "Take one of the three spots." When he didn't respond, her tone became pleading. "No, you don't understand, you *have* to come back. I can't see Morland's future without you. Almost like it's missing. You have to come back. Do you understand now?" she asked.

Morland didn't need him. Nowhere needed him. He was a friendless murderer, but if Derek didn't wake up… Peter turned away from Emmaline's words. He still felt like it was her premonition that had led to Derek's death.

"Oh, one more thing," she said grabbing Peter's hand again as he turned his back to her. "She still has some of the Goodness with her. That's the key. The Goodness is the power of change. She could use it if she wanted to."

"What does that mean?" Peter asked.

"It means what it means," she said. She suddenly went rigid like a metal rod had been inserted into her spine. Her eyes turned cloudy and she squeezed his hand so tightly he yelped. "There are more. There are many. The Darkness will rise again," she said in a voice that gave him chills and then she just walked away. Just walked away. *Great. Can't wait for that,* Peter thought shaking his head but let the world burn if Derek stayed dead.

Peter couldn't stop himself from looking to see if Elinor had noticed Emmaline's premonition or kiss but Elinor's grief oozed from her, her gaze roaming aimlessly before settling back on Derek.

Winter

She still couldn't believe the battle was over. The battle was over and she had done nothing, well almost nothing. She'd had her stupid swords and her stupid strength and that had been all. The stones were silent when she most needed them and her hair was growing in white and she hadn't made the Queen remember her dead family. So her life had no purpose and no point. She walked a couple steps into the woods and out of sight of everyone. She couldn't look at them and their dead prince.

Ryan found her and she could see the fire in his face from a way off. She wished he'd just run home through his stupid tree or whatever it was. She didn't need to hear whatever he had to say, she could read the contempt on his face.

"So did you kill her?" Ryan asked and Winter almost growled in response. If he wanted a fight she could fight.

"She's dead," Winter said. "No thanks to you."

He motioned to his body that was covered in a black slime. Whatever that meant. She was glad he was mad and self-righteous; it was easier. She understood those feelings. He'd never really known her or understood her. But then he reached over and took her hand.

"Are you happy?" he asked and the fire in his eyes had softened to an ember. She meant to say something smart and cruel that showed him that she had been right, that now that her vengeance had been paid it had all been worth it but instead she clenched her fists as tears spilled from her eyes and truth from her mouth.

"No," she said unable to look at him. She'd never been so unhappy. She'd been angrier and sadder but never this unhappy. Everything had been for nothing. The Queen hadn't faced judgment. She'd just been obliterated by the Goodness. There hadn't even been a drop of her blood spilled in the conservatory. It was like Morland wanted to pretend she'd never existed. But she had existed and so had Winter's family. And who was going to remember them now?

She heard him exhale as he grabbed her roughly and pulled her to his chest.

"You are infuriating. You know that?" he said with a ghost of a smile in his voice. "I had a whole speech. I'd been working on it since you left. I was going to tell you 'I told you so'. I was going to make you hear me when I told you that there was more to life than vengeance. I was going to be really self-righteous and unbearable but then when I asked if you were happy you said 'no.' That wasn't in the script," He sighed and she took a couple shuddering breaths to stop crying.

"Remember when we were at the river that night?" Ryan asked without letting go. "You told me you were nothing more than the promise you'd made. Winter, did you promise someone vengeance? Did someone make you promise to kill the Queen for what had happened? Because no one had the right to claim your life like that."

Winter released Ryan and sank to the ground. She didn't want him to hold her like that or to talk to her with that voice. Because he was leaving and she wished he was gone already. But she found herself telling him anyway as he sat down across from her.

"When I got back to camp that night, I was too late. Everyone was dead already except my cousin, Oak. He told me to remember them. With his dying breath he said 'remember us'. But he had to know that I would never forget, so I needed to make sure no one could forget, that she could never forget. But… The Goodness has forsaken me and my magic is gone and my blessing is gone and it all means nothing. It doesn't mean anything. Ryan, you don't mean anything!" she said with her face only inches from him.

"What did you argue with Emmaline about the day you left?" Ryan asked.

Winter huffed into his face. How could he know these things? How could he ask these questions?

"She wouldn't tell me how to get it back,"

"Get what back? Your magic?"

"Yes," she said through tight teeth. "It's gone. Completely now. It had started to fade when we arrived at the Glen. I was so close. So close and… Emmaline told me to wash off the blood or the stones would stop listening. She told me to wash it off and let it go. But she speaks in riddles and my magic is gone so what does it matter now."

Ryan took her hands. "You know exactly what she meant, Winter. Your cousin didn't ask you to remember how he died. Because you were right, who could ever forget that. No, he asked you to remember that they lived, how they lived. They died helping others. You have forgotten how they lived and instead shaped your life around how they died. They didn't want this. You know that. You know that, Winter."

She pulled her hands to her face. "It's so much harder." It was easier to remember the blood. The blood fueled her rage and it gave her strength. But to remember how they lived hurt. It tore her into pieces. It didn't get easier. But what was she now without that hate and vengeance? If she wasn't 'Warrior Winter', who was she? And it hit her. She could be who she was before.

"My parent's names were Rose and Flint. I haven't thought of them as people in so long. I am their daughter and they… they would never have chosen this path for me. But Ryan how can I go back?"

It had to be too late. She'd killed men. She'd killed them with her sword and stone. Her parents would be ashamed of her. She'd used her power for only evil since the day they'd died. Why hadn't her magic left her *that* day? Instead it had waited until… until she was going to use it for cold blooded murder. Every man she'd killed had been in self-defense. But the Queen was different. Winter had had bloodlust and had planned to the smallest detail how she'd kill her. Winter had had weeks to change her mind. She'd seen Elinor's pursuit of the Goodness first hand and had chosen the wrong path over and over. She didn't deserve her magic. She should have died today. She'd planned on dying today.

"Forgive yourself and forgive the Goodness," Ryan said. "If I've learned anything in this whole mess, it's that the Goodness is real and it's never too late. You've seen my sister change. You saw her from day one. Do you even recognize her now? I don't. She let go of her bitterness and became the amazing woman I know you can be too. The Queen is gone. If you ever had an obligation for vengeance it is paid in full. You are free."

Free. The only freedom she'd ever expected was with death's embrace. She had been slowly turning her back to the Goodness, killing as she pleased and then raging when her magic weakened. Winter closed her eyes and took a breath. She was scared. What if she couldn't be forgiven? What if it was too late? But when she cried out to the Goodness, it answered her.

The stones around her rose into the air and she gasped as she felt Morland's foundation. She opened her eyes in a flash and laughed. Ryan's face held bewilderment and confusion but she grabbed his face and kissed him hard. She was surprised when his arms wrapped around her waist and her laugh turned to stone in her stomach, first and last kiss. *Well*, she thought, *I'll just have to make it count.*

Elinor

There was little gentleness available while shoving a limp, lifeless Derek back though the tree portal. Peter and Jol had gone down first to catch him while Ryan and Garrison eased him through.

Elinor stared at the portal and she watched it dim with each passage. It was true. Its power was limited and almost gone. Elinor went through last to make sure everyone was successful.

The pain was instantaneous and monumental.

It felt like getting hit by a truck full of bricks. It made her sway on her knees and forget everything. Had it ever really been better? Had this pain ever not existed? Tears streamed from her eyes and she couldn't think of anything but the pounding and the horror that it was back. It was all back. Her hand ran across her unblemished stomach and she looked around to see that everyone was back to how they were before they left except...

Elinor pushed her headaches down because the thing she should have noticed first was that Derek still hadn't woken up. Elinor released a shuddering sigh and walked to Derek. His body was perfect. Not a scratch or drop of blood. His hair was cut short again and she hardly recognized him. He wasn't hurt here so why hadn't he woken up? No one was touching him as they watched and waited. After two minutes Elinor kneeled beside him and held his face between her hands. *Wake up. Please wake up,* she begged as her tears dropped on his face. The blood was gone and his neck wound was gone but he didn't wake up.

"D...Derek," she said softly. She could see Peter in her peripheral looking on and wringing his hands.

"Please wake up," she said. How long should they wait before... Before what? The question terrified her. Before getting Derek's parents? Before calling an ambulance or undertaker? She sat back on her heels staring as his chest didn't rise.

"Peter," she said turning to face him with a quivering lower lip. "What do we do now?" Peter just stared on, silent and horrified.

"Jol?" Elinor asked turning to the Mage. His years had indeed faded but his blank face was the same. But even so she could guess his thoughts. His plan had failed and he'd killed Derek as surely as Peter had.

"Please, Derek. You need to wake up. Please. You are home," Elinor whispered into Derek's ear. "You are home on Earth."

Derek's eyes opened slowly blinking as he focused on his surroundings. He settled on Elinor and smiled.

"Hello, my little mist girl," he breathed.

"Oh!" Elinor said covering her mouth as one sob escaped her lips. "James?"

"He's back," Derek said closing his eyes. "My soul is back. I'm back," he said as tears fell from his eyes.

"I didn't know they could do that," said Jol smiling broadly helping Derek up. "It's good to see you awake."

"Did we win?" Derek asked.

"Yes. We won," Jol said.

Derek

They'd won. Derek couldn't believe it. His soul was back. The Queen was gone. A shout of pure exultation burst from this lips. He was free. He knew the Darkness was no longer in his blood and he wanted to crow again but turning he saw Peter kneeling on the ground.

"What is it? Are you okay?" Derek said grabbing his shoulder and looking him over.

"Am *I* okay? No, are you okay? Are you really alive?" Peter said hopelessly.

"Yes," Derek laughed. He laughed. He was laughing. Derek was amazed at how different he felt already. He'd thought he was whole when his soul returned but then the Darkness had still been inside him. But now he could feel it was gone. He was himself again after so long a time. "I can honestly say that I have never felt better."

"Derek, do you know what happened? At the castle?" Peter asked still not rising.

"Bits of it. I know my soul came back and then the Darkness was inside me. Then Elinor came with the light," he said turning to look at her. "Oh Elinor. Thank you," he said pulling her into a hug without thinking. Was that his soul or him? As soon as he'd woken up he'd suddenly known all of James's memories, especially the ones about Elinor. He released her quickly when she appeared to be very startled.

"Yes but what happened next?" Peter interrupted.

"Then I guess the Queen tried to take my soul and I don't know. But we won, right?" Derek said looking between them all.

"Yes. The Queen disappeared and the Darkness fled the land," Jol said.

"So why aren't we celebrating?" Derek said taking Elinor's hands in his as he swung her around. "Why aren't we dancing?" he laughed.

"Derek, I killed you," Peter said and Derek stopped. "I slit your throat with a knife. You were dead and I killed you."

Derek took two steps toward Peter.

"Your friend saved your life and the whole world," Jol said looking the youngest Derek had ever seen him. He looked between fifty and sixty. But his eyes were steel and he was watchful of what Derek would do as he spoke. "He used you as the sacrificial lamb to defeat the Queen and it worked. You came back and without the Darkness. Peter is why we won."

Derek ran his hand along his throat and taking another step pulled Peter into a hug. "You only did what you had to do. I think that I can understand what you did more than anyone else. Do you need to hear that I forgive you? Because I do. I'm alive and whole. Thank you, Peter. We did it!" Derek shouted pulling back. "I can't believe it worked! I can't believe we are home!" he said smiling turning around to view the Waxhaw woods and his house just visible through the trees. But Derek stopped suddenly and his face paled. Ryan was struggling to stand and then fell down as he started vomiting. Vomiting up blood.

"Ryan!" Elinor yelled as she ran to hold him up as he started to collapse. "Ryan, what is it? What's wrong?" But he couldn't answer as more blood poured out.

Chapter 29

Derek

Derek hadn't planned on telling his parents anything. No time had passed again and he had no proof that he'd been anywhere. Again. But they sure were startled when Derek, Peter, and Jol walked into the house covered in Ryan's blood.

Derek hadn't prepared a lie so a bit of the truth fell out.

"Derek! Derek, are you alright?" His mom said rushing over to check him for wounds.

"Oh this blood isn't mine. I'm fine," Derek said brushing her off.

"Well whose blood is it?" his dad said. "What is going on? What happened? You've only been gone twenty minutes. And who is this?" he asked motioning to Jol.

"This is Elinor's grandfather," Derek said. "Is it okay if he stays with us for a couple nights until things get settled over at her house?"

"Okay but Derek, who's blood is that if it isn't yours?" His mom said moving closer to him slowly with her hands raised.

Jol and Peter stood silently behind him and Derek continued with enough of the truth. "It's Ryan's blood. I don't know what happened. They were walking home and all the sudden he started vomiting blood. We heard the commotion and helped Elinor carry him back to the house. They rushed him to the hospital and that's all we know."

"That's terrible. But you are okay?" his mom asked.

"Yeah. I'm fine. You guys are okay, right?" Derek asked looking at Peter and Jol. They each had their share of Ryan's blood on them. It had taken all three of them to lift him once he'd passed out.

"I'm good," Peter said unconsciously rubbing his fingers into his palm but the blood held fast. Derek wondered if some of that was his own blood but no, that body and all that blood were Morland property. His Earth body was as unblemished as ever. His hand rose to his tattoo. He could not think about that yet.

"Yes. I am fine also," Jol said. But Derek just stared at him. It was so strange to see him younger. Derek probably couldn't call him old man anymore. He'd probably lost at least fifteen years. Portal magic was strange and Derek didn't have the brainpower to work it out right then.

His dad was the first one to recover from the awkwardness and stretched out his hand. "Hello, I'm Nathan and this is my wife, Jenny. And you are Elinor's grandfather?"

"Yes. My name is Jol. My son is Elinor's father."

"Well it's very nice to meet you, Jol. And you are welcome to stay here as long as you need to. Hopefully we'll hear some news about Ryan soon," his mom said trying to reassure him. She assumed that that was why he seemed so out of it. And that was probably part of it but Ryan wasn't his blood and Derek had a feeling that it was more the shock of really being back on Earth that was throwing him.

"I think we'd probably all like to get cleaned up," Derek said leading Jol and Peter upstairs. "Jol," Derek said opening the door to the bathroom, "Everything you need should be in here and I'll find some fresh clothes for you. And take your time. I think we'll have a while to wait yet."

Peter was about to speak when Derek's parents came down the hallway and motioned for him to follow them into the bonus room.

"Could you spare a change of clothes for Jol, Dad?" Derek asked as he stood standing while his parents found seats on the couch.

"Yes. Of course," his dad said leaving the room and returning quickly after he'd set some clothes outside of the bathroom door.

"And Derek, that's what we'd like to talk to you about," his mom said when his dad had joined her on the couch. Peter lingered in the hallway behind him and Derek grabbed his shoulder and pulled him into the room with him. He wasn't doing this alone again. Derek didn't sit down even though he knew it was making his parents a little uncomfortable.

He had wondered sometimes if his soul ever came back if that would fix things with his parents. He'd wondered if his bitterness and anger towards them was a result of his absentee soul. But facing them as a whole man, he didn't feel magically reconciled to them. He was tired of acting and lying and he didn't have the patience to try again.

"Yes?" he said.

"Derek, where did you find Elinor's grandfather? Was he in the woods?" his father asked.

Derek sighed and kneaded his forehead. He'd thought his parents had mastered the art of ignorance and distraction. For so long they had just let him live his life and pursue whatever hobbies he liked without question or notice. He really hadn't anticipated this line of questioning. He should have been happy that they noticed what he did but he was irritated that they were forcing him to lie to their faces when he was so tired. He wanted to take a bath, talk to Elinor, and then sleep for a week. But Peter was a good friend and spoke first.

"We rescued him from a prison a couple weeks ago," Peter said nonchalantly.

"What prison?" his father asked in a steady voice.

"Umm... It's just called 'The Prison'. Does it have an official name?" Peter asked Derek.

"I think it was called 'Mountain Keep' before it was a prison," Derek said. "But that was a long time ago. Seventy years at least, before... you know."

"So an escaped prisoner has just been walking around behind our house for a couple weeks?" his mother asked in disbelief. Derek didn't know how he should feel that his parents didn't doubt that he was capable and inclined to break a person out of a prison. He supposed it was a compliment to his skills that they didn't think it was ridiculous.

"Um. Not *these* woods. But you could say he has been walking around in *some* woods since we freed him," Peter said carefully choosing his words. Derek was shocked that he hadn't lied yet. Maybe it was possible to tell them the truth in a way they could swallow. But then he saw the look rising on his father's face. No, they were never going to believe him.

"Derek, what is this? What is going on? Are you having another... episode? You need to tell us if you are," his father's tone of worry and resignation snapped Derek.

"I knew it! God! I knew it," Derek said angrily. It wasn't the red-rage that filled him but just regular human anger and hurt. "You'll never change. You can't. You had me there for a moment. I thought maybe... but no. I don't know why I tried. Thanks, Peter," he said letting Peter know that this wasn't his fault. "I appreciate you trying. But they cannot hear."

"Derek. You need to calm down. How can we hear if you won't tell us?" his mom said pleadingly. "Tell us what happened and we will listen to you."

"Really? You promise?" Derek said sarcastically.

"Yes," his mom said. "We will listen for as long as it takes. Please let us in, Derek. What is going on?"

"Fine. You asked for this. But you'll remember that I'm nineteen and an adult now and you are no longer my legal guardians."

Both of his parents flinched and Derek felt guilt rack through him. Guilt was new. It had been a while since he felt truly sorry for causing someone pain. It felt nice and bad.

"Okay so when we got back from Boone, we all went to Morland. Remember Morland?" he asked rhetorically at his parents' paling faces. "I had to go back because Elinor got attacked by a creature of the Darkness and her soul was going to die if we didn't go back through the portal. But once we were through we got captured and I was recognized. Remember I'm a prince in Morland?" he asked without stopping. He was going to get it out. All of it. They said they'd listen and he was going to give them every bit of truth they could stand.

"Well I was taken back to the castle, where the Queen, she calls herself my mother, was planning on flooding me with the Darkness and ripping out my soul on the full moon. But my friends came through for me at the last minute. Elinor invaded my brain and helped me to embrace the Goodness and Peter slit my throat. Those sound like bad things but they are really the sign of good friends.

"Then I'm dead for a little bit. Or not really dead, kind of. We don't know everything about it. Anyway they shove me back through the portal and I wake up good as new with my soul nicely packed back inside my body. Then Ryan starts vomiting blood and here we are."

Derek exhaled loudly and waited. He knew what they were going to say before they started. His stomach was tight and his eyes felt full.

"Derek..." his mom said but before she could continue Jol walked into the room with fire shooting out of his hands.

Jol

Jol couldn't sit back and listen to that for one second longer. Elinor had told him all about Derek's life as they'd journeyed together and he couldn't believe that Derek's parents hadn't believed him. And witnessing it in person was profoundly sad. He understood how two normal non-magical people couldn't believe their son had traveled through a portal to another planet but he'd hoped for Derek's sake that they would at least try. So he'd decided that he'd give them a little show and tell.

"You'll forgive me," Jol said after a moment showing them that the fire hadn't burned him. He turned it on and off a couple times and then formed a perfect fire ball that he let hover between his hands.

"I'm not just Elinor's grandfather. I'm a Morlander and a fire mage. And your son is not a liar. He is a brave man and I'm glad to know him. Everything he has said is the truth. I can do this all day," he said turning the fire off and on again but then he sat down suddenly. "Oh I forgot that Earth doesn't like Morland magic. I *can't* actually do that all day but it's real and I'll keep showing you until you believe your son. Is it so difficult to believe that there can be life on another world? That there could be a way to travel to that world? Do you really think that you know everything that is possible in the whole universe? Is there not even a slim chance that your son is telling the truth?" Jol said and the fire roared in his hands mirroring his mood.

"It's real? Morland?" his dad asked Jol.

"Yes," Jol said exasperatingly. "It's all real. Every bloody word he's ever told you about Morland is real."

"Oh God!" his mom said crying, covering her face as sobs racked her body. "I'm sorry," she said standing up as she pulled Derek into a hug. "I'm so sorry, Derek. How could we have known?"

"Can you tell me it again?" his dad asked Derek. "All of it. Can you tell me everything again?"

Derek

Elinor pulled in the driveway a little after midnight. He guessed her parents were staying the night with Ryan at the hospital. The little kids were asleep in backseat. She had just started to lift Katie out when Derek walked out of the woods. Elinor looked at him, sighed, and then continued to lift a sleeping Katie into her arms. Derek carried Colton and followed her.

"Thank you," Elinor said sitting in the living room in the dark after the kids had been tucked in.

Derek sat down next to her and waited.

"I don't think I can say it," she said bringing a hand to her mouth as she looked past him into the kitchen. "I can't imagine what it was like for my parents seeing us carry a bleeding unconscious Ryan into the kitchen." She exhaled deeply.

"It's really rare. Colton hadn't even heard of it," she said with the ghost of a ghost of a smile. "Ryan was exposed to something at school, a bite from a rodent or a scrape against something infected. It spread in his blood and into the tissue in his lungs. The doctors said we would have had to catch it immediately to have made any difference and he's had this for a couple months. He'll be home tomorrow."

Derek exhaled the breath he had been holding. "So Ryan is okay, then?"

She looked at him as if was speaking another language. "No," she said. "He is not okay. He... is very sick. The doctors say," she swallowed and tried again. "The doctors say he has months... at the most," she said staring at him unblinkingly.

Elinor

She wished she hadn't said it out loud. The word 'months' had been rattling in her brain since the doctors had first said it and everyone had started crying. *Months. Months. Months.* Her brother would be dead in months. She wished she hadn't said it. It made it real. She didn't realize she'd started crying until she felt her sobs muffled on Derek's chest. He was holding her and it felt like he had released the pressure valve. She had been holding it together for hours for the little ones. Her despair was too real and too raw to show the children. Derek just held her and she breathed him in.

"You are different," she said after many minutes passed. She didn't pull back. She just spoke into his shoulder. "I'm glad you aren't dead."

"Me too," he said. "Is there really nothing they can do?"

She pulled back to look at him then and said, "They are going to make him comfortable."

"Oh Elinor," Derek said pulling her back as she started to cry again. "I'm so so sorry."

"It wasn't supposed to be like this," Elinor said leaning back with fierceness in her eyes. "He was supposed to be okay. He was away at school and protected from all my craziness but I pulled him right into it, just like I did with everyone. I say I want to bear it alone but I keep dumping this on everyone," she said reaching for a tube of Bengay that she kept in the coffee table drawer. She had them hidden all over the house. She stared at it and clenched her fists. She was so angry to be using it again. She was so angry to have a broken head again.

"I can't believe it was ever gone," she said massaging the blue gel into her temples and then all over her face and neck. "It was just a dream, wasn't it?" she said running a hand across her smooth stomach. "If it was all just a dream then why does *this* feel like the nightmare?" She stared at him with anger in her eyes and dared him to answer. She wanted a fight. She needed Derek to tell her that everything was her fault and that she was just a dumb girl who ruined everything. She would feel better if she could yell at someone but Derek wasn't the man he was and instead he took her hand and pulled her back to settle her into the couch.

"This is not your fault," Derek said as Elinor shook her head but she still settled next to him. "None of this is your fault. Ryan was infected before you even went to Morland, right? Didn't you notice him acting strange?"

And Elinor had. She remembered the night at the beginning of the school year when they had played poker and he told her he was just so tired. He'd seemed spent and empty and she had just assumed it was a heavier school load.

How could she not have known that he was on his way to dying even then? She should have noticed. But all she'd cared about was herself. She might have stopped this. But maybe all she'd have been able to do was buy him some time. Tears just kept falling from her eyes and she didn't know how to stop them. She had to stop before the kids woke up. What if she could never stop crying, ever? It felt like that.

"There is no chance that it has anything to do with Morland, right?" Elinor asked Derek. She needed to hear someone say it. Not that Derek knew everything about Morland but he did know more than most. Elinor was grateful for the moment Derek really took to think it through.

"No. I'd say ninety-nine percent no," he said. "You say he was acting off before you went and I remember him saying how good he suddenly felt crossing over into Morland. I think it hit him so hard coming home because it was a sudden shock to his system to have a sick body again. Did your headaches feel worse when you first came back?"

She nodded. Her head had hurt so terribly at that first moment of crossing over. It felt a more normal horrible now but that first moment had been a shock. It was just the sudden presence of pain where there had been none.

"Do you think he would have had more time if I hadn't pulled him across the universe a couple times? Maybe I made it worse."

"I think you gave him an adventure."

Without looking at her, Derek pulled her close and tucked her into his shoulder. She stared into the back of the couch and cried into his shirt. His arms hung loose around her and she found that she couldn't actually move. She was so tired and her head hurt so horribly bad and it was really nice to be the huggie instead of the hugger. Elinor dumped all her despair and rage on him and he just took it. When she woke up with the sun creeping through the curtains she had forgotten to close, she was alone with a pillow under her head and a blanket wrapped around her. He'd even taken off her shoes. *Who is this man?*

Chapter 30

Elinor

Ryan was back the next evening and he was drugged to the high heavens. Her parents looked about as poorly as he did. Her dad hugged her long and hard and said, "Elinor, we need to know what happened." She nodded her and texted Derek.

Elinor turned to face her family and said, "I know these have been the worst longest days in created history but y'all need to hear the whole truth of things. I'm sorry to bring company over but I couldn't possibly tell you all of it on my own."

Elinor wondered if she should prepare her father somehow but while she was still trying to find the words to say "So this is your dad. He didn't leave you. He just got sucked back to his home planet and he's never found a way back until I brought him and he's also the exact age he was when he left so..." Jol, Derek, and Peter were already there. She stared at her dad and waited. Would he even recognize Jol? He'd only been twelve when Jol had left. But as the rest of her family looked to her to start, it hit her dad like a punch in the stomach.

Colton spoke first, of course. "Who are you?" he asked Jol.

Her father spoke in a choked whisper. "That, Colton, is my father. Today is not really a good day," he said to the world.

"What?" said her stepmom. "And where have you been?"

"It's a long story," said Jol looking between his son with longing and his granddaughter for help.

"I'm sure it is," said her father. "How did you find my daughter?"

"She found me actually. Rescued me from a prison cell."

"What?" said her stepmom again. "What is going on? I thought you all went to Boone for the weekend?"

"We started in Boone…" said Elinor trying to find a way to diffuse the situation a little. "But we only stayed about eight hours before we came back." She brought her hand to her forehead. She wished she had thought about how to explain this properly but she just took a deep breath and plunged in.

The story wove together in bits and pieces that Elinor hoped made a semblance of sense. The guys added in explanations and for the most part her family sat silently as they absorbed the mass of information being dumped on them.

"So that's it. It's the truth, really…" Elinor said when they had finally revealed all her secrets and adventures and ended the story at the present.

"Honey..." said her stepmom and Elinor recoiled as if she'd been slapped.

"It's the truth," Elinor said as tears started to pour from her eyes. Elinor was a little surprised she had tears still in there. She'd been pretty sure she'd cried them all out on Derek last night. "I knew it. I knew you wouldn't believe me." She looked to Derek and wished she didn't see understanding on his face.

"Is there anything you can prove? Anything you brought back?" asked Colton, the scientist as always.

"No, you can't bring things from one world to another. My eyes change colors a little bit," she said. "Wait, my ring. I brought this over with me, from Morland. It changes colors."

"Stop it! Everyone," said Katie standing on the couch. "When has Elinor ever lied about anything? When? If she says she sees a different world when she blinks then she does! If she says she went to a magic world and brought back our grandpa then she did!"

Elinor reached over to squeeze Katie's hand. "Thanks, Katie." Jol met Elinor's eyes and he opened and closed his hand. She shook her head. Showing them that magic was real would only distract everyone from the story that had been told. But it did comfort her knowing that she did have proof, if they still didn't believe her when she was done.

"Do you have any questions?" Derek asked, taking the attention off Elinor, which she silently thanked him for. He was a so different but still Derek.

"So, you fell through a portal and went back to your magic land and never came back? And now you come back with my daughter looking... looking exactly the same as when you left," her dad asked Jol.

"Not exactly," Jol said. "I came through a portal to get to Earth but I never wanted to leave. I came here on accident the first time. My portal landed me in Ireland and I met your mother. She was studying abroad and... She was it. I came back with her at the end of the semester and we got married. I was older than her but she didn't seem to mind. Your mother knew that I was from somewhere else. Somewhere other.

"I think there is a time limit. That your home world wants to pull you back," Jol continued and Derek turned to look sharply at him. This theory was new. "I started to feel it towards the end. One day, I was sitting in the chair in the living room when a pull came. Like a million hooks deep inside pulling me backwards. I tried to fight back but I didn't stand a chance. The next time I opened my eyes I was back in Morland. The same age I was when I left. I spent years and years trying to find a way back but the portal I had come through was gone and everything I tried failed. I never stopped trying to come back. I know you don't believe me but you and your mother were my life. I love you, George."

Her dad started to choke up as he said, "I think we've had enough for today." He got up from his couch and came over to Elinor. "I believe you, El. I don't know anything more than that but I know you and I believe you. Do you need anything?"

"No, Dad," she said accepting his deep, long hug. "I think we all just need some sleep."

"Jol, where are you staying?" her stepmom asked.

"He's staying at my house, Mrs. Lirdin," said Derek. "Just a couple houses down if you need us. I know you know this but you have really amazing kids. Goodnight."

Elinor walked them down the back steps. "Goodnight Grandpa," she said giving Jol a hug goodbye. He kissed the top of her head. "I know he'll come around. He is just going to need a little time."

"Goodnight, my girl," he said and then added to the guys. "I'm going to take a walk. I need a little air."

She hugged Derek and Peter. "Thank you, guys. I couldn't have done it without you. Tonight or any of it. We haven't really had a chance to talk. Soon. But go home, sleep in real beds in houses with electricity and plumbing. Goodnight."

She pulled Derek's sleeve just as he was going out, "I really am glad you are okay. I don't know what I would have done if you hadn't woken up. Oh and thank you. For saving my life."

"Goodnight, El," he said giving her hand a squeeze as he joined the dark night.

Derek

It was late, well after midnight, and Derek wasn't able to sleep. And neither was Elinor. She was up there. Her curtains were open and the light was still on in her room. Derek hated creeping outside, watching but he needed her. Ever since he had woken up on this side of the portal, he'd felt his need for her like a magnetic pull.

He had fallen for her twice now, each part of him had separately. But now that he was whole, now that his body housed his mind and his soul again, the love he felt for Elinor felt like too much. He had the love of two men, stuffed into one heart. He was glad that she could tell he was different. He had never stood half a chance before, either part of him. But now... he hoped he was enough.

It was so selfish of him, he reminded himself as he almost called her again. She must be so tired and if she needed him she would call. But her light was still on. It was the only one on in the house. She must be exhausted after the days she'd had. She should be fighting to keep her eyes open but it was three a.m. and she was still up and he couldn't stop himself. She had left her curtains open, after all.

It rang twice.

"Derek?" Elinor said from her lit bedroom.

"Hey."

"I'm glad you called," she said after a moment.

"I was in the woods and I saw your light was still on. I... took a chance that you wouldn't mind too much."

"I've been thinking on impossible things," Elinor said without preamble.

Derek stopped his pacing and settled down at the base of a thick tree and gazed up at the light.

"Like what impossible things, little Alice?" he said smiling.

"Like that a couple days ago I was on another planet. I had a large wound on my stomach and a deep puncture from an arrow in my leg and claw marks all over but now... I don't bear a single scar. Is that why you tattooed her name? Because the lack of a scar made it feel like it might have never happened."

"Yes," he said and wondered how she could know him so well. How she could possibly understand his brokenness?

"I was thinking about," she continued not acknowledging that he had spoken, "how my brother could be dying. How he could be dying today when he wasn't yesterday. How in any world, ever, my brother could be dying." She wasn't crying but her voice was so empty and cold. He wanted to make that voice go away.

"No one had mentioned it yet," Elinor said. "But there is only one choice from here and I'm terrified that I might just be too selfish to say it out loud."

"That he might not be sick if he went back to Morland," he guessed.

"Yes," she breathed out as a curse. "You know that he'd been through the portal last year, right? When we first moved here he popped over just for a minute and then came back. We never talked about it. I didn't really put it all together until an hour ago. A couple months ago Ryan was complaining about cleaning out the basement of his rental house at school and he showed us this big cut on his elbow he'd gotten in the process.

"When we first crossed into Morland I noticed the scar was missing. I thought maybe it had healed but... It had disappeared because Morland had put Ryan into the previous body they had on file like it had done with you. How does Morland do this? Aren't we just traveling through a portal, like a magic door? Obviously not, I guess. Why is my body back to normal? Why is yours? We should be covered in scars from Morland but we aren't.

"But honestly the how doesn't really matter. Because Ryan will be better if he goes back. The original file of Ryan was from before he got that cut. If he goes back, he'll be healthy like he was during our Morland adventure. But I can't... I don't ever want to go back there. Oh Derek, I understand you so well now. Why you were the way you were. I feel her too. *Morland*. She's never done with you. I've been telling myself that the worst parts of it are over, the Queen and the Darkness and…"

He was wondering when she was going to mention *him*. He'd known the truth from James as soon as he was whole on Earth.

"How much do you remember of James's adventures?" Elinor asked reading his mind.

"All of it," Derek said and he wondered if that made her blush but her next comment made him realize that she was thinking of another man.

"Then you know about Ian and..."

"Yes. I remember with perfect clarity what that bastard did to you. It was a spell, Elinor. None of that was your fault. If it didn't mean going back, then I'd make sure he paid for it." Derek wondered if she had really cared for Ian. That night when they had danced had been so painful to watch and then when she sent James away... Maybe if Ian hadn't turned out to be the horrible human he was, she might have considered Morland as an option. But Ian was the worst sort of man. He'd put Elinor under some kind of spell and she'd kissed him and... But that hadn't been real.

"It feels like my fault," she said quietly. "Maybe this is weird to talk to you about."

"It's not weird for me but I understand if you don't want to tell me," Derek said but he wanted nothing more than to hear her every thought on this subject. He wanted to know what she'd felt for Ian and what she'd felt for James. But he didn't ask her that. Instead he said, "It was not your fault. None of it. That necklace was dark magic and he used it to manipulate you."

"Yeah," she said. "But if I'd been stronger it might not have worked. It was so powerful. It made me... But you are right, as soon as the necklace was gone my mind was clear and I knew the truth. James, I mean you, saved me that night. Thank you."

She was quiet for a moment before she said. "This stupid ring feels extra heavy." He imagined her staring into its color-changing depths. "Why do I still have this? I shouldn't. Nothing else from Morland has come over. It's just another piece of this puzzle that makes zero sense. Nothing makes sense."

"You don't have to go back, Elinor," Derek said. "You owe Morland *nothing*."

"It would be easier if that was true," she said. "Morland wasn't the worst *all the time* but it was the worst a lot of the time. It's really hard there, everything. Not just the technology gap but so many little things that make Morland not the right choice for me. But Morland gave me a lot. Morland freed me even if it feels like my shackles slammed right back on the moment I returned."

"How is your head?" he asked.

Elinor's deep breathing carried across the yard into his ears.

"Worse... or the same, maybe, but I don't think so. Having been so long without the pain was intoxicating and cruel. While I was gone I had started to tell myself that going over to Morland had just unflipped whatever switch has been broken in my brain or that using my magic would lessen the overflow and maybe it would take a while to slowly build up into what it was. But nothing has changed for me. I still have Morland blood running through my veins. I still have Morland magic in that blood and Earth doesn't want anything to do with it.

"Maybe it would have been different if we'd never moved here. The open portal woke up my blood. Like calls to like. Maybe if I'd stayed in Atlanta none of this would have happened. Maybe I would have just stayed normal Elinor. Who knows? But... I really think it is worse now. Like using my magic exercised the muscle and it's stronger."

"Can you scry from this side?"

He could imagine her trying. Her eyes would blink and then they would change hues in strong pulses radiating from the center.

Elinor exhaled forcefully.

"Oh boy. Yes, I can but it hurts very bad. Way worse than just blinking. The castle is just how we left it. No one has come through. Maybe everyone is at the parade singing *"Ding Dong the Witch is Dead."*

"I'd go back for that," he said smiling in the dark and she must have heard it.

"Yeah, maybe I would too. But..."

"But Morland is the worst," he said and she let free a small laugh.

"It really is. Morland is the flipping worst. But I have to go back. That thought is... I guess only you could understand. Is this how you felt when I made you go through that dumb portal? I'm going back to Morland. I never thought I would. The whole time we were there and I didn't have headaches I just knew when I came home things would be fixed. Everything would be fixed. And then they weren't. Oh, Derek... This isn't the future I wanted! But I'd come right back, right? With no lost time? Maybe it would be okay. I'd spend a couple decades in Morland, get pulled back, spend some time with my family, and then pop back and forth for all eternity or until I died."

"I don't think it will work like that," Derek said. "We know practically nothing about portal magic. Jol says he got pulled back after seventeen years, that does not mean it would have happened to me. I might have stayed in Morland until the day I died. You can't count on coming back."

"Oh," she exhaled. "So Morland forever, huh?"

"But Elinor, you don't have to go back to Morland," he said.

"Don't I?" she scoffed. "I can't stay here and be that broken hurting girl forever. You've told me plenty of times that I'm not really living. That this thing I call a life doesn't mean anything. That I am nothing but the monuments I build to my pain."

"Elinor, please stop," Derek pleaded. "That wasn't really me. Please don't remind me."

"I know... I'm sorry. But you *were* right. If I stay it'll be the same battle every day and I'll lose for real this time because I'll know without a doubt that I'll never ever get better. That nothing on this planet can fix me. Knowing that... Knowing that there really is no hope. I couldn't do it. I can't do it. I keep telling myself that Morland won't be that bad. It'll be better. It'll be better this time. I have so many friends there. The Queen is gone and the Darkness is gone and the world will be changing into something better but..."

"But what?" Derek asked.

"You would never go back, would you?" she said after a breath.

He knew that she must know the answer but she had asked anyway. No, he never wanted to go back. Never in a million years. It didn't matter how long his mother had been dead, the whole world was tainted by the pain he had felt there. But there was Brigitte. He didn't let himself think about her. It was too much. It was too big.

And what about Morland itself? He'd be lying to himself if he didn't admit he felt some responsibility. Who would step up to fix things? Garrison? He might have the skills but Derek didn't think he wanted it. There was no other candidate he particularly trusted with the job and burn it all, he was still the prince. The last prince. Was it not his twisted birthright? His cursed burden to bear? Let anyone else take the rotten husk of a land, it would not be his grave but... what if she went back? The thought made his stomach roil. Elinor being a whole world away from him. Being in Morland when it was the last place she wanted to be. Going back for her head and her brother... He closed his eyes and said the truth.

"If you went back, I would go with you."

"Derek?" she asked.

"Elinor, I love you. I've loved you for a while. I loved you with my broken soul and all my emptiness. And I still do now. I would go to the gates of hell to be with you. I know this is catching you by surprise and I know you are too spent today to say anything back so don't. Just leave these words hanging between us. Think about it when your brain lets you think about things again. I'll be down the street, waiting. Goodnight, Elinor. I love you," he said again. He hung up and left. He turned back once as he headed towards home but the light was off.

Peter

"How is she?" Peter asked when Derek came back into his room. There was only one place Derek would have gone.

"Not great. Really bad actually. Her headaches are back in full force. She has realized that Ryan has to go back to Morland *and* that she has to go back to Morland."

390

"Morland won't be so bad now," Peter said.

Derek just raised his eyebrows.

"I know you both feel that way but Morland has such potential," Peter argued. At Derek's substantial eye rolls Peter changed his vein of conversation. "So there are only three spots. Ryan obviously takes one. Elinor takes one and then what?" Peter said.

"If Elinor goes, I go," Derek said.

"No! No, Derek! You go and leave me here?" Peter asked shaking his head. "That's not how this plays out." He rested his head in his hands because he knew that was exactly how it would play out. Peter wouldn't get that spot. But if Elinor was going to Morland then Peter wanted to go to Morland. He wanted it. He wanted it more than Derek did. Peter wanted Morland almost more than he wanted Elinor. It was... a dream come true. Morland with Elinor. He wanted one of those spots.

The moment he heard the portal had a limited number of uses, he had felt an overwhelming desire for one of them. He wanted it *almost* more than anything. But one of those spots was never going to be for him. Because then Derek would be alone. Peter couldn't do it. It was just like Derek had said, he was incapable of being a bastard but oh Peter wished he could try.

But if Elinor *picked* him... If Elinor chose to go to Morland with Peter, then Derek wouldn't feel the need to go. That was the only way Peter got to go, if Elinor asked him. But if she didn't then Derek would go to Morland and Peter would be trapped on Earth alone. That thought brought him to the brink of true despair. He wouldn't survive it. He would...

"If she picks me, do you let me go?" Peter asked.

"Yes but... I told her that I loved her tonight."

"You what?" Peter said as his mouth fell open. "And what did she say?"

"Nothing. I told her she didn't have to answer."

"That was a jerk move, Derek. You know that I love her."

"I didn't do it to hurt you, Peter. I swear. I just needed her to know. She knows that you love her, whether you've said it or not. I just needed to tell her. I'm sorry."

"Whatever. We'll just cross that bridge when we get there. Whatever," he said shaking his head. "For now, there has to be a way for her to stay if she wants to. There has to be. We need to talk to the old man or the less old, old man." It was really weird seeing Jol with a couple decades knocked off. "He has to know something. He still has secrets up his sleeve; I know it. There has to be a way to keep Elinor on Earth." *with me.* Peter added to himself.

Jol, of course, said there was no way. But Peter knew better. He pestered the old man all night. He repeated everything he knew about magic and the portals and Elinor's gift. They would think of something.

Derek

"So Jol just to review," Peter said. "Your portal looked like a regular meadow. You walk through and end up in Europe. Your magic disappears after a year like you'd emptied the tank and couldn't refill it. And then after you've been here for seventeen years you feel a tug and then you are popped back in the meadow as your younger self," Peter said flipping through the charts and lists he'd created over the last couple hours.

"We have been over this so many times. You know that's what happened," Jol said finally losing his patience after longer than Derek would have expected. Maybe he wasn't the only one who was different now.

"To sum up what we know about portal magic," Peter said unruffled as he riffled through the papers. "When a person travels from Planet A to Planet B via a portal, Planet B takes a snapshot or makes a file of that person at *that* moment and uses that version of that person exclusively.

"When person returns to Planet A, they are put back in their original body. That has been stored somewhere, somehow. The body that they used on Planet B is somewhere waiting for their return.

"Every time person travels to Planet B their previously used Planet B body is used. It's like the first time they cross, the portal *makes* a body and then saves it for the next time. Okay now according to Jol's story the Planet B Body cannot last forever. After X amount of years, seventeen in this case, he was pulled back to Planet A having had no time pass.

"And when *we* took the portal back we returned to our A bodies also with no time having passed. Where are our planet B bodies? In magic limbo? If we went back right now, Derek would probably turn into his prince self with all his scars. Ah it hurts my brain so hard. And you never met anyone besides Derek who has used a portal?" Peter said looking up from his notes to flick his eyes to Jol.

"No. Only Derek," Jol said.

Derek had been prepared to let it go. He was back. He was safe and it shouldn't matter what happened eleven years ago but somehow it still did.

"Why?" Derek asked the Mage, studying his eyes. He knew them well enough that he wouldn't miss a lie this time.

Jol sighed and Derek saw the lost years slide back into his eyes making him look like his old bitter self again.

"At first it was just caution. I didn't know you. You almost raved like a madman. I heard the words you were saying but I couldn't understand or believe them. But you were so earnest and young and scared I finally couldn't doubt you. Then later I knew you but I didn't trust you. Why in the world would I share my greatest secret with a whiny petty boy? What if you told someone? What is she found a way here? No, you were too big of a liability."

"We might have found my portal then and there," Derek said.

"I won't lie. I did look for it later but my first thought was to get you away from anyone who might hear you. And I honestly didn't believe that the portals were two way doors. I'd tried to recreate mine a million times. And my portal could only have been in a single meadow. Yours could have been any tree in the whole bloody forest. It was an impossible endeavor and maybe… maybe I didn't want to come back. I wasn't a good man anymore and I couldn't bear to have the memories of my family tainted with the fact that they would hate me now. Better that they remembered me as I was."

"What about at the end?" Derek could feel his old anger and rage trying to find a foothold but he fought it down. He'd asked for this and he was going to take it.

"I'd always hoped that you'd get pulled back to Earth after enough years passed. I'd hoped you could just wait it out. Then I'd never be in danger and nature would just take its natural course. But after Brigitte… I couldn't let you leave until you'd finished it."

"So you were keeping the flower from him so he could be your assassin? So he could clean up your mess?" Peter asked. Peter's anger was hard to awaken, Derek sure knew, but once it was there it filled the whole room. "You are a selfish coward! Why didn't you give him that bloody flower on day one? Why make him wait? You were going to make him live seventeen years in Morland. Why?"

"You know why I waited. Was the cost worth it? Was the cost of the flower worth six years of freedom?" Jol asked Derek.

His soul… It had been more difficult than Derek could have put into words having his soul trapped a universe away. And now he *knew* how hard it had been on James. He'd been completely alone for those six years. A ghost. His cost had been worse. But was the cost too high? No. Because the only other option had been to become one of her soulless children of Darkness and any cost was worth avoiding that.

But Derek just said "Maybe."

They talked about magic and every kind of mage Jol had met and killed. They talked about Emmaline and her cryptic words. They searched for a loophole, a way to release Elinor from her magic but none of them knew of a way to destroy the magic in someone's blood.

But then it hit Peter like a lightning bolt. Derek saw it the moment it flashed through Peter's eyes.

"Energy cannot be created or destroyed," Peter said sighing as he closed his eyes in relief. "Elinor doesn't have to go to Morland." Derek caught his train of thought a moment later, the law of conservation of energy. Peter was a bloody genius.

"Good job, boy. You've just freed her," Jol said yawning as he finally headed for his bed.

Peter

Derek gave Peter's fist a pound and then began to settle on his pallet on the floor. He'd given Peter his bed, which was a first.

"You are a genius, Peter. Did I say that out loud already?" Derek said yawning as his breathing fell into a steady rhythm in a matter of moments.

Peter was tired but euphoria was washing over him. Elinor could stay. But the euphoria only lasted a moment before he realized that her staying on Earth didn't mean she was staying with him. But it did mean he'd have time. It did mean he'd have a chance to win her and maybe convince her to go to Morland with him anyway. He turned off the clock.

She would be so happy when he told her. He wished he could call her now but he'd see her in the morning. It was exactly what she wanted. But it wasn't really what *he* wanted. If Peter got to choose then it would be him and Elinor, and Derek, in Morland. That was Peter's best case scenario. He didn't know why he'd worked so hard to find her a loop hole because it wasn't what he wanted but that was love wasn't it? Doing what he knew Elinor wanted even if it might kill him.

Chapter 31

Elinor

Elinor read Derek's text with sleepy eyes, "If you are up, your grandpa would love to see you for coffee over here." She considered staying in bed but reality settled into her mind and there was no going back to sleep once she remembered all the horrible truths of her situation. So she went.

Elinor knocked on the front door, feeling a hundred years older than she had the last time she had done so. Mrs. Jensen opened the door and nearly barreled her over in a hug.

"Thank you, Elinor!" she said crying a little. "Thank you." Mr. Jensen gave her a solid pat on the shoulder.

"Um you're welcome," Elinor said. She assumed that some semblance of the truth telling ceremony that she'd had at her house had happened here. She was happy for it. Derek's parents' unbelief had truly been the most horrible part of things for Derek.

Elinor walked into the kitchen and hugged her grandfather. She had wondered if things might get weird between them and she wasn't going to let it happen. No matter how things sorted out, she wasn't going to let him slip away again.

"Good morning, my girl," he said.

"Good morning, grandpa," she said smiling.

"How are things at home?" he asked handing her an empty mug.

"Everyone is sleeping except mom. I don't know if she slept at all," Elinor said as she moved to fill her mug with hot water. Someone had turned on the electric kettle and the water was already hot. Derek came out of the pantry with a wooden box. He opened the lid and offered her her pick of the teas. She blushed. He stared at her so openly. Everyone in the room could read his feelings.

"Thank you," she said. "Is Peter still sleeping?"

"Yes. We had a late night here as well," he said.

"How is your head?" Elinor asked touching Jol's hand. "Do you get headaches like me when you use your magic here?"

"It's not pleasant using magic but as soon as I stop, the pain stops. And if it's anything like last time, in a year or so I won't even be able to light a match. It's not a headache. It feels more like poison in my veins or like an electrical jolt. How is your head?" he said.

She turned away shrugging. "I cannot stop seeing it. It is what it is." Jol looked like he would have said more but she stopped him and turned to Derek.

"Does everyone agree that Ryan will be better if he were to go back?" Elinor asked looking between Jol and Derek.

"Yes, from what we discussed, in great length, last night," Derek said sitting next to her, "passing between worlds takes a snapshot of your body that first time, a scan of who you are at that moment. When you go through again it pulls up the 'last version' so to speak. That's why I looked like my old self when I went to Morland and why Jol is fifty-seven again now.

"If Ryan went back to Morland it would pull up his original body, the one that leaned into Morland a year ago when the two of you were exploring the woods that day. His body in Morland was clean and healthy. I see no reason why going back would wouldn't return him to optimal health but only as long as he remained there." He stopped when Elinor laid her head on the table and cried.

"What's going on?" Peter asked as he walked into the kitchen.

"It's going to destroy them when I leave," Elinor said as tears fell in big drops from her eyes. "Ryan and I both leaving. They will *never* recover from it. They will never let us go. Or they'd try to come with us. Oh God," she said. "I could never let my family go there. What do we do?" she said looking to her grandpa.

"Did you know that we stayed up all night last night trying to solve that exact problem? Elinor, you know that a bit of the Goodness is still in you, right?" Peter asked.

Elinor nodded. Her power wasn't just scrying. It was supercharged. It was unlimited. Maybe that was why her headaches felt worse.

"Does Derek still have any on him?" Peter asked.

"No," Elinor said looking at him closely. She laid a hand on his arm just to make sure. But she didn't feel anything. She felt her face flushing and didn't meet his eyes.

"I thought so," Peter said. "When Derek woke up all traces of the Goodness vanished after the web that had been keeping him alive was no longer needed. I think it's still attached to you for a reason."

"What reason could that be? My headaches aren't gone?"

"I think it's to set you free," Peter said smiling.

Peter

"What?" Elinor said looking between everyone.

"Okay, so we just figured it out like three hours ago," Peter said beaming and yawning.

"Actually Peter figured it out," Derek said. Peter was surprised that Derek let him have the credit. But Derek wasn't the same guy he'd always known. It was going to take some time to get to know the man Derek really was.

"Yeah. So Emmaline said before I left that there was some Goodness still with you," Peter said. "I didn't think anything about it at the time. You know how she speaks in riddles, so she says something like 'Elinor, can use the power of the Goodness for change.' And you can, Elinor. You can use the Goodness to change things."

Elinor just stared at him with an expectant look.

"We think that you can remove the magic from your blood. We think that your connection to the Goodness allows you to make changes to yourself and the world. You teleported eight people like it was nothing. You bend space as easily as breathing. You expel the Darkness wherever you go. We can't even guess the limit to your power."

"But I can get rid of my magic?" Elinor said. "And that would take away my headaches, right?"

"Well you can't get *rid* of it exactly," Peter said. "You can't destroy it. Your magic just has to go somewhere. And what better going away gift for Ryan than a magic power?"

Elinor lips started to quiver. Her eyes turned to Derek and said "Is this true?"

"Yes," Derek said simply. A light started to unfold in Elinor's eyes as she shared a silent moment with Derek. When she heard she could be free, that her cursed blood could be removed, her eyes had sought the person she wanted a future with. Peter had lost in the span of five seconds. He felt his heart break in two. She had already made her choice. When had that happened? They had been home for three days. Derek had been dead for a day before that and she hadn't seen him since he'd been captured. When had this happened? *James,* he thought. He felt his breath getting short.

"So I can stay here?" she asked Derek. What did Derek know about any of this? But she needed to hear him say it. It was Derek's opinion that mattered and it was killing Peter to watch the silent message their gaze was sending.

"Yes," Derek said.

Peter got up and went outside without a word. He had to get away from them. He had to get some air. This couldn't be happening. He hadn't saved her for Derek. He hadn't spent all-night looking for a solution so Derek could have her. Maybe it wasn't too late. Maybe she just didn't know how he felt.

After a couple minutes, Elinor poked her head outside. "Hey what's wrong?" she asked bumping against him before she leaned against the brick next to him.

"Nothing. Nothing is wrong. I'm just tired."

"Uh-huh," she said not believing him. How could she see some things so clearly and not others. "We can talk about it later, if you want," she said. "But I want to head to my house to explain this to my parents. Please come. I know you'll explain the magic parts better than I could," she asked.

"Yup. I'm there," he said following her as he tried to force all his feeling down.

Elinor

"How are you feeling?" Elinor said to Ryan. She was glad he was awake and alone. They had some things to talk about.

"Like garbage. Thanks for explaining everything to the family. Remember how when I came home at the start of the semester and I was feeling really tired and out of it. I think that was the start of it. I don't even think I knew how bad I was feeling until I went to Morland and felt so well. By the look of you I'd say we both aren't the better for wear. Your headaches are back?" he asked.

She nodded.

"So hit me with it," Ryan said.

"With what?" Elinor asked.

"The hair-brained plan you and your nerds have thought of. I know you have one. But saying how all of your plans have failed in the most *monumental* ways, I'm not sure it will be more pleasant than this."

401

Elinor smiled. "We have a couple ideas but you aren't going to like them."

"Do they involve dying in a month?" he said.

"Not exactly."

"Then I'm in."

"They are super weird," she said grinning like a Cheshire. "You are gonna hate them."

"Shocking but somehow my weird tolerance is through the roof. If you said I had to find a unicorn and marry a mermaid, I'd say done and *done,*" he said with a wink.

"So," she said starting, "we all think you'll be better if you go back to Morland."

Ryan nodded solemnly.

"And option one, is I go with you," she continued. "I won't have headaches. And we can make a new world. I'll have my magic and that will really help us. But…"

"But you don't want to go," Ryan said.

Elinor nodded. "I don't want to go. But I could never let you go alone. I couldn't."

"It would kill them if we both left."

"Then there is option two, we all go."

Ryan paled and she was glad he didn't like that idea either. The thought of Katie and Colton being raised there was enough to turn Elinor's stomach and she believed Emmaline when she had said the portal was going to disappear. Trying to force all six of them through was not a good plan.

"Okay this last one better be good," Ryan said.

"You go back alone but I give you a present."

Chapter 32

Elinor

"Okay," Elinor said once both her and Derek's families were assembled. Everyone had seen Jol's magic and had grudging accepted that *maybe* it all was real. "What happens next involves everyone," Elinor said. "And everyone gets to choose. Ryan, of course, has the final say because it's his life. There is no getting around it, if Ryan wants to live he needs to go back to Morland. He'll be healthy and live a long life. Maybe he'll get sucked back her after twenty years or so and no time will have passed but who knows. This is the only non-negotiable part of the plan." Elinor's mom was already shaking her head.

"You've all read Derek's story, I'm sure, so you know that Morland isn't a picnic," Elinor continued. "But the truth is it's better now. The Darkness had fled and the country wants to flourish and rebuild. It will be hard work but Morland is better already." She wasn't sure if she was lying or not but it felt almost true. She wanted it to be true.

"Okay so Ryan moves to Morland and we visit for Christmas and his birthday," said their mother crying already.

"Um. No. Okay, so here is the bad part," Elinor said. "The portal is weakening. Whatever our decision is it will most likely be a permanent one. Anyone who goes to Morland may be stuck there forever. It's not a decision to make lightly. Also this is only a guess but Emmaline says only three can cross. This isn't science but she's never been wrong. And from my view the portal doesn't look strong."

"I'm sorry but we are all coming with you," their mother said to Ryan.

"Mom," Ryan said speaking up for the first time. "If I stay here, I will die. Morland is no one's first choice, it's not. I do not choose Morland for my family. I can't let you. You'd be giving up everything in this world. Besides I don't want the little ones growing up there. I don't believe this would be goodbye forever. Because it's not. It's just sending me on an adventure. An extended trip that lets me live. And only three can go through the portal. Who do you send? Are you going to leave my siblings without a mother? I am a grown man. I will be fine over there."

She left the room unable to stop crying. Their father left with her.

"Who takes the other spots?" Mrs. Jensen asked tears already sliding down her face as she looked at Derek and he answered her "If Elinor is able to pass on her magic to Ryan then only Ryan will cross. If Elinor's transfer doesn't work, I'm going back with her."

"No," said Katie burrowing her head into Elinor's lap.

"No," Peter said looking at Derek. "Either way. If Elinor's magic transfers or not, I'm going to Morland."

"Peter!" Elinor said staring at him across the room. "You don't have to do this. You can't mean it!"

"I think we'd best let you all talk this out some more," Mr. Jensen said leading his wife from the room. Mrs. Jensen pulled Derek in for a hug. "You don't leave without telling us. Promise? You don't leave without say goodbye this time," she said looking at him through tear soaked eyes.

"I promise, Mom," Derek said kissing her cheek.

"Let's take this outside," Elinor said to Peter and Derek leading them to the patio and away from her eavesdropping siblings.

Peter

Peter steeled himself for Derek's rage and Elinor's sadness and.

"You've got to be kidding," Derek said. *Rage, check.*

"I'm not," Peter said.

"Peter... You don't have to go. You don't have to do this," Elinor said. *Sadness, check.*

"Elinor, I know Morland treated you harshly but I'm going," Peter said.

"Why? Tell me why!" Derek said getting in his face. Peter was amused. Derek wasn't really scary when he had a soul. "Give me one reason," Derek growled. "Prove to me that you've thought this through. You'd be giving up everything. There is no coming back, Peter. You'd be in the equivalent of a third world country living in the past. There is no electricity. There is no internet. There is no modern medicine. The country is on the verge of collapse. The monarch has just been assassinated and the people will not look kindly on anyone who tries to bring order. It won't matter to the populace that you had a hand in killing the Queen and that you were there to purge the world of Darkness. You are a foreigner. You only know what I've told you about Morland."

"I will learn," Peter said.

"Is it because it's a magic land?" Derek asked

Peter flushed.

"It is, isn't it? Peter, please, did you not see the truth of it? Did Morland not show you her ugly underbelly? The fact that there is magic there doesn't redeem it. It's not a fantasy land," Derek said.

"I know what Morland is and I know what it isn't. I've been looking for Morland with you for years," Peter said. "I won't deny that living in a world with magic is my dream come true. Morland has a chance to be something really amazing. And I want to be a part of it. I want to help shape the new Morland and bring it into the future. She has good bones. She's not beyond redemption. But the fact that there is magic is only the icing on the cake. It's not the main reason," Peter said.

"Then why?" Elinor asked her eyes pleading with him.

"The truth is I've been looking for a way out for a while. Before you, Elinor, my life was unbearable. I had my dad and Derek. Both of them were broken and violent, distant and unable to really see me. I don't know that I would have ever really hurt myself but... I hated my life. There felt like no escape. I didn't have the money to go to a school out of this city. I didn't have the grades for a full scholarship with room and board allowance. I was stuck like a pin in my hell of a life. My dad wouldn't have even cared that I was gone," Peter turned to Elinor and took both of her hands in his. "Elinor, how can I thank you for picking me that day, for telling me your secret? You changed everything."

Derek took the hint and left the porch in a huff. It was very reminiscent of who Derek used to be. He must be *very* mad. But Peter didn't care because now might be his only chance. She needed to know everything before she made a permanent life changing decision.

"Elinor, I know what Derek told you last night. On the phone." The words flew out of his mouth before he could stop them. He hadn't meant to say them but he found himself watching closely for her reaction. She blushed and he exhaled. It didn't change what he had to do but it did make him worry about her answer.

"Elinor, there is a lot I have wanted to tell you. But the timing has just never been right for us. First you had your headaches and then your stomach was being cauterized and then you were training and then your soul was bonded to the Goodness and then Derek was dead. So I've got to force it now and I don't like it. But here goes," he said smiling rubbing his thumb across the back of her hand. "Have you already picked Derek?" he asked.

"I... I don't know. I haven't really thought about it," she said looking down.

"Oh Elinor, don't lie to me. If your headaches don't go away Derek is going with you to Morland isn't he?"

"He said he would."

"I've seen you look at him. There is something between you two."

"Oh Peter. I really don't know. My brother is dying. I promise you that little else has crossed my mind since that thought became my world. Do we really have to sort this all out now? Can't we wait? If I get to stay on Earth, then we'll have time to see if we are the right fit. You don't know what I'll be like cured of my headaches forever. I won't be this frail pitiful thing I am now. You might not like me. I would need you in a different way."

"Elinor, there is nothing you could become that I wouldn't love. But... I want you to come to Morland with me."

Elinor

"What?" Elinor said.

"Come to Morland with me because that's where I'm going. I thought I could stay here with you. But I can't shake Morland. I want to go back. So let's start a life together in that brave new world. Whether your head is fixed or not, I want you there with me." Peter slid a hand around her waist and pulled her close. "I love you. Pick me," he said kissing her lips softly. This kiss was so different from their kiss in the clouds. This kiss spoke of the promise of a thousand kisses to come. This kiss didn't need to give it all, it was an invitation. When he pulled back Elinor stared into his eyes looking for answers.

"Peter, I don't want to go to Morland," she said. Her head was swimming.

"Not even a little? Not even for a second? I know you had some good times at the Glen. I was there; I saw you. I saw you laugh and make friends. Morland isn't always the worst. I know things went south... Derek told me about Ian. El, I'm so sorry. I had no idea what he was. I feel sick just thinking about it. But don't judge all of Morland on him," he said. "If you went back I would be there to protect you and you wouldn't have to give up your magic. We could really discover what you can do. We can make the world into everything we've ever wanted. You were born with this magic. It's who you are. You were *meant* to have it. You don't have to change who you are if you come with me to Morland. You'd also get to be with Ryan. And what about that ring, Elinor?"

She flushed as he hit on her biggest guilt about staying.

"You are the Màithrean of the South nomads. You don't get to just stop being that. You have people waiting for you. People expecting things from you. Morland needs you. You could do so much good."

"You are going either way?" Elinor asked.

"I don't know. If you told me that you wanted me, if you told me that staying with you here on Earth was the only way you could be happy... I could give up Morland for you. But I won't give it up for a maybe. If you are unsure that you could love me that way or unsure that it's not Derek... I need to know, Elinor. I can't just be your friend anymore. This is our crossroad. The only way I'm staying on Earth is to be with you but it's not my first choice. I'm going to Morland. Come with me.

"El, you saved me from my own Darkness. I think I loved you from the first moment I really saw you. I knew what you were. You are something rare. You are beautiful and brave. You didn't let this never-ending crapfest break you. You stayed good and kind. Elinor, I love you," he said. "I know I've been passive, waiting for you to come to terms with your headaches but you need to know that I don't love you less because I tell you this second. I love you. So I have to ask you to pick me. If you don't that's okay but I can't stay here.

"This world isn't worth it if I can't be with you. I need you to decide if you could really love me. I know it's not fair but time is ticking. Ryan needs to cross over soon and I don't know that the portal will last forever. Maybe it will just fade and fizzle into nothing before I could use it. So I have to ask you to decide now. I think you already know. I feel like you know it's Derek but... pick me," he said raising his hand to her cheek. Elinor found herself melting into it. Peter then pulled her into a hug and just held her. She did love Peter but it was so much he was asking.

"Can I think about it for a little bit?" Elinor asked.

"Of course," Peter said not letting her go. "Is there anything I can say to remove your worries?"

"You know that I've had feelings for you for a while?" she asked listening to his heartbeat.

"Yeah. I'd guessed as much after my proposal," he chuckled. "How much do you like me Elinor?"

"A lot."

"How many 'a lots'?" he asked.

"All of them. I do love you, Peter," she said as he moaned a little under his breath. "But I don't know if it's enough."

"It could be, if you wanted," he said kissing the top of her head.

"I promise I'll have it sorted out soon."

Elinor felt torn. She was basking in Peter. His arms around her were divine. She wished he could just hold her forever locked in that moment. With no consequences and no decisions being made. Forever just being always nine fifteen on a cool night in October with Peter's breathing as the only sign of time passing allowed. But that wasn't how the world worked. She didn't get to pick a moment to live in, she had to live them all. And Elinor needed to decide which life she wanted to live.

"I've got to go home and pack," Peter said. "Text me what time the festivities start."

Derek

Derek stared at Peter's back. Derek had been pacing in the woods unable to really leave and give them the privacy they deserved. They looked like a matching set and it almost weakened his resolve. They were the same kind, both good. Their blond heads kissing had been a moment of rare intense pain.

When Peter went back inside, Elinor just stared into the woods looking like she'd been hit by a bus. He *could* give Elinor up for Peter. He could but he didn't want to.

"Elinor," Derek said after he walked through the gate and up onto the porch.

"I don't want to go back," she said not looking at him.

"I know," he said turning to stand beside her.

"I feel like a horrible person. How could I send my brother there alone? I understand my mother's rage. Letting Ryan go feels like he dies anyway. I may never see him again."

"But he won't be dead. That's the point. We don't know how long he'll stay. Maybe he'll pop back over in an instant like I did. Maybe he'll come back after having lived a great life with a beautiful wife and a dozen children. Whatever the rest of us decide, Ryan will be happy. You need to decide what makes you happy. I'd kiss you now but I think you've still got Peter on you," he said smiling. "I hate to repeat what I'm sure Peter just told you but I hope you choose me. But you need to know that you can also just pick Earth. You can just pick "Elinor." I'll understand after everything I've done to you if you don't want me…" Derek said stopping when Elinor reached for his hand and kissed his knuckles. She'd done that with James and it sent a shiver through him feel it himself.

"I'll text you later when my family sorts everything out. Right now I just need to think," she said.

Ryan

"Ryan," Colton asked sitting next to Ryan on the couch in the bonus room. "Do you want to go back?"

"Yes," Ryan answered. He saw Elinor pause as she came up the stairs and she stared at him a moment.

412

"Yeah but would you still go back if you were okay?" Katie said.

"I don't know. The first time I had a chance to think on it, I wasn't okay. I can't really experience that idea again without the taint of being sick. I didn't really hate Morland," Ryan said.

"But you didn't like it," Colton said. "I've read the blog. I know it's bad."

"I only disliked Morland because it kept trying to kill Elinor all the time," he said smiling. "I had made you all a promise to bring her home safe and she was literally falling to pieces every time I looked away. You know how delicate she is," he said winking. "But I think Morland isn't so bad when there isn't an evil Queen. I think it could be a very popular vacation spot."

Katie crossed the room and gave Ryan a hug. "You did a really great job bringing her home," she said. "You are a good brother." Ryan exhaled. He hadn't realized he needed to hear it until he did. Katie had a way of knowing just what needed to be said. He'd brought Elinor home. Against all the odds and forces of Darkness, he had brought his sister home.

"You really did, Ryan," Elinor said trying not to cry. "I owe you my life a dozen times. Thank you. I mean it. I didn't get a chance to tell you but I am so glad you came with me."

"No, Elinor, you saved me. If you hadn't seen the portal that day a year ago, I'd be dying for real," Ryan said.

"Okay. Enough feelings," Colton said taking charge of the pow-wow with a notebook in hand. "It's time we hashed this all out. What do you plan to do for money when you get there? What skills do you have that are transferable? I'm preparing several bags of literature and resources that will help you. From what I know of the conversion system it will be a stretch if they'll make it but we'll see. So what will you do?"

Elinor let a deep laugh free and Ryan found himself laughing as well. She then turned on him and said seriously. "Yeah Ryan, have you even thought about your future? You are such a delinquent. How will you support your wife?"

"Your wife?" Katie said sitting on her tiptoes.

"You got married? You were only there a couple weeks!" Colton asked incredulously.

"I am not married," Ryan said scorching Elinor with his eyes. She grinned bigger.

"Well they aren't married yet…." Elinor said. "As far as we know. But I don't know *every* nomad custom. Maybe kissing in the woods outside the portal makes you married."

"Who? Who? Who?" said Katie bouncing.

"A nomad? I don't know, Ryan…" Colton said.

"Ugh!" Ryan groaned and then pretended to fall asleep.

Chapter 33

Elinor

Ryan was crossing over in the morning. Elinor didn't have long to decide her future. She would transfer her magic right before Ryan went into the portal. She had a peace and a certainty that it would work. Once she had given him her magic, he'd have to leave soon since it would probably also give him her headaches. So she needed to decide now. And her biggest worry was that maybe she didn't even know what love was.

The horror of the whole Ian situation would wash over her at different times. If Ian hadn't suggested they go for a walk, she wouldn't have stopped. In that moment she'd loved Ian. He had consumed her whole being. She'd never felt anything like that before. She'd been so weak. She felt like such a stupid fool. She'd confused love with an enchanted necklace. If James hadn't have come, she didn't know if she'd be alive.

She probably didn't deserve either one of them. But she told herself again that Ian had had her under a spell. She'd felt it, that magnetic pull that made her *have* to do what he suggested. That wasn't what real love was like. That was false and wrong and evil. She knew love because it was the opposite of that. Love was putting the other person's needs before her own. Love was still passion and fire but it was consent and pure. The Bible had told her what love was.

Love is patient and kind. Love is not jealous or boastful or proud or rude. Love doesn't demand it's own way. Love is not irritable and keeps no record of when it's been wronged. Love isn't glad about injustice but rejoice when truth wins out. Love never gives up, never lose faith, is always hopeful, and endures through every circumstance. Love will last forever.

Elinor couldn't stay inside. She couldn't think inside. Her family would want to know her decision but she didn't know her decision. She loved Peter and she loved Derek. Each love was as different as the men attached to them. Peter was safety and kindness. He was a soft spot to fall. But she didn't get to only choose him she was choosing the whole world that went with him.

She made herself face the truth that Morland could be okay. It would probably stop trying to destroy her when they were on the same side. And if she was honest in her own heart, she loved the land. She loved the nomads. She hadn't forgotten everything she had learned in the Glen but did that mean Morland owned her forever? Hadn't she earned the right to have a life, the life of her choosing? She hadn't asked for that ring. She hadn't asked to have a power that was necessary to battle the Darkness. After all she'd done, and all she'd given, didn't she deserve the right to choose her own path?

The best thing Morland had going for it was that Ryan would be there. He had always been her best friend. She literally could not imagine living the rest of her life without him in it. It blew her mind. But if she left, she'd be leaving Colton and Katie and her mother and father and... Derek.

Derek. It had taken her a long time to solve that impossible puzzle. He had been cold and hard but his soul had been the funniest, sweetest being she had ever encountered. Derek had been so horrible at the start and in the middle. But now...

She admitted to herself that she would never have thought she would fall in love with him. But it had happened slowly. Thinking back, it had really started the first night his soul had sat and silently talked with her at the board game party. But that had been the night things with Peter had first started. It horrified her how her brain was able to completely compartmentalize loving two different men at the same time. It shouldn't be possible. She should just know. People usually just knew.

But the truth was Elinor did know. She'd known for a while and she'd been fighting it. Because it didn't make any sense. Because it felt like the hard choice. Elinor called Peter.

"Well?" he said after the first ring and Elinor could hear the smile in his voice. When she found that the words wouldn't come out Peter guessed. "No?" he asked sadly.

"I'm sorry, Peter. I can't go to Morland with you."

"Oh Elinor. Please think about it some more," he said. "What if I stayed?"

"But you aren't staying."

"Do you still pick him if I stay?" Peter asked

"It's not like that really," Elinor said searching for the words. The words that were true but wouldn't hurt him too badly. She was silent for a moment. "Peter, I will always care for you. I do love you. You mean so much to me." But couldn't she make herself love him *that* way. She'd been skirting it for some time. Dipping her toe in the water but now that she needed to, she couldn't make the plunge. She hung on to the edge as if invisible restraints were making it impossible for her to lean in. She couldn't will herself to love him that way

"Was it always him?" he asked.

"No. It was mostly you until…"

"Until James?" Peter asked.

"Yes. I would have never have picked him as he was before. He's a different man now. He's who he always should have been."

"If it were anyone else…" Peter said. "I would have won you if he'd stayed broken. If he'd stayed only half of himself… It's pitiful that I'm only slightly better than half of Derek."

"No, Peter," she said. "You are amazing. You are kind and good. You are a hero. *You* saved Morland with your love and courage. You are not half of Derek. You are a whole Peter. In another life it would have been us."

"But I'm not enough to leave Earth behind?" Peter asked.

"No. I don't know that I could ever leave the little ones or my parents and I'm getting a second chance at my life. It's what I've always wanted."

"Then I can be happy for you and let you go. Maybe Emmaline isn't as crazy as she seems," he said chuckling. "Does he know yet?"

"No. Not yet," Elinor said.

"So I guess I'll see you in a couple hours. Sleep if you can. Bye Elinor."

Derek

Derek had wanted to call Elinor as soon as he received the text that Ryan and Peter were crossing over in the morning but he made himself wait. She said she wasn't going with Peter and that she'd talk to him after Ryan and Peter left. *That was something.* But she hadn't said she wanted him. She hadn't said that she picked him. He made himself focus on his best friend who was leaving him. When Derek entered the woods in the early morning, everyone was already assembled.

Peter pulled Derek aside and they each struggled for words.

"He knows I'm gone," Peter said. "I left a note. I don't think he'll hassle you about me but you know how my dad is. Everything with school is handled and my paper trail is cleared up. If I ever come back you'll have to take me in because I'll be a poor homeless man," Peter said smiling.

"You are always welcome wherever I am," Derek said. "You know that you are the best friend a guy could have. I have never deserved your friendship. You are a good man. I hope you are happy. I hope you fix Morland. I wish you every good thing. Thank you for saving my life. I love you, my brother. I pray we meet again. Maybe in the next life."

"You better take care of her," Peter said starting to choke up. "You need to swear it to me. I know you have your soul but you can't ever hurt her again."

"I swear, Peter. Oh God. I swear. She is my life. I will never hurt her again," Derek said clasping Peter's arm and hugging him. "What will I do without you? Have fun over there. Tell Garrison 'thank you' from me.

Ryan

"Please, try not to cry too much," Ryan said hugging his mother. "Isn't it better knowing I'm alive somewhere, even if it isn't here?"

"You know it is," she said crying anyway. Ryan had spent all night talking to his family. When Elinor finally came inside from finding herself and announced she was staying, Ryan could have sang '*Hallelujah*'. She was getting her life back. He wouldn't let her give it up for him. He'd be fine.

"I'll always love you. And who knows maybe I'll only be gone a second," he said kissing his mom's cheek. He had kissed and hugged his mother more in the last few days than he had in his whole life combined. She knew he loved her and he knew she loved him. He couldn't ask or give anymore than that.

He moved to hug his stepdad. "You are my real father," Ryan Micheals told George Lirdin. "You are my dad and I'm going to miss you, too."

"I love you, son. Have an amazing life. God bless you."

Elinor, Colton, and Katie were already tearing up waiting their turns. "Come on guys! You are killing me. Please don't make this harder on me. This is almost worse than when I left for college the first time."

Katie barreled into him hiccupping her tears. "I'm sorry," she said. "I'm trying to stop. Really I am. I love you. I love you. Don't ever forget me. You promise?" she asked looking up with a trembling lips.

"You know how much I love you, little sister? All of it. All the love," Ryan said finally breaking down. "I remember the day you were born like it was yesterday. You were so beautiful and perfect. I finally felt like our family was whole. We'd just been waiting for you. Be strong and kind like Elinor. Marry someone who loves you for who you really are. I will think about you every day," he said hugging her tightly before moving onto Colton.

"You are the man now," Ryan said. "You really always have been. I love you, Colton. You are so smart and good. You will have the most amazing life. You will do things no one has ever dreamed of. Elinor is well now. You need to live your life for you. Help everyone not to be too sad, okay?"

"I love you, Ryan," Colton said as he went to join Katie in their parent's arms.

Elinor stomped her foot as tears poured down her face. "I'm so mad," she said. "We were supposed to go to Chapel Hill together. How can I ever go there now?" she said laughing and crying as he held her.

"Elinor, I love you. You are a great sister and you've turned into the most beautiful strong woman. I am so proud of you. Be happy and catch up on all the living you've missed. Don't miss me too much. You deserve to be really truly happy."

"I love you, Ryan," Elinor said trying to catch her breath. "Enjoy every second. Don't miss us too much. We will be thinking of you and loving you forever. Oh God, please protect him," she said pulling herself away.

Elinor

"Okay let's give this a go," Elinor said taking a couple deep breath and wiping her eyes. She walked over to Peter to distracted herself from the tears that wouldn't stop trickling out. "Any tips on how to pass the magic?" she asked him.

"I think that all you'll need to do is access the layer of Goodness that hovers around you like when you go into the spirit world. I mean this is all a guess but..."

"I think you will be able to feel the Morland blood pulsing inside yourself and that's what you'll pull. I feel the fire in my blood and I think you'll be able to feel yours," Jol added.

"Will I still be your granddaughter?" Elinor asked.

"Nothing in all the worlds could change that, my girl. You'll just be free of the genetic magic gene. But there is something else I want to recommend. I think you should put your gift on Peter as well. It will probably manifest a little different with each of them getting a share but I think it will help them both. If Peter wants it, of course?"

Peter's wide eyes and smile were answer enough but he nodded anyway.

"If it works," she said holding Ryan and Peter's hands, "you both might start understanding me a good bit better and I'm sorry. Okay. Close your eyes," she said closing her eyes too. She imagined that she could see inside herself like how she'd felt looking for Derek's soul, that she could see the golden shimmer of magic floating through herself. She imagined pulling it towards the surface, towards the magic that had settled on her skin. Then she pushed it away from herself and into each of the guys, praying that it would help them, that it would finally do some good, that her gift would aid the Goodness and fix the world.

The absence of pain left her gasping for air. She'd forgotten already how intoxicating it was. Peter and Ryan each fell to their knees.

"It sure is horrible," Ryan said, his eyes instantly watering. "And that from a man who is already dying."

"Yup. Maybe you weren't exaggerating," Peter said winking and then grimacing at the pain that the wink probably gave him.

"So did it work?" Jol and Colton asked at the same time.

"It worked on me. I've never felt better. Try to see Morland," Elinor said.

"You do it, Peter. I feel like garbage already," Ryan said.

Peter blinked his eyes and they turned gold around the edges.

"I can't see Morland but Jol is lighting up like a Christmas tree and so is Ryan," he said.

"Well, I have no idea what that means," Elinor said smiling. "But I know a bunch of nomad leaders who would love to help you understand your new powers." She pulled off her ring and handed it to Peter. "I'm only lending this to you," she said unable to stop her lip from quivering. "Wear it until our fight is done. I think Morland could use a really amazing uncle," she kissed him on the cheek and couldn't resist one last hug. Would she ever see him again?

Peter

Peter nodded one last time at Elinor and she nodded back. Peter and Derek helped Ryan up the tree and then Peter followed him. The moment his feet struck Morland the headache was gone. It had worked. He looked around at Winter, Emmaline, Brigitte, and Garrison. Ryan was stretching and smiling. Peter and Ryan grinned at each other. They were new men in a new world.

Derek

Derek watched the tree. She probably wouldn't come. He counted the seconds. He hoped… He had thought about sending a note through the tree a thousand times. But in the end he couldn't do it. He had heard what she said, that she forgave him but maybe Brigitte had just said it so he would accept the Goodness. Maybe it was a calculated move because how could she really mean it? And if she did mean it, it didn't mean she'd come. Why would she leave Morland? Why would she ever want to see Derek again after all the evil he'd done?

Since coming home, Derek had wondered long and hard if Brigitte's magic would give her headaches like Elinor. But Derek believed that the Goodness was everywhere. He knew it was true the moment Elinor had helped him in the conservatory. The Goodness was the most real thing in the world. It gave Derek the greatest feeling of relief that there was a power for good in the universe and that it cared enough to save him. So if Brigitte did come, she'd probably be fine. If she did come... He watched the tree, waiting.

There was one charge left. One more passage through that dumb tree. But maybe she wouldn't take it. Maybe the portal had run out of power too soon. Maybe there was only enough energy for two passages but then he saw a slender dark foot and his sister scaled gracefully down the tree. Derek had watched the multitude of tears falling earlier and he had just been an observer. But when Brigitte started walking towards him he fell to his knees as tears fell freely. She was really alive. She was really alive. She kneeled in front of him and took his hands.

"Hello brother," she said pulling him into a hug.

Elinor

They didn't come back. Every other time a portal had been used the person came back with no time lost. They came back the moment they left having lived for days or years on the other side. Elinor had gone to Morland for three weeks but when she came back through the portal no time had passed on Earth. And when Jol had come to Earth he had lived seventeen years but had been pulled back to Morland to the moment he had left.

But Ryan and Peter didn't come back.

Elinor told herself that was a good sign. If Ryan had come back, he would still be dying. It must be good that he was still gone. She wondered if they stayed because the portal was used up. Maybe they would never come back. She hoped her family would recover.

Chapter 34

Elinor

Later that night as the sun was setting, Elinor watched her phone. Derek hadn't called. She'd texted him to call when he was free and he didn't call. Maybe he had changed his mind. Maybe having Brigitte was enough. Maybe it was more than brotherly love. Maybe a whole, healed Derek had no need of her.

After her family finally cried themselves to sleep, Elinor went to the woods. She walked to the portal and just stared at it. No amount of blinking would let her see what her eyes couldn't see. Brigitte had delivered a note from the guys. It had been hastily scribbled on a bit of fabric.

It said:

'Safe and Sound. We love you all, Peter & Ryan.'

"I took a chance you'd be here," a voice said from her right.

Elinor jumped but she shouldn't have. She knew that voice. "You scared me," she said as Derek walked up.

"I'm sorry. I was going to call if you weren't out here but I had a feeling."

They stood in silence. Elinor's fear grew inside her.

"Derek," Elinor said at the same time Derek said, "Elinor." They both laughed nervously. Somehow they'd gone back in time and they each seemed so unsure about the other.

"Let me go first," he said. "You don't have to be with me. I don't know if you only didn't choose Peter because he was going to Morland or if it was something more but you owe me nothing. Ryan was right. You get a second chance at your life. You can pick to be alone. You owe me nothing."

Elinor couldn't stop her smile. That was all he was worried about? She spanned the difference between them in two strides. She grabbed his hand and said, "I choose you. I would choose you if you were going to Morland. I'd choose you if you were going to the moon. Having Peter go to Morland only removed any doubt I'd felt. I do love him but it's not the same."

"How can you say that?" Derek said tortured, looking down at her hand as if it were a hot poker. She didn't let go.

"How can you doubt it?" She didn't understand. When he'd woken up and called her 'my little mist girl' it had set Elinor's heart pounding. James was in there. It was everything she hadn't even dared to hope for. James and Derek together. And then the phone call… He'd seemed so sure then. He'd said that he loved her without hesitation or calculation. It came out as the simplest statement of fact from him but then something had happened. He'd slipped away from her after that. Maybe he'd thought she really loved Peter or maybe he'd said those things without thinking them through. Maybe he'd changed his mind. But she hadn't.

"I have every cause to doubt it," he said breaking away. "How can you love me after everything I've done to you? I see my past deeds with horror and disgust. I was a monster. When I think it was these hands that strangled you, I want to throw up. How can you look at me the way you are looking at me?"

"Do you remember when I came to you with the Goodness and you were covered in Darkness but I found your soul anyway?" she asked. He nodded miserably.

"I was covered in Darkness because I was weak. Because my bitterness and anger made me weak," Derek said.

"I saw your soul, Derek. I saw all of you and it was the most beautiful thing I've ever seen," she said reaching towards him as he shook his head and backed away. "I saw you for who you are. Your goodness and loyalty radiated from you like a beacon. Your capacity to love. I was seeing you with your soul for the first time and I fell in love with you. Derek, I know you. I know you and I love you. Who else has ever seen your heart and soul? Am I not the judge for what is in there, for what it looks like? It's true that before…"

He visibly flinched.

"Before when you were not whole, I was attracted to you. Your feral beauty was magnetic. But I didn't love you," she said taking another step. "When you held me at Boone, my body did want you but I didn't love you." She took another step, so close he had to look straight down to see her. His face was raw and she dropped the only balm she had. "I fell in love with your soul. With the clear, bright light inside of you. It's just really pleasant that you are so handsome," she said smiling but when Derek didn't soften she finally pulled back.

"Do you not love me anymore? Was it only the thought that Peter might have me? Or was it my headaches that made me fragile and broken?" she asked trying not to cry. She was a new person again and she knew it would take her a while to figure out who she was now. Maybe Derek wasn't interested in a healed, healthy Elinor. Or maybe without her magic she no longer had a pull on him. "Or is it Brigitte?" she asked. Brigitte was beautiful and Elinor adored her. But then the spell was broken and Derek moved.

"Brigitte is as much my sister as Ryan is your brother," Derek said striding forward so she was only inches from him, not yet touching but Elinor felt the charged air. "Do you really love me?" he asked. She felt his fingers grip her shirt as if he could pull the truth out of her. But she gave it freely.

"Yes. With my whole heart," she said.

Derek's sigh gave her goose bumps. Derek's hands around her waist made her knees weak. And Derek's lips on hers made her feel like she was finally home. His lips were soft and still gentle as if he were testing the waters. But when Elinor raised her hands to his face, Derek exhaled and the dam burst. Then she felt his strength. He erased the distance between them and Elinor's escaped gasp made Derek chuckle softly.

"I'm going to have a lot of fun trying to make that noise come out of you again," he said kissing her cheek, her nose, her forehead. "Elinor, do you really love me?"

"Yes," she said laughing softly. "Yes, my dear prince. I love you." She pulled his face towards her and released her need. She kissed Derek. Derek kissed her back. It was as heady as a drug and as sweet as heaven. Elinor hadn't dared to hope for a happy ending, especially one including Derek. The pure bliss of the moment broke the kiss and she burrowed into his chest. She just needed to soak him in. To feel his arms around her and to reassure herself that *this* was real. She exhaled deeply without letting him go.

"I love you, my little mist girl," he said pulling her chin up to stare into her eyes that she knew were only blue. "I will love you forever and ever."

Neither of them could quite finish the task of leaving the other. Elinor had this horrible fear that she'd wake up in the morning to find it had all been a dream. And she wondered if that was why Derek was hesitant to leave as well. But part of why she stayed was because of how fun it was to kiss Derek. It was really amazing to kiss someone she was in love with. It woke her up inside. It made her feel new, again. She never wanted to stop kissing Derek James Jensen.

Derek

When Elinor yawned in Derek's arms as they sat at the base of the tree, he squeezed her once and said "I guess that's our cue." He didn't want to let her go and she didn't move to rise. He didn't ever, ever want to let her go. He still couldn't really believe that it was true. He was holding Elinor in his arms and he could kiss her whenever he wanted. Derek kissed her neck just to check again and he *heard* her smile. Elinor was in his arms with a smile on her lips. If he didn't already, it was enough to make a man believe in God.

Derek had replayed their precious conversation word for word, over and over in his head. He knew he'd do it for a long time yet. She loved him. Derek had never thought he'd stood a chance, not against Peter, not against his own sins but fate always worked in a way he didn't expect. But it was more than fate. He knew that now. It was the Goodness. It was God and He'd given Derek a greater gift than he deserved, Elinor. He locked both of his hands in hers as they rested on her stomach. She was leaning against him with her back pressed close against his chest. It made him close his eyes.

"You know I'm stubborn," Derek said and he could feel Elinor's torso shake in a laugh.

"Oh, I am well aware," she said running her thumb across the back of his hand.

"I'm sorry to say that that means I'm not going to be able to ever let you go," he said as he made his body be still to feel whatever response she was going to have.

But all she said was "Good," as she pressed closer into him. *Good?* Derek thought in shock. *Good? That's all she has to say to that.* A shaky breath escaped his lungs and Elinor turned around. She was on her knees in front of him and she gripped his face in her hands. "Which of us is more stubborn, do you think?" Elinor said trying and failing to keep a straight face.

"Definitely me," Derek said raising an eyebrow. It was not a competition.

"No!" Elinor said. "I am. You were nothing but trouble and I couldn't stay away from you."

"Ha, *you* were nothing but trouble, my dear and I stalked the woods behind your house every night. I knew you were dangerous but that only drew me closer." Elinor eyes grew wide and Derek felt his stomach drop. Had he not told her that he'd stalked her house? Was that the final straw? Had he been too horrible and obsessed with her before? But then she just tucked her head on his shoulder and whispered "You called me 'my dear'." He let the worried breath out in a gust and pressed her tight against him. *I'm never going to let her go,* he vowed to himself. *I'm going to love this girl forever.*

Epilogue

Next Fall

Elinor

"I don't know about this place?" Elinor said dropping her box down on the naked floor.

"It'll be great," Brigitte said. "It's ten minutes from campus and five minutes from my GED class and it's only one minute from Derek," she said knocking on the wall to the apartment next door and laughing when a knock came back.

"Oh Brigitte," Elinor said pulling her into a hug. "Have I told you lately that I adore you?"

"Not lately enough," she said chuckling.

Derek came in from next door smiling wide. Elinor still wasn't used to looking at him. She couldn't believe he was hers. And he was almost hers forever and ever.

"You'll have her all to yourself next year. But this semester she's all mine," Brigitte said unwilling to let her go. Elinor spun her engagement ring around on her finger and shrugged her shoulders at Derek. But he was not to be deterred. He simply encompassed both of them in a giant hug.

"You are both all mine. Forever," he said kissing Brigitte on the cheek and Elinor on the lips.

"Bleh," Brigitte said as she squirmed out of the group hug. "You made it weird."

"You are very sneaky, my love." Elinor said burrowing into his chest as Brigitte moved around them humming as she unpacked.

"I know," he said kissing her neck. "I just can't seem to get enough of you."

"Do you think they are okay?" Elinor asked for the umpteenth time over the past year.

"Yes. They haven't come back. I think they are both living really great lives. Just like us. I think they've changed Morland so much we wouldn't even recognize it. I think things are happening there that we could only dream about. Who knows maybe someday we'll all be there together again," he said kissing her on the lips. Elinor looked out the window and saw the beautiful city of Chapel Hill and nothing more. She was sure of it...

THE END

IF YOU ENJOYED THIS BOOK, PLEASE LEAVE A REVIEW ON:

Amazon
&
Goodreads

Reviews make the world go round and help other readers find my books.

Your reviews make a big difference for indie authors like me.

Thanks, my friend!

About the Author

Megan Allen lives in North Carolina with her husband, daughter, and two giant Ragdoll cats, Poppet and Moxie. She writes books about magic, headaches, and magic headaches. She draws a funny blog about her battle with chronic headaches.

Come find her here:

Website:

www.MeganAllen.com

Book Club/ Discussion Questions:

1. Would you want to go to Morland? If yes, for how long? A week? Seventeen years? Forever? And why?

2. Of the magic seen so far, which kind would you like to have? (Elinor's scrying, Winter's earth magic, Brigitte's goodness barrier, Jermaine's truth detector, Emmaline's future/dream magic, or Jol's fire magic)

3. Would you rather live every day with a headache that will never go away and have to see Morland every time you blink but you can never go there or spend forever on Morland (pain-free) but you can only bring one family member and one friend?

4. Were you happy with Elinor's final love choice? Why or why not?

5. Without looking at the following page choose a number: 5,6,7or 8

Husband
1. Derek
2. Peter
3. Ryan
4. Garrison

Number of Children
1. 3
2. 4
3. 5
4. 7

Location
1. Morland
2. Waxhaw
3. Chapel Hill
4. Behind the door in the mines

Magic Ability
1. Fire
2. Earth
3. No Magic
4. Scrying

Occupation
1. Queen/King
2. Doctor
3. Writer
4. Gypsy Leader

Best Friend
1. Brigitte
2. Elinor
3. Winter
4. Emmaline

Rules:
1. Using your number from the previous page count from the top (starting at the M.A.S.H) and cross out the line every time you hit your number. Continue until there is only one answer under each category. This is your future. Enjoy!

M=Mansion (Castle)
A= Airstream (Travel Trailer)
S= Student dorm
H= House

www.ingramcontent.com/pod-product-compliance
Lightning Source LLC
Chambersburg PA
CBHW051540250626
47157CB00001B/123